ACCLAIM FOR THE GUARDIANS OF ASCENSION SERIES BY CARIS ROANE . . .

"Roane's world building is complex and intriguing, and in addition to her compelling protagonists, she serves up a slew of secondary characters begging to be explored further. The Guardians of Ascension is a series with epic potential!"

—*Romantic Times* (4 ½ stars)

"A great story with a really different take on vampires. This is one book that is sure to be a hit with readers who love paranormals. Fans of J.R. Ward's Black Dagger Brotherhood series are sure to love this one, too."

—*Red Roses for Authors Blog*

"*Ascension* is like wandering in a field of a creative and colorful dream. There are many interesting, formidable, terrifying, beautiful, and unique images. They surround and envelop you in a story as old as time."

—Barnes and Noble's *Heart to Heart Romance Blog*

"A super urban romantic fantasy in which the audience will believe in the vampires and the world of *Ascension*...fast-paced . . . thrilling."

—*Alternative Worlds*

"Incredibly creative, *Ascension* takes readers to another level as you learn about two earths, vampires, ancient warriors, and a new twist on love. I felt like I was on a roller-coaster ride, climbing until I hit the very top only to come crashing down at lightning speed. Once you pick this book up, clear off your calendar because you won't be able to put it down. Best book I have read all year."

—Single Titles.com

"Tightly plotted and smoking hot . . . a fantastic read."

—*Fresh Fiction*

St. Martin's Paperbacks Titles by
Caris Roane

ASCENSION

BURNING SKIES

WINGS OF FIRE

BORN OF ASHES

CARIS ROANE

This is a work of fiction. All of the characters, organizations, and events portrayed in this novel are either products of the author's imagination or are used fictitiously.

BORN OF ASHES

For information address St. Martin's Press, 175 Fifth Avenue, New York, NY 10010.

ISBN: 978-0-312-53374-8

Printed in the United States of America

St. Martin's Paperbacks edition / January 2012

St. Martin's Paperbacks are published by St. Martin's Press, 175 Fifth Avenue, New York, NY 10010.

10 9 8 7 6 5 4 3 2 1

To Kathy and her Warrior
An ocean of blessings

ACKNOWLEDGMENTS

Thanks as always to Jennifer Schober for a thousand conversations.
And as always, I bow to the wonderful Rose Hilliard.
Danelle Fiorella—a million thanks for the *best cover ever!*
Laurie Henderson and Laura Jorstad, thank you for nudging this book into shape.
Liz Edelstein, you rock!
Many thanks to Anne Marie Tallberg and Eileen Rothschild for expanding the markets.
And once again, many thanks to Matthew Shear, Jen Enderlin, and the wonderful team at SMP.

I hold him in the palm of my hand,
He presses me to his chest.
His heart thunders through my mind.
Oh, my beloved bleeds for me,
One drop, then another
Until he is spent
And I am satisfied.

—*Collected Poems,* Beatrice of Fourth

CHAPTER 1

"You're standing in front of the grid, Jean-Pierre." Fiona Gaines tried to push her warrior away, her formidable Guardian of Ascension, but for all his leanness the man was a rock.

"Because you do not listen to me, *chérie.* And I need you to listen. I do not think you should go to the christening today."

She finally looked up at him, something she avoided as much as she could. The vampire was a pain in the ass, but if she met his gaze her mind started sinking into a pile of mush—not because of his enthrallment skills but because he was, well, Jean-Pierre.

He was tall, a beautiful six-five to her five-ten. When she wore heels, she matched him so perfectly that her lips reached his neck, so of course she avoided wearing heels. His eyes were the color of stormy seas, a gray-green-blue. He had strong cheekbones and reckless long golden-blond hair, which he held back in sculpted scraps of pastel brocades, a leftover affectation from revolutionary days in France.

But his body was one powerful thrill waiting to happen, a warrior's body so muscled, so lean, that her fingers trembled when he was close. She avoiding touching him, but sometimes in her dreams she would spend hours roving her hands over every solid inch of him. *Every* inch of him.

Worse, however, was that he had a scent that kept her very female body in a state of almost constant arousal, a scent that was completely ridiculous. He smelled like the best cup of coffee ever brewed on the face of two worlds, yet at the same time that coffee was laced with something so male that even standing here, looking at him, her tongue tingled.

A smile touched his lips, those full lips with the upper points that were so kissable. Damn him. He knew exactly what she was feeling, since for him she had the scent of a French patisserie. The universe could often show a surprising sense of humor. They were almost a cliché: coffee and doughnuts. Okay, so he said she smelled like light buttery croissants. Still.

"Fiona." A Militia Warrior across the grid called to her and, thank God, broke the spell.

She had to step around Jean-Pierre to actually see Eric. "What have you got?"

Her heart rate kicked up a notch. She knew Eric well because of how much time she spent at Militia Warrior Headquarters in Apache Junction Two. Three others worked the grid, at least four on deck around the clock. With satellite hookups, the grid could be moved to any set of coordinates around the globe day or night, searching for anomalies.

Central Command, attached to the ruler of Second Earth, also had a grid, but they kept theirs fixed on Metro Phoenix Two, hunting for death vampire sign.

"Something just outside Bangkok Two. Thailand."

She rounded the grid, which measured the size of a small car, to join Eric on the opposite side. She wasn't surprised when Jean-Pierre followed after her. To his credit, he let her work. She had no doubt, however, that the subject would rear its ugly head again.

After her release from blood slavery five months ago,

Fiona had been a woman on a mission. She obsessed about finding Rith Do'onwa, the main instrument behind the heinous slavery system, and she obsessed about bringing home as many of her fellow slaves as possible. Out of twenty-two known facilities, they had found six, and brought home a total of forty slaves, all women.

Eric had already enhanced the grid and there it was, the signature, so hard to read but fast becoming familiar to her. She had a gift, she knew that. Eric and the other MWs could find the infinitesimal smudges that constituted an anomaly, but only she could see the hint of blue-green, the color of the inside dome of Rith's mist, that indicated they'd gotten a hit.

"Get Gideon on the com." She didn't need to ask if Gideon and his team of thirty-two warriors was ready to go. That would have been an insult to one of the Thunder God Warriors, the nickname for all Militia Warriors.

Nor did Eric ask what, when, or why. He made the call and spoke in low tones.

A minute passed.

"Ready on your mark," Eric said.

She met his gaze and smiled. "Let them fly." It was kind of a joke, vampires having wings and all. And they couldn't exactly *fly* through the dematerialization fold, since wings were too fragile to bear the process. But Eric smiled as he gave the order.

Eric set the communications system on loudspeaker. Colonel Seriffe, the leader of the Thunder God Warriors, wanted it that way. If there would be a battle, they'd all hear it. Seriffe was all about keeping everyone connected, informed, and aware.

Fiona glanced the length of the room. Over two dozen women staffed the communications along with MW section leaders, like Eric, like Gideon. Most turned in her direction, solemn, waiting.

Gideon's voice, low and quiet, hit the airwaves. He issued orders then said, "No DV sign here."

Fiona didn't know when she had actually backed up into

Jean-Pierre, but his presence calmed her. He had a hand on her hip, and she felt his deep breaths. Her heart rate had doubled. She couldn't help it.

She knew exactly what all these women were going through, the despair after usually decades of serving as a blood donor—the polite euphemism for a process that involved taking a woman once a month through death and resurrection by defibrillator to get at the addictive dying blood. Death vampires, by the nature of their addiction, had to drink their victims to death in order to get that last euphoric substance.

A hundred and twenty-five years ago Fiona had been out shopping when two death vampires, whom only she had been able to see, had abducted her from Boston the day after her eleventh wedding anniversary. She had been the first mortal woman to be partially ascended by Darian Greaves and experimented upon. Back then the draining of her blood had involved big steel needles and rubber tubing. Greaves would drain her blood, taking her to the point of death, pump more blood back into her veins, and bring her heart back to life with what she now understood to be powerful hand-blasts from his palm.

Shortly after, Rith, who also had a great deal of preternatural power, had taken over. Fiona rarely saw Greaves after that.

Over the loudspeaker, she could hear Gideon breathing hard as well as the sound of his battle sandals pounding up a flight of stairs. She saw movement to her right. Seriffe emerged from his office, a heavy scowl on his face as he, too, listened.

Gideon's voice, too loud for the speakers, became a shout. "We've got eleven women here!"

HQ erupted in cheers and shouts.

Fiona's eyes filled with tears.

Jean-Pierre leaned down. "Congratulations, *chérie*." She caught his hand and held it tight. She struggled to breathe and not to cry, but tears escaped anyway.

She could hear Gideon speaking, but not what he was saying.

"Settle down, people," Seriffe called out.

Gideon relayed the information that all eleven were alive and healthy.

Fiona slipped her BlackBerry from her pants pocket, touched the screen, and connected with the rehab center. She let reception know that they'd be getting eleven new arrivals.

The woman gave a little cry. "We'll take it from here, Fiona. Well done."

Well done. She wanted to rejoice, she really did, but that meant there were still fifteen other facilities, *that they knew of,* and how many more women to rescue before she could really begin to celebrate.

"Take a moment, Fiona," Jean-Pierre whispered. "This is a good thing you have done."

How did he know? Could he read her mind?

She drew away from him and looked up at him. She saw the deep compassion in his stormy eyes and then she understood. He was a Warrior of the Blood. He had fought for over two hundred years, from the first year of his ascension, against the ongoing depredation of death vampires. He knew the victory that the slaying of each death vampire meant, but he also knew the persistent frustration and despair that accrued because right now there seemed to be no end in sight. The enemy, Commander Darian Greaves, encouraged the creation of death vampires, since he used them as a significant weapon in his bid to take over two worlds, Second Earth and Mortal Earth.

She nodded. She glanced at the clock on the wall. The hour was eleven at night. She would have to go home soon with Colonel Seriffe, her son-in-law, at which time Jean-Pierre would join the Warriors of the Blood as they fought at all five dimensional entry points in the Metro Phoenix area.

"Where will you be tonight?" she asked.

"Thorne likes to keep me at the downtown Borderland."

She nodded. She knew why. The downtown Borderland was the closest location to Colonel Seriffe's home, where Fiona now lived. Thorne knew that the situation for Jean-Pierre, serving as her guardian, was something of a nightmare. He looked it, too, with faint circles beneath his eyes. Even relatively immortal vampires could show signs of strain if they had to guard a woman twelve hours of the day, battle death vampires another six, then toss and turn through a restless sleep cycle.

Damn the breh-hedden, she thought. The former mythological state of vampire mate-bonding had also reared its ugly head. She was afflicted with what she thought of as an inconvenient and terrible disease, but for whatever reason, the *breh-hedden* really took a toll on the men, as though it put all that testosterone on high alert constantly.

Hence, even in the perfectly safe environment of Militia Warrior HQ, Jean-Pierre stuck close.

"Now, *chérie,* we must talk about the christening tomorrow."

She cocked her head and planted her hands on her hips. "I'm going and I don't care whether you think it's a security problem or not. Alison has been a good friend to me and bringing this baby into the world was no picnic. She's a new mom, and I remember what that was like. She needs my support and if you think that I would bail on her at this late hour, after having been a slave for over a hundred years, because of the threat of death vampires, then you don't know me at all."

Jean-Pierre Robillard, out of France in 1793, saw the familiar stubborn glint in the eye of his woman and his hopes sank that he would have the smallest chance to change her mind. She was so beautiful, her long thick chestnut hair wrapped in a twist at the back of her head, her lovely cheekbones well on display, the silver-blue of her eyes shining in the dim lights of the central grid room.

Her scent rose to drift into his nose and command his senses, a delicate bouquet of pastries and woman combined, a heady combination that tended to strip him of all rational thought.

His breath caught and held. He felt as he had from the

first, that he could lose his soul in the eyes of this woman, his woman.

His woman. *Mais quel cauchemar.* A nightmare that would not end. The *breh-hedden* had done this to them both, bound them together when neither of them wanted to be bound.

"I'm going to baby Helena's christening, Jean-Pierre. And that's that. I will not discuss it further."

He could not move her. Whatever her slavery had been, her recovery had been swift. From the withdrawn, despairing woman had emerged a vampire with a dedicated mind-set intent on rescuing all the remaining blood slaves and seeing Rith Do'onwa into the grave.

He applauded her determination but the sheer stubbornness that had arisen, the willfulness, was a thorn in his side, night and day. He would not call her reckless, but certainly *fearless.* His job would have been so much easier if she had been a wallflower that wilted. Instead she forged ahead, ignored his opinions, and was like an Amazon to the problems in front of her.

He served as her Guardian of Ascension and had from almost the day of her rescue. He was both grateful for and hated the assignment. Grateful because he could not have tolerated any other warrior being close to her. Yet if he was to have a chance to not feel so very bound to her, only distance would answer—and distance he could not get.

Worse, she had emerging powers, which meant that the enemy would soon discover her worth, and would want her very dead. For that reason, he had tried to persuade her not to attend the christening, which he had learned just a few hours ago, and much to his horror, was to be conducted in the open air.

Merde.

Seriffe commanded the room again. "We have another situation, people."

"Oh, no," Fiona whispered.

Without thinking, he moved in close behind her once more,

something she allowed, and he was not surprised when she leaned against him for support. As much as neither wished to be close, a friendship had developed, and he knew that to some degree she relied on him.

Once more, he put his hand most carefully on her hip and worked at his breathing. This close, his arousal was only a thought away. But in the past five months, he had learned some new skills in tolerating the presence of *his woman* without constantly sporting, as the Americans liked to say, *a raging hard-on.*

Seriffe had a remote control in his hand. He aimed it at the large central monitor and clicked. "I recorded this a few minutes ago."

Greaves came on the screen. Jean-Pierre could not restrain a soft growl. More than any other creature on the face of the earth, he wanted this vampire dead, set on fire, burned to ashes, then cast over at least five different bodies of water.

"My fellow ascenders," Greaves began, "I have learned this very morning of a grave situation. My staff, in their ongoing efforts to better regulate a world that has fallen into massive decay under Madame Endelle's unfortunate leadership, has uncovered the existence of several blood slave facilities. We are even now in the process of searching these facilities out and ending the reprehensible activity of procuring dying blood from enslaved females.

"I am hereby offering a reward for anyone who can locate the creator and director of these facilities, an ascender by the name of Rith Do'onwa, who has built over the past ten decades an entire black market for this truly heinous commodity."

A picture appeared of Rith, and Jean-Pierre felt Fiona stiffen. He could only imagine how the sight of the vampire affected her.

Greaves continued, "The unfortunate circumstance of the highly addictive nature of dying blood is a problem that the scientific community, attached to the Coming Order, works on relentlessly day and night.

"I wish to set the record straight on one pertinent fact;

many decades ago, I had a brief association with ascender Do'onwa, in which as a joint effort we attempted to create an antidote for the disease. When I saw that such efforts would prove fruitless, I ended the project as well as my association with ascender Do'onwa.

"So serious is the nature of this situation that I'm offering one million dollars to anyone who can provide information that leads to the capture of ascender Do'onwa."

He ended the press conference, refusing to take questions, and left the staging area with the flash of lightbulbs glittering off his shiny bald head.

"Fucking brilliant," Fiona muttered. "He's set Rith up as the fall guy. Bastard."

She was using one of his favorite words to describe Greaves.

Fiona continued. "But do you think the world is buying this?"

"He has great presence, and who would not believe those big, innocent, round eyes of his?"

"Yeah, he looks so sincere. I loathe him, Jean-Pierre. I never thought in the course of my life to hate anyone, but that's all I can feel for him."

"I understand," he said. And he did. He truly did.

As he glanced at the clock next to the monitor, his heart tightened. It was past eleven at night. His woman worked long hours and so did he. Fiona needed her rest and he needed to get into the field. But he did not want to leave her. As hard as it was to be around her most of the time, this was the hour he despised the most: Until he met with her again the following morning, he would be separated from her and unable to get to her if she needed him.

So, shit.

"You must go home now," he said, leaning close and dipping down to smell her neck. He took a long sniff and heard her swift intake of breath. "May I see you home?"

She stepped away from him as a strong roll of her delicate croissant scent struck his nostrils. *Oui,* they were both trapped inside the *breh-hedden.* He also knew she was a woman quick to experience the little death, the place of ecstasy. He did not understand the why of it, but he could *bring* her with just a kiss. The first time had occurred the day she was in the hospital just after her release from the New Zealand blood slavery facility.

She turned to face him and he watched her swallow hard. She had a beautiful long neck. Her vein pulsed. He held back a groan. He longed for this woman in every way. He craved her. He wanted her blood.

She shook her head. A wisp of her hair had come loose. She pushed it behind her ear. Even the shape of her ears was beautiful—as if everything about her was designed to torment him.

"I don't think that's a good idea, Jean-Pierre, do you?"

He shook his head as well but his heart tightened a little more. He did not understand all that he felt. Was he experiencing love or was this just the terrible lure of the *brehhedden*?

From his side vision, he saw Seriffe move in their direction. Seriffe would fold her back to his house, where she lived with his family, in a guest suite all her own. That had been the one piece of grace that had come out of Fiona's enslavement, that when the Warriors of the Blood rescued her and brought her to Metro Phoenix Two, she had discovered that the daughter she had lost so long ago, because of her abduction, had ascended in 1913 and was now married to Colonel Seriffe and had birthed three small boys.

But as Seriffe drew closer, Jean-Pierre's heart rate increased. He did not want to leave Fiona. His instincts kicked into high gear and he stepped in front of her, his chin lowered, his gaze fixed in a hard stare on the colonel.

Seriffe shook his head. "You're still going to do this?"

Fiona pushed at his back. "Jean-Pierre, this isn't necessary."

Fuck them both, he thought. How could either of them know what he experienced right now? "You must promise me this night that you will watch over her and let no harm come to her. You must promise, Seriffe, or by God I will tear your heart out."

Seriffe sighed. He put a hand on Jean-Pierre's shoulder. "By all that I hold sacred, by the lives of my wife and my children, I do so promise."

It was the best Jean-Pierre could do.

He turned to Fiona and though feeling that his heart would break, however absurd, he caught up both her hands in his and kissed her fingers. "Tomorrow, *chérie*."

She had tears in her eyes. *"À demain, chéri."*

He loved her for that. She showed him such kindness. Whatever else she might be, however stubborn, however obsessed with finding Rith, Fiona Gaines was kind.

The following morning, Fiona stood before the mirror in her bedroom. Colonel Seriffe and Carolyn had given her a suite in their sprawling home where she had lived for the past five months, from the time she learned that her daughter had ascended.

Dressing to go to the christening, she contemplated changing her clothes one more time. The woman she was before her captivity would have had no trouble selecting an outfit to wear. Though she'd adjusted to many things about her new world and her new life, she couldn't quite seem to find the right kind of clothes for herself. She despised the quandary and saw it as a weakness, something left over from her century-plus of living under Rith's thumb.

She needed to be patient with herself, but sometimes she wanted to scream her frustration.

She wore pearl earrings and a cream silk tailored blouse tucked into a navy pencil skirt that had a small slit up one side, topped by three covered buttons. Around her shoulders she wore a light blue cashmere shawl.

The baptism ceremony was being held in mile-high Prescott Two and this time of year, in early March, at ten in the morning, the outdoor ceremony would be on the cool side of fifty, as opposed to the perfect seventy of Phoenix right now.

Still, she worried: Was she overdressed, underdressed, too matronly, too young, was the slit too much? She was uncomfortable in these clothes but she wasn't certain why exactly, except of course that her back itched like crazy and there wasn't anything she could do about it.

Except . . .

She turned away from the mirror and moved to the nightstand on the far side of her bed. She drew the deep drawer open and took out . . . a ruler. She hated doing this because it made the wing-apertures weep but she needed some relief . . . now.

She lifted the heavy fall of her hair and shoved the ruler down the back of her shirt. She closed her eyes, and as she reached the uppermost wing-lock on the left side of her back she gave a little cry. It felt so good.

She rubbed the end of the ruler back and forth over the swollen tissue. She couldn't describe the relief she felt but her eyes rolled back in her head. She moved from one wing-lock to the next until she could no longer reach them from an upper stroke. She dropped the cashmere to the bed and pulled the blouse from the skirt.

She tilted the ruler and shoved it up under the hem of the blouse until she reached the first of the lower wing-locks. She performed the same ritual and winced and uttered little muffled cries the whole time.

She was getting her wings but it was not fun. The itching had gotten so bad that two weeks ago she'd seen one of the doctors who had tended her in the hospital five months earlier.

He'd spent a good half hour with her, asking her questions about the wing-locks: When had they appeared, did she ever experience any burning sensations, had she tried mounting her wings . . . all the usual.

The problem was, he'd been concerned because by all appearances she should have been able to mount her wings weeks earlier, maybe even the first week after she'd gone through her formal ascension ceremony with Madame Endelle, the Supreme High Administrator of Second Earth.

Now her back was wet. Of course. She removed her shirt and went into the bathroom to dry off with a towel. She returned to her closet and put on a new blouse similar in style and color.

As she tucked the shirt in, she wondered if Jean-Pierre would like this conservative look on her or if he preferred a looser style. She shouldn't care, but she did. She had a very strong affection for the warrior, which didn't help the situation *at all.*

An odd little vibration moved through her mind and suddenly, without warning, because she had been thinking of Jean-Pierre, now she could feel him, where he was, what he was doing. He was in Prescott, scoping the outdoor chapel where the christening would be held. She felt as though she stood right next to him, as though she could be inside him, inside his mind and his body, which made no sense. She knew, *she knew,* that with just a thought she could complete this process, be in his mind despite the fact that he was a powerful ascender and his shields nearly impenetrable. Yet she would have no difficulty, not even a little, pressing her mind inside his, as though he had no shields at all!

But then from the beginning, from her ascension all those decades ago, her primary gift was her telepathy. She had abilities that far surpassed most ascenders'.

Of course she would never intrude in Jean-Pierre's mind, or anyone else's, without their permission. On the other hand, knowing him, he would have welcomed the invasion.

She shook her head back and forth. What did this freakish sensation mean? He'd already told her he thought she had emerging preternatural powers, which in turn meant she could be in greater danger than ever of hitting Greaves's radar, the last place any ascender wanted to be.

Great. This meant she needed Jean-Pierre more than ever and she didn't want to need him, or anyone for that matter. She wanted a normal life on Second Earth, to have charge of her own home, to engage in work she enjoyed, and perhaps one day to fall in love in a *normal* way.

She really had come to despise the *breh-hedden.*

As she moved back to the mirror, her wing-locks eased

for the moment, and she settled the light blue cashmere once more around her shoulders.

She had only one thing left to do. On the table beside the mirror sat the gold locket her long-deceased husband had given to her on their eleventh wedding anniversary. She had kept it with her all through her years as a blood slave in Burma and even in Toulouse until Rith had moved his slaves unexpectedly. She'd been in a drugged, mindless state, unaware that the precious necklace was being left behind.

Yet somehow, miraculously, Jean-Pierre had discovered the locket behind an antique armoire in Toulouse when the warriors had stormed the facility. Later, he had returned it to her, at the palace, the same night as the rescue.

Yes, a small miracle.

The locket had helped keep her sanity all those decades. She fingered the chain now, running it over and over her fingers.

Colonel Seriffe was her protector in the off-hours when Jean-Pierre wasn't pinned to her side. Seriffe had several squads of Militia Warriors constantly patrolling his property even though Endelle had covered the house in a dome of mist—that extraordinary cloak, invisible to most ascenders, that confused the mind and made even huge buildings seem not to exist.

"Mother, may I come in?"

Carolyn's voice still had the power to undo her and tears rushed to her eyes. She was back in Boston in 1886, Carolyn was a girl of ten, and she was combing out her light brown curls. Another miracle that Carolyn had actually ascended, then eventually married Colonel Seriffe.

"Mother?"

The sound of her daughter's voice pushed her heart around in her chest and she smiled. How she loved her.

She blinked back the usual tears and strove to calm herself. These past few months had been hard on Carolyn as well. She'd had to adjust to a mother, long thought dead and now *risen*. No, nothing about her rescue from blood slavery had been simple.

When she could breathe again, she called out, "I'm decent, sweetheart. Come in."

As she looked into the mirror and settled the gold locket between the lapels of the shirt, she watched the door open behind her, and a moment later her daughter's adult face emerged. She remembered the child's face with the same shy smile. Carolyn's hair was still honey-and-brown in color, with streaks of blond, not so different from Jean-Pierre. Of course, the color now came from a salon in Scottsdale Two. Carolyn was a beautiful young mother of three, even if she was 115.

Ah, Second Earth. Time had a different meaning here. Carolyn could be her sister.

She moved to stand behind Fiona. They were tall women, the Gaines women.

"The cashmere is beautiful," Carolyn said, "and you should always wear this icy shade of blue. It's a lovely contrast for your chestnut hair and the silver-blue of your eyes. I think Jean-Pierre will like it."

She met her daughter's gaze in the mirror. "Now, why would you say something so provoking?" But she laughed.

"Because you're being ridiculous. He loves you and you love him and you should be together. You should at least let him date you once a week. At least throw him that bone."

Yes . . . that bone. She had restricted their dating to once every two weeks. So for the past five months, every two weeks, Jean-Pierre took her someplace special, and the whole time Fiona worked to keep her hands off him.

Fiona's gaze fell away, drifting lower and lower and falling swiftly into the past, into being strapped to gurneys once a month, drained of her blood, then brought back to life with defibrillators. She didn't know how to explain to Carolyn that she didn't want a relationship, she didn't even want to date Jean-Pierre, and she certainly didn't want the terrible *breh-hedden*. She didn't want to be tied down again. Ever.

She'd reached an impasse and she knew it. She couldn't go back but she didn't know how to go forward. She pushed Jean-Pierre away but she kept dating him, kept longing for him, for his presence, his touch, his kisses. Oh, God . . . *his kisses.*

Her gaze traveled back to Carolyn, and there were tears in her daughter's eyes. "I shouldn't have teased you, Mother. I'm sorry." Her arms traveled around Fiona.

Fiona caught them hard over her chest and gave her daughter an awkward hug, a back-to-front squeeze. "I'm lost," she whispered.

"I know. And it's only been five months. I don't know why I keep pushing you."

Fiona nodded. She took another breath. "Are Seriffe and the children ready?"

"Yes."

"We should go."

Carolyn pulled back and Fiona turned toward her. Carolyn smiled suddenly. "I made Seriffe a bet."

"About what?"

"Well, I am convinced that Warrior Kerrick will weep at his daughter's christening. My husband said, *Not a chance.*"

"He's a man," Fiona said. "He has to say that on principle. So what did you wager?"

"That if Kerrick sheds even a single tear, Seriffe will have to take me to Dark Spectacle Phantasmagoria."

"No," Fiona cried. Seriffe was adamant in refusing to buy tickets to an event that he insisted was all smoke and mirrors though it was billed as a preternatural experience.

Seriffe appeared in the doorway. He was as tall as Jean-Pierre—just a few inches shy of the top of the doorjamb. Certainly his shoulders filled the space. "Are we ready?" His deep warm voice boomed into the room.

"Yes," Fiona said.

"I just received a call from Central. Endelle has given permission for Carla to give us a fold as a group to Prescott."

Fiona's brows rose. "Endelle is letting Central help out? Has she gone soft or something?" Madame Endelle had a python's temperament: Circle, squeeze, devour, ask questions later. That she was permitting Central Command to fold groups to baby Helena's baptism was, well, *unusual* to say the least, which only made Fiona worry more. Was Endelle expecting trouble or just being cautious?

Seriffe chuckled. "The day Endelle goes soft is the day we all buy ice skates and take a dozen turns around a frozen rink you-know-where. Apparently Endelle has some security concerns and frankly, I'm with her on this one. Did you know the sisters are holding the service in that really shitty—I mean in that really awful—outdoor chapel?" He glanced behind himself. Young ears were listening and he tried really hard, though often unsuccessfully, to curb warrior-speak.

"No," Carolyn cried. "The one with the graffiti on half the benches?"

"Bingo."

"Don't they have a chapel inside that could pay for a small country?"

"Yep."

"Well . . . shi . . . I mean, that's really too bad." This time Carolyn looked down the hall. Her boys could be heard calling to each other. Carolyn, too, had picked up some of her husband's bad habits. Fiona hadn't exactly been exempt herself.

His gaze shifted to Carolyn, and he straightened his shoulders. "The baby needed a change but I took care of it. Just wanted you to know."

"I suppose now you want a medal."

"Hell, yes! You've changed his diapers. Whew!"

Carolyn went to him, drew close, pressed herself against his chest, and kissed him on the lips. "Sorry, Ethan gave him some of his chili last night." Ethan was the oldest of the three boys and enjoyed tormenting his family in as many creative ways as he could conjure. Fiona adored that about him.

"That explains it." But he laughed.

He turned his wife into the hall, smiled at Fiona over his shoulder, then herded Carolyn in the direction of the main rooms. In the distance, one of the boys started to scream, a very normal sound in the Seriffe household.

Fiona smiled. Maybe there was a lot about her life that she couldn't figure out right now, but being part of this family had brought her great joy.

So, yes, as she followed Carolyn and Seriffe down the hall, as she watched her daughter bend over and pick up her now wailing toddler, as Seriffe took the hands of both his older boys, as the family turned almost as one to look at her, yes, she knew joy.

Whatever else ascension held for her, this moment, this pleasure, made every struggle, every difficulty worthwhile.

The thought that once she folded to the outdoor chapel she would begin a new day with Jean-Pierre, however, left her caught once more in that in-between place: longing to move into the future, but clinging to the past.

We are born of ashes
In the spiritual death and rebirth
Of ascension.

—*The Creator's Handbook,* Sister Quena

CHAPTER 2

Jean-Pierre stood on the periphery of the small outdoor chapel, shook his head, and muttered, *"Mon Dieu."*

His disgust was profound. To call what amounted to an ugly collection of rough-hewn wooden benches a chapel was ridiculous. The entire space defined *security nightmare.* How could he, or the other Warriors of the Blood, protect the women and children who would attend the christening today?

There were no walls, only a slight inclination of the hill and dense forest beyond. He glanced in a slow half circle from right to left, at the slope of the hill near Thumb Butte, rising not steeply but littered with large boulders and flanked by tall ponderosa pines. He stretched his preternatural senses hunting for the enemy but he found nothing, *merci à Dieu.*

But would it remain the same throughout the ceremony?

If he were the enemy, *oui,* he would strike.

The benches were bolted to cement slabs like a Mortal Earth picnic ground. Pine needles covered everything. There was nothing in his opinion that was right for this ceremony. He did not understand why the High Administrator of the Convent, Sister Quena, did not send some of the sisters to at least sweep the needles off the benches.

His ire rose but then these days he was never far from a certain portion of rage. *Pissed off.* He loved the American phrase. *Oui,* he was fucking pissed off.

The air near him moved, setting his warrior instincts on fire. He thought the thought and brought his identified sword into his hand.

Had the enemy arrived so early to do battle? Very well.

He dropped into a crouch. Even though he had battled half the night, give him more, give him much, much more. He was a Warrior of the Blood and he was ready.

As Thorne materialized, he touched down on a thick carpet of pine needles and met one pissed-off-looking warrior. He smiled, planted his hands on his hips, then laughed.

Jean-Pierre drew upright and his sword vanished. He released a long breath and rattled off a few French words that probably composed one fine string of French obscenities.

"You look a little tense," Thorne said, then he laughed again but even to his own ears the sound had a dark, bitter ring. He glanced around. "What a shithole."

"*Exactement.* So why are Alison and Kerrick having the baptism here? Is there not a proper chapel inside the building? I understand the convents have some of the most beautiful chapels in the world."

"The head sister here wanted it this way." He thumbed behind him in the direction of the locked-down facility. "Sister Quena runs this place like the inmates are convicted felons instead of devotees." Well, not all of them had arrived here *devoted.* He knew of at least one who had been consigned here by her parents and who was now restrained with an ankle guard to keep her from folding out of the facility.

"Yeah, the chapel here would have made better sense. I've seen it. The walls are covered with gold and pearl mosaics. I guess we're not good enough to be inside, our hands being covered in blood."

Jean-Pierre shrugged. "Then the sisters are hypocrites. They would not be so ungenerous if death vampires invaded their precious chapel."

Thorne snorted. "Oh, they'd need us then, but Sister Quena would no doubt tell us we were merely the instruments of the Creator."

"Of course."

Thorne sighed. He turned in a circle. He couldn't exactly tell Jean-Pierre the other truth: that he knew about every foot of the inside of the Convent, that he'd been within the walls a thousand times, maybe ten thousand, and not because his sister resided here. Grace had lived in this place for over a hundred years, by choice, because of her intense spiritual devotion. But that wasn't why he'd been here so much.

His woman lived here as well, Marguerite, his sister's cellmate.

Marguerite. Oh . . . God. He had loved her for a century now. His self-proclaimed celibacy? One big fat motherfucker of a lie. He'd been buried between Marguerite's legs from the first day he'd met her. She was irreverent, proud, full of venom, a hellcat. She adored the male body, and he loved her, he goddam loved her. No, he *craved* her. Given the recent rise of the *breh-hedden* among the ranks, he had for a while suspected that Marguerite was his *breh,* but the two of them lacked one critical quality essential to vampire mate-bonding: They didn't share a special scent with each other. Jesus, even Medichi said Parisa smelled citrusy. Oranges or tangerines, something like that.

Whatever.

He wanted to contact Marguerite right now, and he could do it, too, with just a properly aimed thought, especially this close to the facility, but the two of them rarely communicated telepathically. For one thing, he had a telepathic link with Endelle and she had enough power to track his private communications if she wanted to. The last person he ever wanted to know about Marguerite was Endelle. If she got wind of Marguerite's extreme Seer capability, she'd use his woman as leverage and work out a deal with the High Administrator of the Superstition Mountain Seers Fortress. His woman would get shipped to an even worse prison without a second's thought.

Endelle was nine thousand years old and the most powerful vampire on the planet. She ruled him and she had the right to send any Seer she deemed worthy straight to the Superstitions without anyone's permission.

Thorne could never allow that, never risk it. The last place Marguerite wanted to be was in a Seers Fortress. He felt the same way but for a different, quite selfish reason: If she got moved out of the Convent, he'd never see her again, and for the past one hundred years she'd been the sole reason he hadn't lost his ever-lovin' fucked-up mind.

"Are you okay?" Jean-Pierre asked.

Thorne shot his gaze back to the warrior. Shit, he'd been staring at the low stone building that went on for a quarter acre downhill. He'd probably been making a growling sound. "Fine, I'm fine. I just . . . really hate this place."

"You are thinking of your sister, *non*?"

Thorne's pause was just a little too long but he finally managed a gravelly, "Of course."

Jean-Pierre frowned slightly. "I never understood. I knew Grace all those years ago. She had so much *joie de vivre.* Why did she ever choose this life?"

Thorne shrugged. He relaxed a little. He could talk about Grace. Sort of. "The hell if I know. Whatever spurred her in this direction, she never really shared with me, only that she felt a calling. But she seems happy enough. I guess." He shrugged again.

He didn't get it. However, his comprehension of his sister's actions wasn't important; only that she seemed content. After the first decade of her internment and after about a thousand arguments on the subject, he'd learned to rest his concerns about what the hell she was doing in a convent.

Again . . . whatever.

He glanced around once more. "I guess we're the first ones here. Is Fiona coming?"

"Oui." The warrior's voice sounded flat but it wasn't from disinterest.

"Anything you want to talk about?"

Okay, as the leader of the Warriors of the Blood—and by the nature of the job, the one in charge of Jean-Pierre's overall well-being—he had to ask. But so help him God, if Jean-Pierre actually unloaded on him, he'd make a couple of quick excuses and fold the hell out of there, christening or no fucking christening.

Jean-Pierre, however, gave him a skewed smile that covered only one side of his mouth and lifted ever so sarcastically. "About as much as you want to talk about why the Convent is really bugging the shit out of you." Thorne shook his head. What an accent. *Shit* sounded like *sheet.* He might have laughed but dammit, suddenly he was painfully aware that Jean-Pierre had been going through hell for the past five months.

The man was stuck in between worlds. He had a *breh,* but he wasn't bonded to her. He felt the call of that lousy *myth-that-wasn't-a-myth,* the intense *breh-hedden,* but he couldn't do anything about it. Fiona was all wrapped up in helping Colonel Seriffe hunt down that bastard Rith Do'onwa, the one who had held her captive for over a hundred years, and she'd been keeping Jean-Pierre on tenterhooks. She allowed him a couple of dates a month, which clearly ended up being some weird form of torture for the brother.

Jean-Pierre looked it, too. He had circles under his eyes, something an ascender shouldn't be able to get, but then he was pulling double duty. On his off-hours he stuck close to Fiona—Endelle had assigned him as her Guardian of Ascension—but for half the night he worked the Borderlands, making war against death vampires like the rest of the Warriors of the Blood.

"Will Medichi and Parisa be here?" Jean-Pierre asked.

Thorne pursed his lips. Medichi used to serve as a Warrior

of the Blood but with his recent completion of the *breh-hedden,* he had new obligations. "I don't think so. Endelle has the pair of them on ambassadorial duty to every single Territory still aligned with her. I think they're in Somalia Two right now."

Jean-Pierre nodded then shifted his gaze over the outdoor chapel. "This place is too open."

"I agree. That's why I asked all the warriors to come."

"It was the right thing to do." He suddenly put a hand to his forehead and squeezed his eyes shut.

"Hey. What is it?"

Jean-Pierre opened his eyes and looked at nothing in particular. He seemed to be concentrating hard. After a moment, he said, "*Rien.* I mean, I am almost certain I felt Fiona reaching out to me with her mind."

"You don't have a telepathic link, do you?"

"*Non, pas du tout.* She would not allow it."

"Well, shit. What the hell does it mean?"

Jean-Pierre met his gaze. His eyes were blue-gray like the ocean. "She has emerging powers, something I have felt for weeks now."

Oh, God. "You know what that means?"

"Yes. The enemy will want her."

"Or want her dead."

"*Oui.*"

Jean-Pierre saw a large shimmering on the opposite side of the grounds. Once more he drew his sword into his hand, but Thorne told him to take a chill-pill, an expression he still did not quite understand.

And there she was, with her daughter next to her.

Fiona now stood on the far side of the outdoor chapel, with Seriffe's family, and acknowledged him with only a dip of her pretty chin. She was much too far away. He was going mad. Always when he saw her, he wanted to run to her, slide his arm around her waist, drag her against him. He wanted to kiss her and do so many other things to her.

God have mercy on his soul.

He shifted his gaze away from her.

Thorne told him to put his sword away and relax, because the rest of the warriors were on the way. He sent his sword back to his weapons locker in his house in Sedona Two. Another three seconds passed and his brothers-in-arms arrived. They immediately spread out, each man turning in a slow circle to do as Jean-Pierre had done earlier: to scope the territory. He was not surprised when a few expletives left each mouth.

"What a fucking crap-house," Zacharius said. He touched a cloth to his swollen lower lip. "I can't believe that Kerrick and Alison's baby would be christened in a place like this?"

Luken snorted. "You would think someone destined to open the pathway to Third Earth would be treated with more respect, even by a self-righteous witch like Sister Quena."

Jean-Pierre knew that Luken spoke of Alison. When she ascended, not only did she battle a former Warrior of the Blood in an arena, but she became in her own right a Guardian of Ascension with the prophecy attached to her that she would do just as Luken had said: She would be the instrument by which the portal to Third Earth, closed after millennia, would at last be reopened.

There were even Seers' prophecies indicating that once she accomplished this feat, the war on Second Earth would end for all time.

The warriors were now ranged to his right in a protective arc, all standing because who would sit on such miserable benches, some of them marked up with graffiti and all of them buried beneath pine needles. The warriors were bruised, just as he was, from the night's battling. Santiago had a black eye and held his arm with his free hand.

Zacharius's left cheek was swollen and his upper lip split and bleeding. He kept pressing a dark cloth to his mouth. His large blue eyes were cloudy with fatigue, much fatigue.

Luken moved with a limp to stand beside Zach. The pair spoke in low tones.

It never used to be like this.

Something had gone so terribly wrong.

An unseen force had taken to battering the warriors when they were not looking, an invisible force, something that must be from an Upper Dimension and completely illegal, but neither Endelle nor any of the warriors could prove what was going on. Even if they had proof, COPASS would do nothing. The corrupt committee that oversaw the judicial element of all Second Earth was useless.

But worse for him, his own suffering was eased by dwelling on the impossible situation of the Warriors of the Blood.

Pathetic.

The final group arrived: Kerrick, holding baby Helena over his shoulder, Alison beside him, accompanied by Marcus and Havily who stood as godparents. Helena held her head up and eyed the guests, her mouth an O. She had a shock of black hair, the color like her papa's.

Jean-Pierre shifted his gaze once more to Fiona. She had her arms draped over the eldest Seriffe boy, who leaned his head back against her stomach and looked up at her. She smiled down at him. She was maternal, this woman. She had birthed two children of her own so many years ago, and she cared for the recovering blood slaves like a mother hen who gathers her chicks beneath her wings.

Ah, so much love in this woman.

His vision narrowed to a fine point that always stopped where *she* began. He had become as the men who had gone before him—Warriors Kerrick, Marcus, and Medichi—all those men, each a powerful Warrior of the Blood, who had become bonded to their women. As they had been in the early stages of courtship, so he was now: easily distracted by Fiona's presence so that soon he saw only her and cared only that he would draw his sword for her and battle the gates of hell to protect her.

But she stood apart from him as she always did, pretending her immunity, her indifference, as though she did not suffer the way he did. But he knew better. He knew because her scent came to him in soft waves of desire even now. She could not shield that from him in the same way he could not keep from her the intensity of his passion for her, his lust, his cravings, *oui,* his desire.

She stood as far away from him as possible, a shoulder just barely turned in his direction. He measured the angle of that presentation like a careful architect. Had she stood in just that manner so that part of her would connect to him, if just the shoulder? He thought yes, *oui,* because he knew her. After five months of absurd *dating,* yes, he knew her very well.

He saw the clean line of her jaw, the angle of her beautiful long throat, her chestnut hair in waves down her back, her chin lifted, so proud, so determined. He knew her thoughts. *Ah, oui,* after five months he knew her obsessive thoughts and they were not fixed on him as they ought to be. *Non,* they reeked of her constant need to find Rith, to see him imprisoned and tried for his crimes, to see him dead.

What was left for him? Little bones she cast at his feet every two weeks. He hungered for them and jumped at them when they came. He tore them to bits, sucked on the marrow, chewed them with sharp hard teeth until he had devoured each small piece. But until the bones came, he waited as one suspended in time, caught as if between dimensions, waiting for her smiles and her frowns, the soft clearing of her throat, the words spoken from tender lips.

How he despised the *breh-hedden* that had brought him to this terrible place, into the power of another woman. He had fought for over two centuries to keep his heart and mind free of the shackles of any sort of love. Love had betrayed him once, love that had felt eternal, love that he had given his heart to without restraints of any kind.

He had believed himself loved but in the last month before his ascension, his wife had grown distant, even cruel at times, weeping uncontrollably, enraged, perhaps even insane—he would never know. But in her unstable state, she had betrayed him to the revolution, spoken of his crimes, of secret but false alliances with the court of Marie Antoinette.

He had been for the revolution. He had been on committees to create a new government based on *liberté, égalité, fraternité.* He had renounced his lands, his position in society. How could anyone have doubted his sincerity, his patriotism, his dedication to a new France?

But Robespierre was another kind of monster and so he had found himself confronting Madame La Guillotine and all because his wife had betrayed him. He could not imagine what the crowds thought when he simply disappeared off the guillotine just as the angled blade made its terrible descent.

No, his wife's betrayal and the revolution's betrayal had slain his heart, had changed him. Gone was his innocence, his belief in *l'amour,* in the equities of life. He had departed from a country caught in civil war, as well as an encroaching war with all of Europe, to ascend to a new dimension also at war. This time, he became a warrior and no longer a fool hoping for political change.

So Fiona could never truly be important to him. His heart was too broken. But as he watched her, *mon Dieu,* sometimes, he thought his heart beat in unison with hers, trying to call to her from the depths of his soul, summon her, *beg* her to hear him, to turn toward him, that he might see in her eyes the same need he felt.

He was so fucked, another perfect American expression.

Of course, her scent rolled toward him in heavy waves, which meant that she knew exactly where he was and that she was thinking about him, just as he thought of her.

The trouble was that the more her scent rolled, the more it afflicted his lower body as though fingers played over him.

Merde, would this agony never end?

Fiona felt *his* presence like a strong wind against her back, pushing and shoving. She resisted. Of course she resisted. *He* was the real danger in her life, not ten death vampires, not a hundred, not a thousand. They could only steal her life from her, but Jean-Pierre, oh, *Jean-Pierre,* he could steal her heart, her mind, her soul . . . her freedom, her precious freedom.

Ethan had returned to the circle of his father's arm. She

crossed her arms over her chest and grasped the edge of the soft cashmere as though holding on to a lifeline.

She would not look at him.

She would not look at him.

The ceremony would begin soon and she would be free, at least for a few minutes, of Jean-Pierre and the coffee scent that flowed over her in a constant teasing breeze of sensory torment. She wanted a taste, maybe her tongue licking down the center of his chest, over his hardened nipples, biting into his pecs . . .

She brought a hurried fist to her lips.

Quiet your thoughts, she commanded, *or he will know.* She suspected it was already too late for that, but she didn't want him to know just how much she longed for him, how much she *craved* him. Still, the moment her navy heels had crunched pine needles, she had been aware of him.

He was far away from her, maybe thirty feet. She could measure the distance in her mind, one inch at a time. She wanted him next to her, his fingers resting lightly on her shoulder, the shoulder she had deliberately turned toward him. All she could give him was that shoulder. She wanted to give him so much more. Her throat grew tight with longing and tears, with frustration . . . such deep frustration. But she couldn't give him more than the *little bones* she cast at him. Yes, he called them *little bones,* their dates.

They would have a date soon. It couldn't be too soon for her because she was in agony. He would kiss her and his kisses were like heaven and hell combined, because much to her great humiliation his kisses *brought her.* He knew it, too. He savored the moment. She knew he did. What power did a man have that a mere kiss would swell an orgasm through her body like a stream of lightning flying up and up?

Oh, God.

She had to think of something else or she would go mad.

The ceremony. Yes, the ceremony. She would think of the ceremony.

Warrior Kerrick held his daughter, now three months old, in the circle of his powerful arms. She was holding her head well, and he kept a hand balanced lightly against her bare back. The baby wore an infant flight halter because at any moment Helena could do the unexpected and mount her tiny wings.

Fiona shook her head. Apparently, babies with the ability to mount wings were unheard of on Second Earth. Usually wings emerged somewhere between eight and ten for Twolings, those children born on Second Earth. But Helena's wings were essentially a Third Earth manifestation, the result no doubt of her parentage.

Alison clung to his other arm. She kept dabbing at her cheeks, which brought a rush of tears to Fiona's eyes. She had come to know Alison quite well and from her history understood that before her call to ascension, she had been celibate, even resigned to being without a mate the rest of her life. Her powers were simply too strong for a mortal to bear.

If Fiona understood the problem exactly, Alison's power would have been too much for even most ascended males to bear, which caused Fiona to ponder Jean-Pierre once more. If she was his *breh,* did that also mean that her advanced powers, especially her level of telepathy, would be something few men on Second Earth could handle? Was Jean-Pierre in that sense the only man she could ever truly be with?

Okay, she really didn't want to think about this very sore subject right now.

Focus.

Once more she brought her attention to the ceremony.

Baby Helena, born to Alison Wells and Warrior Kerrick just three months ago, was being presented to the Creator in a simple baptism of oil and ash. The mark of the oil at the base of the throat, a place reflective of life and growth, would hold the ash, which in turned symbolized the spiritual death and rebirth of the soul into the service of Second Earth.

Yes, so much better to think of baby Helena and the joy of the moment.

From the stone building to the left of the altar, a tall woman appeared wearing a red robe.

Fiona drew in a breath that sounded almost like a hiss. For a woman given in service to the Creator of all six dimensional worlds, she had a face pinched like a withered fig. There was nothing of love in this woman. She looked strangely ancient, even though the relative immortality of Second Earth kept everyone looking thirty-ish.

How much Fiona pitied anyone living in submission to what she could only describe as a very sour-looking hag.

"Who stands for this child before the Creator to support the parents, Alison Wells and Warrior Kerrick?"

Jean-Pierre heard Thorne growl faintly as Sister Quena spoke. He glanced at Thorne. Why did he despise the woman so very much?

Jean-Pierre glanced at the tall figure with the sharp cheekbones and strangely lined appearance. Most ascenders were youthful, age being irrelevant past thirty.

She wore a red robe heavily embroidered with designs of wings in gold silk. What a strange counterpoint to the lack of care given to the so-called outdoor chapel.

She stood before a heavy wooden altar, two small brass pots in front of her. The sleeves of her robes had wide swaths of fabric that hung almost to the ground and which, when she lifted her arms to the heavens, created another winged effect.

She rolled her strange black eyes back into her head often when she spoke, as though overcome with spiritual fervor.

In response to her query, Marcus and Havily each took a small step forward. Havily held her *breh*'s arm and smiled up at him. Marcus's voice boomed around the bowl-shaped space. "We support the baby Helena, Havily Morgan and I, Marcus Amargi."

Sister Quena's eyes rolled once more as she lifted her arms and the wings waved back and forth, quite absurd. The woman could perform in spectacle, if she wished.

Thorne released another growl as though he could not contain his dislike of the High Administrator.

Sister Quena made her pronouncement. "The godparents have been approved. Now give me the child."

"Don't do it," Thorne muttered.

Kerrick and Alison approached the altar. Kerrick slid a hand beneath Helena's neck and supported her bottom with his other hand. The sister took the baby—and it was as though one door closed and another opened. She held Helena in a tender cradle of her arms and smiled. Most of the lines and frowns left her visage. The infant smiled back and made small noises. She kicked her feet.

Sister Quena looked at Kerrick. "Warrior, you will place the oil at the base of the child's throat."

Kerrick moved but Jean-Pierre was too far away to see anything. "Yes, there. Good. Now, Alison, please touch the ash, just a little will do, and rub it three times in a circle over the oil." She scrutinized Alison's movements. She nodded. "Yes, very good. Now you will both repeat after me. As the Creator has designed us for service . . ."

The combined voices, male and female, rose into the air, to the tops of the pine trees. "As the Creator has designed us for service . . ."

"So we serve this child."

Again the parents spoke. "So we serve this child."

Jean-Pierre thought it beautiful, very beautiful. Some ritual did bring good things to earth, any dimension.

"And offer ourselves a living sacrifice."

Kerrick and Alison looked at each other as they repeated, "And offer ourselves a living sacrifice."

"Amen."

When the final amen floated through the air, Sister Quena lifted her eyes and let her gaze scan the warriors and guests. "For those of you who have witnessed this baptism, will you join with me in repeating the Holy Affirmation?"

Jean-Pierre had been a mildly observant Catholic during his mortal life, but the French Revolution had stolen the last of his faith.

In this dimension, he had been inside a Creator's Dwelling, as the places of worship were called, a mere handful of times, nothing of significance. But the Holy Affirmation he could believe in, and since it was often used in ceremonies such as this, he'd memorized it. As one, the group spoke: "Oh, most Holy Creator, make of me an instrument in our beloved dimension, of peace, of goodwill, and of service, for as long as the years are given to me. Amen."

Yes, he could believe in peace, goodwill, and service.

Fiona wiped her cheeks. The ceremony had been very short but for some reason, even though the elements weren't known to her, they moved her. Somehow, the giving of the child to God, to the Creator, eased her heart, and she smiled.

It was also a joy to watch the devoted sister holding Helena and obviously delighting in her. Her demeanor preceding the moment of taking the baby in her arms had been one of near-hostility, as though she disapproved of everyone gathered in the outdoor chapel. Perhaps she did. Maybe that was why the ceremony had taken place outdoors instead of in the richly appointed chapel.

As it was, Sister Quena smiled down at the child, her expression rapt. She didn't seem to want to give her up, but at last she rounded the altar and with a heavy sigh placed her in Kerrick's arms once more. Alison still pressed her handkerchief to her face. Her blue eyes glowed with pride and an unearthly light, her smile as warm as sunshine.

She met her *breh*'s gaze and leaned up to kiss him on the lips. Fiona couldn't hear her but she felt certain the words she spoke to Kerrick were, *Thank you.*

Fiona's heart hurt. She had thanked her husband once for giving her their two beautiful children. Together they had presented Carolyn and Peter in baptism a long time ago, when they were infants, a different kind of baptism but still much the same in spirit.

Because the ache grew and grew, and made her think and wonder once more about Jean-Pierre, this time she did not stop from turning and looking at him over the tightly directed shoulder.

He met her gaze and for once she let all that she was feeling just flow toward him, holding nothing back: all her fears, her frustration that they had still not caught Rith, the depth of her loneliness, her wish that they did not live in a world caught in a war, her longing for another family, a different life, even the breadth of her desire for him.

He put a hand to his chest. He held it there and closed his fingers into a fist as though he was holding all her thoughts close to his heart. He was unexpected, this warrior. He possessed a soulfulness that constantly surprised her.

Please come to me, she sent.

He nodded and moved toward her. *I do not think I can do anything else but obey you. What have you done to me? It is as though I am bound to you by a leading rope.*

She smiled, loving how he put words together.

His eyes, blue and gray and green, so beautiful, loomed closer and closer. He was here now beside her. She looked up into his face.

"Warrior Jean-Pierre!" The second eldest Seriffe boy, Alexander, lifted up his arms, a silent plea to be picked up and held.

Jean-Pierre didn't look at him. Fiona didn't think he could. But without breaking their locked gaze, he leaned down, slid his arm around the boy's back, and hefted him to hold him as a father would hold his son. But not once did he shift his gaze from her.

His warm hand settled over the light blue cashmere, and she sighed.

"Do you love my grandma?" Alex asked.

The boy had dipped his chin. His black hair curled at the ends. He looked angelic. He had one arm around Jean-Pierre's neck.

"We all love your grandmother," he said. "All the warriors."

The boy smiled. "She was a blood slave, but now she lives with us."

"All that is very true."

Fiona met Jean-Pierre's gaze and as had happened so many times before, her heart swelled with affection—but why wouldn't it, since he was so kind to Seriffe's children. Jean-Pierre would be a good father. Her husband Terence had been like that as well, kind to children. He had been a strong man, powerful in business, but he knew how to leave his sword at the door when he came home at night.

Sister Quena's voice once more sounded in the strange outdoor chapel. "And now, if the assembled guests would approach Warrior Kerrick and his family and profess once more the pledge you have made to the Creator, our ceremony will be concluded."

Marcus and Havily began, and the warriors that ranged behind Jean-Pierre moved down the three rows of benches, stepping from bench to bench with long, heavily muscled legs.

Carolyn looked back and smiled at Jean-Pierre. She nudged her husband, who turned around and held his arms out to the boy. "Come, Alex, we'll greet baby Helena."

He went willingly, and Seriffe slid him to the pine needles. "Is she going to mount her wings?" Alexander cried. "I want to see her mount her wings."

"Hush, Alex," Carolyn said. "Be respectful. You know we don't ask anyone to mount their wings. It's not polite."

Fiona didn't turn away from Jean-Pierre. She could have. But now that she was near him, she didn't want to be apart from him. He was close and she surrendered to it.

As her family stepped away from the benches to the right and moved down the incline toward the altar, he leaned close and asked, "Speaking of wings, how are your wing-locks doing?"

She shook her head. "Right now, I would give my life for one of those silly small bamboo hands with a long handle that you shove down your shirt."

He laughed. "If you turn around, I will scratch your back."

She closed her eyes and shook her head. "I am so tempted," she whispered.

"I will be very discreet. If you turn to face the altar just a little more, I can do it. We are the only ones up here now. No one will know."

She couldn't help herself. Whatever else he might be, he knew exactly how to relieve the terrible itching—and it was at least one harmless way she could allow his hands on her without losing control. She shifted as he suggested.

He moved in, much closer, and his hand slid beneath the cashmere. He petted her back through her shirt in a long gentle sweep.

She withheld a groan, not because he meant to give her relief but because his touch was heaven and the scent of him, delicious coffee and earthy male, filled her knees with water. "Ohhhh," she murmured.

He began at the lowest wing-lock on the right side of her back. With the exact pressure she needed, he rubbed back and forth.

She groaned softly.

Heaven, heaven, heaven, heaven . . .

"Oh, Jean-Pierre."

He moved to the next wing-lock and with the tips of his fingers pushed the fabric of her shirt over the offending aperture. He continued this from one wing-lock to the next, up and up, then descended the other side. The relief was so profound that by the time he finished she was nearly weeping.

Oh, God . . . thank you so much, she sent. She turned toward him and smiled. "You don't know how much I've wanted to rub my back against the bark of one of these trees."

He smiled. He had the most beautiful smile.

He laughed. His laugh made her heart ache.

Without thinking, she leaned up on her tiptoes and kissed him, a soft brief kiss on his full lips.

His eyes widened. Did he stumble a little?

Fiona, he sent.

I shouldn't have done that.

No, no, he responded straight to her mind. C'était parfait. Absolument parfait. *I expect nothing.* Rien.

She nodded briskly several times. She was about to tell him if he wanted another date, sooner than the allotted two weeks, she would allow it, but at that moment she heard a very faint ringing of bells.

"Do you hear that?" she asked. "It's very beautiful."

He glanced around. "No, I hear nothing except the warriors greeting *petite* Helena. What is it? What do you hear?"

"Well, it sounds like old-fashioned church bells, very soft, the lower registers, deep, sonorous, like a man's voice."

She searched his eyes but still he shook his head.

A headache suddenly broke over her mind and she put her hands to her head. She struggled to draw breath.

"What is it? What is the matter? Tell me, Fiona."

"I . . . I'm not sure. I think it's my telepathy." She released her telepathic shields just a little and directed her attention to the Convent.

A woman's mind suddenly shrieked within hers. *Help me, goddammit! Help me get out of this fucking place!*

The headache released and she opened her eyes to once more meet Jean-Pierre's. "I think a woman inside the Convent is asking for my help. Her mind . . . wow, it's incredibly powerful, although for a moment there she sounded just like Her Supremeness. What do I do?"

He shrugged. "If I were you, I would try to contact her. There must be a reason for such a sudden, unexpected event."

Fiona closed her eyes and directed her mind once more toward the Convent.

Beyond the military parade,
War has no luster,
Just gore.

—*Collected Proverbs,* Beatrice of Fourth

CHAPTER 3

Marguerite paced her cell, the ankle guard banging around her leg. She had calluses now, thick ones. She could feel that Thorne was maybe a hundred yards from her and she couldn't get to him. She couldn't reach out to him telepathically, either, since she had a guard dog monitoring her and she didn't want to give away the fact that she had a very close, personal, hot-as-hell relationship with the leader of the Warriors of the Blood.

But she could send out random cries into the void, cries that her poor guard dog could hear, but no one else.

"Devotiate, I beg of you," Henrietta said. She was stationed just outside Marguerite's door. "Please do not send another telepathic plea. I realize no one is there to hear you, but you know the rules. Sister Quena was most specific. No telepathy of any kind. I do not want to get you into trouble."

Marguerite always tested the waters, even when the waters

were boiling hot. She'd test them and test them. She would test them until she was blistered up to her elbows.

Henrietta was too much of a do-gooder doormat to be a real threat so Marguerite powered up her telepathic ability and all but shouted out into the universe, *Someone help me get out of this fucking shit-box!*

The groans from the hallway pleased her to no end. She smiled.

"Please, Sister Marguerite. You do not understand the level of your powers."

"*Sister* Marguerite? You would say that to me, Hetty? That's a goddam laugh. I'm not a sister. I'm a prisoner."

A long-suffering sigh followed. Henrietta sat on a hard stool outside the cell. She wouldn't even appear in the small barred window near the top of the door. Although to be fair, Hetty had cause. Marguerite had enthralled her once, made her unlock the heavy cell door, and Marguerite had invaded the kitchens and gorged on pastries until Sister Quena found her sitting on the floor, a blanket of flaky crumbs covering her chest.

She laughed when she thought about it. Her pleasures were simple these days if *very* short-lived. She'd spent a month in solitary for that little stunt. Of course, Sister Quena didn't call it solitary. *Private meditation* was her euphemism for being forced to fast for a month in a room that had a bucket for a toilet, no bed, and no light whatsoever.

She paced the ten feet that formed the length of the cell. The ankle guard jumped up and down a few times. God, she hated everything about this place including the way the stiff handwoven fabric caught around her legs.

She wanted Thorne.

She wanted him now.

She wanted out. But if she couldn't be out, she wanted Thorne in her bed. Knowing he was near was causing her serious agony of a purely sexual nature. She flopped down on her back on the stiff mattress that lay cradled on ropes, beds from the dark ages. She had to tighten the ropes to keep the mattress from eventually sagging to the floor.

Thorne had been her saving grace for how many decades? Oh, yeah, ten, since she'd first gotten dumped in this joint by her loving parents.

Who are you? A voice sounded through her head, a woman's voice, an unknown woman's voice.

What the hell?

Marguerite sat up. Someone had penetrated her mind, but who? How? Her shields were said to be like flint. Holy shit. She was careful, however, not to answer. "Henrietta, did you say something to me mind-to-mind?"

"No, Sister. Of course not. I would never disobey Sister Quena, you know that."

The new voice flowed through her head once more. *Are you all right? Are you in danger? I heard your call for help.*

Her call for help? Someone else had picked up on her telepathy? What the hell?

Now who the fuck was trying to communicate with her? Was it a trick? Could Hetty detect this new voice? Apparently not, because she didn't interfere.

She lay back down and rolled her thoughts inward. She closed her eyes and began searching for the origin of the telepathic questions. As far as she knew, no one could invade her mind. She had extraordinary shields and she knew it, so how had an unknown woman gotten inside her head without even a hint of her presence?

She took her time following what proved to be a gold stream of light. She traveled slowly, hoping to avoid Henrietta's scrutiny. After a good long moment, she got very close and realized that here was a woman of tremendous power situated near Thorne, which meant that the woman had attended baby Helena's baptism.

Marguerite lifted her brows. Well, well, well. A woman, who was somehow connected to the Warriors of the Blood or at the very least to Alison or Warrior Kerrick, was actually communicating with her. *Damn.* This had possibilities.

She opened her eyes and stared up at the wood-beam ceiling. But she remained buried in her mind and wondered just what she should do. Should she risk punishment by contacting the woman?

I can feel you, the unknown woman sent. *I sense that you're very close, in the Convent, right? Did you call to me? Are you in danger?*

Shit, yes, this ascender had power. Ah, what the hell! She couldn't help it. She had to know, had to communicate even if Hetty would figure it out and alert Sister Quena.

So you heard me yelling for someone to get me out of this place?

A pause, maybe a faint gasp. *Yes, I did.*

And you can sense that I'm in the Convent?

Another pause. *Actually, I'm right next to you. Do you have a sense that I'm there?*

I have to say I don't. So this isn't just telepathy.

Something a little more involved than telepathy, yes.

No shit? she sent.

"Sister," Henrietta called out. "You are forbidden! You must desist at once!" Sister Henrietta could sense the telepathy the way a good bloodhound could smell prey—one particle in a million—even if she couldn't actually register the nature of the communication. Dammit.

Marguerite ignored her as she focused on her new friend. *You're very powerful. What's your name?*

Fiona. And yours?

Marguerite. I'm Thorne's woman.

Silence. Long silence. Finally, *Thorne's woman? But . . . we all thought he was celibate.*

Henrietta now pounded on the door. "Sister, cease, or I will have to summon the regulators!"

Marguerite blinked. She was also hearing something else, something that should have been lovely to her ears but which gave her a profound sense of unease. *Do you hear that, Fiona? Church bells?*

Another silence, then, *Yes, but apparently only you and I can hear them. I heard them earlier. Did you?*

Yes.

A dark, dark feeling flowed over Marguerite. She tilted her head back and the future streams were suddenly upon her, a fierce pressure demanding her attention *now.*

She rode them, because she knew she could sense that something terrible was on the way, something menacing and evil, something that had the preternatural taste of death vampires.

She searched quickly, riding fast. The church bells grew stronger and within the space of three seconds she found a ribbon of light, a shimmering green, a vibrant emerald green, iridescent and exquisite. But she began to tremble on the bed, and perspiration beaded on her forehead, her neck, and beneath her breasts. Sweet Christ, what was going on, and who did this emerald ribbon belong to?

She mentally grabbed hold of the ribbon. At the same moment, she sent a message to Fiona. *Stay with me. Trouble's on the way.*

Of course, returned to her. Definitely possibilities.

She rode the light and saw a figure hovering high in the air, looking down, well above the Convent and the outdoor chapel. He floated but he had not mounted his wings. Levitation? Very powerful levitation, and he maintained invisibility without the use of mist.

The unknown ascender was very handsome in a dark way; thick, blackish brown hair flowed away from his face in waves and curls and hung very long, past the middle of his back. His nose was strong but narrow, almost hawkish. He had large deep brown eyes framed with thick black lashes. He wore a black leather vest that revealed a feathering of matching chest hair. His pants were white and so snug that Marguerite's brows rose. Here was an ascender who knew how to *display.* And she was a vampire who loved to *look.* Whoa, mama!

He wore embroidered white leather ankle boots with some kind of insignia on the sides, she couldn't tell. But his hair was the main feature, since it floated away from his face, as though responding to the obvious excitement he was experiencing.

Well, shit. If an air of malice hadn't clung to him, he was so the sort of man she went for.

He wasn't exactly a death vampire, though. Her instincts told her as much and she always trusted her instincts, but neither was he a Second ascender. He was higher than that. Holy shit, an Upper ascender. Well, what the fuck do you know? Huh.

The pealing bells returned and floated around the vampire. Interesting. The sound of the deep church bells, which so far only she and Fiona could hear, belonged to this Upper ascender. She wondered which dimension he was from. Third? Fourth?

But what was he looking at and where the hell was he? The sky around him was a sharp blue, a mountain blue. Shit, he must be close by. But just how far in the future was this little episode?

She drew near and positioned herself beside him. She turned in the air and looked down as well, knowing that she needed to see exactly what had put such a satisfied smile on his face.

Oh, hell. From this position, she could see the outdoor chapel below, one couple off by themselves, the rest clustered by the altar and that bitch of a witch, Sister Quena.

She shivered, then the time frame kicked in. This was hardly the future . . . *this was twenty seconds from now!*

She scanned the surrounding forest and finally figured out why the bastard next to her was smiling. From every point of entry to the outdoor chapel, death vampires moved into position, even some from the direction of the Convent.

Suddenly the ribbon of light disappeared and she was brought back to her present not-so-great situation.

Hands and arms grabbed at her, pulling her up and out of the Seer trance. Palms slapped her face. She opened her eyes.

Oh, shit, the regulators had already arrived. She felt a pinprick in her neck. Dammit! She only had seconds now.

Fiona! she cried.

I'm here.

Death vampires . . . in the forest . . . now . . . all around the outdoor chapel. Her mind slipped away as she flopped back onto the hard mattress.

Marguerite, Marguerite, Fiona called to her.

Her last thought was of Fiona, and that perhaps at long last she had found the key to her escape.

Jean-Pierre did not understand what was happening to his woman. She looked blind, as though held in a trance of some kind. He had told her to attempt to connect with the woman, but he grew concerned. Perhaps she was just concentrating very hard on something, a vision, maybe, inside her head.

He put his hand on her neck and rubbed her cheek with his thumb. He stared into her eyes, but she was not focused on him. She merely dipped her chin in response. At least she could acknowledge him. That was a good thing.

He did not wish to disturb whatever was happening, but his skin crawled in some kind of warning. She was upset now. He could see it in her eyes. His gaze flitted to the forest. He was uneasy—or maybe it was just Fiona and her strange behavior.

Finally, she blinked. Yet she did not hold his gaze. Instead she turned to stare at Thorne, who smiled at Alison as he drifted his forefinger over baby Helena's cheek.

"Thorne," she called out. "Death vampires in the forest. Now!"

Thorne glanced around. His gaze landed on the Convent then back to Fiona. A split second later he called out, "Marcus, Kerrick, Seriffe, Jean-Pierre . . . get the women and children out of here."

The next moment, Jean-Pierre felt the hairs on his nape lift, a certain sign that Fiona's warning was accurate.

He prepared to fold Fiona away from the chapel, but she shook her head and placed her hand on his arm. "I must stay. The woman issued the warning. I must speak with her."

"No, I must get you to safety. You do not know what this will be like. You have listened to the battles over the loudspeaker at headquarters, but this you have not seen."

Seriffe folded his family away. Kerrick, Alison, and their

baby vanished. Marcus had his arm around Havily as they dematerialized together. Sister Quena folded as well.

Thorne shouted, "Jean-Pierre! Get Fiona the fuck out of here!"

"I won't leave," she cried. "I'm needed here."

"Fuck!" he shouted in response, as warriors changed into leather battle gear and swords flew into waiting fists. He added, "Jean-Pierre, manage your woman."

"With all due respect, Warrior Thorne," Fiona cried. "Like hell."

Jean-Pierre met Fiona's hard stare. He recognized the oh-so-stubborn glint in her eye. "I wish you would not stay. This will be very . . . messy." He tried to put into that last word everything a battle against death vampires could be.

She shook her head, but he saw the fear in her eyes as her gaze strafed the surrounding forest. "I can't explain it, Jean-Pierre, but I can't leave this place. Not yet. If I can reach the woman again, I must."

"Very well." To Thorne he called out, "Fiona believes she must stay and I will not force her to go."

Jean-Pierre waved a hand, and gone was his finery. He now wore a black leather kilt, weapons harness of the same sturdy black leather that held two daggers, studded wrist guards, black battle sandals, and shin guards.

His sword was in his hand as Thorne shouted at Fiona, "Goddammit! Fiona, get the hell out of here! You don't understand what's about to happen."

Fiona turned in Thorne's direction and in a loud voice responded, "Marguerite issued the warning."

Thorne's complexion paled. "Marguerite warned you?"

"Yes," Fiona responded.

"Who is Marguerite?" Jean-Pierre asked.

But it was too late now. In the distance, deep into the forest, there was movement everywhere, a dozen, two dozen, more. *Mon Dieu.* "Fiona, let me take you from here. I have never seen so many."

She shook her head. She squeezed his arm. "No, no. This is where I belong."

Jean-Pierre slid his arm around Fiona's waist and pulled her tight against him. "This will be very bad. Are you sure?" He heard the running feet of the death vampires. "There is still time."

"I will stay. I must."

"Very well." He turned his gaze. "Luken! Zacharius! Fiona believes she must stay. Will you help me protect her?"

The men answered by drawing close to Fiona, or as close as they could with all the awkward benches in the way. With swords drawn, they formed a protective triangle around her, facing away from her.

What he feared the most had come upon him. His woman was at his back and dozens of death vampires moved forward on swift-running feet through the forest. How could he keep her alive against so many?

They came.

They were so beautiful, dark hair, bluish translucent skin, dark eyes, muscled like gods, fierce, fair of face. *Mon Dieu.* Even after more than two centuries of battling them, he could still be almost mesmerized by such incredible beauty.

But he knew their beauty served them in exactly that way—for what mortal or ascender, other than trained warriors, could withstand such magnificence? They were designed to enthrall, to trap, to kill the mortal in order to quench their addiction to the powerful effects of dying blood.

He lowered his chin and dropped into a fighting stance.

Three attacked him at once, but his sword flew in swift arcs and at preternatural speed, leaping over the bench in front of him, and before he had even struck steel two pretty-boys were on the ground cut, bleeding, and flying toward death on swift wings.

The third was older and much more skilled with his sword. He matched strike for strike. Jean-Pierre focused his attention on his adversary's waist and, noting the direction of movement, he countered, struck, and decapitated him.

He did not dare look behind him but he heard Fiona softly within his head. *Five to the left.*

How calm his woman sounded in the midst of battle.

Five to his left and another three to his right. *Merde.*

He had never seen so many death vampires in one place before, not even at the Borderlands during the night.

To Fiona, he sent, *Make yourself very small, low to the ground, near a bench if possible.*

What he had to do next would require skill and much movement. He did not want a blade to touch her accidentally. He folded, materialized behind the ones to his right, and took out three along the hamstring, then resumed his place in front of Fiona.

The remaining two were bewildered by the maneuver, but they gathered their fighting wits and approached. He could not risk leaving Fiona again.

He drew a deep breath, plotted his course, and moved like a whirlwind, spinning and striking with preternatural speed. The other warriors did the same. He brought them all to the ground but none were dead and they would heal.

What he had to do next, he did not have time to issue a warning to Fiona.

He moved from one to the next and took each head in a barbaric series of moves. This he would have protected her from if he could have.

More came. On and on he fought. He caught glimpses of Fiona crouched, keeping herself low to the ground, but moving away from the warriors when needed. She never once uttered a sound. Luken and Zacharius fought as well, in the same manner, with speed, agility, and the training of centuries.

Fiona's determination shaped itself into a rock. The beauty of the death vampires meant nothing to her, had no power over her, because she knew what they did to arrive at such beauty. After all, her blood had fed them for over a hundred years. The only thing that really surprised her was how much they looked alike—not completely, but there was an overwhelming resemblance. She knew this was true of the monsters, but she'd never seen it before.

Rage boiled in her blood, in her chest, in her lungs until she felt choked with it. She wished for a sword in her hand and the ability to battle as the warriors around her were battling. These creatures deserved death and as each Warrior of the Blood took death vampires to the ground, something primal within her rejoiced, even savored the blood that now poured over the pine needles and into the hard ground beneath.

Her heartbeat pounded in her head, loud, hard thumps. She should have been horrified by what she saw around her, but she knew how these men fought. She had heard tales for months now, and she had listened to the battles of the Militia Warriors over the loudspeaker at HQ.

On her dates with Jean-Pierre she had asked him many questions about what his battles were like. He had been reluctant to speak at first, but in the end her persistence had been rewarded and more and more he had opened up about the thrill of slaying the enemy, because he knew each kill meant that he had saved lives.

So it was that she rejoiced with every death now.

The number of death vampires that came began to diminish. The fighting had extended farther away from her since there were bodies everywhere. She recalled what Jean-Pierre had told her about Central Command, so she made a phone call to Alison who connected her. Central Command served Endelle and the Warriors of the Blood, while HQ served Seriffe and the Thunder God Warriors, as the Militia Warriors were known among the ranks.

"Carla here, Fiona. How may I serve?" How calm she sounded even though no doubt Alison had told her what was going on. Carla worked Central during the day while her counterpart, Jeannie, served the warriors at night. Both women were utterly adored by the Warriors of the Blood.

"We need cleanup. There have to be at least thirty, maybe forty, death vamps on the ground, but some are still half alive so the morgue should have Militia Warriors on standby." She heard the clicking of fingernails on a keyboard.

"We've still got a battle going, right?" Carla asked.

"Yes." The women at Central were so calm.

"Small bursts. Let the men know. Just say those words so everyone can hear."

Fiona had never done this before but she called out in a loud voice, "Small bursts."

Thorne, who had a break in the fighting, echoed her. "Small bursts."

"Done," Fiona said into her phone.

The flashes of light were almost blinding, but by report she knew it was nothing compared with the comprehensive cleanup Central was capable of doing.

Bodies disappeared, body parts, severed heads, debris she didn't want to put a name to, mostly big stuff.

Another wave of death vampires came, almost as heavy as the first. The battle raged.

The circle closed nearer to her again. Thorne and Santiago formed another wall around her. She knelt in the pine needles, her silk skirt a very thin layer of protection against the prickly needles and rough ground.

In intervals, Fiona made her calls to Carla. Small bursts of light kept everyone's eyesight safe. Debris vanished.

Not until a good fifteen minutes had passed did the last of the death vampires fall. After one last conversation with Carla, all that remained was Fiona surrounded by five warriors. Each of the men bent over, gasping to catch his breath from the sudden harsh exertion. Each pointed his identified sword toward the dirt to protect the others. Sweat streamed and mingled with blood spatter on bare skin.

Fiona rose to her feet.

"Madre de Dios," Santiago cried. "There must have been over seventy, maybe eighty."

"Shit," Luken stated succinctly.

"Lady present," Thorne said.

"No, please," Fiona cried. "Don't hold back on my account. I'll say it, too. Shit!"

Jean-Pierre met her gaze. *"Ça va?"*

"I'm fine, really. I am. You . . . you were all wonderful, really wonderful." She met each gaze. She wanted them to know she approved, that she wasn't upset by what she'd seen. "I only wish I could have battled alongside you."

Zacharius nodded his understanding. "You, above all, would want them dead."

"Yes," she cried, her voice splitting resonance. *"Oh, yes. All of them. All of them."*

"Did you hear that?" Luken pumped his fist in the air. "She fucking split resonance."

"Split-resonance," Jean-Pierre said. "That is power, Fiona. Much power. So, *oui,* your powers are emerging."

For some reason, the image that ran through her head was one she had carried with her all her life as a blood slave, one of the face of every woman who had died because she'd been worn out by being drained of her blood and brought back to life month after month, year after year.

Fiona had memorized each face, each name.

Throughout the decades of her captivity, she had often recited those names and promised retaliation if it was ever within her power to destroy those who had taken all those precious lives.

This was what lived in her, a dark storm, the thunder and lightning that possessed her soul. This was why she kept Jean-Pierre at bay: because she didn't have room for him. But would he ever understand? So long as those faces lived in her mind, so long as she had breath, she would work to eliminate all the death vampires from the face of the earth, any dimension, so help her God.

She blinked and realized that the men were all watching her, each pair of eyes, each face full of concern. She took a breath and dipped her chin. "Thank you" was what came out of her mouth. And she meant it.

"Jesus," Luken murmured. "Fiona, we're so sorry you had to see all this, to be afflicted again."

But heat invaded her heart and she stared at him hard. "I'm grateful they're dead, Warrior Luken. Every last one of them. I never thought I would be this person, this woman, to be grateful that any creature died. But don't you see, my blood may have fueled them all for who knows how long.

"Do you know the anguish I feel because of that? Do you know how enraged I am that my blood, through no fault of my own, may have been the cause of the deaths of the innocent? No, do not tell me you were sorry that I witnessed this slaughter, because I'm grateful on so many levels. So, I will say this again, *thank you.*" She knew she had split her resonance again, and more than one pair of brows rose because of it.

Luken folded a dark towel into his hands, wiped his face and neck down first, then went to work on the blade of his sword.

Thorne cleared his throat after which his rough voice hit the airwaves. "You spoke of a warning. You had a warning this was going to happen. Can you tell me about that?"

She met his gaze. She saw the wary shift of his eyes away from her, in the direction of the Convent building, then back. "One of the sisters called to me telepathically and issued the warning just before the death vamps arrived." There was more to tell, a lot more, but this was not the time, nor the place, especially given the haunted look in Thorne's eyes. Since everyone present thought he was celibate, and she knew by Marguerite's admission that he wasn't, she had no intention of talking about the woman in front of the other warriors.

His gaze slid to the carpet of needles. "Shit," he murmured.

"I feel compelled to try to contact her right now," Fiona said. "With your permission."

He gave a small shake of his head then stopped himself. "By all means."

With all the men still watching her, she closed her eyes and focused on the Convent once more. She lowered her telepathic shields and at first was bombarded by the thoughts of every woman within the building. One by one, she shut them down, searching for Marguerite, until the last mind disappeared. Then there was nothing. Just nothing.

She shook her head. "I can't find her. I don't hear her."

"But you communicated with her mind-to-mind before?" Thorne asked.

"Yes."

He whistled. "That's a helluva lot of power, Fiona. But as you know, my sister, Grace, lives here in this Convent. She's said that not only is telepathic communication forbidden, but if it's discovered by one of the administrators, punishment can follow."

"You think that's what happened to . . . this woman? The one called Marguerite?" She'd spoken her name before and felt compelled to say it now.

"Given all that Grace has told me over the years, yes, I believe that's what happened. The Convent has numerous barbaric policies, and a band of enforcement sisters called regulators administer justice for every infraction."

Fiona felt ill, her stomach turning over. She held Thorne's gaze. "Is it possible this woman is kept imprisoned here?"

He shook his head. "It's not as simple as that. Some of the women are placed here by well-meaning relatives. This might have been the case with the woman who contacted you."

Again her stomach writhed. She had been within the woman's mind, and though she detected a certain wildness of spirit, there was nothing cruel about her. The fact that she had gone so far as to deliver the warning spoke of her character more than anything else could have. "Whatever the case," Fiona said, "this woman saved all our lives here this morning."

"Hear, hear," Zach said. Each of the men followed suit.

She met Jean-Pierre's gaze and offered a half smile. "But what I'd really like right now is a drink." She shifted her gaze to encompass the group. "Any of you boys have an idea where I could get one?"

"Hell, yeah," Luken said.

"To the Cave." This time, Santiago lifted his fist in the air.

The warriors all shifted to look at Thorne, since he always had the last word. Fiona knew that generally women weren't invited to share a drink at what was essentially the private, very male-oriented rec room.

But he met Fiona's gaze for a long tense moment, then nodded. "To the Cave."

After the warriors folded their swords back to protected lockers, the men one by one lifted arms and vanished.

Jean-Pierre took Fiona's hand. She met his gaze and nodded to him. His ocean-blue eyes were lit with fire. "Shall I do the honors?" he asked.

He was polite, and she valued that. "Yes, please."

He returned her half smile and the vibration began.

Once at the Cave, a large building in downtown Metro Phoenix Two, Fiona accepted a vodka and tonic from Santiago.

She took a deep breath and let the tension of the recent battle go.

Casimir held a chilled martini glass by the stem; Dubonnet, London dry gin, a slice of lemon. He struggled to understand exactly what he was feeling.

He held the mass of his hair back and sipped. He stood on the balcony of his room at the Plaza Athénée and since it was already night in Paris he had a view of the Eiffel Tower, glittering like a diamond. He loved the noise of the Mortal Earth city below. Nothing like this existed on Fourth Earth Paris. The population of the fourth dimension did not begin to approach Mortal Earth so there was no need for Paris Four to have this delicious crammed-together sensibility.

He was a vampire of simple emotions. Lust usually led the way. But ever since he'd agreed to assist Commander Greaves in his efforts to take over Second Earth, something within his soul had shifted. In the five thousand years of his absurd life, he'd never been quite this driven to see a task accomplished.

He had to admit he was pissed off by events of an hour ago, in real-time Arizona Two. Eighty death vampires and not one Warrior of the Blood so much as scratched.

He'd been convinced there would be at least one kill, but apparently he was shit out of luck.

Fuck.

Julianna slid her arms around him from behind. "You are very tense. Let me braid your hair."

"Do you need me to hunt tonight?" Hunting would be a good thing to do given his current state.

"Yes," she whispered against his shoulder. "I'm hungry for all the prey you bring home and everything we'll do together. You have seduced me, Caz. Please hunt tonight."

"Maybe."

"You're tense," she said, biting his bare shoulder. He still wore his leather vest. "Didn't the slaughter at the Convent go well?"

He was angry and something more. "Not by half." He turned into her, holding his martini glass aloft. Her hand slid low, right where he wanted it. She squeezed a little too hard, just the way he liked it.

He hissed.

"Tell me everything," she cooed. "Let me make you feel better." She rubbed. He kissed her forehead.

"You ease me, Ju-Ju. I didn't expect this when I bartered for you." She was the price he had required of Greaves in order to come on board.

She pouted and stopped her ministrations. "Please don't remind me."

She walked away. She was still unhappy about having left Greaves, but he didn't know why. He knew she was relatively content, even satisfied being with him, that she enjoyed him, yet she would express her displeasure and he was always surprised.

She wore a loose white silk top, cut to reveal her perfect cleavage, and matching flowy pants, very wide at the ankle. She had on strappy white heels with little squares of gold down the instep. She curled up on the gold silk couch, her hands clasped around one elevated knee.

"You can't love Greaves." He sipped again.

She lifted her chin. "What if I do? What of it? You took me to punish him. But don't you see, Caz, that you've punished me instead? I think it grossly unfair, ungentlemanly."

He threw his head back and laughed. "I never said I was a gentleman, *ma petite idiote*."

She huffed for a moment, then patted the seat next to her.

"Come sit beside me and let me braid your hair." She was a woman of vast appetites. That he'd introduced her to the pleasure of hurting mortals almost to the point of death while taking their blood had given her a new taste that she needed satisfied . . . often.

He smiled. He was happy to oblige. There was truly so much to like about this woman. For a hedonist, she was a perfect partner. She might pout, but she never truly complained. "Very well."

She smiled. He joined her on the elegant sofa. Pity. The expensive fabric would be very stained by the end of the night. But then he had resources and could pay for the repairs.

Julianna began pulling his hair back, away from his face. She used her fingers to comb through it, quite soothing. She created a very appropriate French braid. He always wore his hair braided, out of the way, when he hunted.

Just when she'd folded a stretchy band to secure the bottom of the braid, he heard the sound of small running feet.

He set his now empty martini glass on the coffee table and opened his arms wide. His two young boys, Kendrew and Sloane, ran toward him and leaped on him.

He caught them up, rose to his feet, then spun them in a circle, delighting in the chortles that came from their young throats. He loved being a father, a real surprise since this was a first for him in all these millennia.

He had loved their mother as well, a deep love, one that almost made him human. Almost.

He returned to the sofa, holding each boy on a knee. He ignored Julianna who now scowled. She didn't like his children, but he didn't care.

"Tell me what you did today?"

Kendrew, recently turned five, talked about the park, having a pastry and café au lait. Sloane, not quite three, looked at him and asked. "When is Mama coming home?"

He kissed Sloane on the cheek. "She had an accident, remember? A car hit her and took her life. She can't come back to us, ever."

"Why not?"

Kendrew became impatient and flicked his younger sibling on the cheek. "Because she's dead, stupid. Dead people don't come back. Ever."

Sloane started to cry. Caz gathered him up close, holding him over his shoulder, the way Warrior Kerrick had so lovingly held his daughter, Helena.

Kendrew didn't cry. He just stared off into space and sucked on his lower lip.

"Remember, *mes enfants,* life is very difficult and sometimes bad things happen to wonderful people. But your papa will always make certain that you are well loved. Do you understand?"

Sloane nodded against his shoulder.

"Kendrew?" The five-year-old looked up at him, his eyes wet, his lips pressed together hard. He nodded as well.

Caz drew the older boy up over his empty shoulder and hugged them both.

A sliver of fear, a prescience, a knowing, passed through him, that the bargain he had made with Greaves in haste and out of sheer boredom would cost him something very precious in the coming months.

He took deep breaths and held his boys harder still. Something had happened in Arizona that he still didn't quite understand. How did the woman Fiona, *breh* to Warrior Jean-Pierre and former blood slave, know to give the warriors a warning that death vampires were in the forest?

It would appear he had a mystery to solve, and at that he smiled. Mysteries were a good thing to hedonistic, easily bored Fourth ascenders. As for the sense of approaching doom, he mentally set it on fire until it turned to ashes. A Fourth ascender could always direct his path away from danger.

He needed to consult with Rith, whom Greaves kept very close these days in his Geneva penthouse. At this point, Rith was more a lapdog than a useful tool in the war, but he had a well-developed Third ability to ride the future streams and had predicted a slaughter at the Convent, something Casimir hadn't taken seriously since it was only one of several outcomes that had shown up in the future streams.

Yet the slaughter had happened, which was why Caz needed to figure out what had intruded to disrupt his moment of glory.

For just a moment, he pondered Fiona Gaines, the woman Warrior Jean-Pierre obsessed over in the growing tradition of the *breh-hedden*. Caz knew she had emerging powers.

But what kind of powers? How had she known to warn the warriors about the attack? He had read her powers previously, more than once. She had tremendous telepathic ability. However, beyond that, she was truly a disappointment. She could barely fold from place to place. She couldn't throw a hand-blast. She had no preternatural speed. In some ways, her connection to the Warriors of the Blood was a complete mystery.

And yet, with all that lack of power, she had saved them all.

When Sloane's crying ceased and when the boys grew relaxed against his shoulders, he lowered them to their feet and, taking each hand, walked them back to their bedroom, where their au pair stayed. She was a Second ascender, quite a gifted horticulturalist, great with children, and lovely to behold.

Greaves had recommended her when his beloved wife died. Of course, he'd abducted her and made a little mischief with the memories of those closest to her. He kept her partially enthralled all the time so that she would remain content with her surroundings. The effort required some energy because she was very powerful.

But enthrallment couldn't answer for her character. A mean person enthralled was still very mean. Greaves had been right. The woman was, therefore, kind, loving, firm when necessary and never vicious, the perfect babysitter.

As he watched her draw Sloane onto her lap and stroke his unruly blond hair, he marveled at the airy waves of her long curly red hair. If not for the color, she would have looked positively angelic.

"Tazianne, I'll be leaving for a couple of hours. Make sure the boys have their baths then put them to bed."

"Very good, *monsieur.*"

He closed the door and headed out to hunt. At some point, he felt certain he'd solve the mystery of Fiona's warning, but for now he turned his attention to the pleasures before him.

Time to hunt.

Some choices just suck.

—*Collected Proverbs,* Beatrice of Fourth
Translation into the modern vernacular

CHAPTER 4

At eleven thirty in the morning, Thorne held his tumbler of icy Ketel One in his hand and tried to keep the damn thing from shaking. He wasn't sure if it was post-battle adrenaline or the fact that Fiona had communicated with Marguerite. He took a sip and let the fire burn down his throat. He drew in a deep breath.

Hands still shaking.

He leaned his hips against the pool table, which had somehow miraculously escaped damage in the last few months since it had been replaced. Must have been a record, but then with Marcus out of the picture but two nights a week, Medichi traveling the globe, and Kerrick anxious to get home to his wife and baby after battling till dawn, there was a helluva lot less testosterone being thrown around these days.

He sipped again, savored another burning slide, and finally his fingers were a little less shaky.

He'd rarely taken his eyes off Fiona from the time she touched down at the Cave. He was trying to figure out how to separate her from Jean-Pierre so he could talk to her for a couple of minutes, find out exactly what she knew about Marguerite.

The whole situation was eating him alive.

Damn but Fiona was another beauty, all right. She had dark wavy hair, though not quite as dark as Parisa's or Marguerite's for that matter, more reddish gold. Fiona's eyes were blue, but much lighter than Alison's, and on the silver side. If she hadn't been a loving kind of woman, her eyes could have been called icy. But with a face that always measured everyone else with expressions of concern, *ice* was the last word he'd ever use to describe Fiona Gaines.

She was also tall, like the three other women who'd become *brehs* to their warriors. Was height some sort of indication the women were meant for the *breh-hedden*? None of the Warriors of the Blood was shorter than six-five. Jean-Pierre was no exception. So, Fiona, at close to six feet, was a match for him.

Marguerite, on the other hand, was a full foot shorter than Thorne, only five-five, so it looked like she couldn't be his *breh* if height were a requirement. Of course, her lack of height hadn't made one damn bit of difference in bed. He'd taken her every which way from Sunday over the decades. He took a sip of Ketel to keep from smiling. Marguerite was an experimental sort of woman, always game for the most outrageous gymnastics.

But she wasn't tall.

And she didn't have a special scent, either, which of course meant that even though Marguerite had become his goddam raison d'être, she could never be his *breh*.

He should have felt relieved. Instead, the whole thing bugged the shit out of him.

And what the hell did it mean that Marguerite had been able to contact Fiona and deliver a warning about an attack at the outdoor chapel? He knew his woman was an extraordinarily gifted Seer, but had she really been in the future streams just before the attack? And how had she been able to contact Jean-Pierre's *breh*?

He was as confused as hell.

One thing he did need to know, however, was how much Fiona knew about Marguerite. No one knew about her, certainly not her name. But here was Fiona, not five months in the Metro Phoenix Two area, and she knew his woman's name.

Jesus H. Christ.

For the past five minutes, he'd been trying to figure out how to approach her and have a private conversation without Jean-Pierre listening in. Damn preternatural hearing.

For the past century, since he'd first hooked up with Marguerite, he'd been keeping her a secret from the brotherhood. He didn't exactly care if they knew, but he feared Endelle knowing more than anything. Yeah, she'd have shipped Marguerite off to the Superstition Fortress in the blink of an eye—after, of course, a significant negotiation with the High Administrator of that hellhole, Owen fucking Stannett.

He suspected Fiona knew something he didn't want her to know, and he had to swear her to silence. God help him if Endelle found out about Marguerite because he honestly didn't know what he would do, where his loyalties would fall. Truth? He couldn't lose Marguerite. Even thinking about it made him feel like he was flying apart inside.

Sweet Jesus!

When Fiona glanced at him, he held her gaze for a long moment. He knew he was frowning, but he was trying to get a message to her without opening a telepathic channel. Holy hell, if Jean-Pierre knew he'd tried to converse with his *breh* mind-to-mind, without permission . . . well, let's just say the shit would hit one big motherfucker of a fan.

You didn't mess with a warrior's *breh* on any level, and that included telepathy.

She returned his frown with one of her own then turned to Jean-Pierre. He could have listened in, but he kept his hearing tight.

He wasn't surprised when, after an exchange of words,

and a scowl directed at him by the Frenchman, she crossed the rec room to him.

She didn't exactly smile; more like an uneasy curve of lips. "I thought you might want to talk," she said quietly as she drew near.

He could feel the frown between his brows. He crossed his arms over his pecs, holding his tumbler off to the side. "So," he said in true brilliant fashion since nothing else came to mind.

Fiona's gaze shifted away from him, maybe trying to figure out what to tell him. She blinked several times. Finally, she looked back at him. "Shall I tell you everything?"

He released a heavy sigh. "Yes. Please. But keep it low."

She nodded then laid it out. She had a measured way of speaking, restrained. She was very careful. Again, no doubt the result of having lived in captivity.

When she told him that Marguerite had said she was *his woman,* he mumbled a few curses then spoke through pinched lips. "No one knows."

"I figured that much since it was the first I'd heard of it. I won't say anything if you don't want me to but, is she your *breh*?"

He shook his head back and forth, and his Ketel sloshed around. "No, I don't think so."

"Have you been together long?"

He met her gaze. Now that the cat was out of the bag, and because she'd somehow gotten stuck in the middle, he said, "About a century."

Her brows rose. "You're kidding."

"Nope, not kidding." His thoughts darkened as he thought about the last hundred years. Shit.

"I got the feeling she's desperate to get out of there."

"Yeah, more so lately. Her abilities to ride the future streams have become more . . . pressing for lack of a better word, even taking her over at times. She isn't so much riding them as they're riding her. It's getting to her." He was surprised, suddenly, at how good it felt to just talk about his horrible situation.

"Is that how she knew to warn me about the attack?"

"I think so. She's . . . gifted."

"What do you think it meant that we both heard church bells? At first I thought they were the Convent bells, but Jean-Pierre couldn't hear them."

"I'm not sure." He shook his head back and forth. "We don't have anything like that on Second Earth. It might be some kind of Third Earth ability."

Thorne got a really sick feeling that the woman in front of him and his woman were connected somehow. This couldn't be a good thing. The last year had been a nightmare, what with Alison's frightening ascension and all the trouble that had ensued since: the increase of death vamps at the Borderlands, the attempt on his own life, Parisa's abduction and recovery, a horrendous battle over the Grand Canyon that took the lives of a thousand Militia Warriors.

But this, Fiona having conversed telepathically with Marguerite without ever having met her, then having received a warning from her, smacked of *convergence*. And convergence always meant escalation . . . like today's battle at a goddam baptism.

He needed to tell Endelle that they were in for it but if he did then he'd have to explain about Marguerite. Revealing his woman's Seer power would blow his life all to hell. And yeah, he was being selfish, but he just wasn't ready to do that.

He uncrossed his arms and with a string of harsh gulps he downed the rest of the Ketel.

"What do I do, Warrior Thorne? Jean-Pierre will want to know more and we . . . well, we tend to share things with each other. He's my guardian, after all."

"Shit," Thorne muttered. Mentally, he let loose with a really long string of obscenities, but for Fiona's sake he kept his trap shut. "Well," he said at last. "I think you'd better tell him everything, but I'm asking that both of you keep all that we've discussed, especially anything concerning Marguerite, close to the vest. Okay?"

"Of course. Of course."

He supposed that if anyone would understand discretion

and restraint it would be this woman. She was really lovely, her complexion like milk, her eyes a silver-blue, her brows arched and so pretty.

Suddenly all he could think about was that she'd been used as a blood slave. "I'm so sorry, Fiona. I'm so sorry."

"For what?"

"For that whole thing, being trapped like you were, your blood harvested like some kind of farm animal. I'm so sorry. If we'd known, we would have come for you. I promise you that, but we just didn't know."

He heard her gasp, a faint sound from deep in her throat. She lowered her chin and her gaze. He hadn't meant to upset her, and it didn't surprise him that Jean-Pierre picked up on it and moved with preternatural speed to get to her side and put his hand on her shoulder.

He glared at Thorne. "What have you done? What did you say to her?" He let loose with a really long string of French. It couldn't have been a compliment.

Fiona put her hand to her forehead.

"What the fuck did you say to her, Thorne? Why is she so unhappy? *Merde.*"

"I . . . I said I was sorry that she'd been used as a blood slave. I didn't mean to cause her pain."

Fiona turned toward Jean-Pierre and put her hand on his cheek. "It was kindly meant. He just took me by surprise and sometimes, I'll confess, *sometimes* certain things, at unexpected moments, have the power to take me back there. I was back there. But I'm not now. It's okay. Alison said it would happen and it does, but Thorne was expressing a great kindness, nothing more."

"Shit." Sheet.

Thorne wanted to apologize again and again, but now he feared that another *I'm sorry* would once more have the opposite effect and remind of her where she'd spent the last hundred years.

His gaze flicked to the ratty brown leather sofa against the back wall adjacent to the bar. Luken, the biggest of the warriors and as muscled as hell, sat on the couch, his head back at an angle. He had a beer in one hand, propped on his thigh. His eyes were closed. The beer listed sideways and Luken snapped awake, righted it, then closed his eyes again.

Santiago was slumped on one of the bar stools, and Zach was stretched out on the floor yawning.

Thorne shook his head. They'd battled all night, stayed up a little longer to be at baby Helena's baptism, then battled some more. "All right, you men," he called out. "Head home. Now. Get some sleep."

Heads bobbed. All three struggled to their feet and with each lifting an arm, they disappeared. Luken took his beer with him.

"I'll say a good night or good morning or whatever the hell this is. We'll see you at midnight, Jean-Pierre." The warrior worked a split shift so he could stay on guardian duty, so yeah, the brother had circles under his eyes.

His gaze once more met Fiona's. "I'm here if you need me. Central can reach me day or night, okay?"

"Thank you, Warrior Thorne."

He got that sick feeling again but hell, he needed some sleep, too. First, however, he had to make his report to Endelle. This would be no fucking picnic. Okay, maybe one or two more belts before he folded to administrative headquarters.

Endelle leaned her hips against her marble desk, the thick slab cutting across her ass but hardly making a dent through the thick boar's-hide skirt she was wearing. The thing was bristly as hell but she loved it. In the past five months, she hadn't changed much about her wardrobe except to add a little embroidered leather. That bastard, Owen Stannett, High Administrator of the Superstition Mountain Seers Fortress, had actually inspired her; the man had some serious kick-ass embroidered leather shit goin' on. He made her feel like a fashion slacker.

Other than her admiration, however, of the last leather ensemble he'd worn, she hated his guts. He was a narcissistic care-for-nobody and she still didn't have access to his

Seers, the only Seers on the planet she was supposed to have access to.

A century ago, COPASS had started establishing the rules of warfare between her faction and Greaves, but had somehow been manipulated into giving Stannett sovereignty over the fortress. She'd been future-blind for ten decades and it was the most powerful reason why Commander Darian Greaves was winning the goddam war.

Of course, all that wasn't what troubled her in the here and now.

She sighed, and the sound was a rush of wind through her administrative office. Even the door rattled. Yeah, she was just a little upset.

And it was barely noon.

She stared at the zebra-skin rug closest to her desk and flipped the edge with the pointed toe of her black stiletto.

She always wore stilettos.

She could wear them day and night because she was ascended and could heal her feet constantly.

Otherwise she'd be screaming. And fucking crippled.

Right now, though, she felt like screaming anyway. She wanted to pull every last goddam strand of her long thick black hair out by the roots until she was bald and she'd do it screaming the entire time.

Yeah, that's what she wanted to do.

She couldn't, though. She had to maintain her composure for the sake of all of Second Earth. She was the Supreme High Administrator and this was her job.

So instead of screaming, she gripped the edge of the marble, one hand on either side of her hips, and with the toe of her stiletto she lifted up the edge of the zebra skin then put it down, patting it in place then lifting it up again. Lift, release, pat. Lift, release, pat.

She'd done this maybe a thousand times in the past half hour.

She'd lost track because her mind had shifted back to the fiasco at the Creator's Convent. Earlier, she'd gotten a sick-gut feeling and, using her preternatural voyeurism, had checked in on the doings with no one the wiser.

Everything had been fine until Fiona, their newest *breh*-candidate, had gotten a funny look on her face and told Thorne they had incoming.

The battle had been okay. A victory, actually.

The fighting hadn't bothered her and yeah, she was glad so many death vampires had bit the dust, or bit the pine needles as it were. Her men had performed admirably, and she was surprised as hell at Fiona's calm under pressure.

No, that's not what had bothered her.

In fact, she would have tuned out the whole damn thing except Thorne had looked at Fiona and his expression had been . . . guilty as hell.

Something was up with her second-in-command.

Something *big* . . . and not his oversized cock.

Her internal alarms had sounded like an enormous bell ringing on a mountaintop; Himalayas maybe.

So, instead of getting back to work at her desk, and reviewing Marcus's latest reports on which of her High Administrators around the world were most likely to turn traitor and align with Greaves, she'd followed Thorne back to the Cave using her same voyeuristic powers.

Flip. Release. Pat. Flip. Release. Pat.

That's when she'd listened in on one little horrific conversation between Thorne and Fiona.

She'd been dreading this moment for a long time, a century maybe, and right now she wanted to scream or cut her throat.

Marguerite.

Endelle had known about her almost from the first, having seen the glow of a memory deep within Thorne's mind. She'd pushed her way in when she shouldn't have. Thorne had hooked up with a powerful Seer in the Convent and was keeping her hidden.

But now that the Seer had become a player in their little

thing called "the war," Endelle would have to act. And she didn't want to. She didn't want to hurt Thorne.

"She wants to see me now?" Fiona asked. Thorne looked pale, his bloodshot eyes blinking strangely.

Thorne nodded. "Ten minutes. Both you and Jean-Pierre, and no I don't know what it's about but my guess is it has something to do with what happened at the christening."

"What does she know?"

Thorne shrugged, but his lips parted and for a good long moment she watched him dragging air into his lungs. He rubbed his forehead. "Okay. Okay. We can do this. She's in her office at HQ." He looked at Jean-Pierre. "Bring Fiona with you when you're ready. I'm heading for the shower. See you there." He lifted his arm and vanished.

Fiona turned to Jean-Pierre. "I don't want to do this." She shook her head back and forth. Endelle on a good day was hard to take, but Fiona suspected Her Supremeness would want to investigate everything that had happened at the christening.

She shuddered. She understood now that she truly did have emerging powers, that what used to be a simple form of telepathy had escalated into something more, something much more. Endelle, on the other hand, collected powerful beings around her, but the last place Fiona wanted to be was near the scorpion queen.

The woman might have had a few endearing qualities a couple of millennia ago. But the intervening centuries had worn away any superficial charm, any means by which the ruler of Second Earth could pass through the world with a nod and a smile.

Another shiver traveled through her. She'd rather be bitten by rattlesnakes than spend ten minutes in the woman's presence.

"She is not all bad," Jean-Pierre said.

Fiona looked up at him, but the quirky smile that played over his lips didn't give her confidence. "You're so not helping."

He chuckled. "She possesses a good heart. Unfortunately, it's buried beneath layers and layers of concrete." He glanced down at his stained battle gear and skin. He looked at her as well, his gaze sliding down to encompass her shawl and blouse, her skirt, her legs. There was nothing of desire in his expression; instead he frowned. "You will want to wear something else as well."

He didn't think her somewhat conservative ensemble would please Madame Endelle. Then she glanced down and her brows rose. Several dark streaks and smudges also marred her clothes.

A gasp caught in her throat and for a moment she couldn't breathe. She nodded several times. "I should change." Evidence of the battle combined with thoughts of having to meet Madame Endelle battered the support beams beneath her composure.

She took a moment and calmed herself, taking deep breaths. To Jean-Pierre's credit, he didn't try to touch her or in any way attempt to settle her down.

When she looked back up at him, his gaze held more speculation than compassion, and again she was grateful. "Thank you for that."

"For what, *chérie*?"

"For not jumping in and trying to make me feel better."

At that he smiled. "I have extended my hand to a biting dog on enough occasions to know better."

She put her hand to her chest. "Am I that bad?"

"Oui," he answered. "Vile, actually. Nearly as bad as She Who Would Live herself."

Fiona laughed. She thought he must be one of the kindest, most perceptive men she had ever met.

She Who Would Live. Madame Endelle. Her Supremeness. She had another name, one that apparently only Thorne could pronounce, one with three clicks from ancient times, one that gave rise to her abbreviated name and to her nickname, She Who Would Live.

Nine thousand years.

Unfathomable.

Perhaps if Fiona lived to be that old, and carried even half the responsibility that Endelle did, she would also turn into a fire-breathing dragon.

Whatever.

"Why don't you fold me to Militia Warrior HQ and I'll stay there until you're ready, then you can take me back to Seriffe's house to change. Will that do?"

He nodded. "You have a very organized mind."

She snorted. "You mean controlling and obsessive."

But at that, his gaze grew intense. "I like your mind, Fiona, very much." A wave of rich, aromatic coffee rolled in her direction.

She stared into his eyes, and all her well-ordered plans faded into the background. She was struck again by the varied shades in his eyes, the dark blue, the gray, the grayish green and just a few flecks of amber, sun glinting off the ocean.

What she felt couldn't be just about the *breh-hedden*. He had taken pains to understand her, to know her, and that meant something. Perhaps the absurd call of vampire mate-bonding had sunk its claws into both of them, yet it would be so easy to simply turn away from the man right now if he had been mean or surly or disrespectful. Surely, the profound desire she felt for him would wane in the face of such unhappy qualities.

Right now, however, because he hadn't crowded her, because he kept the reins light in his hands, she liked him all the more. Her body responded, a swell of sensation rising from deep within, like a wave rippling up her body, tingling, warm, thrilling.

His eyes closed and he listed, jerking a little to right himself.

When he opened his eyes they came only to half-mast. "Fiona," he whispered, low and deep, his accent dipping then rising over her name, a caress.

She became acutely aware that she was alone with her vampire boyfriend in a room that had several large empty couches.

She swallowed hard. When he took a step toward her, she

planted her hand on the center of his weapons harness, which meant she connected with the hilts of two daggers.

That forced her to draw back and to blink several times.

"Take me to HQ, please."

Half an hour later, Jean-Pierre stood just inside the door of Endelle's office. He trembled in rage at the ruler of Second Earth, but he could not interfere. He would give his life for Her Supremeness, but there were times, like now, when he wished to put his hands around her neck and squeeze.

Thorne remained next to him, keeping him from acting when he should not act, as Endelle continued her interrogation of Fiona.

"What are you not telling me, ascender?" Endelle shouted.

Fiona once more drew her shoulders back, her head up. She wore black slacks, black heels, and a lavender silk blouse, snug at the waist with a small bow in the front. "I've told you everything that happened and in the sequence in which it happened." Her voice was sharp and strong. "How many more times can I say this: I heard a woman's voice in my head calling out for help, I extended my telepathy to her, located her, and started to communicate.

"Her name is Marguerite, and yes, she sounded desperate to escape from the Convent. Then, while still connected telepathically, she seemed to disappear for a moment, but not really disappear. And when she came back she relayed the warning that death vampires, a lot of them, were making their way through the forest toward the outdoor chapel.

"But there was one more thing, something I forgot to tell you. We both heard church bells, very deep, lovely."

"Why the fuck didn't you tell me? Goddam, that's a Fourth Earth signature and your ability to hear it, that's Third shit." She nodded several times. "What else?"

"The rest, the attack, Thorne has told you about. After the battle was over, I tried to reach her again, but couldn't. I've been given to understand that telepathic communication is forbidden inside the Convent and that she was probably punished."

Endelle got in her face, not for the first time. Jean-Pierre took a step forward, and as many times before, Thorne threw an arm in front of him, hitting him square in the chest. He had changed from battle gear and his hair was still damp from the shower. He wore a Gaultier jacket and loose comfortable slacks. But there was nothing comfortable about watching Endelle grill his woman.

"Relax, Jean-Pierre," Thorne whispered, spitting the usual gravel as he spoke. "Fiona is doing just fine. She's got a lot of spirit."

Endelle finally turned away from Fiona and Jean-Pierre released a heavy sigh.

"That Quena is such a bitch," Endelle said. "She uses a rod to discipline her devotiates. I'd like to take a rod to her. Goddammit! I just wish I knew what the hell this means."

She started to pace, although a new word should be created for this movement, since every third step lifted her into the air, probably a form of levitation.

She wore a very bristly skirt that could not be comfortable, but it was short so her legs could move. Her halter was composed of small white feathers and *oui,* the room smelled of poultry. *Mon Dieu.*

"Do I smell chickens?" Thorne asked in a low voice, leaning close.

Some of her long black hair was piled high, while the lower parts swung in perhaps a dozen braids. Would she perform acts of voodoo next?

Endelle paced and levitated her way to the enormous plate-glass window that overlooked the eastern desert. She returned to stand once more in front of Fiona, her brown eyes so strangely lined, as though the years of service as the ruler of Second Earth had disfigured them.

"Well, Fiona, you're not going to like this but I'm going to have to read your powers. I've got to figure out what we're dealing with here. Thorne tells me you have emerging powers and I believe him, but this latest thing really has my thong in a few dozen knots, if you get my drift."

Fiona backed up.

Endelle's thick black brows rose a notch. "What the fuck?"

"I've heard tales about you, Endelle, and I'm refusing to have you read my powers. Let Thorne do it."

Jean-Pierre's temper, already simmering, shot like a rocket into outer space. Before Thorne could stop him, he now stood in front of Fiona, his arms spread wide. He glanced from Thorne to Endelle. "I will not permit Thorne to read her powers." He felt a thumping at his back, which he ignored. He knew what reading someone's powers could entail, a full-blown mind-dive, and the fuck he would let Thorne in his woman's head.

"Goddammit, Jean-Pierre," Thorne cried.

More thumps at his back. "Move it, Jean-Pierre," Fiona cried. Another thump. She was using her fists and trying to get his attention. "Get out of my way, now."

He looked back at her, surprised at the flush on her cheeks. Her silver-blue eyes looked almost dark. "What is it, *chérie*?" He lowered his arms and turned to face her. "Why are you angry?"

She planted her hands on her hips and cocked her head. Her eyes flashed a little more. "I don't need you to fight this battle for me and if I want Thorne to read my powers, then he'll read my goddam powers. Are we clear?"

"You go girl," Endelle said.

Jean-Pierre ignored her. "No, we are not clear. I will not have another man inside your head. *Pas du tout. Jamais.*" He waxed long on this theme only vaguely aware that he had lapsed into French.

She planted a hand on the T-shirt beneath the jacket. "English, *s'il vous plaît, monsieur.*"

That brought him up short. "*Oui,* of course. I am sorry, but I cannot allow this."

"Hey, Jean-Pierre," Endelle called to him.

He turned around, a heavy scowl pulling at his face. "*Quoi.*"

He didn't even see her fist coming. The next thing he knew he was spinning around and falling, his head just missing Thorne's booted foot.

"Better, asshole?" Endelle asked.

Jean-Pierre sat up, felt his jaw and worked it back and forth. The woman could throw a punch.

He sighed. His shoulders sagged. He wrapped his arms loosely around bent knees. "Fuck," he muttered.

"Nice coat, by the way. Gaultier?"

He looked up at her. He saw the amusement on her face, the quirk of her lips, and the odd compassion in her eyes. He had needed her fist to his face. He lacked control and to be challenging her? *Mon Dieu,* what the fuck had he been thinking?

Fiona just looked at him and shook her head, bewildered. He stared at the floor then pulled his *cadroen* from his hair. He turned the pastel green braided brocade in his hands, his own take on the *cadroen,* a memento of his years at court, a snub to the revolution that betrayed him.

"My apologies. I will not interfere." For good measure, he remained sitting on the floor. He was afraid if he stood up, he would succumb yet again to the cursed *breh-hedden*'s claim on his soul. God help him.

Freedom has only one master,
Emerging power.

—*Collected Proverbs,* Beatrice of Fourth

CHAPTER 5

Fiona frowned at Jean-Pierre. She hadn't meant for Endelle to flatten him. At the same time, she really needed him to stop with the caveman stuff. She could manage her own battles, thank you very much.

But as she looked at Endelle, she sighed. She had to accept one single fact: No way in hell would she ever win this one, not by a long shot.

"I'm not bustin' your balls, Fiona. I think we might be in big-ass fucking trouble here. I need to know what's going on with you—or do you not understand how remarkable it was that you connected with this Marguerite woman?

"I don't know of any other ascenders who could receive a telepathic communication like that, from out of the blue, from some unknown woman in another location. But it also sounds to me like she had foreknowledge of the battle, which also means she could have serious Seer ability.

"You've been here long enough to know that if she does,

I can use her. She'll have to go to the Superstitions, of course, but by God I won't turn her over to Stannett without some conditions." She looked away from Fiona, her gaze flitting around as though working out exactly how she was to manage the High Administrator of the Fortress. Her gaze stopped for a brief moment, settled on Thorne, then launched again. Fiona knew that the nearby Seers Fortress had become a nightmare for Endelle.

She heard a strange hissing sound behind her. Great. Now what was Jean-Pierre freaking out about?

She turned around and looked at him, but his gaze was fixed up and sideways toward Thorne. When she shifted to look at Thorne, she withheld a gasp. Thorne was doubled over and making the strangest sound, like the combination of a gasp and a grunt. He looked like he couldn't breathe.

"Ah, Christ," Endelle muttered. Then added, "Fuck. Thorne, you okay? You need a glass of water? More Ketel, maybe?"

He rose, his face red like he'd been choking. He drew in a long struggling breath and cleared his throat. "Ketel would be great. Thanks."

Endelle held out her hand, let it sit in the air for a few seconds, perhaps kinetically pouring vodka into a glass in another room, then, *voilà,* a tumbler of clear liquid appeared.

Thorne pushed away from the wall, crossed the few feet, and took the glass. His hands shook but he drank it down.

Fiona glanced at Jean-Pierre, but he merely wagged his head back and forth a couple of times. He still sat on the floor, which was probably a good thing. He swept his hair back and secured the *cadroen* in place.

When the flush on Thorne's face dimmed, Endelle once more focused her lined brown eyes on Fiona. "We're wasting daylight, missy. Let me put my hands on your face and see what you've got."

Fiona huffed a sigh. There was nothing for it.

She moved close to Endelle and closed her eyes. Not staring at all the braids and the ancient-looking eyes made it easier. She relaxed, and as Endelle's cool fingers touched her cheeks she strove to lower her shields.

"Good," Endelle said. "Stay as relaxed as you can."

It wasn't that the woman took a ride through her mind exactly, but it did feel like preternatural fingers poked at her. "Now show me the memory of your interaction with Marguerite."

Fiona realized that no detail would be spared. *The truth shall out.* Shakespeare had said that. She hoped that Thorne could at least take some comfort in the fact that he'd been able to keep his affair with Marguerite a secret for a hundred years. That had to be some kind of record.

The fingers prodded and poked and scraped and dug, until the sensation became almost painful. She knew when Endelle reached the memory of the recent battle.

Lower your shields, ascender, Endelle sent into her mind. *I already know the truth so stop worrying.*

About Marguerite?

And Thorne. Yes. And can I just say your telepathy has a beautiful intonation, almost like music, very powerful? Shield?

Fiona hadn't thought she'd kept a shield up, but then she'd been worried about Thorne so maybe that was all it took. She focused inward and let the last of her shields fall.

Endelle stayed within her mind for several minutes. She explored the memory, especially the entire scope of her interaction with Marguerite.

I'm right about one thing: This woman picked up a ribbon in the future streams, an iridescent green ribbon. Huh.

Can you see the future stream? Fiona was shocked that Endelle could determine so much. Even Fiona hadn't been aware that Marguerite was engaged in reading something from the future streams. She had deduced it later, but at the time she hadn't had a clue.

Not exactly, I can just feel the resonance of it, like an afterimage. Now I need you to be strong for me.

Uh-oh.

Why? Fiona asked.

You've got a layer here I've never seen before. I may have to punch through. Ready?

Shit. Fine. Just do it.

Endelle drove her mind down and down and the pain struck like a bolt of lightning. Fiona started screaming, at least within both their heads. She hoped it would give Endelle a clue to let up. Instead, the woman pushed harder, like solid punches within Fiona's mind. She was certain her brain would either explode or implode. Had to be one or the other.

Then there was a flash of brilliant gold light everywhere, sparkling, iridescent. And underneath a swell of heat, but not the usual red-hot heat—something different, something dark, something *powerful.*

At the same moment, she could feel Endelle, all of her, and know her. She understood her voyeur powers, her kinetic ability, which was incredible, her telepathic capability between dimensions, the level of her hand-blast, her darkening capacity, that ability to move within nether-space. More arrived, a knowledge of the woman herself: that she had been unattached for millennia, that she hadn't known real love in that long, that her duties as Supreme High Administrator had stripped her not just of a capacity to love but of desire as well. So that in the depth of the woman's being, she did not feel loss so much as utter resignation.

The heat began to rise, like black incomprehensible flames, and she began to scream again.

Then nothing.

Jean-Pierre held his woman in his arms. She was limp, almost lifeless. He wanted Endelle to help, but she was tearing around the room, shouting something like a fierce triumphant call, a wild sound, an animal sound. She raised her fists to the ceilings, she leaped on her desk, she screamed until she was hoarse.

Thorne didn't know what to do, either. He knelt beside Fiona but didn't touch her. "Is she breathing?"

"Just barely. Please bring Horace here."

"Yes. Yes," Thorne murmured. "Alison, as well." Yes, Alison. She was a healer of the mind.

Jean-Pierre clutched Fiona to his chest. He rocked her. He murmured softly in her ear, words in his birth language that soothed his mind but probably did little to help her. "I cannot lose you, Fiona. You must fight."

Horace folded into the room a moment later. Thorne gave up his place to the healer. He asked what happened.

Jean-Pierre shook his head. "I am not certain. Madame Endelle was trying to read her powers, but she must have gone deep. Now you see the state Her Supremeness is in. I do not know if she is in some danger as well."

Horace glanced behind him, in the direction of the desk, then he smiled. "Our leader is experiencing euphoria. That's all. Exultation."

"Exultation? What the fuck do you mean by that?"

Endelle jumped off her desk and crashed her hand on Thorne's shoulder. Thorne buckled to the floor. "What the fuck?" he cried.

Jean-Pierre had never seen Endelle so wild-eyed. For a moment, even the striation in her brown eyes had blended to a smooth beautiful brown. She looked so young.

She shook her finger at Fiona. Her hand trembled, her arm, her body. "She . . . she is something I have never seen in my entire life. She was never supposed to exist. She has come and not just her, but two more. Oh, God, two more because the myth says they come in threes, a triad of power."

She started tearing around the room again, jumping, levitating, squealing.

"You see?" Horace said. "Exultation."

"Do you mean, she is happy?"

"And excited about possibilities." Horace sat back on his heels and focused on Fiona. "You do not need to worry, Jean-Pierre. Physically, she is perfectly fine. If you had that much power in your head"—he jerked his thumb in Endelle's direction—"you might need a few minutes to recover as well."

Jean-Pierre released a quavering sigh. "Good. That is good. Thorne has called for Alison."

Horace nodded. "She is what is needed here."

Jean-Pierre met his gaze. "Thank you, my friend." Horace served the Warriors of the Blood every night. He and his team healed their physical injuries in the field, sort of a preternatural medic.

Horace settled a hand on Jean-Pierre's shoulder. "Be well." He rose to his feet, exchanged a few words with Thorne, lifted his arm, and vanished.

A minute later Alison arrived. She stood frozen for a moment at the sight of Endelle, doing a happy dance on her enormous marble desk.

But the moment her gaze shifted to Jean-Pierre and Fiona, Alison dropped down beside Fiona. "What happened and why does Endelle look like she's been mainlining crack?"

"We are not sure. She was testing Fiona for her emerging powers and this was the result. Fiona started screaming, then stopped for a time, then screamed again, terrible cries of agony. Finally, she crumpled."

Alison put her hand on Fiona's forehead. Even at that distance, Jean-Pierre could feel the warm energy flowing. He could breathe once more.

Time passed. Despite Alison's healing efforts, to the point that her forehead grew damp and she trembled, Fiona did not begin to return to herself for several more minutes.

By then, Endelle sat on the edge of her desk, her bristly skirt a lumpy line at the hem, her gaze fixed on Fiona.

"Tell her to wake up. Now."

"Endelle," Thorne barked. "Haven't you done enough?"

"You don't understand, but you'll know in a few minutes. Dammit, you'll all know." She clapped her hands together and cried, "Hah! We have something now. Goddammit!"

Then she laughed.

Maybe it was the laughter, but at that moment, Fiona's eyes fluttered and finally opened. She met Jean-Pierre's gaze, but there was no light in her eyes, as though she were turned inside herself. She did, however, struggle out of his arms and sit up, her hands limp in her lap, her legs straight out in front of her.

Alison put her hand on Fiona's back and drew close. "How are you feeling?"

"Fine. Weird. At least I'm not in pain anymore." She turned her head to look at Alison then up at Endelle.

Jean-Pierre shifted so that he could see Fiona's face. She was very pale.

"Damn that hurt, Endelle."

"Well," Endelle mused. "Ascension ain't for sissies."

"No, it's not," Fiona said. Then she started to smile, a very slow curve of her lips, wider and wider until she grinned and her eyes took on a light he had never seen before.

Endelle nodded.

Fiona nodded back.

What had the women discovered? What had made Fiona scream in such pain? And why was she smiling now?

"What is it, *chérie*? What did you see?"

"A fountain of gold light. No, a flame of gold light, a shimmering light, unearthly, supported by black flames. Yes, that's what I saw. Black flames, dark, so very dark, but powerful. So much power. I can't explain it."

Thorne joined Endelle by the desk. "But what does it mean?"

Endelle hopped off her desk and moved to stand in front of Fiona. She extended her hand down and Fiona took it. Endelle lifted her to her feet. Both Jean-Pierre and Alison rose with her.

She put her hands on Fiona's cheeks again. Jean-Pierre wanted to protest, but something in Endelle's demeanor stopped him.

"I can't believe it," Endelle said. "I just can't believe it." She stared into Fiona's eyes.

Then the most impossible thing of all happened: Tears trailed down Endelle's face. She pulled Fiona into her arms and held her and wept.

Jean-Pierre exchanged a glance with first Alison then Thorne but they each shrugged, uncertain why Endelle was so overcome, when she was never overcome.

Finally, Endelle released Fiona, folded a thick wad of tissues into her hand, then blew her nose like an elephant trumpeting.

"Chérie?"

Fiona turned to him, her expression beatific. Tears also shimmered in her eyes, but hung suspended as though unwilling to fall and destroy what he could see was her happiness. Then she, too, did the unexpected. She moved into him and as he opened his arms wide, she pressed herself against his chest, slid her arms around his waist, and held him.

She had never done this before.

If ever a moment had been designed to feel like heaven, this was the moment. He engulfed her in his arms and embraced her. Whatever had happened, something essential within his woman had changed. He could feel it.

Fiona shifted slightly and held out her hand to Alison. When Alison took it, she gasped and arched her neck slightly, then relaxed and cried out, "Oh, my God. Fiona." This time *her* eyes grew wet.

Jean-Pierre was holding Fiona, but he felt nothing from her that would cause such stunning sensations.

"All right, ladies," Thorne said at last. "I've had about all the suspense I can take. What the fuck is going on here?"

Endelle punched him in the arm, not too hard because he actually remained upright. She swept her hand in Fiona's direction. "Thorne, you're looking at a goddam obsidian flame, apparently the gold variety."

Thorne turned and stared at Fiona. "But I thought it was a myth. That book we all go by, that tome by Philippe what's-his-name, must be full of shit. He called obsidian flame a myth, now you're saying it exists."

"Don't blame the author. We all thought the *breh-hedden* was a myth, but Jean-Pierre can tell you it exists."

"Unfortunately, it is very alive and well. But what does it mean, Endelle? What is obsidian flame?"

It was Fiona who spoke. "A duty and a purpose centered on power, a lot of power."

"What sort of power?" Thorne asked. He scowled fiercely.

Endelle moved in a circle, still apparently overcome. When she once more stood in front of the small group, she waved her hands about and shook her head, the bottom of the braids flipping back and forth. "The power always comes from the woman, from her most essential power. I think with Fiona it will begin with her telepathy, which is really at Fourth ascender level, and it will flow from there. I believe she has the capacity, even now, to communicate between dimensions as well. But that's beside the point."

"What will this mean for her in the immediate future?" Jean-Pierre asked.

"Practice," Endelle said. "Lots of practice. She'll also need a mentor to help bring this power online. Alison, I want you to do it because you're mental. Shit, that didn't sound right but you know what I mean."

Alison shook her head. "I don't think this is a good time for me." The moment the words left her mouth, though, it was as if the other shoe fell and hit the floor hard.

"What the fuck is that supposed to mean?" Endelle asked. "Since when does something being 'a good time for you' matter *at all*?"

Thorne glanced up at the ceiling. Jean-Pierre pretended to find a speck of lint on the sleeve of his jacket.

"I've only been ascended for a year," Alison said. "What do I know about bringing powers online?"

Endelle snorted. "Tell you what, princess, either you do it or I do it."

At that, Fiona took a step toward Alison and Alison took a step toward Fiona. "Oh, no, no, no," Fiona said.

Endelle laughed. "That's what I thought." She glanced at Alison. "Besides, anyone with a turd's brain can see that Fiona's still got that post-traumatic-bullshit-disorder going on. She's doing better, but she needs to get over herself and that's your fucking specialty, right? And I'm so sick of the whining! Alison, I expected better from you."

"Fine." Alison rolled her eyes. "Fine. Whatever."

"That's the spirit," Endelle said. Once more she clapped her hands together. "Well, damn my pussy, obsidian flame! Now we'll see some serious shit. Mark my words."

Jean-Pierre watched her glance from one to the next but two seconds later her expression hardened. "All right, you two." She met Jean-Pierre's gaze then shifted to stare at Fiona. "Enough of this nonsense. I'd tell you to complete the *breh-hedden,* but I already know you're both stubborn enough to fight me to the death over that one. But let me tell you how this is going down. Fiona, you're moving in with Jean-Pierre and no arguments. You're going to need his protection. And Jean-Pierre, no more battling at the Borderlands until further notice."

Thorne intruded. "Endelle, we can barely hold the line as it is, what with Medichi roaming the planet and Marcus only available two nights a week."

Endelle grew thoughtful. "You've got some strong Militia Warriors coming up the ranks. Gideon for one, and I think Duncan has got some chops. Send them each out with a contingent of thirty-two. That should take care of business. But no arguments. We need Fiona safe. Shit, obsidian flame."

She spaced for a moment, then looked back at Jean-Pierre and Fiona. "Take her to your Sedona rabbit warren and keep her there. Now that I know what we have, it won't be long before you-know-who finds out, then we'll be in the crapper all over again."

Fiona turned and looked at Jean-Pierre. He felt so strange, dizzy, and did not at first recognize that what he felt was very close to exhilaration—exactly what Endelle had been experiencing a few moments ago.

For the past five months, he had wanted her beneath his roof . . . in his bed. But what would she think of being there, with him, all the time. Oh, *mon Dieu, tout le temps.*

But Fiona weaved on her feet and when her scent, the light buttery croissant scent, rippled over him, he knew her thoughts had traveled the same path as his own. He was still surprised, however, when instead of recoiling, instead of stepping away from him and creating distance, she once more drew near. When he opened his arms, she again stepped inside.

Mon Dieu, mon Dieu, mon Dieu . . .

Something had changed within his woman, some miracle

had happened, that she appeared to welcome the thought of being in his home.

How ironic, though, that at the very moment of receiving what he wanted most in the world, he felt nothing but blind panic, a desire to run. Endelle was right. If she had ordered them to complete the *breh-hedden,* he would have fought her, to the death. Fiona as well.

He did not want this intimacy, yet he craved to have her near him. He was torn apart, as though he were two men who never stopped battling each other.

But when her sweet scent, of croissants and woman, drifted once more beneath his nose, he let himself fall into the moment, into his desire, embracing what he craved. What would it hurt to place himself on the altar of passion with Fiona, to sacrifice himself, his body, for her pleasure?

"As for you, Thorne," Endelle said, cutting into his thoughts. "Looks like we've got business to discuss."

Thorne didn't meet her gaze. He seemed to stare in the direction of her marble desk at nothing in particular. His shoulders dipped. "Yes, I suppose we do."

"There's one more thing," she said, glancing at Jean-Pierre. "I've been thinking this for a long time and I might as well share my thoughts right now. I believe we have a Third or Fourth ascender causing all these fuckups with you men when you're out fighting. Now that I know about Fiona, it all makes sense. Greaves wouldn't take chances, not this late in the game. I believe he's brought someone of power on board to help out."

"Well how the fuck are we supposed to battle a Third ascender," Thorne asked. "And don't even get me started on a Fourth asshole?"

Endelle shrugged. "Beats the shit out of me. Looks like he's stuck the way Greaves and I are stuck. He may have some Upper ascender babysitters keeping tabs on him, which is a good thing. The bad news is, of course, that this vampire will have a boatload of power and a dozen tricks up his ass. So let the warriors know and we'll just keep on keepin' on." She planted her hands on her bristly skirt. "All right. The rest of you get out of here. I need to talk to my second-in-command."

Jean-Pierre held the door for Alison and Fiona. He intended to leave the decision up to his woman: whether to go first to Militia Warrior HQ and continue the hunt for Rith throughout the afternoon, or whether they should head straight to his home in Sedona.

Much to his surprise, she chose Sedona, and for a reason that touched his heart. "You haven't slept enough today. We're going to take care of that right now."

He could hardly believe it: After five months, not only was she ordered to stay in his home, but she wanted to. He was in no doubt about that. No restraint, no holding back. *Oui,* something had most definitely changed for her.

Alison and Fiona discussed when they should meet up for the first training session. With late afternoon settled on, Alison lifted her hand and folded home to be with her baby for the rest of the day.

Jean-Pierre was finally alone with Fiona. "*Chérie,* I wish to know so much what happened. You seem changed, different."

Fiona's lips parted, and that former light entered her eyes. "I am changed but I'm not sure I can explain it."

"You were screaming, Fiona. Were you aware of that?"

"Oh, it hurt. Endelle had to push through this place deep within my mind, like a barrier between the mind and the soul. I can't explain it. I really can't. But when she did, it was like geysers of the most beautiful shimmering gold exploded in my mind. I wish you could see it, Jean-Pierre. It was magnificent. But the beauty was only part of the experience. I felt as though something enormous had been released inside me, as though I could do anything, and what I thought, what went through my mind, was, *Now I can really go after Rith.* Yes, that's what I thought, that now I had sufficient power to hunt him down, to find him, to bring him to justice."

"Your eyes are filled with fire." When had his arm slid around her waist? When had she put her hand flat on his chest just inside his jacket? He wanted to kiss her, but not here, not in the hall outside Her Supremeness's office. "Shall we go to my house?"

"Yes." Just like that, after five months of keeping him so far away, she said yes.

He nodded, and, holding her against him, he lifted his free arm and thought the thought.

The ride through nether-space was smooth as silk, a swift glide, then a touching down on the red-brick patio of his front yard. To the left was a small wooden bridge he had built over a dry wash that directed overflow to Oak Creek; to the right was a curved grassy area.

He looked around and extended his preternatural senses, hearing and vision, hunting for the enemy. But all that returned to him was the sound of a hawk high in the air, beyond the tips of the Arizona sycamores that surrounded his house.

"So this is your home?" Part question, part statement.

"Oui."

"And you built this, by yourself, over the past two centuries since you have lived in this part of the world."

He had told her about his house over the course of their dates but she had not seen it before. He was proud of his "rabbit warren," as Endelle so aptly called his home. He had never had a plan, but just built rooms and stairs and windows, letting his soul guide him. The only thing he had been definite about was that in the very center was a large round room, a type of space meant for meditation, but very large with a glass ceiling open to the sky and a glass floor to allow a view of the creek flowing below.

Beyond the desire for that room, the house was truly a work of impulse year by year.

He loved it.

But would she like what he'd created?

As these doubts twisted his stomach into a knot, his sheer desire for her, to share his home and his bed, overcame everything. He needed to know her thoughts, her reservations, her present wishes.

"Will you come inside? Be with me, Fiona?"

He meant the question to be frank, even obvious. How much better to know what he could expect than to stumble and offend her by a careless kiss or embrace.

He watched the most exquisite blush climb her cheeks. He knew her past, that she had only known one other man in her life, her husband of many decades ago.

She had been born in a different time, in old Boston, which would have had very strict ideas about sex. And sex would never have been discussed, probably not even between husband and wife.

"I do not mean to push you, *chérie*."

She met his gaze at last. "I just need you to know that whatever we do together, during this strange time of transition as I learn what it is to be an obsidian flame, I can't guarantee that it will lead to anything permanent between us. I know the *breh-hedden* has us locked into these really terrifying but wonderful sensations, but my heart is fixed on a different path. Do you understand?"

"Finding and prosecuting Rith. Serving this new world."

She nodded. "I am determined, Jean-Pierre."

These thoughts did have the wonderful effect of calming him down, at least sufficiently that he could pivot and offer his arm to her.

She took it, but she said, "I want to sleep with you."

His eyes closed as though he could not keep them open. He released a soft sound, something like a sigh and a gasp at the same time. More than anything in the world, he wanted to take her to his bed and keep her there, slide over her body, into her secret places, feel her, experience her wetness, the taste of her.

She laughed. "You smell like a Starbucks right now."

He huffed a small piece of laughter. "No doubt an entire plantation of coffee beans, a factory, smokestacks billowing my scent."

"Yes. But it pleases me so very much."

He squeezed her arm. "Come. Let me show you my house."

He moved forward with her, but her steps slowed. He

stopped and turned to watch her. She seemed surprised, her brows high on her forehead. "What is it?"

"When you told me about your house, how you had built it, I didn't realize you'd used so much glass. I had come to think of it like a cabin in the woods, but it's not at all like that."

"*Ah, oui.* But if you look around, you can see the why of it, that I put the house in the middle of a woodland of sycamores. And on the opposite side of the house is Oak Creek, which you can hear from this place. I wanted views of it all."

"It's . . . *beautiful.*" She spoke the words slowly as though she savored each syllable, which of course made his heart swell.

The front entrance was set at an angle to the body of the house and had a steepled porch that served as protection from the weather. Sometimes there was snow in Sedona and during the summer, heavy monsoon rains.

He released her to slide his arm about her waist and held her close. Only then did she move forward with him.

He opened the front door and swung it wide, letting her precede him.

When she crossed the threshold, something powerful inside him opened and spilled out, leaving behind a pit of relief—as though he had been holding his breath all these months and now he could finally breathe.

Oui, the *breh-hedden* was a terrible master.

But she was here, in his home, with him, and she was safe.

"A piano," she cried. She turned to look at him over her shoulder. "Of all the things I expected to see here, this wasn't one of them. Do you play?"

Such astonishment. He shrugged. He knew he should not be offended but somehow he was. "*Oui. Bien sûr.* Of course."

She closed her eyes briefly. "That sounded so . . . wrong and I apologize. But I haven't seen a piano yet on Second Earth, not that I've been in many ascended homes."

Of course she had not. Perhaps only a handful, since he

kept her close and she only had encounters with Madame Endelle's administrative headquarters, Militia Warrior HQ, her daughter's home, or Alison and Kerrick's. Once she had been to Medichi and Parisa's villa. But that was all . . . and no pianos in any of these homes. Perhaps one day.

She turned back to the small grand piano situated in the angled foyer, and said, "It's just that all of the warriors battle so hard. Even Seriffe is gone so much working with the Militia Warriors. I didn't think anyone had time for such things, for even a modest hobby."

She had a lovely shape; her shoulders were neither narrow nor too broad and she had a small waist. He longed to put his hands around her waist and see if his fingers met. He had long fingers. He thought they might touch, fingertip-to-fingertip, but such thoughts put a trembling in his thighs.

He drew close to her from behind and fingered the lavender silk of her blouse. Her hair hung just a few inches from her waist, so thick and beautiful, chestnut streaked with dark golds and reds.

He worked to set aside the trembling and the desire. "There was a time when we did not fight as we do now. We were called to service by Central throughout the night, at different hours, but not every hour until dawn as we do now. We were able to do many things when I first ascended; that is how Medichi built his villa and vineyard and how I built this house. But the war has changed in recent decades, grown much more intense. Yes, at one time we were able to do many things."

She looked back at him, her smile teasing. His breath caught in his throat at such an expression. He did not think he would get used to her beauty and how it made him feel, especially wearing a smile that reached her eyes.

"Many things, huh?"

He smiled as well, not dwelling too much on her meaning, for his fingers were now smoothing the silk of her blouse in a line up to her neck, beneath the wavy fall of chestnut hair until he found skin. He stroked the nape of her neck slowly.

"*Oui*. Many things. I will not lie to you. I am a man."

Her smile dimmed just a little. "And did you bring many of those *activities* here?"

He shook his head. "Here? No, Fiona. *Jamais*. Never. I swear it. I could not have brought you into my house if I had."

All the teasing left her lovely face, and he leaned close. He drifted a kiss over the line of her cheek. "I never wanted anyone here, not until I saw you in Toulouse."

She blinked and looked down, a most certain sign that the old horrible memories had surfaced.

He cursed himself for bringing up Toulouse. Had he lost all his skill? All his finesse? *Merde*. Toulouse was where that monster, Rith, had taken her and the other blood slaves when the Warriors of the Blood had rescued Parisa from the Burma facility.

He decided to simply shove the conversation in a different direction entirely.

"Come," he said. He stepped away from her but took her hand at the same time. He drew her toward the door behind him, to the right of the front door. "I wish to show you something."

She followed and did not protest.

He opened the door for her. "Be careful. The steps are a little steep." Much of the house was built on a slope and there were many short flights of stairs throughout the progression of the house, some up, some down.

The smell of wood and her scent flowed over him. The room below was cool and dark. He touched one of the switches to his right as he descended the stairs.

Inset ceiling lights just around the perimeter lit the room in a warm glow.

"Oh . . . my." She put her hands to her face. "You keep . . . surprising me."

He looked around at his woodworking shop and could not quite understand what she meant.

She turned back to him. "Don't you see, Warrior? You are not a simple man."

"And you thought I was?"

She shook her head slowly back and forth. "I have not

seen past the battling you do. But this—" She turned in a circle. "Every tool is hung on the wall in a specific place. And there must be hundreds of them. It's all so . . . organized."

"It keeps the process very simple, to know where one's tools are kept."

She walked to the table in the center of the room and ran her hands over the top. She touched the place he worked and he was moved. He could feel his heart pounding. She was telling him something. She spoke with her actions more than her words, perhaps more than any woman he had ever known before.

She stood next to the table now and turned to him. "I want you here," she said. She rested her palm on the table and tilted her head just so.

Surrender is only a beginning.

—*Collected Proverbs,* Beatrice of Fourth

CHAPTER 6

Jean-Pierre's chest expanded at the sight of Fiona with her hand on his worktable, the place he had laid each timber of the house: measured, sawed, planed, sanded. It swelled again, as though with her words and the things she did, she kept breathing life into his heart, almost more than he could bear.

He did not refuse this invitation. He did not remark that the table, though not dirty, was not clean, either. He did not suggest his bed or even the soft couch in his living room.

No, he went to her thinking that this was good and right in a way his soul could understand even if his mind would have suggested other places to take this step on their journey.

He had built his house with his hands and now he would put his hands on her, and build something new.

He drew close, standing in front of her. He touched her face, her skin soft beneath his callused warrior hands. She turned her face into his hand and kissed the toughened ridges, shaped by the leather-wrapped grip of his sword for two centuries.

"You honor me," he whispered.

Her lips were swollen now and her scent filled the room, buttery pastries. He knew what would happen as he leaned toward her. Little puffs of air left her mouth. Her scent thickened the space between. A light groan met his lips as he kissed her.

Jean-Pierre, she sent. *You will make me come.*

Come. He deepened the kiss, sliding his tongue between her lips. She cried out and he bored deeply. She clutched his arms as he brought her. She cried out again and again until she could barely stand. He slid his arm around her waist and drew back just enough so that he could look at her flushed cheeks and liquid eyes.

"How do you do that?"

"You ask me that every time. I think the better question must be, how do *you* do that, *chérie*? Was it this way between you and your husband, between you and Terence?"

She looked down, and he wished the words unsaid. Some memories took her back to unhappy times; this was one of those memories.

He put the side of his finger beneath her chin and lifted, forcing her to look at him. "I value your love for your husband."

"Oh, Jean-Pierre, how you please my heart." Tears swam in her eyes, a little ocean of pain. Then she laughed and wiped at her cheeks. "Terence used to tease me. I was always so ready for him. I seemed to be a little pile of kindling just waiting for the strike of a match. But doesn't it bother you to hear that?"

He shook his head. "Of course not." He smiled. "Well, perhaps a little but that is just the *breh-hedden* being absurd."

She searched his eyes. "I don't want you to take this moment too seriously."

He shook his head. "I believe we feel the same way, desire but restraint, *non*?"

She nodded.

He put his hands around her small waist. He smiled because his fingers touched.

He unbuttoned her slacks and since he dipped his chin to work the front zipper, she leaned close and sniffed his skin all along his temple until chills chased one another down his neck and his chest.

His muscles flexed and released.

He pushed her pants to the floor, and she stepped out of them then kicked her heels off as well. He looked down, not at the floor but at the expanse of lovely pale skin, thigh to ankle. He ran a finger across first one warm thigh, then the other. She hissed softly and put her hands on his shoulders.

She leaned forward and nuzzled his neck again. "Take your hair from the *cadroen,*" she whispered. "I want to see your hair, to feel it between my fingers. I have wanted to do that for so long. For so long I've wanted to do so many things with you."

She kissed his neck and licked and kissed. These small kitten-like ministrations built a fire in his body and weakened parts of him while strengthening others. For that reason, he had difficulty lifting his arms in order to obey her command. But he succeeded at last and freed his hair. He folded the *cadroen* to his bedroom.

Using both hands, she drew his hair forward. It was long now, in somewhat wild waves with a few errant curls here and there. The Warriors of the Blood all had long hair, an ancient ritual, the keeping of long hair to reflect strength and dedication. Her fingers sank into his hair on both sides and she dragged her hands lower and lower, the tips of her fingers poking through and connecting with his jacket.

But her fingers became knotted, of course, so he took her hands and untangled them. He held her gaze as he lifted both hands to his lips and kissed each finger, one after the other. Her breaths were light again and very quick.

Her lips parted. Her breath flowed toward him, a sweet scent of the *patisserie.* Shivers chased over his body. What she could do to him!

She was killing him so sweetly. Did she know how she

affected him? That her gaze never strayed told him she did. She must have pleased her husband very much, and all, no doubt, without the smallest awareness of the effect. This he knew to be so very true about her—she had no guile and he loved her for that.

He released her hands and untied the small bow at her waist. He unbuttoned her blouse until he could push it apart. Her bra was cut low and made of a very fine cream lace. She had full breasts, and his breathing changed at the sight of them. He dipped low and a soft sound swirled from her throat as his lips kissed each mound in turn. His hands became restless as he continued to kiss.

He thumbed her nipples through the fabric and made them into hard beads. His touch, of lips and hands, drove new sounds from her throat, new cries and whimpers.

Her fingers worked through his hair again. "Jean-Pierre," she murmured. He felt her lips then kisses on his head.

He pushed the bra over her left breast and took the nipple in his mouth. She gasped and cried out. "You will bring me again," she said, panting.

Good, he sent.

He suckled, hard and fast.

Her body writhed. He vowed he had never known a woman to come so quickly but he suspected that these were but faint shadows, very small *petits morts,* and but a prelude to what he could accomplish with her body.

Would she let him? Could he sweep over her as he wanted to, a heavy wave across her body, of great pleasure, perhaps like nothing she had ever known?

Fiona was draped over Jean-Pierre, her arms wrapped around his bent shoulders as he slowed the suckling of her nipple. Her breath came in shallow pants, and her body had that sweet drift of lethargy that always accompanied such a swift climax.

She stroked his hair then unloosened her arms to drift her fingers once more through his long half-curling, half-wavy locks. He released her breast and rose so that her fingers could travel all the way to the tips.

Jean-Pierre had magnificent hair. It wasn't blond or brown, but someplace in between. All the outer layers and long tendrils were gold, especially in sunlight; what lay beneath was darker, heavier, as though he were these two qualities blended, a soft more playful layer over the toughness that characterized all the warriors.

He was infinitely gentle with her as well. Did he know how much she needed his gentleness? Her pursuit of Rith had toughened her and brought her courage. But in this quiet intimate moment, her fears returned. She was reminded of all that she had lost when she'd been taken from the streets of Boston so long ago.

He placed a finger between her eyebrows. "Why so worried, *chérie*?"

She shook her head then laughed, that falling laughter of frustration. "I fear waking up bound again."

"*Oui.* Of course you do. That will not go away very soon. So tell me, what more can I do to ease you?"

His smile was soft, almost teasing.

She should be thinking of him. After all, he had already given her two lovely light releases. "Kiss me," she said.

He didn't wait for further invitation but swept the few inches of his extraordinary height down to meet her lips. This time, he was not gentle and she leaned against him, against his hard chest, and slung an arm around his neck, across his thick glorious hair. She took what he gave and gave more in return until he released her with a groan.

He waved a hand. She wasn't sure what he meant by it until he lifted her up on the table and instead of feeling wood beneath the thin silk of her underwear, she felt a soft fleece blanket. He was so damn thoughtful. Her heart began to hurt as she put her hands on his shoulders.

He looked down very low and eased her knees apart. The crook of his finger drifted over her clitoris. A gasp left her throat.

He met her gaze. "Your body, *ma chérie,* is a finely tuned, delicate instrument." She kept gasping as he gazed into her eyes and continued that soft intimate drift.

His fingers spread and she felt a very strange movement then realized he'd folded off her underwear. She giggled then swallowed hard.

Fear began to move in a circle in her stomach, like a living creature that his touch, his nearness had awakened. Were they going to do this? Were they really going to make love?

She didn't understand that small creature but the movements quickened and the creature began to swim up and up, paralyzing her stomach, her chest, her throat.

"*Chérie,* what is it? What is the matter?"

She shook her head and clutched at her throat. "I don't know. I don't know." Strange tears burned her eyes.

He covered the hand over her throat. "*Regarde-moi.* Look at me."

She fixed her gaze squarely on his but she couldn't breathe.

He searched her eyes for a long moment. "I can feel your pulse racing." He eased back from her. "I will stop."

She gasped and shook her head. "No. This wouldn't be fair to you."

"I do not care what is right or fair. I worry only that you are in such sudden distress."

Fiona forced herself to breathe, to move past the tightness around her throat, the grip of something like steel bands around her chest. She forced the creature back into her stomach but she could not make it stop moving in swift threatening circles.

She should leave, but she hated the idea of leaving like this. Something was very wrong with her. Something hadn't worked right since she'd been rescued. Even after five months, she lived with such agony and fear.

Something had to give, had to change.

When he took another step back, and his gaze fell from hers, when she could feel not just his despair but his resolve as well, she thrust her arm forward and caught his neck at the nape. She would not let him go. "Enthrall me," she cried.

"What? I do not understand."

"Put me in thrall. I've heard tales of it. I know you can do it. All Militia Warriors enthrall the women they dance with and make love to at the Blood and Bite. Enthrall me."

He shook his head. "*Non*. I will not take you like this."

She understood what needed to happen next if they were to move forward. She understood the way the sun rose and set each day, the way the tide came in and went back out. She had to be enthralled. Her fears, not of her own making, wouldn't allow her one more step with him.

Her resolve deepened and she let her arm fall away from his shoulder. She met his gaze in a hard stare and overlaid his mind with her thoughts. *I have been held captive by a quiet monster and made to feel powerless. I know that I could not bear your weight on me without having those fears overpower the moment. But, Warrior Jean-Pierre,* mon homme, *who would be my* breh, *you must do this for me and for us.*

I want your weight on me more than anything in the world. I want to be connected body and soul with you more than anything in the world, here and now, on this table from which you built this house. I beg of you to enthrall me and make me yours. Please.

The last word had resonance, and she watched him close his eyes and weave on his feet.

When he opened his eyes, she saw his new resolve and the creature fled to the darkest recess of her soul. His mind came to her through his gaze in waves of exquisite peace.

Jean-Pierre had bedded so very many women in this way, putting them in thrall and taking them into the red velvet booths at the Blood and Bite, the club designed especially for the warriors of Metro Phoenix Two.

But even as he felt Fiona begin to sink, as his vampire mind, that which was truly and purely vampire, began to send *you will do my bidding* thoughts over her mind, he knew this would be different from anything he had experienced before. And not just because of the *breh-hedden*.

Fiona was unlike any of the mortal women he had seduced. As he held her mind in a gentle seductive grasp, he felt her power. Waves pulsed toward him, over him, like fingertips exploring not just his mind but his body as well.

He was firm within his slacks, ready for her, ready to pleasure her. With a thought, he folded off his clothes, which brought a sharp cry from Fiona's throat. Enthrallment didn't mean a diminishing of experience, just an easing of fear.

He slid one hand to the back of her head and one behind her back as he laid her down on the soft dark blue blanket he had folded from his bed. He could not bear the thought of splinters in her ivory skin.

Her silver-blue eyes were glazed, her lips parted, her breaths coming once more in little pants, which swept her soft *patisserie* scent over him, which in turn was like a new set of fingers rubbing ever so lightly over his cock.

With great care he positioned her, lifting and adjusting until her hips were low on the table and he had arranged her legs carefully over his shoulders.

He trembled now, not from exertion, but because what he had wanted for so long, for five long months, was within a few inches from his tongue.

She had a perfect chestnut triangle of hair and as he sank to his knees, not caring that the cement floor was hard and cold against his skin, his lips finally met her lower lips. Her hands now pressed into his scalp as though urging him to go where he needed no urging to go.

He kissed her long and deep and made use of his tongue. How he had wanted to be here, to taste her, to feel her rippled flesh over his tongue.

Her hips rolled beneath him. He used his forearm over her hips to keep her seated. The heels of her feet pushed against the muscles of his back.

For him, a woman's nest was a place to savor, to take his time, and for once she did not rush to a climax. He smiled and licked a long line from her sweet opening to the apex of her nest. Yes, for once she was in no hurry and he began to build her fire with each kiss and lick. One upon the next, he felt her urgency grow as well as the elegant flow of power that moved in waves over him now.

He groaned and, in response, his mind filled with her thoughts, *Jean-Pierre, thank you, thank you. I feel so peaceful and your tongue and lips, like heaven.*

He made love to her with his mouth and tongue for a long time, driving her to the edge, then pulling back until her heels pushed harder and harder into his back and her whimpers turned to cries.

Jean-Pierre, she cried out in his mind.

He pushed into her now, deep thrusts with his tongue. He shifted one hand to press on her nest, pushing and pressing. Her cries grew lower in timbre until she groaned and arched her back. He drove his tongue hard now, deep inside, faster and faster until she screamed. But on he pushed, so that he brought her again and again.

At last her hips settled. He kissed her very low once more, slowly and with reverence, savoring each delicate fold.

He rose up and saw that her eyes were still glazed, but in his mind, her thoughts were coherent. *How you satisfy me. I have never felt like that before. Always, it's a quick rush, and pleasant, but not like this . . . oh, Jean-Pierre.*

He responded, *Your power, Fiona. It is as though you possess my mind, as though you are inside my mind. It is so beautiful. And I feel your power in a flow of waves over my body. I have great need of you.*

Her lips tried for a smile but enthrallment tended to keep the face very quiet. *Then take me,* chéri.

He carefully repositioned her legs, drawing them around his waist as he stood up. She locked her ankles.

He looked down and shuddered because he was so close to possessing her as he had wanted to, ached to, since Toulouse. Using his hand, he guided himself and began a gentle push. She was very tight and moaned at the presence of his cock.

He pushed a little more, and began to enter her, slowly, so slowly, savoring this first taking. She gave little cries and tugged on his arms, urging him on. He watched his long thick hardness begin to disappear into her body. He trembled now, the muscles of his arms shivering like a stallion ready to run.

He curled his buttocks and took her another inch. He rolled his hips and pushed from side to side.

She cried out and her hips arched off the table. Only then did he lift his gaze to her face and saw that tears trickled from her eyes. Only then did he realize his eyes were wet as well.

There was great beauty in making love.

Once more he looked down between them. The dark hair of his body now shielded their connection from sight. But he had to see more and he pulled back. His cock was wet so that when he pushed back in it was a smooth glide and he collapsed forward, catching himself with his hands on either side of her. His hips would not stop as he wished them to and he was hard, so very hard.

Fiona was lost, deep within her mind, because Jean-Pierre held her in this magical place. She was at the same time so at peace yet stimulated and alive as she had never been before. He was thrusting now, into her, and rubbing over a place inside her body that was bringing her such pleasure. She wished he would continue forever, thrusting and driving.

She rolled her head from one side to the other.

Fiona, he whispered inside her mind.

She could hear him, but she couldn't focus on him. *Oui,* she sent.

She heard him groan, and his thrusts were faster now.

I want to remove you from thrall. Will you allow it? Will you try?

I'm afraid. This is so wonderful. You don't know. I'm afraid. Afraid.

Never mind. His voice was but a whisper. *Are you close?*

Close? Close to heaven? Yes, she was. Close to ecstasy? Oh, God, yes. She had never felt anything like this before.

But there was one thing she desired, something very specific to the vampire world in which she now belonged. She wanted Jean-Pierre to take her blood.

Jean-Pierre, she sent.

He groaned. *I love your voice in my head. Tell me what you desire. I will do anything.*

Take my blood. There she had said it and the moment she did, her internal muscles tightened around him.

Cherie, I wish for nothing more than that, you know I do. But after all you have been through—

She cut him off. *It's not the same thing at all. You have to remember, what was done to me was done with needles and machinery.*

But are you certain you are ready? Blood is what was taken from you all those years.

Jean-Pierre, you're not "taking" my blood, I'm giving it to you and I want this more than I can say.

"Shit," he said aloud and his body stilled.

The trouble was, she was so ready and thoughts of his fangs in her neck so aroused her that she played him, deep within, as though the well of her had fingers and he was her instrument. She couldn't exactly control what she was doing, but the feel of him, so still, so hard, brought deep groans from her throat.

"You must stop. I'll come. Fiona." He gasped each word. "Please stop."

She sucked in a deep breath and grew as still as he was. She panted lightly, trying not to feel so much. The only thing she regretted was that she had waited so long to give herself to him.

After a long, long moment, he relaxed his shoulders and seemed to take a deep breath. He leaned over her now and nuzzled her ear, her throat, her neck.

He began to lick right above her vein. Each stroke of his tongue sent shivers down her shoulders, her breasts, over her abdomen, and caused her to tighten around him. He began to move within her once more, slowly now.

The enthrallment surprised her, that she could feel so much, almost acutely, and yet her mind could be so relaxed.

She felt her vein rise to meet him and before she could prepare, he struck deep and began to suckle.

The sharp sting passed so fast and the suckling, as he took her blood down his throat, was an erotic ballad. She savored the sound and loved that what she gave him would nourish him in a way that was a mystery on Second Earth. She knew that her blood contained her power and that in some way, his power would be affected by hers.

His hips moved, his thrust grew quicker. Her heart sped up and he groaned, drawing harder at her neck.

You taste exquisite, chérie.

Her hands drifted over his long hair then found his back. Wing-locks were so sensitive, and she found that his wept with pleasure. She drifted her hands down them so that he writhed beneath her touch, moved faster into her, sucked harder.

His movements grew quick.

Jean-Pierre. So close.

He left her neck and drew back. His lips tinged red.

Kiss me, she sent.

He crashed down on her. The moment that she tasted her blood coupled with the flavor of him, pleasure began to flow, to pull hard within her body, in spasms that sent ecstasy shooting over the folds low on her body, traveling up her well to rise, higher and higher, grasping her abdomen, her stomach, flowing, another kind of geyser.

I am giving you what I have to give, his mind cried within hers. She felt the power leave her body and he cried out sharp and loud, driving into her in hard punches that once more brought her.

Your power is a wave over me, plucking at my skin, my nipples, stroking my neck, now low, so low . . . oh, God. He shouted now, words in French she didn't understand, but it didn't matter. The orgasm flew then retreated to build and fly again until she was screaming at the wooden beams of the ceiling, her back arching, his back arching, his body slamming against hers.

Jean-Pierre. Jean-Pierre.

Fiona. Mon Dieu!

The orgasm drifted away, like the last note of a beautiful song, something French, *"La Vie en Rose,"* perhaps.

His hips slowed and finally stopped. Her body grew slack.

A moment later, he lifted the veil of thrall. Fiona blinked several times. He was poised above her, holding himself away from her but still connected.

She brought her hand to her chest and looked into his eyes, ocean eyes.

She put her hand on his cheek. "Oh, Jean-Pierre, that was so beautiful."

"Only one thing would have made it more perfect," he said.

She nodded. "I know. Perhaps soon I can do this without the thrall—but for this moment, perfection."

He kissed her and she tasted her blood once more and that which was from the depths of her body.

But even as he remained within her and held himself just inches away from her chest, the fierce wild thing in the pit of her stomach began to wriggle around. She fought for her next breath and the next.

"Please," she whispered.

He seemed to collapse within himself, though he did not fall on her. His head dipped forward and in a smooth movement he pulled out of her. But at the last second her body seemed to cling to him, very low and tight. She met his gaze. She was startled that she clung.

His brows rose. "Fiona?"

She shook her head, trying to ignore the swirling in the pit of her stomach. "I . . . I." She covered her face with her hands.

He completed his withdrawal and folded a washcloth into his hands, pressing it gently between her legs.

This gesture, so normal, so absurdly normal had a strange calming effect on her, and she chuckled softly. "Thank you," she murmured. She had forgotten how messy and how embarrassing sex could be and yet as she met his gaze, she saw only tenderness.

With the thrall gone, she looked at him, his flushed complexion, the sheen of sweat on his forehead, his throat, his chest, his eyes very bright and his glorious warrior hair hanging about his shoulders.

"You look like . . . a god, something out of mythology. I swear it."

He chuckled and in the playful manner she'd come to know as uniquely his, he lifted his right arm and flexed his bicep.

The vampire had muscles and she cooed. She lifted up, put her hand on his bicep, and squeezed. A wave of coffee scent flowed over her. She breathed in and her eyes closed. Desire once more swirled over her as though she hadn't just had the best sex of her life.

But this was ridiculous. She sat up the rest of the way. She was suddenly aware how few clothes she wore and that the room was cool. She covered her chest with her arms.

He held out his arm and a moment later another blanket appeared. He wrapped her up so that she felt warm and safe. He held the front together with his hands.

He was a very attentive man, in every respect, and her heart reached for him, an almost physical leap in his direction. Would it be so very bad to make a life with this man?

Could she? Could she give herself again?

She didn't know. The truth was, she hadn't expected to go even this far. But Endelle had helped her to release a new power and in that release, some of her resistance to the demands of the *breh-hedden* had fallen.

This she could do, making love to Jean-Pierre.

"Now," she said, scooting to the edge of the table and sliding to her feet. "I want to see you in bed. No, stop that. Asleep. I want you to sleep."

A sigh flowed out of his chest. "I think I could, if you were with me."

She nodded. She knew what the last five months had cost him. This she could give him: just a little peace of mind so that he could sleep.

The enemy wears a variety of masks,
But the ascender lacking wisdom cannot discern the difference.

—*Collected Proverbs,* Beatrice of Fourth

CHAPTER 7

"I didn't expect her to be so goddam short," Endelle cried.

An hour after she left Thorne, Endelle stood in the cell that belonged to the now infamous Marguerite. How could Thorne's woman be so short? "She can't be more than five-five or five-six. What the hell?"

Sister Quena's nostrils flared. She held her hands pressed together in front of her. The woman was tall and too lean. She looked scarecrow-like with a weathered face, something that should have been impossible on Second Earth. Maybe she took some really nasty Chinese herbs.

Endelle liked her own height a lot. Though to be fair, she hadn't always been six-five. She'd gained a few inches as the millennia moved along. But at least she'd started out at five-eleven. *Hello.*

Sister Quena, the High Administrator of the Creator's Convent, looked as prim as hell, her thin lips pinched together like she was trying to erase her mouth.

"Yes, Madame Endelle. Sister Marguerite is not as tall as you but she is considered average in height. Not short."

Disapproval reeked from every word, every expression, even the whitening of her compressed lips.

This of course had the worst effect on Endelle. "Well damn my pussy, I never thought Thorne would fall for a shorty. Goddam." She all but slapped her leg as she said it.

Sister Quena's complexion turned the color of a beet and not because she was embarrassed. Endelle smiled. She snorted. "Would you please just relax a little? Can't you see I'm jerking your chain, Quenny? Now, what can you tell me about this ascender?"

She waved a hand over Marguerite, who lay on her back, the skirt of her coarse woven nightgown caught between her knees, her lips parted. The woman was out. Her complexion was as white as Quenny's was red but Endelle suspected the lack of color reflected the drugs that sister-bitch had used on her devotiate.

Sister Quena's hands never left their glued-together state. Her nostrils widened once more as she looked down at the prostrate woman. "Sister Marguerite is a very difficult and a very sad case. Though her Seer gifts exceed any that I have encountered in quite some time, I have not found the key to her rehabilitation. I fear she is perhaps my greatest failure in my three thousand years as a servant of the Creator. Her stubbornness is beyond comprehension. She was consigned here by her parents because of a particular inclination she exhibited in the area of mores. More specifically, nymphomania."

Endelle's brows rose. Where was the problem in that? She'd had her own nympho period around the time of Plato and it had been hot as hell. She'd cooled a bit since then but that's what being High Administrator of Second Earth could do to a gal's libido. "I think I need you to be more specific, Quenny. Why was Sister Marguerite condemned to this shithole . . . no offense intended."

"Madame Endelle, with all due respect, I am completely and utterly offended."

Endelle rolled her eyes. She had never been able to comprehend the soul or the fervor of the religious fanatic. The thought of being so removed from the ins-and-outs of life, literally, gave her the scratch.

On the other hand, what man would ever want to fuck the woman in front of her with her thin white lips, her pointed chin, her disapproval of everything? Maybe it all worked out in the end and who the hell was she to judge anyway?

"Let me try again. Why was she shipped here?"

"She had a love of men, *a lot* of men. Her parents believed it to be a profound defect of character."

"Well, then, exactly how long has she been here?"

"Not long. A century."

"Jesus H. Christ," Endelle muttered. She glanced at Sister Quena, who stared down at the woman. The head sister of the Creator's Convent didn't just frown, she scowled. Endelle would bet every one of her pubes that despite the laws against floggings and canings, the good sister used these methods in the name of spiritual purification.

Endelle didn't like Quenny. They were opposites, of course, although in the sense that each ruled however the hell she wanted to, they were very much alike. But what she really despised about the good sister was her mean spirit and how she completely ignored the biblical scripture "Love thy neighbor as thyself"—a word of wisdom, by the way, that had been carved into the stonework above each doorway.

Bunch of self-righteous, soul-eating hypocrites.

Whatever.

"You may leave us," Endelle said.

Sister Quena gasped. "I do not think that is either necessary or wise." She lifted her stubborn pointed chin and tried for imperious. She damn near succeeded even though Endelle, in her stilettos, towered over her.

Yes, the bitch ruled as she saw fit and no doubt the thought that anyone else would have control, even momentarily, of one of her subjects chapped her ass, to say the least.

But in this respect Endelle still had some power—she could overrule the High Administrator of any of the Creator's

Convents on Second Earth. Not much had been left to her after the creation of COPASS, but she still had some jurisdiction here.

"I don't give a fuck what you think is necessary or wise. Get out." She held the woman's gaze and let her feel the weight of her nine thousand years.

Sister Quena began trembling and her gaze fell away. "Yes, Madame Endelle."

Much better.

Sister Quena left, closing the door behind her. The door was tall, arched, wooden, and had a small window with wrought-iron insets. Bars, really.

She glanced around.

There was a second bed in the room. Both were narrow and sagged oddly. The room was frigid. Thorne had made his confession about Marguerite explaining that his sister, Grace, shared Marguerite's cell, which also explained how he had met his ladylove in the first place.

Thorne had been surprised that Endelle didn't condemn him for holding back. How could she? Thorne carried the load and the load had become the proverbial one-too-many straws. She knew it, but she just didn't know what to do about it. They were a little short on Warriors of the Blood right now.

She shivered. This room was fucking cold and when she blew a stream of air, sure enough, she produced fog.

She reached down and touched Marguerite's feet. Dammit, they were like ice. Had sister-bitch no compassion? What the hell was wrong with that woman?

Endelle waved a hand and folded a thick comforter into her arms, one from her own bedroom. She spread it over Marguerite. Even in her drugged state, the beautiful woman sighed and her whole body relaxed.

The bed was so low that when Endelle sat down at its foot, she could easily reach under the covers and rub some warmth into the woman's feet. Marguerite made soft warbling sounds in her throat.

Endelle didn't know exactly why she was so moved, but

she was. *There but for the grace of God, and all that shit,* she thought.

Because of her age, Endelle possessed a number of Third Earth abilities. Her preternatural voyeurism was almost unequaled on Second Earth. But another Third Earth power Endelle had involved her ability to penetrate minds, even while drugged. There were some things she had to know about this woman before she proceeded with one of the most disloyal acts she'd ever thought to do in her long fucking life. Desperation was its own terrible motivation.

Still rubbing the woman's feet very gently, warming them up by degrees, she slid her mind against Marguerite's.

The split second she penetrated the tough-as-nails head, a voice shouted at her telepathically, *Who the fuck are you? And what are you doing inside my head?*

Endelle laughed and for a moment stopped working some circulation into the woman's toes. *The one who's keeping you from frostbite.*

Oh. Well, I hope you aren't into women because I'm not and if you take one fucking millimeter's advantage of me I'll have you by the short hairs. Got it?

Endelle laughed then chortled.

What's so goddam funny?

Nothing, Endelle sent. *Not a goddam thing.*

Not much anyway, she thought. Except she actually liked Marguerite. So much spirit.

Which meant . . . shit.

Hey, I'm warm, Marguerite sent. *I'm actually warm.*

I brought you a comforter.

What are you, like some kind of angel?

That sent Endelle into another bout of laughter to the point that she had to wipe her cheeks with the back of her hands and she almost peed her boar's skirt. *Not hardly,* she sent. *But I'd better get to the point. Sister-bitch will be back any time. I cowed her for a couple of seconds but you're her property and she thinks I'm here rustling.*

This time, laughter rang through her mind. *Sister-bitch.*

Oh, I like that. I like that a lot. If ever there was a fitting nickname, you just coined it.

Endelle nodded even though Marguerite's eyes were shut fast.

The devotiate remained on her back, as still as a rock, except for a little light breathing thrown in. For just a moment, as Endelle watched the rise and fall of Marguerite's chest beneath the mound of the comforter, she wondered what kind of world Second Earth had become that an obviously healthy young woman, with a perfectly understandable love of the male body, could be kept imprisoned for a hundred years under the guise of spiritual reformation?

Jesus. H. Christ.

Some things just hadn't changed very much in nine thousand years.

Although she rather thought that her own reason for being here was worse in some ways, since she was thinking about moving this gifted woman to another kind of prison. How then did that make her any different from sister-bitch?

The toes were toasty warm now, and she withdrew her hand from under the comforter.

She rose to her imposing height, and because the bed was low to the stone floor, it was like staring down at a doll somehow. Thorne had chosen a real beauty in Marguerite but damn she was short.

She had planned on grilling Marguerite, on finding out the truth, but, man, her heart had started to hurt something fierce. She loved Thorne. He was the brother she'd never had and he was above all her comrade-in-arms.

It was often rumored that they were lovers but that had never been true—much too much an incestuous feel to it. No one, *no one,* could have tolerated what he put up with in her. So how the hell was she supposed to betray him like this by taking his woman out of the Convent and sending her someplace worse?

I'll leave you now, she sent.

What's your name?

Doesn't matter. She chuckled again. *Call me Angel.*

Thanks, Angel.

Aw, shit. *I'm leaving the comforter and I'm telling sister-bitch that if I ever learn she took it from you, I'll feed her to the next death vampire who crosses my path.*

Thanks . . . Endelle.

What the fuck?

She heard that telepathic laughter again. *Hey, you're not the only powerful ascender in this room. I just lack the ability to fight these fucking drugs.*

Well, well, well.

Just . . . please don't take Thorne away from me. He's . . . he's what's kept me sane all these years.

Oh . . . shit. This just kept getting worse.

Bye, Marguerite. Don't let Quenny get to you.

A slight pause. *I won't.*

Endelle didn't wait. Jesus, she was in deep and all she'd done was have half a conversation with a comatose nymphomaniac.

She folded back to her palace. She had thought first to return to her administrative headquarters but damn, she had so much to think about.

She touched down in the rotunda next to the one she used for the major ascension ceremonies.

She paced back and forth with a little levitation thrown in. The domes of her palace were so tall that a death vampire could have been doing a series of rolling loops and not touched any of the walls.

There were only three small white sofas in the white marble room. She had heard her palace referred to as Olympus more than once.

She paced in the direction of the balcony that overlooked the expanse of desert to the west of the McDowell Mountains. The land stretched out before her, mostly made up of oily creosote, the occasional saguaro, prickly pear, cholla. She felt like the desert right now, barren, full of thorns, dry as hell. Her temper had sharpened but lately her chest had been hurting. Since she was an ascended vampire, that ruled out heart attack, so what was going on?

Everything was changing, but nothing seemed to be improving. They were still losing the war to *the little peach,* that self-styled Commander and leader of the Ascension Liberation Army, Darian Greaves.

Endelle had an elite group of warriors at her command, the Warriors of the Blood, and they were still all that prevented the collapse of two worlds. But right now, her little band of men was fragmented with change.

Four of her warriors had bonded with their *brehs.* Maybe Jean-Pierre hadn't completed the process but he was well down the pike. Jesus. Four. *Four.* Would she now lose Jean-Pierre as a warrior?

When Warrior Medichi had completed the *breh-hedden* with Parisa Lovejoy, he'd embarked on a new form of service, traveling the world as her ambassador and performing the ritual of *royle* wings alongside his *breh.* The couple shared the same wings, *royle* wings, which was all well and good and yes, they were helping to improve her image around the globe as a powerful ruler, but in the meantime she'd lost Medichi's sword-arm at the Borderlands.

Her men were in deep shit. They protected the five Borderlands, keeping hundreds of death vampires from escaping to Mortal Earth every night.

Colonel Seriffe and Jean-Pierre had been working with the Militia Warriors, to improve their death vampire fighting skills. The problem—and it was a motherfucker of a big one—was that it took four Militia Warriors to bring down one death vampire. For whatever genetic lottery had equipped the Warriors of the Blood, they were so far superior in preternatural speed and skill that they could easily take on as many as eight death vampires at once. That was a helluva lot of power.

But she wasn't going down that road. That road led to the Grand Canyon of five months ago when Greaves had called her out in battle and she'd lost over a thousand Militia Warriors.

So, no. Her thoughts stopped right there.

She had to live in the here and now or she'd lose her fucking mind.

She shoved both hands into her thick black hair and pulled at the braids dangling past her shoulders. She whirled away from the balcony and paced into the rotunda. She took a deep breath, levitated, and mounted her wings all with one thought. Jesus, mounting wings was a rush, about as close to sex as any other function got.

She rose into the air, plowing in smooth sweeps of her wings so that she rolled beneath the rounded ceiling. She ended up on her back with the tips of her wings flapping ever so slowly, like swimming in a pool and staying afloat with just a sweep of the hands.

What was she going to do? Creator help her, what was she going to do? Marguerite was a gifted Seer and for the first time in a hundred years she had a card to play against Owen Stannett. She could trade Marguerite to Stannett and gain access, at long last, to the information from the Superstition Fortress that could turn the tide of war . . . at long fucking last.

But the price—!

The inestimable value of two souls, one of which she had loved for two thousand years.

Talk about a crucifixion.

Fiona lay in bed beside Jean-Pierre. His back was to her, the dark blue comforter under his arm so that his hair was spread out for her to see. He slept heavily, his breathing almost labored, the sound of someone whose sleep had been uneasy for a long time.

His hand rested on his hip and she kept her fingers on top of his. Without the connection, he would wake up.

The man was in hell.

Whatever the *breh-hedden* might be for her, Jean-Pierre suffered more, as though his male protective instincts had come online with all the subtlety of a summer monsoon.

She owed him this, just to stick close for a while so that he could sleep. Her arm hurt, though, from the unsupported position.

In order to change that, she needed to get closer, something she did not want to do. His coffee scent, even while sleeping, still made her almost anxious to repeat everything they'd just done together. While showering, however, she'd concluded that she ought to be a lot wiser about their relationship. They'd taken a big step, a huge step, a massive leap, but how smart could any of this really be?

For one thing, she knew Jean-Pierre had issues, something she thought had to do with his wife of many decades ago. Then there was her own little struggle: She never wanted to be close to a man again, to get tangled up in the hopelessness of trying to be a couple, or a family, in any dimension.

She shifted her hip in his direction because her arm was close to spasming. She had to get closer, but she so didn't want to.

She rotated her shoulder, which turned her arm over but still kept her connected. A little better.

She put her palm beneath her cheek and watched his thick hair move up and down with his breathing. She huffed a sigh. So she was obsidian flame, a vampire with "a duty, a sense of purpose, built on a foundation of power." Jean-Pierre had posed the question to Endelle, but Fiona had answered it, then Endelle had jumped and levitated around her office . . . again.

Endelle seemed to think that her gold variety of obsidian flame might end up having something to do with her telepathy, since it was her strongest power.

She sighed once more. Her eyelids grew heavy but just as she might have fallen asleep, her bicep, tweaked as it was, started to spasm. Aw, hell, there was nothing for it.

She moved in behind Jean-Pierre, tucking her hips low so she could bend her knees and spoon him.

He didn't exactly wake up. He just pushed backward to get closer still, took hold of her hand, and drew her arm to his chest. She was now so close to him that she had to push all that glorious hair away from his back because her face was also smashed up against him.

She took a deep breath of his exquisite coffee smell. Though desire rolled through her as it always did when she caught his scent, a delicious lethargy took hold of her as well. She closed her eyes with the heat of his body taking her that last final step into the oblivion of sleep.

Sated. Oh, so sated.

Casimir left his nearly comatose partner stretched out on her back, in his Paris bed, her arms flung wide, his fang marks all over her breasts, her abdomen, her navel, and lower. She had taken her fill of the hopeless young gothic woman he'd seduced out of a club an hour earlier.

He and Julianna had drained her almost to the point of dying blood, but neither of them would ever go that far. They might be hedonists, even sadists, but they weren't murderers.

The young woman lay naked and unconscious, bloody and bruised on the fine silk of the sofa. Her short hair was bleached white, her lips tattooed black, and she had piercings in a number of places, most of which Julianna had ripped from her, savoring the screams, in the course of the taking.

Naturally, Caz had misted a tough barrier between the back bedrooms and the living rooms. He would never want his babies distressed by the activity in the living room.

He thought the thought and her skimpy black leather bustier, mini skirt, and torn stockings reappeared on her body. On her feet, combat boots. Cliché, in Caz's opinion, but the ensemble had worked for Julianna.

Extending his preternatural voyeurism, he sent the special window flying back to the club where he'd found the woman and moved to scope out the alley in the back. With no one around, he simply returned her to lean against the wall. With any luck, she'd be well used again before she woke up and their misdeeds were laid at the feet of mortals.

Pulling his voyeur's window back in and shutting it down, he gathered up all the superfluous silver loops, studs, and bars and sent them clinking onto the cement next to the goth.

He stared down at the couch and clucked his tongue. The fabric was a mess. He shook his head. He had so much power. With barely a thought, he had been able to send the fully clothed goth back to the club. But he couldn't seem to remove stains from silk.

The three of them had been very active . . . well, two of them had been active. The goth party girl had lost her smiles about two minutes in, had screamed for about forty minutes, then lost consciousness before the big climax.

Surprise.

Vampires are real.

So was his current dilemma.

The silk used to be gold.

Gold silk.

The color snagged his mind, worked him over, forced him to think.

Gold.

Then suddenly all the pieces concerning the attack at the Convent fell miraculously into place. And sure enough, as he reviewed the battle, as he dwelled in particular on Fiona's aura, he saw . . . *gold.*

Part of him was delighted that his mind had finally figured it out. The other part, the one that understood the implications, was appalled. This kind of power could be *vast*—as in monumentally *vast.* It could also be lethal, deadly as hell.

He hadn't expected this . . . so, shit.

He felt a slight movement of air behind him and stiffened. Without looking around he said, "Hello, Darian. How's tricks?"

He turned to face his co-conspirator, who stood just three feet away and bore a slight sheen on his forehead. Caz smiled. Apparently the man with ambitions to rule two worlds had been forced to work pretty hard to get through the shields Caz had placed all around his hotel room.

Very nice.

Greaves held his right hand in his left and gave his onyx pinkie ring an infinitesimal adjustment.

"Tricks, Casimir?" Darian glanced at the offending sofa and offered a soft grunt of disapproval. He turned away and moved to an uninjured pale cream chair near the window.

He sat down, smoothing the back of his tailored wool suit as he did, as though feeling the length of old-fashioned tails.

Caz knew the sensation well. He often regretted the passing of the very best of men's fashion from the early 1800s.

"Didn't we all look grand in our waistcoats and breeches?" he asked.

Darian nodded. "The neckcloths. Remember the neckcloths?"

"Three feet of the finest linen. I had Brummell himself teach me how to do the little folds. But then no doubt you did not come here to discuss British fashion."

Darian splayed the fingers of his right hand. "No. I wish to understand how the devil you sent eighty death vampires to that absurd, weedy outdoor chapel then lost all of them without even drawing blood once against our enemy?"

"I have asked myself that question at least a dozen times." He crossed to the bar and removed ingredients he'd arranged ahead of time for this little interview: Old Tom Gin, juice of a lime, heavy cream, and a very ripe peach, mashed. It had been just a matter of time before the Commander would come, without the courtesy of an announcement, of course.

Using a stick blender he beat the hell out of the ingredients. He poured the result in a tall fizz glass, added Perrier, and crossed the room to present the result to Darian.

"Do you know what this is called?" Caz smiled down at him, at the man who was called *the little peach* by the opposition because he had won awards for his peach orchards in Estrella Two.

Darian's very arched left brow rose as he took the glass in hand. He held it carefully, his left hand supporting the bottom. He sniffed and closed his eyes. "Lovely. Do tell."

"Peach *blow.* I would have made it just for the name alone."

"Yes," Darian said, "I suppose you would have. It works on so many levels." He sipped. "Very nice. I had this once in Atlanta, I think, around 1900 or so."

Caz, sated as he was, did not partake of the drink. He didn't want to spoil his buzz. The goth's blood, so full of disease and cocaine and some other mood elevator he couldn't quite identify, did cartwheels in his head as he fought off the effects of the drugs and syphilis.

He moved to sit in a companion chair opposite Greaves. He didn't hurry the interview; nor did he rush to deliver explanations, even though he had one. He smiled. Timing was everything.

Greaves licked his lips. "So, as you can imagine, I've been asking myself if the price I'm paying for your services has any value at all."

Caz slipped lower in his chair. He spread his legs a little wider and smiled. He still said nothing.

Greaves tapped the fingers of his left hand over the curved wooden arm of his chair. "Are you flirting with me again?"

Caz shrugged. "Perhaps."

Greaves sighed. "What happened at the chapel? I suppose it was my own fault for getting my hopes up that in one fell swoop you would destroy the last barrier to the fulfillment of my ambitions."

Caz stretched his legs out and flexed his hips. He scooted even lower in the chair. He locked his hands behind his head. He knew he had a powerful body, broad muscled chest, heavy thighs, and other considerable assets. "How do you like the blow?"

Darian, to his credit, never let his gaze slip below Caz's shoulders, even when he flexed his pecs and rolled his abdomen, trying to get Greaves to notice what he had to offer.

"Enough of your games," Darian said. He split his resonance, which sent a shard of pain splitting Caz's mind in two.

Exquisite, he sent. *That felt wonderful.* Aloud, he said, "Are you now trying to seduce me?"

At that, Darian laughed. He set the glass on the marble-topped table at his elbow. "I take it you have something to tell me about the morning's failed battle."

Caz could feel the smile tug at the outer reaches of his lips. Ah, yes, timing. "How do you feel about obsidian flame?"

Darian grew very still. Most people, upon hearing such a deadly pronouncement, would start or gasp. Darian merely turned to stone and stared at him with his large, round innocent-looking brown eyes.

"Which variety?" he asked after a long stellar moment. He visibly forced himself to sit back in his seat. He crossed his legs at the knee; such a gentleman.

Caz chuckled. "Gold, but only you would immediately dissect the situation, draw the correct conclusions, and go to the heart of the matter. The woman, Fiona, the one who has been hunting Rith since her escape from blood slavery, issued a warning. At first I thought she was merely hypersensitive to preternatural imprints. But afterward, when I did a careful review, a closer examination frame by frame of my memory revealed her aura. There can be no mistake. She bears the gold mark of obsidian flame. Given the shields I used in order to disguise the death vampire force, except for an obsidian level of power, she should never have been able to discover my plan.

"You know what this means of course. Tell me you comprehend the scope here."

Greaves's nostrils flared. "A triad."

"Yes, a fucking triad."

Darian shifted his gaze to the thick carpet at Caz's feet. His jaw twitched. After a moment, he lifted his gaze once more. "Do you know who the other two are?"

Caz shook his head. "Only that while I levitated high in the air to watch the unfolding of my plan, I felt a very powerful feminine energy next to me. This energy was very different from the woman who alerted Warrior Thorne to our presence. I couldn't get a fix on her, but I believe she may have a connection to our gold obsidian.

"I confess I didn't make much of it at the time, which might be a flaw I should examine, since my dismissal of the woman's energy reflected the fact that I don't have a very high regard for women. Oh, there I've said it. Now you will think less of me."

Darian smiled. "No, not at all. Women are necessary in so many ways. You and I would not be here otherwise. They are often very powerful, and have control over men in ways

I daresay they truly do not understand, thank the Creator. But when all is said and done, only men know how to create the highest and finest achievements in life."

"I believe that might be the longest speech you've ever made."

Darian shrugged, then asked, "What do you intend to do?"

"The process will not be simple. I'll need to test the woman first, try to understand the direction of her power. Killing her sooner rather than later would be the wisest course, but as you know I am not allowed to do the deed directly." All Upper ascender exiles were monitored for killing behavior, and such behavior meant instant assassination. Another profound annoyance. "I think, though, that given her current obsession with finding our little friend Rith, as well as her intention to destroy as many of your blood slave facilities as she can, my plans will probably flow in the direction of something like a bait-and-switch. How does that sound?"

At that, Darian actually chuckled. "Like perfection." He rose to his feet. "Just get her for me before the other two obsidians emerge and forge the triad."

"You do understand the difficulty."

Greaves nodded. "Her power will be unpredictable."

"And deadly."

"But in the early stages, as now, the power is emerging and at its weakest. If you can arrange it, kill her."

"That's the plan." Caz slid his thumb into the waistband of his white pants and let his fingers rest low on what was now very firm. "Are you sure I can't persuade you into my chambers for a minute or two. I'm very good, better than a peach blow any day."

Only then did Darian slide his gaze lower and lower. "Almost, you tempt me. But not quite, my friend." He lifted his arm and vanished.

O, Beloved,
Take me with your lips,
Take me a thousand times
And I will prepare you a feast.
O, Beloved,
Take me with your arms,
Take me a thousand times
And I will inhabit your bed.
O, Beloved,
Take me with your body,
Take me a thousand times,
And I will build you a house.

—*Collected Poems,* Beatrice of Fourth

CHAPTER 8

Fiona heard a buzzing sound at a great distance, very annoying. She burrowed her head deeper into the pillow and into the mountain of heat that radiated in front of her. She was toasty warm and something more, something that felt like peace.

She fell back into her dreams, of mounting her wings and flying over White Lake, the beautiful narrow man-made lake on the west side of the White Tanks. She flew behind Alison but with two women off to her right, also in flight, which meant that she formed the left flank of the trio.

However, she couldn't see the other women clearly, as though they were blurred through the distance of what she could feel was simply the future.

Her heart swelled. As one, all four of them drew their

wings into what was called parachute-mount, cupped at the top. In increments, she drew her wings in closer so that she eased downward through the air in the direction of the lake.

Her bare toes touched the cool water.

She looked up.

A rush of gold power flew through her up and up, joining with the women to her right. Euphoria flowed as well, such happiness, such fulfillment.

Her power joined the powers of the other women, and what had been three individual obsidian flames became one massive joining of gold, of red, and of cerulean blue, a twist of individual colors and power that blended just at the edges to forge a massive, rainbow-colored beam of light.

With her toes still grounded by the lake, and her wings supporting her, she looked up. There, in a beautiful swirl of blue, the color of Alison's eyes, was what she knew to be the portal to Third Earth. A resounding *yes* flew through her mind. She was ready to help Alison open the gateway to the third dimension.

The dream vanished, like a giant whirlwind being dragged up into the sky higher and higher, growing smaller to the eye as each millisecond passed, then simply disappearing.

The mountain of heat beside her moved, pushing her and rolling her onto her back. The buzzing sound returned. So annoying. She felt groggy and couldn't quite open her eyes. She didn't know where she was.

All she could think about was White Lake, White Lake, White Lake, until the mountain spoke in a whisper next to her ear. "Fiona, your phone is buzzing."

Something mumbled came out of her mouth.

She turned over on her other side and folded her hands prayer-like then placed them beneath her cheek.

A large warm hand found her shoulder and gave her a gentle shake. "Fiona. It is grown late. Alison is probably trying to call you."

Alison had been so beautiful in her dream. She didn't wear a flight suit, but rather the most beautiful ethereal gown all in white and flowing around her as though made up of thousands of sheer long silk scarves, hanging several yards past her feet.

She looked almost angelic, a very strange state for a vampire woman.

The shaking recommenced. She opened her eyes this time and tried to focus. She had fallen asleep. When? Where?

Curved wooden shingles made up the wall opposite her. Why were there shingles in a bedroom?

The memory of being in Jean-Pierre's wood shop, and lying on her back on his table, flowed through her like a wildfire on a dry grassy hillside.

Desire ignited. Her back arched.

She finally started to wake up.

A roll of Jean-Pierre's café-au-lait scent battered her and she heard him groan. His hand was still on her shoulder.

She shifted to look at him and met eyes the color of the ocean, blue, gray, and green, eyes at half-mast. His nostrils flared and his hair hung over her arm and touched her breast, teasing her bare nipple.

His chin trembled. His lips parted. He leaned lower and lower. She rose up and just as his lips would have touched hers, the phone buzzed again.

Alison.

"Oh, shit, Alison! Jean-Pierre, what time is it? How long did I, we, sleep? Oh, my God."

But even though the phone buzzed, he put a hand on her right shoulder and pressed her back down into the mattress. She let him. When she was flat on her back, he planted a hand on either side of her. She thought he meant to kiss her and then do more than that.

Instead, he held her gaze for a long moment, his expression solemn. "I slept, *chérie*. I have not slept like that in decades."

She blinked up at him and drew a deep breath. She nodded, her head sliding up and down on the pillow. "I did, too."

Sleep still clung to her, desire as well, but in this moment, with this powerful warrior suspended above her, she felt like weeping.

Tears rose then slid from the sides of her eyes, drifting into her hair. "Jean-Pierre, how beautiful you are." She lifted her right hand and stroked the length of his long warrior hair, all the way to the tips. Maybe it was because sleep still lived in her mind, but all she could think to say was, "When I mount my wings, will you take me flying over White Lake?"

"Of course I will take you flying, anywhere you like."

He smiled, his big bold smile, full of good humor and something so male, so sexy that once more desire consumed her. She wrapped her hand around a thick section of his hair and tugged him toward her.

But the phone buzzed again, loud and insistent.

Jean-Pierre, closer now, once more remained suspended, his gaze fixed on her lips.

"I have to get that. I really do." She drew in a deep breath, closed her eyes, and began inching sideways toward the edge of the bed, toward the pile of her clothes, and where her phone must be, but she couldn't go farther than where his hand pressed into the bed on that side of her.

He lifted his arm and threw himself backward on the bed, the comforter caught around his waist.

She held the comforter to her chest as she leaned then leaned a little more over the side of her bed to reach her phone. She felt cool air all down her back and her bottom. What a sight she must make.

Jean-Pierre stared at the most beautiful shape in the world. He loved to look at a woman from this position, her body stretched out, on her side, reaching, so that her waist elongated and her hip became a smooth curved line.

The split of her bottom was squeezed together because of her slight contortion, and he wanted his finger drifting along that line and exploring . . . everywhere. His tongue as well.

He almost called to her, to remind her that she could fold the phone into her hand. But his strong male intelligence kicked in and he leaned back to enjoy the show.

She scooted her hip, which made her bottom jiggle so

enticingly. He folded his hands behind his head. Of course he was making a tent out of the comforter, but who cared. His woman was in his bed, creeping along, still caught in her sleep-daze, and pleasing his eyes.

She finally looked back at him and scowled. "Will you please stop with all that coffee?"

"Non," he said, stating his case simply. "How can I when your body is so exquisite, *chérie*?"

She scowled a little more and tried to tug the comforter around her but didn't succeed. That he pulled against the fabric worked a little more in his favor.

A new idea struck. He thought the thought and her buzzing phone appeared in his hand, which meant, of course, that she flipped over and turned in his direction, reaching out.

Pure genius.

He groaned at the sight of her full bare breasts, nipples peaked. Her long hair flowed around her shoulders, some in front and hanging to disguise what he longed to put his lips around.

"Jean-Pierre," she cried. But he kept the phone at a distance, his arm extended away from her so that she had to reach into him. He leaned forward at the same moment, and pressed his chest against hers then crashed his mouth against her mouth.

She made a tactical error, parting her lips to protest. He thrust his tongue deep inside and just like that, her body stilled and her lips began to work, kissing him back, thrust for thrust.

Her stillness melted and he dropped the phone on the other side of the bed.

He was just about to lie back and pull her on top of him when once more the phone buzzed.

Fiona pushed away from him. "Enough. We have people depending on us." She scooted off the bed on the opposite side and, in a terrible sequence of quick thoughts, dressed in her black pants and heels, her lavender blouse. She was tying the bow by hand when he rose to stand naked on the other side of the bed.

Her gaze fell to what was hard and ready for her. He watched her brow crumple and a small whimper leave her mouth. Then she simply turned around to face the wall, her shoulders slumping a little, as she continued to fiddle with the bow.

Jean-Pierre's thoughts became fixed on one thing: His woman had been in his bed, had slept beside him, wrapped around his body. And he had known such wonderful peace.

He waved a hand and with the practice of centuries went from naked to fully dressed, not in flight battle gear, but in a long-sleeved ribbed T-shirt, jeans, and loafers. He would not be fighting tonight and they would head out soon to Militia Warrior HQ.

By now Fiona was on her phone making her apologies to Alison, but then she said, "Oh. I see. Well, that's good then." She paused. "Yes, we slept all afternoon, can you believe that?" Another pause. A chuckle. "Okay, see you in fifteen minutes at HQ."

She touched the screen of her phone and turned back to him. "She's still feeding baby Helena."

Jean-Pierre nodded.

"You look so nice. Navy is a good color for you."

"Merci."

She looked down at her own clothes. "Do you mind if I take a little time to fold some of my things here before we head over? I'd like to change. I usually don't go this formal at HQ."

"Please. Make yourself at home."

Fifteen minutes later, Jean-Pierre had his arm around Fiona's waist as he folded them both to a secured landing platform at Militia Warrior HQ in Apache Junction Two. Because of the possibility that death vampires could fold directly into the facility, the entire complex was shielded with an electronic system that only allowed folding directly to designated platforms. Technology was a good thing.

Before the shield and platforms, many Militia Warriors died when death vampires folded straight into the facility and began slaughtering at will.

The ascender on duty knew Jean-Pierre well and actually looked a little bored as he waved them both through.

Jean-Pierre kept Fiona close as he guided her down the ramp and into the long building.

The Warriors of the Blood rarely met up at Endelle's Central Command. Jeannie and Carla kept the grid humming and had decades ago worked out the perfect communications system among the warriors, all orders traveling through Thorne unless otherwise designated. Central Command also answered to Endelle. But because there were only eight Warriors of the Blood—seven on active duty because of Medichi's ambassadorial assignment—a large-scale operation just wasn't necessary.

This was not true for the Militia Warriors who were led by Colonel Seriffe.

The Militia Warriors numbered in the thousands in Metro Phoenix Two, serving as a police force for the ascended city as well as a hardened battling force in the ongoing war against death vampires. Every Territory on Second Earth also had fighting units of Militia Warriors so that worldwide, they were a brotherhood of half a million.

Jean-Pierre knew what the Militia Warriors called the Warriors of the Blood behind their backs: WhatBees, after the initials WOTB. As was typical of the male spirit, one group insisted on holding territorial rights against the other. It was just human nature, ascended or mortal. For that reason, he politely ignored all but the most blatant of pissing contests, another American expression he enjoyed very much.

There was, however, much mutual respect since all warriors battled the same enemy: Greaves and his army of death vampires.

Fiona led the way, but he knew exactly where she was going and why her chin had that familiar stubborn look. Before she did anything else, even before she began to explore her new power as obsidian flame, she would check the Militia Warrior HQ grid to see if any more anomalies had been sighted that might in turn lead to the discovery of yet another blood slave facility. In hunting for the facilities,

Fiona was convinced that one day she would find Rith and bring him to justice.

As they passed the offices of the numerous Section Leaders, Jean-Pierre caught Gideon's eye and nodded to him. Gideon had led the most recent group of Militia Warriors, bringing home eleven blood slaves to freedom.

Gideon nodded back but returned immediately to his computer, as though avoiding Jean-Pierre. The vampire had reason. He was approaching Warrior of the Blood status but anytime the subject came up, he got his back up. More than once he said he would never leave his service as a Militia Warrior.

Gideon was as tall as Jean-Pierre now and even perhaps more heavily muscled. Thorne felt certain he was only months away from a WOTB calling.

God help them, but Endelle's forces needed more Warriors of the Blood. The difference in battle was profound and truly without explanation. But when a vampire achieved WOTB status, he could outperform his fellow Militia Warriors by incredible lengths. For the most part, a WOTB could battle eight or more death vampires at once, while a typical Militia Warrior had to be part of a squad of four to survive the attack of just one death vampire.

There was no comparison, so it was not unusual for Endelle or Thorne or any of the Warriors of the Blood to track the sudden development of a Militia Warrior. Gideon at this point in his life was known to battle two and sometimes three death vampires at once. It was not a small thing for Gideon, therefore, but the man fought, and even appeared to despise, his emerging status.

Jean-Pierre wished more than anything that he could help facilitate the emergence of more WOTBs, but nothing at present had transpired to hasten the process.

Once at the grid, he stepped back and let Fiona do what she did the best. She checked each of the anomalies that the grid-keepers found, searching for a special shading that only Fiona could see, which had in the past five months never failed once to produce a blood slave facility.

A few minutes later, she turned back to him and shook her head. She shifted to lean to her right then waved. When Jean-Pierre looked over his shoulder, he saw Alison through the windows that flanked the hallway as well as the grid room. She smiled, stopped, then waved an arm forward, beckoning Fiona to join her.

Jean-Pierre accompanied Fiona to the room Alison had decided to use to begin the strange sort of obsidian flame training. Once inside, he closed the door, but he moved to the glass windows that fronted the hall and turned the two closest blind slats up so that he could see movement in other parts of the facility. He might not be able to see everything, but he could make certain assessments just by watching who travelled the halls and at what speed.

"What's wrong?" Fiona asked. The moment she had taken a good look at Alison, she knew she had to ask.

Alison rolled her eyes but she turned in a complete circle, threw her hands wide, and said, "You were a young mother once, right?"

All the tension Fiona had been feeling drifted away. She had expected something about death vampires—or worse, Endelle, since Alison worked most days as the scorpion queen's executive assistant. But babies? Yes, she knew something about that.

"It's hard, isn't it?" Fiona offered.

The office was bare of furniture except for a handful of chairs against the wall nearest the door. Alison moved to sit in one and crossed her arms over her chest. "I never thought I'd feel this way. I mean I always wanted a baby, but I didn't expect this." She lifted her eyes to Fiona, her lovely blue eyes rimmed with gold. She put her hand above her heart and rubbed. "I ache when I'm away from Helena, and it's really getting to me."

Fiona chuckled. She had raised two children. "That's so we bond really well with them. It's a beautiful trick of nature, because in about two years, you're going to want to kill her."

Alison smiled. "The Terrible Twos."

"Or Threes. Some children don't assault your humanity until they're three."

Alison leaned back in the chair and took a couple more breaths. She relaxed her arms and let them dangle at her sides. "It's just that this is a really hard time to bring children into the world."

There was so much Fiona could have said, about how she'd lost her beloved Peter forever when he was eight, how she'd lost 115 years with Carolyn. But she went to something else. "A friend of mine and her three children died of typhoid fever in 1883. I know that most of the diseases from my era have been eradicated on Mortal Earth in the United States, but I can remember saying exactly what you just said, so I would suggest this: When has it ever been truly safe to bring a child into the world?"

Alison shook her head. "Never, I suppose."

Fiona moved to sit beside her and took her hand. They shared a few things in common. They were both powerful in ways neither had expected to be.

More than once, Alison had talked about her ascension experiences, stunned by what she had accomplished and what she was supposed to accomplish in the future.

And now Fiona was grappling with something called obsidian flame.

They also had their men in common. Warrior Kerrick had immense power in his own right. His preternatural speed was unmatched.

Fiona glanced at Jean-Pierre, but he wasn't looking at them. He held the vertical slat aside with two fingers and scanned the activity in other parts of HQ. She wasn't quite sure if he did this to give them some privacy or because he was in a constant state of concern about issues of security. She suspected the latter.

"Endelle says Helena needs to learn to be tough so that I shouldn't worry about being separated from her this much."

Fiona started to laugh and couldn't seem to stop.

Alison finally said, "Hey, what's with you?"

Fiona giggled some more. Tears ran down her cheeks.

"I'm sorry, but that's the funniest thing I've heard in a long time. Do you really think you should take parenting advice from a woman who's never had children, who wears a mini skirt that I'm pretty sure was taken from an animal that likes to roll around in the mud, and who is known to use the oh-so-elegant expression, *damn my pussy*?"

Alison sported a smile that turned into a bout of laughter. This led to a discussion about how, during the few days surrounding her ascension, Endelle had worn a bodysuit made entirely from some kind of weird gray snakeskin.

And so it went, until Fiona was doubled over and Alison expressed her fear that if they didn't stop, she was going to pee her pants.

"I hear she's into embroidering leather," Alison cried, wiping her face and barely able to get the words out, "because Owen Stannett wears embroidered leather."

This sent Fiona into whoops, until she was slapping one hand against her thigh repeatedly.

Fiona remained beside Alison for a good long while, chuckling when Alison chuckled, catching Alison's eye and laughing some more.

Finally, Alison said, "Well, I guess we'd better find out what the hell an obsidian flame is."

But this only caused Fiona to laugh all over again. This life of hers was just so freaking weird.

As Fiona wiped away another set of tears, Alison addressed Jean-Pierre. "You must think we've lost our minds."

He now stood facing into the room and smiling. His eyes held a beautiful light. He leaned against the closed door, his arms over his chest. "I love that you are both laughing. I think it wonderful. We do not laugh enough in this world I think?"

Alison sighed. "No, I guess we don't."

Fiona stared at Jean-Pierre. Her heart squeezed tight. This was something she loved about him. He always knew the right thing to say, and he said it.

Alison stood up. "All right, ascender, we'd better get started because the moment we're done here I have to report to you-know-who. I also need to relieve Kerrick on babysitting duty before he heads to the Borderlands tonight."

Fiona stood up as well and blew the air from her cheeks. So this was it. With any luck, between the two of them she would learn exactly what it meant to be the gold variety of obsidian flame.

Caz materialized into the grand black marble foyer of Greaves's penthouse in Geneva. Rith waited for him next to a freestanding holy water font.

So Rith had foreseen this meeting. He couldn't explain the man's presence otherwise.

"You been dipping into the future streams again?"

Rith just stared at him. All that Asian stoicism. He certainly didn't smile. He was so odd looking, straight black hair almost to his shoulders, a wide forehead, broad nose.

Still, no answer, not one word.

Caz flexed his pecs, something he did when he was plain mad. He had no patience for this ass-licker. He cleared his mind—the specialty of Fourth ascenders, so that anyone with powers approaching Third level wouldn't be able to read his thoughts or his intentions. Only then did Rith show a sign of emotion, a faint startled ripple that swayed his black hair in a wave right to left, very faint, barely a movement at all.

Caz walked toward him, holding his gaze then burrowing into Rith's brain, sort of a mind-fuck, something he loved to do. But damn if this bastard didn't just sit lotus-style in the middle of his head, forearms balanced on his knees, thumbs and fingers touching.

He wasn't sure which emotion struck first, more anger or plain old disgust. This man didn't live. Maybe he had never lived. He sat in his head, cool as a cucumber and twice as useless. But with just a little preternatural magic, Caz mentally walked over to the meditating image and gave him a solid karate kick to the head, one solid foot-jab.

Caz withdrew from Rith's mind and wasn't surprised to

find the bastard spread out on the floor, screaming and holding his head. At last. A little emotion.

"Let's talk, shall we?"

Rith looked up at him, his dark eyes darker still. More emotion? Fancy that.

"Did I cause you distress?" Caz asked.

Rith gained his feet. A sheen of sweat covered his face and neck. "What do you want?"

"You've been in the future streams, my friend. You tell me."

Rith pinched his lips together. He looked away from Caz, his eyes shifting back and forth. When they settled, staring at some object on the wall, he said, "You wish to know about the woman, Fiona. You wish information from the future streams. What I can tell you is that you must seek the other obsidian flame first, the one who was beside you while you levitated above the outdoor chapel in Prescott Two." He paused and met Casimir's gaze. "Does any of this make sense to you?"

Caz nodded. "Where do I find the woman?"

"Her name is Marguerite and she is locked up in the Creator's Convent. There is one man who has access to her, however. High Administrator Owen Stannett."

"Stannett? Fuck." Just to be sure, he added, "Of the Superstition Mountains Seers Fortress?"

Rith nodded.

"Now, was that so hard?" Caz asked.

But a strange light entered Rith's eye and a smile curved his lips. "Do what you will, make as many bargains with the devil as you will, but you are not long for this world, Casimir of Fourth Earth. You are not long for this world."

Caz rolled his eyes. "Fuck off, Seer."

He lifted his arm and got the hell out of there.

When he landed outside the tall, rusted iron doors of the Superstition Mountains Seers Fortress, he shook his head. Another shithole. What was wrong with these powerful administrators that they insisted on squalor?

He sent his voyeur window on a quick hunt for Stannett

and found him in . . . well, what do you know . . . a nicely appointed office. Pieces of Stannett's character fell into place. Clearly, the man saved the best for himself.

Caz could respect that, of course.

He folded to the end point. Stannett turned and said, "Right on time." Another fucking Seer. It made Caz want to spit venom.

Caz did not like Owen Stannett. He never had, not in all the centuries he had known him.

The little prick, as he would always think of Stannett, stood framed by a plate-glass window. Beyond lay a garden that vied for beauty with any of the gardens at the White Tank Resort Colony itself.

The Superstition Mountains Seers Fortress was situated not just within the mountains but near a famous geographic landmark called Weaver's Needle. Stannett's office, as part of the fortress, overlooked a sharp incline of what should have been desert terrain. Stannett, however, had altered a section of the land to create a dome of microclimate beneath which a garden more suited to the Mediterranean had emerged: Flowers cascaded over stone walls; stone paths led among sculpted beds full of lavender, succulents, and roses. Throughout, tall Italian cypruses punctuated an intense blue sky beyond.

Breathtaking.

A man with a horticultural sensibility should have been someone Caz could appreciate. Instead, his Fourth ascender instincts clanged in awkward counterpoint to the beauty of the garden. Something was not right with Owen Stannett, and this from a self-proclaimed sadist-hedonist.

Stannett wore his short and very thick dark brown hair in a strange wave on the right side of his head. Blackish chest hair protruded in clumps from the deep V of his embroidered red leather vest. His jacket was of a similar ilk, but white and embroidered with flowers in the primary colors, plus green and splashes of violet.

He looked western in a Liberace sort of way. He even wore cowboy boots.

Caz turned to sit in a stiff brown leather club chair across from the desk.

"Why so glum, Owen? I thought you'd be glad to see me. We used to have some fun together."

Owen drew a shallow breath. "That was three centuries ago."

"Oh," Caz drawled. "Seems like yesterday, yet you actually appear upset. I thought you enjoyed sharing my bed."

"When you weren't hurting me, it was pleasant enough."

Caz clucked his tongue. "Never hold a grudge. Besides, how can you possibly be mad when I helped you get this gig? Hasn't it turned out well, especially from the time COPASS came into being?"

"I confess that it has."

"Then I think you owe me a little favor or two."

Stannett's shoulders dropped an inch. Caz was impressed. Stannett had been something of a baby all those centuries ago, always complaining when something *hurt,* always wanting to be set free. But here he was in command of himself and so much in charge of the Fortress that he'd single-handedly hamstrung the ruler of Second Earth.

"What do you want?" Stannett asked.

Straight to the point. Again, Caz was impressed.

He gave him the essentials about the fiasco at the Creator's Convent. Stannett nodded a couple of times. Caz spoke of Fiona and obsidian flame and *the little prick* didn't flinch, not even a little. So the sly bastard knew about the emergence of obsidian flame.

"I'm not certain how I can be of use to you, Casimir." He held his hands out, as though helpless, then sat down in his chair behind his desk.

Caz narrowed his eyes. "So how well do you know the High Administrator of the Convent?"

"A little."

"Oh, I think you know her a lot. How sly you've become." He paused and sifted through time zones as well as night and day. "Yes, that would have been this morning, Arizona time. How time flies.

"As you can imagine, I'm trying to reconstruct events, trying to discern connections. I've been trying to figure out how a woman so recently rescued from a blood slave facility would suddenly be able to give warning about an attack when she just doesn't seem to have either clairvoyant ability or Seer skills. Sort of a mystery, don't you think? How did she know there were death vampires in the forest?"

Like Rith, Stannett held his face immobile as he waited.

Caz continued, "So I got to thinking. Obsidian flame always comes in threes and yes, we have more frequent occurrences of the phenomenon in the Upper Dimensions, so I am somewhat familiar with them. But while I was levitating above the battleground, I sensed a presence beside me before the battle occurred. That was when I put two and two together. I thought, what if there is a powerful ascender inside the Convent who somehow alerted Fiona to the encroaching danger."

"That would make sense."

Caz felt his temper harden and he knew a sudden and profound desire to launch on Stannett and literally tear him, limb from limb. He took two very deep breaths. He despised all this insidious pretense, as though Stannett didn't have a clue.

"Cut the crap, Owen. Tell me what you know of the devotiate, Marguerite. Tell me everything and tell me now."

Only then did some of the former Owen Stannett return. His chin even shook a little as he patted the wave on the side of his head. "She is the most gifted Seer I have ever known."

"Then why haven't you moved her here?"

"It's complicated."

"Try me. I don't lack for intelligence."

"She belongs to Warrior Thorne."

This, Caz would never have suspected. "Marguerite is Thorne's woman, as in he fucks her, a devotiate in the Convent?"

"He has, I believe, since early in her internment."

Caz had a sudden new respect for Thorne. Who would've thought? One of those do-gooders molesting a Convent devotiate? But then, talk about a juvenile fantasy come to life. His mind drifted to Julianna and a swift scenario flipped through his mind of the woman in a severe Convent gown, innocent and so afraid of what was about to happen to her.

Lest he go too far down that intriguing road, he brought his attention back to the present. "I still don't see why you haven't brought the woman here. You had every right under COPASS law."

"I never moved her for fear of what Thorne might do, how he might react. He has great need of her."

"Don't tell me you're protecting Thorne?"

Stannett shook his head. "I'm protecting myself and my interests from what might happen if Thorne believed his woman to be in danger."

"More future stream bullshit?"

Stannett didn't try to argue his position. He merely nodded.

Caz drifted his gaze to the ceiling. Stannett had a ceiling made up of slate tile squares and mirrored squares. How very strange. Although the mirrors did lend themselves to certain advantages when engaged in certain acts.

The scales fell from his eyes. Caz started to laugh. He should have known. He should have known. There was only one reason a man locked a building down: privacy and secrets.

"Have you ever fucked Marguerite?"

"No." Clear, sharp, direct.

"What about your Seers here? You keeping them pure or are you helping yourself to whatever delights come your way?"

Owen shifted his gaze in the direction of the garden.

"Oh, don't look so dismayed, Owen. I approve. And if you recall, I even encouraged you to explore your hidden desires and needs."

Stannett remained silent, not a bad move.

"Well, you shouldn't be so distressed. And who could blame you? After all, women in cells, a few men, too. Such temptation." He narrowed his gaze. "Everything seems so clear to me now. A few moments ago, you were nothing but a puzzle. Now, an open book." He clapped his hands together and rose to his feet. "This is all just as I had hoped. So here is what you're going to do for me. I want you to go to the Convent and have a little session with Marguerite. Put her through her paces, only this time, when she goes into the future streams, have her pick up her own ribbon of light and find out what she sees."

Stannett nodded. "As you wish."

He always was an obliging bastard, when it suited him.

"But there's one thing you should try to remember. At some point, the Commander will want her disposed of. So even if she ends up here, please don't think you'll get to keep her forever.

"Are we in agreement?"

Stannett's nod was slow, the wheels of his mind turning. "Yes."

"Good. Now please go directly to the Creator's Convent and see if you can find out if Marguerite is the second of our troublemakers. I want confirmation because I want to know exactly what I'm dealing with."

"And what will you be doing while I'm at the Convent?"

Caz didn't have to tell him, but he did anyway. "Setting a small trap for Fiona. I just want to determine a few things about her powers before I go much farther down this road."

"Keeping your own hide safe?"

"Always." And that was exactly the truth.

Practice might make perfect,
But more importantly,
Practice makes possibilities.

—*Collected Proverbs,* Beatrice of Fourth

CHAPTER 9

Fiona rested deep inside her mind. She pressed her mind close to Alison's.

I can feel you, Alison sent.

Yes, Fiona sent. *As though I'm right next to your mind. No, not just your mind. I don't understand this. I can feel that I'm next to your arm, your hip, your shoulders. How is that possible? Except this is how I felt when I first met Marguerite telepathically.*

"I have no idea how you're doing this," Alison said.

Fiona drew back and opened her eyes. Alison sat across from her, maybe five feet away in the middle of the room. Fiona sat against the wall. "That's really weird."

Alison opened her eyes as well. "I'm not sure I'm understanding either what you're doing or what this is. I can feel your mind, but not just your mind . . . almost your *being,* for lack of a better word."

Fiona nodded. "It's sort of like a form of advanced telepathy, but it's not really deep-mind engagement, is it?"

Alison shook her head.

"Fiona," Jean-Pierre called from his sentinel position by the door. "I do not mean to disturb, but I have seen Gideon go by and I wish to speak with him. Will you excuse me?"

"Of course." The truth was, she'd been so engaged with Alison that she'd forgotten he was there.

"I shall return in but a few moments."

"Fine. That's fine." She watched him leave but felt her heart lurch, as though her heart left with him. Her gaze stayed fixed on the door for a long time. She looked back at Alison, who smiled at her with a knowing warm light in her eye. "What?" Fiona asked.

Alison shook her head. "No, I shouldn't say anything."

"Okay, now you really have to tell me."

"Kerrick and I have been together for a little over a year now but I remember the early days. It's overwhelming, isn't it?"

"Completely. I never know whether to hug him, or send him to Siberia . . . permanently. I've never been so torn in my life about something as I am about dating Jean-Pierre, about being with him, and now—" She almost blurted out that they'd just had sex, but she really didn't want that known around Militia HQ or anywhere else.

Alison said, "I have to say it would go a lot easier on all us girls if those men were just a little less *built*."

"Oh, amen to that, sister."

Alison giggled. "But it's kind of great, too, like winning the lottery."

Fiona nodded. She looked away from Alison and tried to breathe because for just a moment all she could think about was being on her back on Jean-Pierre's worktable, and his tongue working her over.

When a shiver traveled straight through her body, she swallowed hard and ordered her mind. She blinked several times then forced her attention back to Alison and all the critical matters at hand. "So, obsidian flame."

Alison's gaze narrowed. "Fiona, what if it's not telepathy at all."

"What do you mean?"

"Better that we try something together, rather than attempting to explain it. Do you trust me?"

"Absolutely."

Alison nodded. "Good. Okay, this time, when you feel yourself right next to me, try pushing all the way inside me. And don't worry, I trust you as well, so give it a shot, okay?"

Fiona nodded. "Got it." She closed her eyes and worked her telepathy until once more she felt herself right next to Alison.

She pushed, as though trying to push her being inside Alison's being, but nothing happened. *Are you shielding?* Fiona sent.

No. My shields are flat on the floor.

Fiona tried again, but nothing happened.

She pulled back mentally and once more opened her eyes. "I don't think that's it. In fact, I think it would be a very dangerous thing if somehow I was able to inhabit *your* being—again, for lack of a better term."

"You're probably right. So what else could this be? I mean, if telepathy is your strongest power, then I'm not sure I can begin to comprehend what this is."

"Let's try it again. This time, I want to explore. Okay?"

"Go for it," Alison said.

Once more, Fiona used her telepathy to draw near, but this time instead of pushing inside, she closed her eyes and with tentative mental fingers began to poke and prod at the nearness, trying to determine what it really meant.

As she pushed against Alison's arm, a vibration began that got stronger the farther down her arm she traveled. By the time she reached Alison's hand, Fiona felt an answering vibration in her own hand.

What is that? Alison sent.

My hand is trembling as though filled with a kind of power I don't understand.

Mind-to-mind, she sent, *Can you throw a hand-blast?*

No, Fiona responded. *I've tried but I don't have that capacity.*

A long pause, in which she could feel power building in Alison. At exactly the same moment, the vibration in Fiona's hand got stronger and stronger.

"Fiona, work very hard to stay right next to me exactly as you are but open your eyes and look at me."

Fiona locked herself into the mental position and opened her eyes. She gasped because she and Alison stood in the exact same position, a mirror image of each other, a true mirror image since Fiona's right hand was raised but opposite her, Alison's left hand was raised, palms up, fingers tense.

Fiona looked at her hand. She felt her connection to Alison, her being pressed close to Alison, connected. She felt power in her hand. She looked back at Alison. "What will happen if I release what I've gathered here in the palm of my hand? Will I blow the roof off the building?"

Alison laughed. "No. This is hardly anything. In fact . . . okay, this is what I want you to do. Come back to me and reconfigure what's in your hand."

Fiona closed her eyes and once more drew close. Again, she touched Alison's arm metaphysically, mind-to-mind, then traveled back down to the wrist. She could tell Alison was doing something unusual, but she couldn't tell what.

Got it? Alison sent.

I think so.

"Open your eyes but hold on to this thing."

Fiona once more looked at her hand.

Alison was grinning now as she said, "On the count of three, just feel what I'm doing and follow suit. Okay?"

Fiona nodded.

"Oh . . . but don't close your eyes this time."

"Right."

Fiona looked at Alison, who could hardly contain some sort of secret enjoyment. Then the miracle began. Alison lifted her hand and spread her fingers wide. Fiona felt the motions from deep within and did the same. Alison jerked her wrist. Fiona followed.

The next moment, two perfectly formed gold fireworks burst at the ceiling level and sent a shower of harmless sparks floating toward the floor.

"Oh, my God," Fiona said as gold rain sparkled around her.

"It worked. Wow, it worked. I was pretty sure it would, but still. Fiona, this is fantastic."

Fiona was still looking up at the ceiling, even though all the sparkles had just dissipated.

The next moment an alarm sounded, a shrill ringing of bells. Fiona looked at Alison and at the same moment, they both cried out, "Death vampires."

Fiona turned toward the door, intent on finding Jean-Pierre, when he burst through bearing his sword. He moved in, stepping in front of Fiona. Seriffe was behind him, also with a sword. Gideon followed, yet one more sword.

"There's nothing in here," Seriffe shouted. "What the fuck?"

Jean-Pierre turned to look at Fiona. "The grid registered a surge of power, similar to a fold of several death vamps. Did you see anything? Hear anything? Are you all right?" Once more he looked around the room, holding his sword aloft, out of harm's way.

Fiona was totally confused by what had just happened but Alison said, "Not death vampires. Fiona just channeled my energy and we released two fireworks at the ceiling."

Seriffe looked from one woman to the other and finally settled his hard gaze on Alison. He ground his teeth, then said, "How many times do I have to tell you people not to use that level of power within my headquarters? Goddammit!"

He turned on his heel and she could hear him shouting up the hall. "Bev, false alarm. Shut it down. Shit, motherfucker!"

After five months, Fiona knew her son-in-law well. Seriffe never got that upset except when he thought someone he cared about was in danger. That this time, what he cared about brought tears rushing to her eyes.

Jean-Pierre put his arm around her. "No, no, *chérie.* Do not be upset by Seriffe. He was worried. That is all."

She looked up at him and while pushing the tears off her

face she said, "I know. That's why I'm crying. I love that he cares about me so much."

Alison drew near as well and laughed and smiled and even shed a few tears with Fiona. "Everything is just so intense with these men, huh?"

"Yeah, it is."

Marguerite sat in chapel, that period of devotion required before dinner could be consumed. So much fucking bullshit.

Her cellmate, Grace, sat beside her. Thorne's sister.

Grace was lovely, with wispy, ethereal blond hair and green-gold eyes. She had a straight nose and sculpted cheekbones. Her lips were not full but suited her face. Her chin had a faint dimple.

They were opposites in nearly every respect, beginning with their looks. Marguerite had dark brown hair, very thick, and her eyes were a matching brown.

Beyond that, Sister Grace was all about spiritual devotion, whereas Marguerite thought the whole setup was one big pile of bullshit designed to control as many people as could be brought under the banner called the worship of the Creator.

On the other hand, Marguerite liked Grace. She admired her intelligence and she appreciated the fact that despite Grace knowing all about Marguerite's athletic relationship with her brother, she never judged either of them.

If anything, Grace had shown full support. She had once taken Marguerite's hints to leave the cell for half an hour and had kissed her on the cheek before she left, saying, "You give him peace, if only for a short while, and that blesses and relieves my heart. I am more grateful for your presence in Thorne's life than I can say."

Marguerite had almost shed a tear. Almost. She wasn't much of a weeper, never had been.

Neither was Grace, come to think of it. She met Sister Quena's tirades with a stoicism so at odds with her delicate appearance. For a devotiate, Grace broke the mold.

As Sister Quena droned on and on, Marguerite found her mind drifting to thoughts of Fiona, the woman who had contacted her earlier. She wished she could find out what happened after the regulators stuck her in the neck with their quick-acting drugs.

But the way this institution was run, the outside world didn't seem to exist. Certainly, no one spoke about a death vampire attack, not a single gossipy whisper.

There was just so damn much to dislike about her current situation. She despised the hard wooden benches, and the wall opposite the pews made of gray stone striated with amber. She hated the large slotted circle above the altar, backlit and meant to represent the unity of the Creator and his creation. Mostly, she despised Sister Quena, now and forever *sister-bitch*, as Endelle had called her earlier.

She smiled. *Sister-bitch*. Nice.

There was another chapel, much smaller, and made of gold and pearl. Marguerite had been there more than once, having snuck in. The benches were padded with soft mossy green velvet. No doubt Sister Quena kept the chapel for her private use, the spiritual narcissist that she was.

The High Administrator of the Convent stood at the pulpit to the right of the glowing circle and read from a book of prayers she had written at least a thousand years ago. For a woman who believed that humility was the highest virtue, she was incessantly vain about her spirituality. Imagine reciting from a self-published book of prayers rather than any of a hundred works written by theologians through the ages. Even the Bible or the Qur'an would have made better sense.

The drugs still worked in her system, and her eyes grew heavy. She slid her hands up the bell sleeves of her robe and as Sister Quena droned on, she drifted into slumber.

She was nudged awake by Grace.

A little shot of adrenaline brought her out of the half-drugged sleep. Oh, shit, she was headed for solitary again for sure, especially since Sister Quena now stood at the end of Marguerite's row, glaring at her across the trembling forms of five devotiates, each of whom had bowed her head—probably in deep supplication that she wouldn't get caught in the cross fire.

"You will come with me, Sister Marguerite. Now."

Grace grabbed her before she rose and gave her arm a squeeze. She whispered low, "Just once, bide your tongue, my sister."

Marguerite whispered a very soft, "Fuck off." But Grace wasn't offended, which was why Marguerite loved her. When Grace turned her face away, the hint of a smile was the last thing Marguerite saw as she gained her feet.

Sister Quena turned up the aisle that led to the narthex or, in Marguerite's view, the shithole of a foyer. To the right of the narthex was the long passage back to the cold sleeping cells; to the left were the administrative offices and sanctuary rooms used for prayer. Straight ahead lay the underground solitary confinement chambers.

Marguerite had expected to go forward to suffer another round of solitary, so she was surprised when Sister Quena turned to the left. Maybe all sister-bitch meant to do was give her a good dressing-down then send her to her cell for the night. But when the hell had Marguerite ever gotten off that lightly?

Something wasn't right.

Then she caught the smell of leather, and she almost made a run for it. But there wasn't anything she could do. She wore that damn ankle guard and could be found through GPS, and she still couldn't fold out of the building. She'd tried to escape by physically leaving the place, but Sister Quena had sent one fine pack of dogs to hunt her down. She'd had to heal from thirteen bites, five of them on her ass after that little experiment. Escape on foot? Nooooo, thank you.

So she heaved a familiar sigh and followed her high-and-mightiness to the third sanctuary room on the right and wasn't surprised when the good sister held the door for her, then slammed it shut.

"Well, fuck," she said, facing Owen Stannett with her shoulders back. "Look what the cat dragged in."

"And a good evening to you, Sister Marguerite."

"Cut the shit, Owen. I'm no more a sister than you are fit to run the Superstition Fortress."

Owen didn't flinch. He merely smiled and sat down in a ladder-back chair provided for him. "I see you are your usual charming self." He gestured to the slatted wood lounge.

Marguerite looked at it and something inside her began to crumble. She didn't want to do this again, to be caught one more time in the middle of the future streams. She hated her gift, she hated Stannett, and she hated this godforsaken Convent.

More than anything in life she wanted her freedom. She wanted to live in the open, to live as she pleased, and especially she wanted to drive a car. Thorne had shared the experience with her through a really terrific mind-dive; she'd never driven a car otherwise. So, yeah, she wanted to drive a convertible along a straight stretch of highway for hundreds of miles, with the wind in her hair, and the music on as high as it would go without busting out the speakers. She wanted to drive and drive and not look back, never look back, just move forward and plan a different kind of life, preferably in one of the rogue vampire colonies on Mortal Earth.

She'd heard about them, of course, places where ascender misfits could create a new life, separate from all this Second Earth bullshit called war and domination and death and servitude.

Fuck all of that!

"Please, do make yourself comfortable. I understand you were sedated earlier. I wouldn't want to add to your distress by having to force you to do what must be done."

"Always the gentleman, Owen. You must be so proud of yourself."

"Marguerite, you've always misunderstood me. This is about survival and it always has been."

At that she looked at him and frowned. "You're not usually so forthcoming or philosophical. Some bug climbed up your ass today?"

"Did I ever tell you just how much you remind me of our fearless leader, of Madame Endelle?"

At that Marguerite laughed, but her mind sloshed back and forth. "Only about every other visit."

Shit, she was just too wigged out to put up much of a fight. Usually she got in a few scratches before Owen strapped on his version of preternatural bindings and held her to the wooden chaise. At least he'd never tried to rape her. She'd give him that, the bastard.

She stretched out and put her arms over her head, crossing her wrists. "What will it be tonight, Stanny? You want me to see if you get to win the Mortal Earth Powerball anytime soon?" It was a little joke, of course, since the future streams didn't exactly work that way.

"I want you to pick up your ribbon tonight, Marguerite, and tell me what you see?"

At that, she turned to look at him. She frowned. "You've never had me do that."

"Haven't you been curious?"

"No. I tried it once decades ago, then I ended up here, exactly as I foresaw. You can imagine how I've felt ever since. So, no, I don't want to know the future. I've always thought of my gift as some sick joke the universe was playing on me."

He clucked his tongue. "And your gift is beyond anything I've ever seen, which I would have to agree makes this some kind of terrible joke. Do you know how much I would give to possess your gift? Half my kingdom."

"Then you could take over the world."

He sighed, his lips pinched inward. Finally, he said, "I've never wanted to rule the world. Again, this is about survival and being able to call the shots in my own life."

At that she lowered her arms and leaned up on her elbows. "Then surely you can understand how I feel. I've been in this dump for a century with no way out. Why don't you have compassion on me, remove this ankle guard, and let me slip out the side door."

He folded his arms over his chest. "Why should I do for you what no one has had the slightest interest, ever, in doing for me? Your job is to take care of Marguerite. Mine is to make sure Owen Stannett has the life and future he wants."

"Fine." She lay back down. The funny thing was, she kind of agreed with Stanny on this one. Besides, her head had begun to ache.

She relaxed her mind and drew in a deep breath. She didn't so much find the future streams as fall into them. Her Seer power was enormous, just as Stannett said.

All the ribbons of light were spread out in front of her in a glorious array of shimmering color. If she hadn't despised the process so much, she would have enjoyed the light show.

Still, she shivered at the thought that today, after all this time, she was going to lift the skirts of her own future.

Whatever.

She focused on herself and a ribbon lifted up a few inches, shimmering in a color she had not seen in over a century—the most beautiful shade of cherry red. At exactly the same moment, she felt Stannett's presence as he mentally joined her, the perverted voyeur.

In previous years, she would pick up the future stream ribbons, as if by hand, then examine them. Lately, however, she'd made more of a game of it and dove within. The funny thing was, when she entered the future streams, she also saw the past events of the person belonging to the light ribbon. How strange this time, to see flashes of her own life wink at her: quick-moving images of Thorne and Sister Quena, of Grace, of her really wretched parents who visited her once a decade, of her life before her internment, full of men, lots of wonderful men. Oh, yeah, good times.

Then the present arrived and she saw herself reclining on the slatted wooden chaise.

Suddenly the future rushed at her, the deep cherry swirling over her and around like a great wind.

The wind caught her up from beneath her and forced her into the air higher and higher, a warm wind. No, a hot wind.

She glanced down. Not wind at all, but fire, black at the base and red flames rising. She knew the colors well, two of her favorites, red and black. She still moved up, into the air. She shifted her gaze in front of her and saw a vast swirl of blue deep into the sky, but she didn't know what it was. On and on the black and red flames pushed her, catapulting her into the swirling blue vortex.

But the air was thin and she couldn't breathe. The vortex sucked her up and up. She flailed in the air with no wings to mount, no levitation to keep her up, no way to even fold out of the terrifying event.

She screamed and screamed, crying out for help, but no help came.

When her lungs failed her, she passed out.

She awoke some time later, in her cell, strapped on top of her comforter, unable to move. How clever of sister-bitch. Endelle might have given her the comforter, but Sister Quena still made it impossible for Marguerite to be warm.

She stared up at the ceiling, her mind caught up in the strange future vision. She couldn't imagine Stannett gaining anything from what he might have witnessed.

Then she heard the words whispered through her mind, *obsidian flame.*

Jean-Pierre savored these few minutes with Fiona, watching her work so diligently with Alison to throw hand-blasts that she somehow channeled through Alison. After much bickering, the room's security system had been disconnected and Seriffe had given his permission for the fireworks to continue.

He felt pride. Perhaps he should not. Perhaps he was being foolish, but he was proud of Fiona and her power and the delight she took in learning her new skill.

After launching a sparkling emerald firework to the ceiling, she danced around beneath the green sparks. When the most recent light show ended, Fiona tilted her head at Alison. "So you think my specialty somehow involves channeling?"

"I think so." She glanced at her watch. "Just as I thought. I have to leave now but before I go home I'm going to have to give Endelle a report."

Jean-Pierre watched, again savoring, as Fiona thanked Alison for her help. The women embraced then Alison left the makeshift training room and headed to the right toward the landing platforms.

"I don't even know what to think about this," Fiona said. She stood near the center of the room, hands on hips, and staring at the floor. After a moment she lifted her gaze to Jean-Pierre. "Channeling? Have you ever heard of a Second Earth preternatural power like that? Channeling?"

He shook his head. "Not at all. I am not even certain it is in Philippe Reynard's book on ascension. But perhaps it is a gift of Third or Fourth ascenders. Given all that we know, anything is possible."

"I guess. But how would this work? What would the benefit possibly be of me being able to channel a power like making fireworks with my hands?"

Jean-Pierre moved closer to her. "Do but think, Fiona. If you were ever in a difficult situation, you could channel this ability in possibly anyone. You could therefore throw a hand-blast to save yourself. I think the applications have great potential."

She nodded again, but this time her nostrils flared. "I could take Rith down."

At that he chuckled softly, and because he was close enough, he lifted her chin with two fingers. "Easy, tiger." He smiled.

She returned his smile. "I do seem to have a one-track mind."

"That is not a bad thing." He still touched her chin, and the contact both eased him and excited him. In all the time that she worked with Alison, her delicate croissant scent was a constant pressure on his senses.

But standing here now, the delicate scent deepened. His breathing faltered. The pheromones, meant just for him, assaulted his nose then his brain. "Fiona," he whispered, his voice now deep and very rough.

Café-au-lait, she sent, her nostrils flaring.

Seriffe appeared in the doorway, and Jean-Pierre let his hand fall away.

"You gotta see this, Fiona. Bev thinks she's found another anomaly."

"You're kidding. So soon? That's fantastic!" She headed for the doorway and before Seriffe could move out of the way, she pushed past him.

The two men followed behind.

"There's just one problem," Seriffe said, glancing at Jean-Pierre.

"What is wrong?" Jean-Pierre asked.

"We've got a bunch of power-signatures at the site."

"Death vampires."

"Probably. We've been able to count seven."

"Mon Dieu."

"No shit."

Once at the grid, Fiona confirmed the blue-green shading that indicated Rith's unique mist-signature.

"What is the location?" Jean-Pierre asked.

Without taking her eyes off the grid, Fiona responded, "Honduras Two. Not that far from us." Although distance hardly mattered. A good fold would bring all the women back to the rehab center within seconds of extraction.

Fiona turned to Seriffe. "One of those signatures could be Rith. This could be it."

Seriffe nodded. "Possibly." He then looked around the room. His gaze found Gideon. "Is your team ready?"

"Calling them in now. Ten minutes to fold-time."

"With so much death vampire sign," Jean-Pierre said, addressing Seriffe, "I wish permission to accompany the team. You will need my sword."

Gideon's voice cut across the length of the grid, his voice as hard as steel. "We've got this, Warrior."

Jean-Pierre turned and met his gaze. "You would turn down my sword because of your pride?"

"We don't fucking need a WhatBee on site. No offense. But we've been managing just fine for the last seven extractions. My men are well trained."

Jean-Pierre understood exactly what he was looking at.

Gideon was not just a Militia Warrior marking his territory; he was close to WOTB status, which meant his instincts had moved into overdrive. He even wore his blondish hair long, past his shoulders and shoved behind his ears. He'd be needing a *cadroen* soon, in more ways than one.

"I will defer to Seriffe on this," Jean-Pierre said. "His call. Not mine."

"At least you're making some sense now," Gideon retorted, his voice sharp.

Jean-Pierre felt the tension that now surrounded the grid table. Even Fiona glanced up at him, her eyes wide.

"Gideon," Seriffe said. "Stop being an asshole." He turned to Jean-Pierre. "We'll take you up on your offer and I'll clear it with Endelle since you're on guardian duty. I'll keep Fiona close. But I have to say that I don't like the way this feels. Too damn easy."

Gideon moved to stand across from Seriffe, but his gaze was fixed on Fiona. "What do you think? You know Rith well. Is this something he would do? Try to lure us in?"

Fiona shook her head and shrugged. "I'm not sure. Rith was many things but his mind never struck me as particularly devious. He liked order and routine, everything by the numbers, and he did not like death vampires. So, if they're at this facility, then I think there's a good chance that something else is going on."

"So where exactly is this in Honduras Two?" Seriffe asked, looking up at Bev.

She was on a platform elevated three feet above the massive grid so that she could see the whole picture. She sat on a tall stool, operating the controls. She made a few taps on her computer to her right then called out, "Near the Guatemalan border, a place called Copán Two. On Mortal Earth, the Mayan ruins draw people from all over the world. But on Second, a river, a jungle, solitude."

"Perfect for a blood slavery facility," Seriffe said. "Maybe more like a camp. Lots of vegetation. No wing fighting." He looked up and met Gideon's gaze.

Gideon nodded, his brow furrowed. "Got it. No wings." He glanced at Jean-Pierre. "The landing platform in nine minutes."

Jean-Pierre dipped his chin once.

Fiona was bent over the grid, staring at the anomaly, when Jean-Pierre leaned close. "May I speak with you . . . alone?"

His breath touching her cheek and ear sent shivers down her shoulder, arm, and back. He smelled of coffee suddenly, and male, and she rose up to let him escort her back in the direction of the original training room.

He was close at her back, almost touching her as she walked through the doorway. She was about to ask for a little space, but the door shut with a snap, the two slats he'd opened fell closed, and suddenly she was alone with her vampire.

Her breath caught in her throat as he took hold of her arm in a tight grip. "You must stay with Seriffe the entire time I am gone, do you understand? Seriffe is powerful. If there is trouble, he will be able to help you. And do what he tells you. Also, I do not want you near any of these Militia Warriors."

In the dim light of the room, she stretched her preternatural vision so that his face appeared as if lit by candlelight. She opened her mouth to protest all these commands and was just about to pull her arm out of his grip when she caught sight of the terrified look in his eye.

How many times over the past five months had she seen that look, that haunted expression of complete fear that if he so much as moved a foot from her, she would be taken from him and he would be unable to get to her, to help her, to save her?

At one point, she had made him tell her what was going on with him. He said it was the *breh-hedden,* that he was crazed. All these feelings were new and maddening. He despised them and he despised himself for pressuring her when she didn't need pressure of any kind.

Remembering what he had said just an hour or so ago—that he hadn't slept so well in decades, because she'd been beside him—she relaxed her ready-to-do-battle stance and put her hand on his face. "Seriffe will know what to do," she said.

A long agonized breath left his body. She was so glad that for once she hadn't lit into him and told him to back off and give her some space. He even let go of her arm. *"Bon,"* he whispered. He plunged his hands into his hair, but the *cadroen* held fast, so that now some of his wavy blond curls stuck out from the sides of his head.

She chuckled and tried to pat them down, but it was no use. "You'll have to reset your *cadroen*."

He held her gaze and seemed to freeze at her touch.

He was so beautiful in his god-like warrior way. His features were strong, his cheekbones defined partly by his leanness, and his blue-gray-green eyes large and fringed with thick light brown lashes. His lips, oh his lips, the two erotic points and the full lower lip. She wanted to kiss him, but she shouldn't. She wanted to touch more of him, but she needed to start getting a grip where he was concerned.

Her fear swamped her all over again, of living this difficult life. How simple things had been for her in Boston, the wife of a wealthy man of commerce. She'd been in command of her home, her servants, her children; she was a leader in her social circle.

Then captivity and life had undergone a long series of new definitions. Now, with Jean-Pierre, though it wasn't his fault, she sometimes felt as much a captive of the *breh-hedden* as she had ever felt under Rith's thumb.

"We need to take this slow," she said. Of course visions of what it had been like to make love with him just a few hours ago sort of shattered her *slow* concept. In what way, exactly, could they now take it slow?

He nodded. *"Oui, chérie.* We should take it slow."

At least he didn't argue with her.

"Good, I'm glad you agree, that you understand."

He stepped into her and put his hand on her right hip, very lightly. He held her gaze. "We should take it *very* slow. I would like that."

He would like that? What was she missing here?

Then he dipped down to her and she felt those sensual lips, now very moist, on her neck just below her right ear. He kissed her then moved his lips in a long slow line down her neck, down and down, onto her shoulder and down to the mound of her breast. *Very slow,* he sent.

When she weaved on her feet and her mind started playing *"La Vie en Rose,"* she began to understand he was thinking of something else entirely. Just like a man.

Yet here she stood, desire washing over her in a heavy ocean-like wave, so that she didn't even protest, not when he rose up and rubbed her lips with his thumb.

"Open your mouth, *chérie.*" Another command, and dammit, she obeyed him.

He slid his thumb inside and her knees buckled. But he was a quick vampire and he caught her around her waist. Then he did the most terrible thing: He began moving his thumb into her mouth then pulling back in a slow, deep rhythm.

She couldn't help herself . . . she began to suck.

He groaned and released a whirlwind of his coffee scent, heavy with all that was male.

He went back to her neck, licking in a long *slow* line up to her ear. Once there, he said, "I want you sucking me . . . *très lentement. Chérie,* would you do that for me? Would you enjoy taking me in your mouth and sucking me?"

Oui, Jean-Pierre. Absolument.

Then his tongue dipped into her ear and he Frenched her slowly in a rhythm with his thumb so that she was close, so close. She moaned and sucked harder.

But much to her intense frustration, he drew away from her. "I must go, *chérie,* but we will finish this, oh-so-slowly, when the night's work is done, *ça va*?"

She nodded. Her lips felt bruised they were so swollen. She blinked up at him and he bent down and placed a light kiss on her lips. Then he backed away from her and leaned against the wall. He stared at the floor.

She understood, or thought she did. Arousal was very different for a man, especially one as large as Jean-Pierre.

He needed time to grow calm so that he could change into battle gear and head out to slaughter death vampires. An erection wasn't easily concealed with a kilt.

She needed some space herself, and some air. Maybe a bucket of cold water would help. She smiled and with a little off-site telekinesis, she put a washcloth from Jean-Pierre's sink under a flow of tap water. A moment later she brought the damp washcloth into her hand.

She immediately placed it at the back of her neck.

She heard him chuckle, then she looked at him and in a quick motion she flung it at him. "This is all your fault. What a tease."

He laughed again. He unfolded the cloth and put it over his face.

"And your hair is sticking out in a ridiculous manner. You look like a clown."

He laughed a little more then flung the washcloth back at her. She caught it in her hand. She loved his smile, all those big gorgeous teeth. He closed his eyes, drew in a deep breath. A split second later he wore black leather battle gear. He lifted his now very bare and supremely muscled arms to pop the *cadroen* and take command of the mass of his hair.

Okay, this was so not fair, to be presented with so much male beauty. She wasn't sure who had designed the flight gear but that black leather kilt just did it for her. Of course, it helped to look like Jean-Pierre from head to foot.

She forced herself to remain where she was, she worked hard at it, because all she could think was that she wanted her hands under that kilt, she wanted to fall on her knees and savor what he'd asked her to savor *slowly* just a few minutes ago.

"Your beautiful patisserie scent, *chérie. Mon Dieu!*"

"Jean-Pierre, don't take this the wrong way, but I really wish you would leave right now and please don't come over here and touch me. Okay?"

"Fiona, look at me."

She once more followed his bidding and met his gaze.

He looked so serious, but then a very sneaky smile curved the corner of his mouth. "Slowly," he said.

Then he moved with preternatural speed, crossed to her, kissed her, then left the room.

The bastard!

But she smiled as she touched her lips. He was a tease and much too demanding but then he would smile and disarm her, keep her off balance. And the real problem was, she loved it!

He was so not helping to keep their relationship headed in the right direction . . . as in a very necessary eventual separation.

Just not tonight, when she would return home with him.

Seriffe stuck his head in the door. "I thought we'd wait in the grid room. You okay with that?"

She drew in a deep breath and nodded. She knew what he was really asking. The grid room had the best speakers for listening to the inevitable battle. Was she up to listening to it? Of course she was. But as she headed to the door, she halted.

This time, her man was in the battle.

Sometimes the attack comes from the shadows,
But a clear eye, unfettered by fears,
will always recognize the enemy.

—*Collected Proverbs,* Beatrice of Fourth

CHAPTER 10

Jean-Pierre folded to Copán Two, Honduras. Humidity hung in the air, so different from the desert. He extended his preternatural vision. So much green everywhere.

He folded his sword into his hand. He heard laughing in the distance, deep male laughter.

Gideon was beside him, chin down, eyes scanning.

Thirty-two Militia Warriors ranged behind them both.

Gideon looked at him. "Let my men see to this first. We need the practice in order to get stronger, to battle better. Do you understand, Warrior?"

Another pissing contest. Jean-Pierre stared at the Militia Warrior Section Leader. Although Jean-Pierre felt a bristling down his back, what Gideon said made sense. There would be no reason for him not to observe at a distance.

"As you wish." He could always engage the battle when he was needed.

He slipped into the thick vegetation. Gideon lifted his

left arm high, then dropped his arm, the signal for forward movement.

The Militia Warriors blurred their speed as they shot forward, moving with stealth, low to the ground, swords ready.

Jean-Pierre nodded his approval.

When the last of the warriors faded into the jungle, he looked around and found high ground back and to his right. He moved to the new location in a split second, found a perch in a tree, and extended his vision farther. He watched each squad maneuver around a death vampire, separating the overly confident pretty-boys from one another.

Very intelligent. Gideon was right. His men were extremely well trained.

But when he felt the hairs on the nape of his neck rise, he instinctively knew he was not alone. Slowly, he looked around, scanning the vegetation for any sign of movement. He extended his hearing; nothing returned, yet the uneasy sensation remained.

Then he understood. The Upper ascender. A bare split second later he took the invisible punch to his chin, which threw him backward off the branch. His sword slipped from his hand, spinning through the foliage. He hit the ground on his back.

He rolled swiftly and heard a thump in the empty space he'd left behind. He leaped to his feet. He could feel the presence of *the other* but he saw nothing. Endelle had said this was the latest threat, that an Upper ascender had been causing all the inexplicable bruising and cuts among the warriors over the past five months.

And the monster was here.

Invisible.

"Show yourself." He drew both his daggers, one in each hand. He took a hard kick to his left wrist. He heard the crack of bone breaking and his dagger flew.

Mon Dieu, he was in fucking trouble.

Fiona leaned over the grid as she listened to the battle, every muscle tense as though she had a part in the fighting as well.

She recognized Gideon's voice through the transmitter on his weapons harness as he called out to his various squads. She heard the shouting, the grunting, the victorious screams, the clang and rasp of metal against metal as swords clashed.

But she did not hear Jean-Pierre.

She extended her telepathy the distance of two thousand miles and reached him. She heard his mind in her mind, *Mon Dieu*. He was in pain.

She rose upright. She pressed her newly discovered channeling ability, that part of her that was obsidian flame, and as she had experienced with Alison earlier and even Marguerite before that, she was just suddenly with him, next to him, her being pressed alongside his.

Jean-Pierre, she sent.

Fiona?

I'm here. You're hurt.

Oui.

He moved. She could feel his body, feel him roll, feel the kick now to his sternum. He writhed in pain.

Then she heard the church bells. *The Upper ascender is hurting you.*

Yes. How can you tell?

I hear the church bells. Tell me what to do. What can I do?

My left wrist is broken.

I can have Bev fold you out of there.

No. Not yet. Fiona, think. Maybe if we worked together, we could wound him. He's been hurting the Warriors of the Blood all these months.

She heard the church bells off to his right shoulder. *Right shoulder,* she sent.

He struck my right shoulder.

I think I'm tracking his location and intent. Wait for it.

The bells boomed. *Big one coming . . . your left knee.*

Aw, shit. Sheet.

Jean-Pierre, get ready to use your hand-blast, on my mark and in the direction I tell you, got it?

She could feel him breathing. Hard.

She waited. Tense.

Finally, she heard him. *Ready.*

The church bells sounded right behind his head. *Behind your head, now!*

She felt the blast leave his hand. She felt him flip over and sit up, his body contorted in pain. *We hit the mark. I can see him, our Upper ascender. I hit both legs. His image is flickering. He is gone.*

Did you kill him?

Non, pas du tout. *But I hurt him. We hurt him. That was* magnifique.

Jean-Pierre, I can feel that he is no longer there. How is that possible?

You have power, chérie. *Much power.* He gasped for breath.

What do you want me to do? Do you want Bev to get you out of there?

First, I must find my sword.

She felt him struggle to his feet, to walk, pushing through leaves and branches. *I have got it. I am ready when Bev is ready, then have Seriffe let Gideon know.*

Fiona remained next to Jean-Pierre. No way in hell would she leave him until she was assured Bev had folded him the hell out of there.

But as she waited beside him, she shifted her present gaze to Seriffe.

"What was that all about?" he asked. He looked stunned.

"You could tell something was going on?" But as she glanced around, she could see that everyone in the grid room—Bev, Seriffe, and five Militia Warriors—was staring at her.

"You have a gold aura and we can all see it. That whole time, whatever was going on, you were glowing."

Fine. Whatever.

To Bev she said, "Get a fix on Jean-Pierre and bring him here now. He'll need a healer. He has a broken wrist and maybe a dislocated knee."

"You got it." But her eyes were wide as she tapped on her computer.

Back to Seriffe. "Jean-Pierre needs you to let Gideon know that he's wounded."

He nodded briskly as he pressed the com attached to his left shoulder. He spoke a few quiet words then shifted to stare at Fiona, his gaze moving over her hair and her shoulders. He shook his head.

Fiona looked at her arm. Yep, she was glowing. Glancing back at Seriffe, she said, "So you know I've got this thing called obsidian flame, the *gold* variety as Endelle calls it."

"I could see it working. What happened?"

She explained about extending her telepathy to Jean-Pierre because she could tell he was hurt. She spoke of Alison and Marguerite, of being able to feel their external sensations and of hearing the Upper ascender's unique church bell sound. "It's low, sonorous, really beautiful, but he was hurting Jean-Pierre." She related the strikes against Jean-Pierre. "But we got him."

"Got him?"

"Because of the sound of the bells, I was able to direct Jean-Pierre where to let loose with a hand-blast."

"She is telling it exactly right."

Fiona turned to find Jean-Pierre walking, no, limping into the grid room.

"You look like hell," Seriffe called out.

His mouth was swollen and bleeding. He had a terrible black eye. His hair hung in a mass around his shoulders, no *cadroen.* He was holding his left arm and his knee was, well, *not right.* He shouldn't have been able to walk, but he was, after all, a warrior who had been battling for decades, who was used to a certain level of trauma.

But he didn't seem concerned about much as he rounded the grid table. His attention was fixed on the intercom since the battle was still going on.

"Bev called for a healer," she said softly as he drew close.

Jean-Pierre nodded, but he directed his attention to Seriffe. He jerked his head in the direction of the loudspeaker. "How is it going?"

"Good. I think we're good."

After a few minutes, all that could be heard was Gideon breathing hard, a good sound since the swords had grown quiet. Fiona listened to every whisper of noise coming from the loudspeakers. A wailing sound. A woman.

Oh, God.

Fiona's heart began to thump in her chest. Jean-Pierre took another step closer to her. She met his gaze. Tears touched her eyes. Her prayer, however, she sent skyward: *Please don't let anyone be hurt. Please. Please.*

But Gideon's voice whispered over the loudspeaker. "Oh, God. Oh, God." Then nothing. Then, "How many dead?"

Fiona's chest seized. No. Oh, God, no.

A heavy exhale of air. "All right." Louder. "Seriffe, we have seven to bring home. One is alive, two barely. The rest are . . . gone. Fang marks, throat torn. Goddammit."

Seriffe touched his com. "How many death vamps?"

"Duncan, how we doin' out there?" A pause.

A very long pause.

Tears started tracking down Fiona's cheeks. She knew the truth before she heard the words. "Nine death vamps dispatched." Another long pause. When Gideon spoke next, his voice was hoarse. "We have two Thunder God Warriors wounded. And . . . shit. Greg is gone, no chance of recovery. Fuck."

Sometimes the severely wounded could be brought back to life. *No chance of recovery* meant a mortal wound of grotesque proportion. Fiona knew what that meant. She'd seen death vampires killed in the same manner at the Creator's Convent.

Her gaze skated to the colonel, Carolyn's beloved husband, her son-in-law, her family. He was pale, his hands planted on the thick black edge of the grid. He took long, steady breaths, then finally touched his com. "Get everyone home, Gideon. Good job."

Gideon's voice, strong and sure, began issuing commands about bringing the wounded back first, of sending the death vamp corpses straight to the MW morgue, of getting the surviving blood slaves over to the rehab center since the facility had an MD on staff, of deciding to send the slain women to the morgue at Central Command. Fiona approved. For whatever reason, she couldn't bear the thought of the deceased slaves in the same morgue as their killers.

A healer arrived and began working on Jean-Pierre's arm. The tense lines across his forehead and beside Jean-Pierre's eyes softened as each second passed. He would be out of pain soon, and he was alive.

Fiona swiped at her cheeks. One truth kept cycling through her mind: that according to Seriffe, he lost Phoenix Two Militia Warriors at the rate of one a week.

Too many.

Too goddam many.

Casimir lay on Greaves's black leather couch, in his penthouse in Geneva. He shook from head to toe even though three healers were bent over him, working their magic with powerful hands that emitted warmth and ease. Greaves had enthralled the healers, which meant that once they left the building, they would have no recollection of the experience.

Greaves did possess some quite beautiful telepathic and enthrallment skills. He bordered on a true artist.

"Hold," Caz called out in a voice that quavered. His body twisted sideways as he leaned over the bowl that Rith, kneeling on the floor, held for him. He vomited yet again, though barely anything came out, just some vile yellow liquid.

Christ, his legs hurt. Of course that's what happened when a Warrior of the Blood, bearing a number of Third Earth powers, aimed a hand-blast at your shins.

He was still surprised.

Greaves stood behind Rith, his arms over his chest. His lip curled as he stared down at Caz. "Are you ready to tell me what you learned this proud fine evening?"

Caz still couldn't feel his feet. The muscle and tissue had been burned down to the bone and the healers were rebuilding, so no, he wasn't exactly up to talking. But he made the effort anyway.

"She was there. I felt her presence. I just never thought . . . dammit, how the hell did she know where to direct Warrior Jean-Pierre?"

Greaves made a disgusted sound in his throat and turned away, his arms still crossed over his chest. With a thought, he moved one of his chairs closer and sat down. "The woman has power. Obsidian flame, remember? Rith, do get out of the way."

Rith rose from the floor, but left the bowl behind. He moved to stand behind Greaves.

The million-dollar reward on Rith's life was all part of an elaborate public relations ruse that Greaves had well under way. Because Rith was just so damn creepy, besides about as trustworthy as a fly promising never to eat shit, Caz wanted him out of the picture, the sooner the better.

Greaves had already reassigned the dying blood acquisition process to several of his subordinates. Greaves had to keep the facilities going since he supplied any number of good citizens of Second Earth not just with the blood that the slaves provided, but with the antidote as well.

Caz thought the overall scheme wonderfully diabolical.

He just didn't like Rith.

But Greaves had his own timetable for everything, so in the meantime, Caz intended to use Rith to entrap Fiona as soon as he could figure out how to do it without getting his own sweet self killed. Jesus, his legs hurt.

To own the truth, he was just a touch discouraged.

His stomach boiled all over again. "Rith," he called out.

Rith moved at preternatural speed, fell to his knees, then held the bowl for him once more.

"Hold," Caz called out. The healers as one leaned back, like three blind mice holding up their little paws.

He vomited into the bowl. He wouldn't be quite so sick if the smell of his burned flesh hadn't tainted the air.

"I don't suppose we could open a window," he said, arching his neck to look at Greaves.

"If we can tolerate the smell then so can you," Greaves said.

Fuck.

He glanced down at the healers, still sitting with their hands in the air, and barked, "Continue, goddammit."

Bodies hinged forward as three pairs of hands began more magical work.

He leaned back on the couch and swallowed hard. He strove to take deep breaths.

But breathing like that now brought Rith's strange odor leaching into his nostrils. What the hell was that metallic smell?

He glanced at Greaves, created a powerful shield around his telepathy, then sent, *I think I want to do a preliminary test run of our little bait-and-switch. I need to find out more about Fiona's abilities.*

You would be wise to do so, but if you have the opportunity, please destroy her. The future streams are all lit up about her right now. Her powers are growing. If you can kill her, do not hesitate. I'll send you a pair of death vamps to assist. Is all of this agreeable to you?

Of course.

I've also decided we should move forward with our public relations plan where Rith is concerned. Unless he dies during your test run, please see that he's delivered to the appropriate entities.

Caz smiled. *Happy to. I can hardly tolerate his smell. So what is that? Rust?*

Chinese herbs of some sort.

Disgusting.

Very.

Then he threw up again.

Jean-Pierre sat on the couch in the room he always thought of as the Oak Creek room. He had built the room right next to the creek, on a platform suspended six feet over the water so that with the window open, as it was now, he could hear the rush of water below. The fresh smell of the creek also flowed into the room, a soothing humidity against the arid Arizona land. Sedona was located in what was called "high" country at four thousand feet, but, *oui,* still very dry.

He sipped a glass of Medichi's very fine Cabernet Sauvignon, from his own vineyard on the east side of the White Tank Mountains. His label bore a pair of wings, quite beautifully designed by the horticultural artist known as Tazianne.

Fiona stood by the open window, also with a glass in hand. Her hair was damp from her shower and she wore a flowing nightgown of cream silk, *très jolie* against her wealth of chestnut hair. A deck ran around the outside. She had spent an hour out there first, but in March the temperature in Sedona was perhaps too chill at midnight to be enjoyed.

His wounds, cuts, and bruises were healed, but not his soul. He had gone to Copán Two in order to be of use. Instead, the Upper ascender who had been harassing the warriors for months had been waiting for him. The bastard could have killed him outright, yet did not. Would he have done so if Fiona had not come to him in her miraculous way and alerted him to his enemy's location? According to Endelle, the Upper ascender had rules he had to follow, and he was not permitted to slay lower ascenders. On the other hand, Jean-Pierre never wanted to be in a situation where he must discover if the Upper ascender always played by the rules.

He sipped and let the wine roll around on his tongue, savoring the almost coarse bite, the peppery flavor. He and Fiona had not spoken very much since their return to his house probably two hours ago. In this most essential way, they seemed to be alike. Grief weighed her shoulders down and kept her eyes wet with tears. He felt as though a beam had entered his chest, filling it from one side of his ribs to the other.

He sighed and sipped.

Fiona brought her goblet to her lips then drew it back, her lips trembling. "Come sit beside me, *chérie,*" he finally called to her. "Let me hold you."

She turned to him, a sad smile trembling on her lips. She crossed the room to him, setting her goblet on the table at his elbow. She sat down beside him, very close. He put his arm around her and held her. She put her hand on his chest. She took an occasional harsh breath, as though holding back her pain by force of will.

He turned toward her and kissed the top of her head.

She looked up at him, her eyes swimming once more. "This war hurts me," she whispered.

He nodded. "*Je comprends*. I understand, very much."

"There is something I want to tell you, to share with you."

He stilled. He could imagine many things she might say, but he feared the worst: that because of her suffering she had decided to leave his house despite the current danger she was in. "What is that, *chérie*?"

She leaned into his shoulder, and her hand drifted over his pecs. "I was the first of the blood slaves, the one Greaves experimented on. That much you do know. But what I've never told anyone is that I memorized the name of every woman who was brought into the facility, whether she lived one day or fifty years. I remember them all and when I can't sleep I repeat their names."

"Were you saying them now, by the window?"

She nodded, which made a glide against the T-shirt he wore. She plucked at the front of the shirt.

"Fiona, I would take this from you if I could."

"I wish that I could be rid of it, yet all throughout my captivity, saying their names was sometimes the only thing that kept me from going mad."

He loved her for this, for the tenderness of her spirit that would keep such a memorial in her heart, to those who had died.

"I almost didn't make it back the last time I was drained. Did you know that?"

"Non." Mon Dieu, how his heart hurt thinking of her being drained and not having the will to return. The thought that he might never have known her added new girth to the beam in his chest.

"That day, just a little over five months ago now, I was prepared to die because it was Carolyn's birthday and my will to live was gone. I survived because somewhere in my death-dreams, I came across James."

"James? The Sixth ascender?"

Again the sliding nod against his chest. "I fought my way back and first I met you, then a few days later there was Carolyn and Seriffe and my three grandchildren." He felt her lift her hand and wipe away more tears. "I'm so grateful that I came back but right now my heart is so heavy knowing that more lives were lost tonight. I learned from Bev just a little while ago that Greg had a family. His wife had just given birth to their fourth a few months ago."

"Oh, *chérie*. I am so sorry."

"He told Bev that he had bought tickets to Dark Spectacle as a surprise for his wife. Now that surprise is gone and the thousand more he would have given her over the coming decades, centuries. All gone. I'm so sad."

He kissed her forehead again. *"Chérie, chérie."* He kissed her once more and she lifted her face to him, her sweet, drenched, mourning face, and he pressed his lips to hers, meaning only to offer comfort, as much as he could. How much he valued her tender heart and her openness with him.

But she shifted just a little more and her fingers rose to his neck and she began to stroke very gently. He groaned and pulled back. He looked at her. "I would not distress you for anything right now, but you fill me with desire when you touch me over my vein."

He waited, willing her to understand his dilemma, but a sudden drift of croissant flavored the air. He closed his eyes and shuddered.

"Jean-Pierre, I have need of you right now. I know it isn't proper, but will you make love to me?"

There were so many reasons to refuse her request. The death of the Militia Warrior had reminded him of the impermanence of the fighting man. He was such a man.

If he continued down this path with her, taking her body beneath his, making these intimate connections, where would it all end? What did he truly have to give her? For all this time, he had kept his heart free of the commitment to a woman, any woman. His occupation was one reason, but the other, he believed, touched the core of him: He did not know if he could trust Fiona.

His wife had been so much like her, tenderhearted, kind, perhaps even driven in her own way to shape the world around her to her tastes and liking. She had made a home for them in impoverished Paris, battling for rooms, selling off the ancestral possessions he had brought with him after renouncing his estates—not for gain, but to furnish their new home and to buy food, all the necessities. His activism in the revolution used up his energy. But what had he not seen? Had his obsession with creating a new, freer France blinded him to her true nature? Or perhaps living in poverty had battered at her resolve so that one day, she had given him up to Robespierre. What had he not seen?

And if such a woman, of fine character and worth, could betray him, then why could he ever believe in another woman again, even Fiona, whom he admired?

The answer was simple. He could not.

So what was he to do with these vast sentiments that swelled in his heart when he held her like this, when he looked into her silver-blue eyes, when he felt her need for his touch, for his embraces, for the pleasure of his body?

There was only one answer: He could not deny her. So he suppressed thoughts of the betrayal that had ruined his heart. He rose to his feet and held his hand out to her. When she took it, he lifted her up then bent down to slide a hand behind her knees so he could carry her in his arms.

But he did not take her back to his bedroom. For this, for a time when her heart ached and he still had a terrible beam in his chest, he went to the northernmost part of his house and there began to make a three-story climb up a narrow tower.

"Where do the stairs lead?" she asked, her arms around his neck.

"To the sky," he said.

Fiona would love this. As he climbed, his chest began to ease.

Fiona leaned her head against Jean-Pierre's shoulder. She forced herself not to think about what was lost tonight, but about what was gained: one more night with the man carrying her in his arms, one more day with Carolyn and her children, one more stretch of life in which she had the chance to keep living.

She couldn't have changed the outcome of the fighting tonight. She had acquitted herself extremely well in that she'd helped Jean-Pierre stay alive.

Beyond that, what control did any one single person ever have over the horrors of life, over the chance events that thrust one warrior beneath a blade and pushed the other out of harm's way? No control.

What could she control? That she was safe for this moment in time and nothing more. If the Upper ascender were to come after her, or after her family or Jean-Pierre, could she stand against him? Probably not.

But she was safe, bouncing in Jean-Pierre's arms as he carried her up the winding staircase, up and up. She focused then on what she might find at the very top of these stairs and on losing herself in his body, perhaps even tasting of him for the first time.

As he reached a landing, she opened her eyes and saw that he was pushing open the door. He carried her onto what proved to be an open platform high in the canopy of the tall Arizona sycamores.

The air was so fresh and clean and carried the somewhat sharp scent of the sycamores. He put her on her feet. She looked up. Through the gossamer web of Endelle's mist, stars filled what was a large open space between a circle of branches.

"Jean-Pierre, this is so beautiful!"

"I thought you would like it."

She turned in a circle on the solid deck, looking up. The railing had widely spaced natural wooden pickets, weathered by the elements and time, but beautiful. "I would like to sleep up here tonight. Do you think we could? Would that be possible?"

He smiled and moved her close to the railing. "This will require some maneuvering, but yes, it is very possible." She could tell he was focusing hard so she kept very still.

A moment later a bed appeared—sheets, pillows, comforter, everything, well, everything except the bed frame and the box spring.

He gestured with a sweep of his hands. "Will this do?"

He was turned away from her, apparently admiring his skill. She had a daring idea and thought the thought. "Very nicely, and will *this* do?" she asked, mimicking him.

He turned back to her, then his eyes flared since she stood naked in the cool March air, even shivering. Her nipples responded, pulling into hard beads. His gaze fell to her breasts and he moved into her, sweeping an arm around her back and covering one of her breasts with his hand. He thumbed the hard tip then kissed her.

Fiona let it all go, her grief, her fears about the future, about what had almost happened to him in Honduras, everything. She focused on that beautiful mouth of his, the lips that were pointed and full, so sensual, on his tongue as he invaded her mouth searching out the recesses.

She shivered. Her hair was still damp and the night was cold. She pulled out of his arms and dove beneath the covers.

He laughed and, with another thought, divested himself of his clothes as well. He climbed into bed beside her and looked down at her. "You are so beautiful in starlight."

"You say the loveliest things." She saw him in her preternatural way, as though he were lit by candles. Because he was over her, she had a view of the long column of his throat. She could see his pulse beating and desire rose in a sudden sharp tug between her legs. "Jean-Pierre. I have never taken blood before but I want to, so very much, and I want you to be the first."

He growled softly, but she thought it was a growl not of desire but of ownership. She knew the state he was in most of the time, that she was for him a territory that he had to mark and claim and stake, over and over.

She shifted onto her side and patted the bed next to her. "Will you lie down and let me take you at your neck?"

He groaned a second time, but this was accompanied by a wave of his delicious coffee scent, which made her mouth water. Would his blood be flavored like his scent or would he taste of something more, something exotic perhaps?

Her breathing changed in anticipation. Her gums tingled. She felt her fangs emerge, lowering to make her strike.

He stretched out on his back. She put her hand on his stomach and played with the soft well of his navel until his back arched, then she followed the seductive line of hair that led lower. She didn't get far because he was fully aroused, ready and waiting, and he was big, very big.

Her heart rate climbed higher and higher as she touched the crown of him and felt the wetness that came from him. She felt the need to do what he had asked her to do earlier.

When she pushed the comforter back, down to his thighs, she turned in the direction of what she wanted in her mouth. As she lowered herself to him, his hand found the nape of her neck and he rubbed and pushed, guiding her. She found the commanding touch so erotic. She opened her mouth and took him inside, as far as she could. Jean-Pierre was large and beautiful, so only part of him fit in her mouth. But what remained, she grasped in her right hand.

He groaned as she alternately sucked and stroked him. *I love having you in my mouth,* she sent.

He groaned, louder this time. *I love entering your body any way that I am able.*

She opened her hand and slid her palm over the hard length of him, lower and lower, to the sack that carried what was most essentially male. She savored the ribbed feel of him and the tender, floating bits beneath. She released his cock from her mouth and trailed wet kisses down and down. He let go of her nape and stroked a hand down the center of her back as she reached low with her tongue and licked and sucked and drew as much of him in her mouth as she could.

His back arched again. *Fiona. So exquisite, the sensation like velvet, but wet, so wet.*

His voice in her head brought desire streaming from her. He pushed her legs apart, and her hips flexed. His hand trailed lower, drifting over her buttocks, lower and lower until he found what he had made so very wet. He explored as she licked, pushing aside all her folds.

Her hips rocked as one finger slid inside her. She began a slow journey back up his cock. She needed him in her mouth again, and with a slow sucking motion she stroked him up and down.

His finger went in very slowly, just as he had promised earlier. She groaned. His finger came out equally slowly.

More, much more, she sent.

He removed his finger altogether and she protested with a whimper as she drifted her tongue around his crown and pulled on him with her mouth.

This time two fingers went in. He had the most beautiful hands, this vampire, long elegant fingers, and he made use of them now, stroking her in a slow and steady movement, pushing toward the front of her until she cried out.

"Good," he whispered.

He pushed on that special place over and over until her hips met him with each drive of his fingers, and pulled away as he withdrew. She tightened around him. *Faster,* she sent. Her breathing as she continued to suck him grew harsher. She matched his speed as she pulled on his cock with her lips.

She felt him shift. "Fiona, release me and lie across my abdomen, let me bring you."

He didn't have to tell her twice. She stretched over him.

"Now spread your legs."

She did. Her feet hung off the wide mattress. His fingers found her again. He leaned up on one arm, supporting himself as he began to drive into her once more.

She crossed her arms in front of her and settled her head on her arms. The pleasure was so intense. She cried out and whimpered. He increased the speed and she cried out again and again.

"Jean-Pierre."

That delicious ache began to grow. Faster and faster he pumped his fingers into her, hitting the most necessary spot over and over.

She was crying out, deep throaty cries. She lifted up. She couldn't help it. She pushed up and arched her back and then the pleasure came streaking along her clitoris and gripping her within so that strong grunts left her mouth.

Look at me, he sent. *Let me see your eyes, your passion.*

She twisted just enough to look into his face, and once more he brought her. God, he was gorgeous and she was shouting into the night sky.

She fell forward, her body growing slack across his abdomen. He petted her back and when he touched a wing-lock, she didn't know which reaction affected her more: the sudden need to be scratched or a quick desire to be stroked and sucked on every one of her wing-locks.

She groaned.

He chuckled and then he started at the top, rubbing and scratching. For her, it was a different kind of ecstasy, but ecstasy just the same. He didn't stop until he'd ministered to every single one.

She remained slumped over him, but looked at him over a lazy shoulder. "How much pleasure you give me, Jean-Pierre."

He still rubbed her back.

"You have wonderful hands."

"You have a wonderful body."

Always, he said the sweetest things.

He deserved some good treatment. "So, what's your pleasure, *monsieur*?"

He smiled. His hand drifted lower until he rubbed her bottom in slow smooth circles. "I want you to take my blood. That is my pleasure."

Her brows rose. And just like that, desire rose once more as his savory coffee scent battered her senses. Her gaze fell to his neck and she whimpered. "I've never done this before."

"Come," he murmured, then he eased back onto the pillow

and laced his hands behind his head. "Of course anything else you want to do to me first would be welcome."

Her gaze drifted down his lips, his neck, the hard line of his collarbone to his pecs. His nipples were hard beads. She licked her lips. Once more her fangs made an appearance.

There was more she could do with her fangs. She needed to expand her thinking.

She pushed up and away until she leaned against her heels. He became a starlit feast. The trouble was, it was still March and she was chilled again. She thought the thought and brought her chenille robe into her hands and slipped it on. For what she wanted to do, she needed to take her time. But she couldn't take her time if she was shivering and cold.

"We could go inside, if you want?"

She didn't answer him. Instead, she spread her hands over both pecs and pushed up on his nipples, then brought her hands down rubbing hard. His back arched. "Or we could just stay here."

"I like the fresh air," she said. She leaned down and licked his left nipple. Once more he put his hand on her nape, rubbing and stroking, guiding. She licked and licked.

She knew she could release potions from her fangs so she planted her hand on the mattress, between his rib cage and his arm, to steady herself. She hesitated.

"Just do what feels right," he said. "Trust yourself."

She looked up at him. *Your fangs are beautiful,* chérie.

She held his gaze for a long moment, then looked back at the thick muscles of his chest. Desire once more drove through her and she struck.

A heavy grunt left his throat and his back arched. "Oh, *mon Dieu,*" he whispered.

She thought the thought and when he cried out, she knew she'd done what she'd never done before. She withdrew her fangs and touched the little wounds. She rubbed back and forth.

His back arched all over again. "Oh, God. Oh, God. Fiona. It's never felt like that before. It must be you, the way you affect me. The potion is like fire."

She rubbed his pec and thumbed his nipple. He writhed back and forth.

"What does it feel like, Jean-Pierre? Tell me."

He met her gaze. "A terrible burn. A wonderful burn. An ache that goes deeper and deeper." He took her hand and used her fingers to rub him.

She leaned down and without warning, sank her fangs into his right pec, just above the nipple. He started panting and his eyes glazed over. She shifted away from him and saw that his cock was rigid. He was close.

That he was so close again made her own back arch. Her fangs now throbbed, begging for more. She threw a leg over his hip and eased her body down on him. Using her fingers, she guided him to her opening and inch by inch swallowed him.

He tossed his head back and forth. He panted. "The potion, *mon Dieu.*" He rattled off a string of French words that she couldn't understand. He twitched within her.

She didn't have much time. She leaned over him and pressed his head to the side with her arm. She held him in place. She dipped low and licked his neck until what she needed rose. She didn't overthink the moment; she just shifted her head sideways and struck to a depth that felt right. Then she began to draw into her mouth an elixir like nothing she had ever known before.

Oh. God.

His blood tasted like he tasted and like he smelled, a kind of rich, heady wine, but with a bitter coffee edge, all blended and erotic as hell.

But it was more than just the flavor of him. It was also his power. She drank down his power and as his blood hit her stomach, she felt wonderful explosions begin to erupt within her veins, one after the other, which only made her draw deeper. The well of her was wet, so wet, and began to grip him, tugging on him. Oh, how she needed him, all of him, moving within her.

She felt his hands on her waist. And before she could prepare, he began to pump into her, hard thrusts because he was ramrod-stiff and so ready. He was grunting and growling, more beast than man, and she loved it.

She sucked harder at his neck, holding him in place with her arm. Her body started moving in powerful waves, meeting his thrusts in answering jerks of her hips. He went faster. She followed suit.

His blood hit her bloodstream and she pulled out of his neck, planting her hands on either side of his head and working her hips over his cock, pulling and tugging until rapture burst like an enormous firework through her brain, through her body, and deep, so deep that pleasure streaked through her, up and up, over and over.

She heard screaming but it was his voice then hers and back and forth, as he came and she came, riding him hard, his hips pumping and meeting her downward-pounding gallops.

"Fiona, hold on. I am coming again."

Again. Oh, God.

Once more he shouted to the heavens and once more pleasure gripped her and streaked through her body until she was shouting with him, sending his name flying into the stars, flying and flying, until at last she was spent, and he was spent and she collapsed on top of him.

How do you carry the past into the future?
The question was first asked when Adam and Eve left the garden of Eden.
There still isn't a sufficient answer.

—*Memoirs,* Beatrice of Fourth

CHAPTER 11

"Don't you have anything to say about this?" Endelle stood in her office, in front of her desk. She planted her hands on her hips and rubbed her fingers over the stiff boar's hide of her awesome skirt. It was closing in on one in the morning, she had darkening work to get to, and she felt her scowl drawing all her loveliness into a weird-ass knot.

Thorne shrugged but didn't exactly meet her gaze. Ten kinds of ruined. He always looked like ten kinds of ruined. Maybe eleven right now. Aw, hell, maybe a hundred.

Thorne was a handsome man, hair light brown and permanently sun-streaked. His eyes had every shade possible, wedges of brown and gray, blue and green, a perfect hazel, but that seemed like an inadequate description.

She might have gone for him at one time, like a couple of millennia ago, but from the first he just felt more like a brother than someone she could ride. He was built, oh, dammit-to-hell,the man was built. He had perfect proportions, from his awesome shoulder width to his narrow hips. His thighs were a dream. And he was stallion-big when it came to what men were all about.

But for the last hundred years he'd been proclaiming his celibacy and all the while he'd been shagging that little devil-child in the Creator's Convent.

Which brought her right back to her original question. "Dammit, Thorne, you have to say something. You can't just defer to me, not on this."

He looked up at her. The man was a beautiful six-five, the same height as her, but she always wore her black stilettos, for obvious purposes. If you planned to order around seven or eight of the toughest hombres on the planet, then you'd better give yourself a few artificial advantages.

"You want me to say something? You want me to fucking say something? What? What should I say?" There, a little sarcasm. That was better.

"I don't know, asshole, you tell me?"

"All right. Here's what I have to say. I hate this fucking war and you're the last person on earth who should have ever been allowed to fucking rule." His face was ruddy now—a good match for his red-rimmed eyes.

Her turn to shrug. "That's why I brought Marcus on board as HA of Desert Southwest Two. So tell me something I don't know or don't agree with. I didn't want this gig, but I've got it. And I know you never wanted to be my second-in-command, so the fuck what?"

His shoulders slumped. "What the hell am I supposed to say. I love her? Well, I do. I also know her really well and I know a move to the Seers Fortress is akin to setting her on fire."

"Just tell me you understand why I have to do this. Tell me. I need to hear it from you."

At that he looked at her, really looked at her. "Shit, Endelle, don't make this harder than it is. Just do whatever the fuck you have to do. I'll get over it. I'll move on. I don't know how, but what else is new."

"Can you lay off the Ketel One?"

"No. That I can't do, won't do."

"Shit."

"And don't you have some darkening work to do? As for me, I've got to get back to Awatukee. In case you haven't noticed, we're down two warriors. Any chance you can recall Medichi for a couple of nights? Just until Fiona's out of the woods?"

"Maybe. Shit, I guess I should. I don't know how much good that ambassadorial tour is doing anyway, but Marcus puts a lot of stock in it. He keeps trying to build up my image in the Territories aligned to us, but Greaves has this blog going that shows me at my worst."

Thorne shook his head. "Yeah, but some of those pics have to be doctored, I mean, come on, flashing at Mardi Gras in New Orleans Two?"

Endelle shrugged and opened her eyes wide.

"You're fucking kidding me."

"I'd had a couple of mint juleps. Okay, maybe eight. Besides, don't you think I have the prettiest breasts?"

"Again, I refer back to the not-exactly-ruler material."

She shook her head. "I'm sorry about Marguerite."

"Yeah. Whatever. Well, this has been fun but I have to get back to the war."

"Get me some blue skin."

"I always do." He lifted his arm and vanished.

Endelle stood frozen, completely immobile except for the bizarre tears that rolled down her cheeks. She never cried, but lately, shit, she'd been losing it a lot lately.

Even though no one was in her office to see her, or anywhere else at administrative HQ, by habit she lifted her right arm and dematerialized to her bedroom.

The funny thing was, once there, she couldn't exactly remember why the fuck she'd come. Why had she folded here?

Oh, yeah, to have some privacy while she wept.

Except now she didn't feel like it.

The bedroom was round, another smaller rotunda. She had a bed right in the center, no headboard, just a disco ball suspended from the enormous ceiling to hang about ten feet from the bed. Now, there was an era she missed: mirrors, flashing lights, a lot of bodies gyrating on dance floors.

She felt so low, like she'd been battered over the head a few times with a wooden plank.

She had to get changed for her nightly darkening work. As it was, she should have been here for two hours or more, trolling the dark paths of nether-space for Darian Greaves's light trails, making her way to the end of those trails to prevent the bastard from sending more international death vamps to his Estrella Mountain War Complex.

She hoped when the time came she'd get to send him to perdition herself. She needed that. She needed to know that when he died, he was truly dead.

She turned toward her closet, the one in which she kept a nice sampling of sleepwear and the soft purple gowns she wore when she stretched out on her lounge and engaged the darkening. She had a separate room for her primal fashions: the feathers, the leather, the skins, all the good stuff that kept everyone around her sufficiently off kilter to give her a psychological edge.

She was always looking for an edge.

She waved a hand in front of her current outfit and sent the chicken feathers and hide to her favorite laundry, Murphy's on Central Two. They specialized in leather and did most of the battle gear for the Warriors of the Blood and as many of the Militia Warriors as wanted to pay their inflated prices.

She let a few expletives flow then turned in a circle, naked as shit. She let a few more fly as she stared into her closet, then came to a decision and shouted it into the air. "The hell if I'm sending Marguerite to the goddam fucking Superstition Mountain Seers Fortress. I'm not gonna do it!"

"Nice landing strip, babe."

Endelle stiffened. She knew that voice. James had told her *he* was coming, but fuck! She'd never really believed the tale that *he'd* actually survived his death, that Luchianne had somehow saved his sorry ass.

It couldn't be true. It couldn't fucking be true.

She turned around, like some stupid actress on stage, in a kind of wide arc, half bent over.

But there he was, reclining on her bed, his elbow bent and his hand planted on the side of his head in support. He wore jeans, no shoes, and a wife-beater shirt no doubt to show off his perfectly shaped bowling-ball shoulders, the absolute edible breadth of his biceps, and the sexy drift of black hair down his chest. Her mouth actually watered.

His gaze fell to her crotch and his eyes dropped to half-mast. "Yep, *nice* landing strip."

Endelle knew she had a good body and she wasn't modest, not even a little. *Hello. Mardi Gras.*

So there was only one reason she wanted to clothe herself: to let this arrogant asshole know that this shop was closed.

"You're supposed to be dead, Braulio. I fucking watched you die. Hell, I held you in my arms. I thought I laid you on the funeral pyre myself. So what was it I burned up? Whose ashes did I spread over Lake Tanganyika Two? What was that, some sort of fucking clone?"

He shrugged.

He was reclining on her bed and he had the audacity to just offer a shrug, the raising of one shoulder, so not even a full shrug, but a half shrug.

"Something like that," he said. "Hey, I thought you'd be glad to see me."

"Fuck off."

"Aw, babe, don't be like that."

She turned back to her closet and pulled a purple gown from its hanger. She was pissed off. Royally. *Aw, babe. Aw, babe.* Shit, shit, shit, *shit.*

She waved a hand and a split second later the sleeveless gown covered her, with the exception that her head stuck out of one of the armholes. Yeah, she was that pissed off.

She let out a cry of frustration and waved her hand again. This time the gown went where it was supposed to go.

She lifted her arm and folded straight into her holiest of holies, the small sanctuary in which she engaged in her darkening work. No one could fold in there except, of course, fucking Sixth ascenders.

A movement of air told her what she needed to know.

She ignored the presence of the most formidable Warrior of the Blood to have ever lived, who had also been her former love-slave. She stretched out on her chaise-longue, clasped her hands over her stomach, and prepared to launch into nether-space. Then she felt a hand on top of her hands.

She opened one eye. "Get away from me, Braulio. I don't know if you've noticed but I'm not especially thrilled to see you right now."

"I thought we might fuck, take some sting out of the situation here."

"In your dreams, asshole."

"I have some new moves." He waggled his thick black brows and rippled his abs. "I've learned a thing or two in the last three thousand years."

"Have you learned to fuck yourself, because right now that's all the action I see you getting."

He laughed. "You haven't changed."

"And you're still an arrogant prick. So let me make this easy for you. You can't have me again, Braulio, so if you haven't come to help out with our sucky little war, then I suggest you take yourself and that bulge in your pants anywhere but here."

She closed her eyes.

"Aw, babe," he whined.

She opened her eyes, pressed her lips together, then rose up off her couch to face him. "*Aw, babe*? What are you, sixteen?"

"I can be, if that's what you want."

"You are so full of shit."

"Aw babe."

Okay, he'd fucking done it one too many times. So with all the preternatural speed she could muster, she threw a right hook that blurred with the best of them.

But she found that the only thing she hit was his hand, which then closed around her fist.

"That would've hurt, Endelle."

She was way too close to him. He had a nice scent, something familiar, like sandalwood or a really fresh cologne. He had full sensual lips but like hell she was going to just throw herself at one of the biggest players the northern tribes had ever produced.

She took her fist back then turned away from him. "All right, let's have it. Why are you here? Why did you come to me tonight?"

"To keep you from making a mistake."

She looked back at him, and he held a phone in his hand, her phone, her Droid. "What the fuck?"

"I need you to call Owen Stannett and make a deal with him about Marguerite."

So he knew all about that shit. "I can't and I won't. I've already made that decision. I won't hurt Thorne."

"Your loyalty is touching, but make the goddam call."

At that, she narrowed her eyes at him. "Why? Why should I? Why should Thorne be denied his woman? For what?"

"You know why. You've got to get access to the future streams . . . now." He squeezed his eyes shut like he was suddenly in pain. "Shit. Time's up."

He didn't lift his arm, he just fucking vanished, and at the same time her phone dropped to the marble floor.

She let a few more expletives fall from her lips.

She picked the phone up, surprised it hadn't shattered on impact. She rolled her eyes. She tapped the screen.

When Owen's voice came on the line she said, "All right, you motherfucker, let's make a deal. Just how bad do you want Marguerite?"

In the way-too-early hours of the morning, during that gray part of dawn, Marguerite stood before Sister Quena.

She had been awakened from a deep sleep and her first thought had been, *Thorne*—that perhaps he'd come back and how glad she was. She needed a good tumble after the day she'd had.

But Thorne hadn't come to the room and thank God she'd

had enough sense to keep her mouth shut. The last thing she wanted in this situation was to get Thorne in trouble.

As it was, she had the worst feeling that the thing she had feared the most had finally come upon her.

In a hundred years, she'd never been summoned from her bed by a group of senior devotiates and marched in formal style all the way to Sister Quena's office.

Now, as she faced the High Administrator of the Exalted Order of Religious Bullshit, she slid her hands deep into the opposing sleeves of her Seers robe in order to hide her trembling hands.

Sister Quena rose from her massive burlwood desk. She had deep permanent grooves on her forehead as though she bore responsibilities no one else could possibly comprehend.

"You know how strenuously we have strived to train you for your most blessed service as a Preeminent Seer of Second Earth. Well, apparently the heavens have smiled upon you. Your gifts have become known to Higher Powers." She smiled.

Damn. Sister actually smiled.

Then this couldn't be about Thorne.

And what was all this bullshit about *Higher Powers*?

Oh, God.

Oh, shit.

A sense of doom swept over her. Just as any good Seer would do, she opened her mind, and the images of her impending future swept through her: of being locked away in the Seer domicile in the middle of the Superstitions, ostracized from society, forced to keep strict schedules and vows of silence, and chained to a grinding routine of constantly looking into the future for the sake of Mortal and Second Earths.

Sister Quena continued, "She Who Would Live herself is having you transferred to the Seers Fortress in Thunder God Mountain. Indeed, such an honor! I cannot even conceive of it." Vermillion bloomed on each pallid cheek. "I had always hoped, of course."

Marguerite heard what amounted to a death sentence and shook her head. She kept shaking her head and didn't stop.

"I see you are overwhelmed by the magnitude of the blessing that has been conferred upon you. I understand. You do not believe yourself worthy and indeed, given your general lack of enthusiasm during rituals, prayers, and study, I am not surprised. But your present silence does you honor and I am fully persuaded that whatever your past errors, whatever the deep unassailable flaws you possess, you will rise to the occasion."

"No." She shook her head. "No. I don't want to do this. I won't go. I won't. You can't make me."

"Calm down, Sister Marguerite. Your duty always takes supremacy over desire. You know that. Besides, your parents have already approved the transfer. I spoke with them not five minutes ago. They are very proud of this accomplishment. I have ordered the honoring bells, documents, and ribbons. They will take part in a ceremony to be viewed by all of Second Society throughout the entire world. You seem to have no real understanding of the magnitude of this accolade. You should be happy. To be of service in this manner is all that a woman of your ability should ever desire."

She continued to shake her head. "No. No. No. I won't go. No. You can't make me. No one can make me. I'd rather eat dirt. I'd rather drink Darian's blood."

Sister Quena recoiled in horror. "Sister Marguerite! Desist from such vulgarities."

But Marguerite continued wildly, "No. No. I won't work with a bunch of old farts in permanent cloister. You can't make me. You'll have to kill me first."

Sister Quena began to flutter around her desk. She levitated. She called out loud incomprehensible things. The room filled with red robes that rushed toward Marguerite and restrained her. She felt hands on her head forcing her back, back, back.

Sister Quena laid a hand over Marguerite's forehead.

The paralysis came swiftly.

Even her tongue proved immobile. *Thorne,* she screamed

mentally. Nothing returned to her. How could it? She'd never shared her blood with him or the depths of her mind, only her body. He would never be able to find her or hear her or know what she was going through. She was on her own again, alone. She couldn't bear it.

But there was another who might be able to help. *Fiona!* she screamed. *Help! Fiona, I'm in serious shit! Fiona, you have to help me!*

She couldn't catch her breath. She couldn't even feel her lungs rise and fall.

"She's convulsing."

Fiona awoke flat on her back, staring up at an emerging dawn, a heavy weight on her chest. The air was cool, even chilly on her face and her shoulders.

She blinked and looked down. Jean-Pierre's arm was across her. She pushed his arm away, trying to think what had awakened her.

She sat up.

"What is the matter, *chérie*?"

She glanced at him. He leaned up on one elbow and rubbed his eyes. He rattled off something in French.

"I'm sorry?" she queried.

"Oh. Sometimes when I awaken, French is in my mind. I said, it is dawn already. The warriors would be almost done fighting. Why are you troubled? Did you not sleep well?"

She smoothed the comforter over her lap. "I slept really well, thank you, but I woke up feeling that something was very wrong. I just don't know what."

"Try to relax for a moment. Let your thoughts go very loose."

Fiona released a sigh and closed her eyes. She breathed in the fresh air that smelled of sycamores and Oak Creek. Then, as if from a great distance, she heard a kind of weeping-shrieking sound, very faint, *Fiona, help me.*

Her eyes popped open. "It's Marguerite. She's in trouble."

"The woman in the Convent? Thorne's woman?"

"Yes, but her telepathy is so faint. I'm going to try to get closer to her." Once more she closed her eyes and let her telepathy travel as far as it wanted to go, in the direction it wanted to go.

A moment later she felt herself next to Marguerite. *I'm here,* she sent.

I'm paralyzed, returned to her.

What do you mean?

I can't move. I can't speak aloud. I'm bound in some kind of cloth. I'm in a vehicle of some kind, like an ambulance. Please tell Thorne. I'm being transferred to the Superstition Mountain Seers Fortress.

Oh, no. How is that possible? We'll let Thorne know. He can talk to Endelle and change this.

A pause followed. *Endelle approved this fucking transfer. It was her idea.*

Marguerite, I don't know what to do. How can I help you? Tell me what to do.

Another pause, but this one seemed less frantic, as though there was less telepathic noise in the background. She could *feel* Marguerite thinking.

Finally, Marguerite sent, *Form a telepathic link with me. That way, I can reach you anytime and you can reach me. Will you do that?*

Fiona clasped her hands together in her lap and held on tight. Marguerite wanted access to her telepathy day or night. The link would bind them. She didn't want to be bound. *I don't want to be bound . . . to anyone. I was a blood slave for a hundred and twenty-five years. I . . . I don't know if I can do that.*

Another pause. Marguerite's voice in Fiona's head was softer this time. *I've been trapped for a hundred years. I get where you're coming from. Fuck.* Was that a mental sigh that followed? Marguerite continued, *I won't force this on you. I'm so sick of being forced to do all this shit. Owen Stannett was at the Convent earlier. He made me pick up my own future stream ribbon. I hated it, hated being forced to do it. And worse, that ride was so full of fucking symbols that I didn't get what it meant, red and black flames and a swirling blue high in the sky. I got sucked into that weird vortex. So no, forget the link.* Laughter followed. *Besides, it sounds like all I have to do is start shrieking your name and you'll come to me.*

Fiona laughed. *I think you're right. But—*

But what?

Fiona's heart started to thump in her chest. She felt dizzy. *Did you say black flames?*

Red and black. Why? Wait. I remember hearing the words "obsidian flame" in a recent vision. Do you know what this means?

Fiona felt goose bumps travel all over and she shivered. Jean-Pierre moved up behind her and surrounded her with his warm arms. She relaxed against him. He was so damn thoughtful. He really wasn't helping their present predicament.

But to Marguerite, she took several minutes to explain all about obsidian flame. With Jean-Pierre cuddling her and keeping her warm beneath an ever-lightening sky, she talked about her gold variety and about practicing with Alison; about the recent battle in Honduras and that she had traveled telepathically to Jean-Pierre, even helping him to fight off an attack by an Upper ascender.

Are you with Jean-Pierre? Marguerite asked. *I mean, like you're together? Are you his woman?*

Fiona felt a blush bloom on her cheeks. *Yes, I guess I am. I don't want to be. We're stuck in this* breh-hedden *thing. Do you know about that?*

Yes, and thank God that's not what's going on between me and Thorne. Just another way of being trapped if you ask me.

Exactly. Fiona breathed a sigh of relief. Finally, someone got where she was coming from.

Wait a minute, Marguerite sent. *Can you describe this Upper ascender? Maybe it's the same one, I mean the one at the Creator's Convent.*

Fiona looked back at Jean-Pierre, who at that moment leaned down to kiss her bare shoulder. Another set of shivers, different in nature this time, sped down her back. "Jean-Pierre. Stop that." But even she could tell there was little force behind her command. When he continued, she spoke a little more firmly. "I'm talking to Marguerite. I think she might be the red variety of obsidian flame."

Jean-Pierre's eyes went wide. "Is this true?"

Oh, why did the man have to be so handsome. She licked her lips, swallowed, and worked at focusing on the matter at hand. "Marguerite wants to know what the Upper ascender looked like. She saw him, in the future streams, just before the attack at baby Helena's christening. She thinks they might be one and the same."

"I did not see him but for a second or two. We hurt him, you and I, Fiona. We burned his lower legs, both of them. He was flying backward. He had very dark hair, though. I remember that: very dark and very long and curly. He was quite good looking, I think. A straight narrow nose."

She put her hand on his cheek and nodded, then sent these details to Marguerite.

Marguerite's voice in her head returned as a solid punch. *He must be the same one. I would have described him exactly the way your warrior did. He held himself in the air through levitation alone, high in the air, no wings, so that he could look down on the battle from above. That's how I saw all the death vampires moving on that shithole of an outdoor chapel.*

Let me tell Jean-Pierre.

Go for it.

Fiona drew her mind from the conversation with Marguerite and once more focused on Jean-Pierre. He had pushed her long hair aside and was kissing her upper left wing-lock. She drew in a soft breath and gasped. "Oh, my God," she whispered.

What's going on? Marguerite asked.

Without thinking, Fiona sent, *Jean-Pierre is kissing one of my wing-locks. Oh, shit, I shouldn't have said that.*

But Marguerite growled softly. *It's the fucking best.*

Marguerite, she drawled, attempting to chide her.

Don't get pissy with me. Besides, if he's kissing a winglock, maybe we should sign off.

Not yet. I want to tell Jean-Pierre what you said.

She drew out again, but this time, she twisted sideways and pushed him away from her back. "Would you stop that?"

He chuckled and folded his hands behind his head. "Very well."

"This is important. Okay, so here's what she said." She relayed all the information about how the Upper ascender levitated high in the air.

Jean-Pierre whistled. "There is so much power in the Upper Dimensions. I am not surprised."

"What do you think we should do—with Marguerite, I mean? What if she is an obsidian flame?"

"I think we must speak with Madame Endelle and Thorne. This may change the transfer to the Fortress."

"You think?"

"Which do you think Endelle would prefer to have? A gifted Seer to whom she might have partial access, or an obsidian flame that she could command at all times?"

Fiona recalled Endelle's extreme behavior leaping all over her office when she discovered what Fiona really was. "I see your point. I'm going to tell Marguerite. Would you let Thorne know? I have a profound sense of urgency about this."

"*Bien sûr, chérie.* Of course. I will do it even now." He held out his hand and folded his phone into his palm.

Fiona twisted to face front once more, though she felt Jean-Pierre's warm palm on the center of her back as his deep voice rumbled an explanation to Thorne.

She dove within her mind once more and let Marguerite know all that they were doing. *I'll keep you informed. You know, I just thought of something. Let me try to contact you. Let me move away from you and let's see if I can reach you the way you reach me, okay?*

Sure. I'm not going fucking anywhere.

This made Fiona laugh. She didn't know if it was the fact that both women had shared the same terrible *long* captivity, but she liked Marguerite, profanity or no profanity. She began to pull away, drawing the telepathic thread closer and closer to Sedona until she felt it almost snap back in place. She knew one thing for sure, all this practice was improving her skills.

Marguerite, she sent. She waited. Nothing happened. Great. Now what should she do?

She focused on her telepathic thread and extended it just a little. She concentrated very specifically on what she knew to be the sense of the woman when she communicated mind-to-mind with her. Then she spoke her name in a sharp command, *Marguerite.*

What the fuck! Why are you shouting at me?

Again, Fiona laughed. *I'm so sorry. Okay, I'm going to try this once more, but I think I've figured it out.*

She pulled the thread back until it popped into place. She took another deep breath, closed her eyes yet again, and focused. This time, when she extended the thread, she sent in as quiet a voice as she could manage, *Marguerite, are you there?*

Much better, idiot woman.

You make me laugh.

Good. There's just one thing. Owen Stannett has a lot of power, which means that he's probably got the Fortress shielded. I don't know if we'll be able to communicate.

Okay. Okay. Well, we'll take this one step at a time. Now, where had she heard *that* before?

I'm signing off now. Sweet Jesus, those bitches drugged me last night then paralyzed me this morning. If I ever get out of the Fortress, I'm burning that goddam Convent down.

You go girl, Fiona sent.

You go girl? Really? The sarcasm didn't drip, it flooded.

Hey, Endelle says that all the time when she's impressed with something I've done.

Well, then, if Endelle *says it.* More flooding sarcasm.

All right. All right. Jean-Pierre's tapping my shoulder. I think we're heading out in a few minutes to see Thorne. I'll contact you as soon as I know something.

Good. Was that a mental yawn? *Later, sweet potater.*

Yes, Fiona definitely liked Marguerite. *Bye.*

She pulled the thread back.

Her heart felt ridiculously warm, like she'd just made a new friend.

She turned to Jean-Pierre. His gaze fell to her breasts and he pushed the comforter away from them. He sighed. When he spoke, his gaze remained pinned to her nipples, which she knew had beaded in the cool morning air. "Thorne wants to see us in five minutes. He's bringing Endelle along."

She was about to nod and get up off the mattress, but he pushed her back and before she could protest, he had his mouth around her breast and was sucking at just that right pressure, not too hard, not too light.

Her back arched. Dammit, her warrior could get her going faster than lightning.

She moaned then shoved at his shoulder. "Would you stop that?"

His mouth popped off her breast and he looked up at her with all those big teeth. He looked so beautiful, even happy, and almost relaxed.

"But your breasts are like food to me, a feast fit for the gods, and I am a man who is starving."

He was nothing less than temptation on two legs. Oh, dear God. She swallowed hard. "Now we only have four minutes and thirty seconds to get dressed, brush our teeth, and move our asses to administrative HQ."

"Would you not like some coffee first?" He looked so innocent that she fell for it.

"We don't have time for coffee. Oh, you mean *coffee,* as in . . . Jean-Pierre, what a rascal you are."

She lifted her arm and without one more word of explanation or discussion, she folded straight to his master bathroom and hopped in the shower. Five minutes or no five minutes, she was not going to HQ without showering!

He took me to the grotto,
And explored the damp, weeping walls.

—*The Forbidden*, Devotiate Grace

CHAPTER 12

Thorne pounded on the marble of Endelle's desk. "Do something now! You heard Fiona. Marguerite is obsidian flame."

Endelle sat in her chair, staring up at him, a mulish set to her chin. "She *might* be obsidian flame. We don't know for sure."

"She had a vision of black and red flames," Thorne shouted. "How much more proof do you need?"

Fiona stood beside Jean-Pierre near the never-used fireplace on the west wall. He held her hand because she'd drawn close the moment Thorne's face turned beet red and Endelle sent a shower of brilliant white fireworks in the direction of the tall ceiling.

"Goddammit, Thorne. Take a fucking chill-pill. Fiona, get your ass over here. I want to know how you contacted her. Tell me everything."

Fiona huffed a sigh. She really didn't like the idea of

walking into the middle of the whirlwind, but she didn't have much of a choice. Not really.

She released Jean-Pierre's hand and moved to the end of the desk. The marble slab, supported by woolly mammoth tusks, was the size of a yacht. She thought maybe she'd be safe so long as she didn't stand on one side or the other.

Endelle rocked back in her black leather executive chair. She leaned her head against the Appaloosa horsehide. Even though it was barely dawn, she'd changed her clothes and now wore a beige snakeskin halter, a heavily embroidered white leather mini skirt, and around her neck a collection of rattler tails. Vintage Endelle.

Fiona described how she had awakened to the sound of Marguerite's cry for help then launched into exactly how she had contacted then recontacted the powerful Seer.

"All right. I concede you have a connection with her, but one vision about red and black flames does not an obsidian flame make. I'd have to see her myself, do some serious mind-diving, and I can't do that right now because I have a treaty with Owen Stannett." She didn't look at Thorne, but even Fiona felt the waves of anger radiating from him.

"This is fucking bullshit," Thorne shouted, leaning over the desk so that he was just three feet away from her.

Fiona took a step back. Way too much emotion in this room right now.

Endelle turned slowly in his direction, her eyes hooded. "You know what's bullshit? You. You're fucking bullshit. You could have told me about Marguerite decades ago and we could have gotten access to all the future stream information we needed. We could have shut Greaves down by now. But you kept your woman a secret because she got your rocks off. That's bullshit, Thorne. How many Militia Warriors and ascenders and mortals have died because you couldn't bear to part with your favorite piece of ass."

Fiona didn't need an invitation. She scurried back to her much safer place beside her own Guardian of Ascension. The air in that room crackled with fury and maybe a whole lot of guilt.

"You would say that to me?" Thorne breathed hard. "You would fucking say that to me when I have bent over for you and taken it and taken it and taken it until I'm bleeding from my fucking eyes? You know why we're in this war up to our necks in alligators, because you're the worst at what you do. You've given Greaves all the ammunition he needs, day in and day out, to simply walk away with two worlds and you sit there and tell me somehow, because I protected Marguerite from Owen Stannett, that this entire fiasco is my fault. Go to goddam fucking hell, you *bitch*." The resonance he put in that one word, and that he spoke it from his mind as well as his voice, dropped Fiona to her knees.

She covered her ears and screamed. The pain was beyond bearing, like knives in her head, flipping and slicing. Tears streamed down her face.

Jean-Pierre dropped beside her and petted her back. Then suddenly he was on his feet and moving. "You hurt her, you motherless piece of shit."

Fiona struggled to right herself, to call Jean-Pierre back, but there was nothing she could do. She leaned against the fireplace and rocked, her hands still to her ears as the warriors, like two bucking broncs, went at it.

Thorne head-butted Jean-Pierre. He staggered back, then launched at Thorne, tackling him around his waist and throwing him to the zebra skins. He straddled Thorne and with preternatural speed started landing punches in quick succession until Thorne scissored his legs in a quick jerk and caught Jean-Pierre around the shoulders with his powerful thighs.

The men rolled and rolled, banging into the wall by the door. Jean-Pierre broke free and leaped to his feet. Thorne did the same. They crouched and circled. Thorne moved in and punched Jean-Pierre two times, really fast, in the left eye.

Jean-Pierre caught him low, throwing a hard punch to Thorne's ribs. Thorne doubled over. Jean-Pierre swung up hard and caught Thorne's chin, throwing him up and over. But Thorne gained his feet in time to block two more punches then get in a solid right hook of his own.

Jean-Pierre's head snapped back. Thorne moved in, punching and punching.

Fiona saw a shadow and looked up and to her left. Endelle stood on her desk and boxed along with her men: left, right, left.

Fiona lowered her hands and found blood on them. Thorne had just busted her eardrums. Great.

The men continued to punch and Endelle kept throwing air punches. Fiona drew her phone from the pocket of her cream linen pants. She called Bev over at Militia HQ. "Thunder God Warrior HQ. Bev here. How can I help?"

"Hi, Bev. We have a sitch over at administrative HQ. Two of the WhatBees are going at it."

"Oh, boy."

"Yeah, we'll need a healer in I'd say maybe two minutes. And Thorne used his resonance, telepathy, and his voice. My ears are bleeding."

"Again?"

"What can I say? I'm hopelessly sensitive. I've finally got Seriffe trained not to do that to discipline his men while I'm around but Thorne was a little distracted." She paused and cupped the phone. "He called Endelle the b-word."

"Holy cactus shit. Wow. Okay, let me check things out." Fiona heard some tapping on the computer. "Yeah, it looks like Horace is still over at the Cave taking care of Zach. A skin-burn I think. I'll see that he makes a final house call before heading home."

"Thanks. You're the best."

She put her phone away.

The men were breathing hard and the punches had slowed. Wouldn't be long now. Fiona rubbed her temple, but her head hurt and her ears rang.

Thorne now faced Fiona. She winced and rubbed her ear, and still came up with a whole lot of blood.

Thorne must have seen her because he cried out. "Aw, shit, Fiona, did I do that?"

"Yep."

Unfortunately, his remorse caused him to let his guard

down. She watched Jean-Pierre wind up and was just shouting at him not to do it when he let his fist fly. Thorne flew backward about nine feet, almost hitting the couch by the east window. His eyelids fluttered.

He was on his back and he wasn't moving.

"And he's out!" Endelle shouted. She jumped off the desk and held up Jean-Pierre's arm. "The winner."

Jean-Pierre, however, shook her off and returned to kneel beside Fiona. Fiona looked around his shoulder and caught Endelle's eye. "Horace is on his way."

"Good call, I guess. Fuck, are your ears bleeding again? What is with you?" She rolled her eyes and returned to jump up and sit on her desk.

When Thorne finally gained consciousness and sat up, Endelle said, "I'm leaving her at the Superstitions . . . for now. We'll see if Stannett behaves himself. If not, I'll give you permission to take a tank into that goddam place."

"Well, that's something, I guess."

He put his head in his hands and groaned.

Fiona looked at Jean-Pierre and met his gaze. Both eyes were bruised and swollen, his lips bleeding. "Do you think you could cool the caveman shit for at least one minute? You know my ears are unusually vulnerable."

"I am sorry, *chérie,*" he mumbled, squeezing the words out since his lower lip was about twice its normal size. "But I cannot bear to see you hurt."

At that she smiled. "If you're going to be my guardian, you might want to get used to that."

Endelle busted up laughing. "Ain't it the fucking truth."

Half an hour later, when Horace had Fiona healed and had begun working on both of Jean-Pierre's black eyes, Fiona approached Endelle.

Her Supremeness still sat on the edge of the desk, swinging her legs up and back at the knees, like a schoolgirl. "Well, ascender? How's the obsidian flame training going? I'd like a full report from your end. Alison was here last night for a few minutes. She said you both made fireworks."

Fiona nodded. "We did. It's an interesting skill—not

making the fireworks, that was just a controlled hand-blast and a turn of the mind. What was interesting was lining up beside her, feeling the energy move down her arm, then mimicking the same thing."

"Have you ever done a preternatural voyeur?"

"You mean Parisa's main gift?"

"Yep. I have it, too. Wanna try?"

"Of course." Then she realized what she was saying, that she was offering to get close to the scorpion queen. She almost pulled back but she knew what would happen if she withdrew now. Endelle would hang her up by her ankles and shake her silly . . . for about an hour.

"So how do you do this thing? Do you touch my face or something?"

Fiona shook her head. "No, it's not physical in that way at all. I mean it's very physical, but I won't be touching you. I mean—"

"For fuck's sake, just do it. You should know by now that I'm more of a take-action-and-ask-questions-later kind of gal."

No shit.

Fiona nodded. "Right." She closed her eyes and focused on the most powerful vampire on Second Earth. She took a few deep breaths and tried to believe she wasn't stepping straight into a hurricane.

With a quick thought derived from her practice with Alison the night before, she placed herself against Endelle mentally, side by side.

Nice, Endelle sent. *So how the fuck does this work? What do you need me to do?*

Fiona was surprised that Endelle didn't know, so she sent, *Well, why don't you open your window and we'll see what happens?*

What do you want to see?

There was only one real answer. *The grid at Militia HQ.*

You're a dog with a bone.

Fiona smiled. *I am.*

Fine. Whatever.

But instead of the grid, Endelle zoomed in on the workout

room, which had a host of warriors, in sweaty T-shirts and gym shorts, pumping iron, boxing, running on treadmills. But she kept zooming toward the back of the building.

Endelle, no!

Endelle only laughed and kept moving fast, right past the doors that led to the locker room with more naked male bodies than Fiona had ever seen in her life.

No! Stop it!

Straight to the showers!

Oh, God.

Endelle panned all the way left then all the way right. Some of the men faced front, some back; either way the view was extraordinary. The warriors were very fit, muscled, so much like Jean-Pierre in many, many ways.

Fiona tried to close her eyes but couldn't, since this was Endelle's window. She didn't know what she could do in this situation.

Hubba, hubba, Endelle sent. *Are you enjoying the show as much as I am? The warrior on the left. Damn, is Jean-Pierre that long in the cock? Although I prefer girth myself . . . but, still.*

That did it.

Fiona pulled away and because it wasn't exactly an agreed-upon separation, there was a kind of rubbery snap to the process. At least it was painless.

She opened her eyes and shouted, "Why did you do that? Why did you have to do that? That was such an invasion of privacy."

Endelle just smirked at her. "You could have left sooner."

"I didn't know if I could!"

"What is wrong, *chérie*?"

Fiona turned to Jean-Pierre and her face flamed. There was so much heat that she put her hands to her face. She didn't wait. She just left Endelle's office and started running.

She ran past all the executive offices, past the admin pool, and through the sliding glass doors. She turned to the right where there was a long corridor—no windows, just a dark stretch of hallway. At least none of the admins had shown up for work yet.

She leaned her back against the wall, then bent over trying to recover.

What further surprised her was that soon she saw two pairs of feet, one in brown leather loafers and the other, black stilettos.

She looked up but just shook her head.

"Your boyfriend here insists I apologize. Fine, I apologize, but what the fuck was that about?"

Fiona rose up. She chuckled but still her face grew warm. "I think you keep forgetting that I've had three parts to my life. The first part was in a very conservative Boston in the late 1800s. The second was in captivity where there were only women around, and Rith, but he doesn't count.

"Now I'm here. It's modern times on both Mortal and Second Earths, and things are . . . wonderful in many ways. But how did you think I could tolerate . . . that?"

"*Chérie,* what did she do?"

Endelle held her hands up. "Nothing. We took a trip to Militia HQ."

At that, Fiona tilted her head and raised her brows. "Tell him the rest, Endelle. You owe me that much because at some point he's going to find out and I don't want him to think, on any level, that this was my idea."

Endelle backed up. She shrugged. She didn't exactly meet Jean-Pierre's gaze. "We might have looked in on the men's shower room at the workout center." She pursed her lips and pretended to examine her nails.

"You did what?"

Fiona didn't quite understand what happened during the next few seconds. The air seemed to tighten all around her, Endelle flew back about five feet and landed on her ass, then Fiona had 260 pounds of pure, lean, hardened vampire pressed the length of her and smashed into the wall.

"Jean-Pierre, stop." She felt the strange snake-like things begin to swirl in her stomach. "Stop."

"You are not to look at other men, not like that, not without clothes on. I will not have it."

She tried to push at him, but he was a brick wall. The writhing thing in her stomach rose. She couldn't bear to be held down like this.

In the distance, she heard Endelle say, "Well, then. I'll leave you two kids to it."

She wanted to call her back to ask for her help, but Jean-Pierre's body and something she could only feel as his energy flowed over her and around her, poking at her skin as though seeking entrance. She couldn't breathe.

"You are for me, Fiona. No others." His voice was deeper than she had heard it before, ever.

The writhing, crawling beast climbed up her chest and into her throat. She felt strangled from within.

Then she felt him against her mind. He pushed against her shields. He pushed hard. She looked into his eyes, saw the strange hard glitter. She understood his dilemma, the extreme protective urges, the need for dominance and possession. He needed to mark his territory. She doubted he was fully aware of what he was doing.

Let me in.

Three simple words. Let him in. He wanted in. He wanted inside her mind, to take her mind, to dominate her mind. She had done nothing wrong and Endelle's thoughtless little jaunt to MWHQ had cost her this, a major confrontation between herself and her vampire lover, who wasn't exactly in his right mind.

She held her shields in place so he began to push, slamming against them hard, his body still a wall against her.

Funny . . . all the writhing fears had subsided.

Why?

Then she understood something else. She liked what he was doing and even more than that, she trusted him even in this ridiculous caveman posturing. He ground his hips against her and he was, oh, God, so aroused.

His scent surrounded her but instead of the usual coffee dominating, that which was male was in the fore, very male.

A wind possessed her mind, spinning around and around, and still slamming against her shields.

When he powered against her shields one more time, she dropped them flat.

He bored into her, a deep overwhelming rush into her mind, swelling over her thoughts, her memories, flowing into every narrow recess, swallowing her up.

And still she wasn't afraid.

She met his mind straight-on and let him possess her.

She slid her arms up around his neck, leaned the few inches that separated his mouth from hers, and kissed him.

He plunged his tongue inside, not a surprise. He drove and drove and drove, making his point. His hips flexed and he pushed that hard, thick, rope-like length against her.

A moment later, without warning, she felt movement, a flying sensation, and complete darkness. A glide through nether-space began.

She landed in a very damp space, so at odds with the desert or even Sedona.

She drew away slightly to look around, but didn't get far since he pulled her against him. *Where are we?* she sent since she couldn't exactly speak.

What returned within her mind was a cross between a grunt and a growl. He moved back from her about a quarter of an inch and over her mouth said, "My house. A grotto. By the creek."

He kissed her and the storm in her mind kept moving around, searching, hunting.

He found the memories, the quick preternatural voyeuristic vision that Endelle had forced on her, of men working out, of men changing in a locker room and finally men naked in showers.

He threw back his head and roared.

She didn't know what to do with this beast that had taken her into his grotto. She saw that he was out of control. She felt his desire to do harm to the men she had seen. She felt that he was ready to fly once more through nether-space, to go straight to that locker room and that shower, but like hell was she going to let him do harm to a bunch of men who had done nothing wrong.

She summoned her increased physical power, broke away from the restraints that were his arms, but instead of stepping away from him, she planted both hands on his face. "Look at me," she cried.

He seemed startled and he froze. She could feel the vibration of the fold that almost happened but didn't.

He stared at her unseeing, breathing hard. He had to be in there somewhere. "Fuck me, Jean-Pierre. Right here, right now. Take me, as hard as you want, in whatever position you want."

His nostrils flared. His lips quivered and drew back from fangs that emerged.

She pushed her hair aside and bared her neck for him.

He struck hard and she winced. Shit, that hurt. But as soon as he began a series of heavy lusty draws, her body softened and sank into a deep pool of exquisite pleasure. He grunted over her neck. The word *mine* repeated through her brain.

In small stages, since he still had possession of her mind, she pushed him out of that horrible locker room and directed him to the memory of last night when she was sprawled across his abdomen, with his fingers buried inside of her. She let him relive the cries that she shouted into the cool night air.

He drank his fill from her neck and she kept the memory in front of his mind. He grunted his approval.

But her body ached now, in so many places at once. *I need more,* she sent, her hands rubbing up and down his biceps, to his wrists. She rolled her fingers around in his palms.

He finally released her neck, but he looked wild, his mouth red, blood dripping down his chin. He was in so many respects a gentleman that to see him like this both surprised her then made everything within the deepest part of her body pull into a knot. She needed him and she needed him now.

"Fuck me."

He put a palm between her breasts, his brow low as he stared at her. The next moment her clothes simply disappeared.

Another blink and his clothes were gone.

She looked around, wondering what he meant to do in this place of earth, stone, and water. There was a chaise-longue nearby but she doubted it would hold his weight and hers.

She watched the pad disappear and before she could determine what he intended, he flipped her around and forced her down onto the same pad.

She started to turn over, but his movements were brusque as he pushed a leg wide, then her other leg, her arms as well until she was on all fours and somehow that seemed exactly what she needed.

He was behind her and she thought he would simply thrust into her. Instead, she felt a hand on her hip and the next thing she knew his tongue was all over her, very low, thrusting, tasting, pushing everywhere.

She cried out, arching her back. Oh, God.

His mind, still connected within her, still possessing her, shouting *Mine*. He swept his tongue up her body then licked at her left buttock. She panted and wept. She trembled.

Then his fangs struck deep into the flesh of her bottom and she felt the potion leave fire and pleasure behind that began streaking down and down.

"Oh, God, oh, God!" she cried, long and loud.

He did the same to her other buttock so that she had two lines of intense sensation flowing toward everything that was delicate, swollen, and aching beyond words.

Then he rose up behind her, pushing her legs farther apart. She felt his thighs against the backs of hers and his hard cock poised at her opening. She could hear him breathing in deep draws. *Do you feel the potion?* he sent.

"Yes."

How close are you?

She knew what he meant. She panted, swift short draws of air. Her back arched. *Almost. Oh, God. Almost.*

She gave a cry, which was all he needed. He drove into her, holding her hips to keep her seated in the position he wanted her. Now he thrust, hard bucks of his hips, taking what he wanted, what he intended to mark.

The orgasm barreled down like a sudden waterfall over a cliff. Pleasure flowed in a hard swift wave of sensation and she screamed and screamed, because it kept coming.

She felt his hand at the back of her neck as he wrapped her long hair in his hand and pulled her back toward him so that her back was arched as he thrust into her.

He was still pumping and she could feel her pleasure building again. The potion intensified every sensation. He had one arm looped low now around her waist as the other, holding her hair, arched her back so that his mouth was against her ear. "You must stay away from other men, do you hear me, Fiona? Do you understand?"

She tried to nod but he held her trapped and she didn't mind at all, because pleasure began to erupt. "Yes," she cried out then screamed some more.

That's when he sank his fangs on the opposite side of her neck and began to drink once more as he plunged into her. He held her immobile but it seemed to help the sensations that worked her flesh. She screamed and screamed.

His body tightened and he was so hard. He released her so that she once more supported herself on her hands. He gripped her hips again and as he came he let out another roar, a resonant sound that filled the stone grotto. His roars echoed up and down the nearby stream, and what had been a mad chattering of birds stopped.

The whole world fell silent before the claiming sounds of his voice as he pumped into her, rocking her body wildly, and giving her what only a man could give.

Her arms ached from holding the position, but she was smiling. She tried to think back on her former life. She thought of her husband, but what a mistake since Jean-Pierre was still within her mind and knew her thoughts. He leaned over her, still connected, and growled in her ear. He huffed as well, several times, blowing into her ear and on her face.

She drew out of the memory. *I was thinking only that I had been such a good woman in those days and now I'm here. I thought I was happy then, but civilization robs us of something, I think.*

The only answer he gave was to shift his body while remaining connected low. He pushed away her hair then, without using his fangs, he bit down hard and held her like that, his big gorgeous teeth sunk into her neck and holding her immobile.

His breathing was ragged. She still gasped for each breath. She had the weirdest thought that she wanted to stay like this forever, that no matter what happened, life could get no better than this . . . ever.

In stages, he began to withdraw from her mind and when he left, the sense of aloneness pinched at her. She almost begged him to return.

He took his time leaving the well of her body, almost as though he knew, too, that once separated, life would again swell in a huge wave, flow between them and pull them apart once more.

But when he did withdraw, she rolled on her back on the soft pad, pulling up her legs to maneuver around his since he didn't move. He was on his knees at the very end of the pad. He looked so serious, which made her concerned. What on earth was he thinking?

Jean-Pierre stared at the woman he had just taken. His brain seemed fractured and incapable of pulling together in order to once more start forming rational, sensible thoughts. He had taken her roughly, as someone who had become more beast than man. He had brought her repeatedly, so he knew she had been pleasured, but what must she think of him now? He hardly knew what to think of himself.

"The *breh-hedden* is an exacting master," he said at last.

She nodded, her lips parted. She had bruises on both sides of her neck. She looked well used, her eyelids low, her lips swollen and bearing a faint curve. She was still breathing hard, as was he.

Her gaze moved over him in such a way that he swelled his chest and tightened his abs. She lifted up on her elbows then leaned forward to extend a hand to the dark line of hair below his navel. She drifted her hand lower until she touched his cock, which hung both satisfied and still partially erect off to the left.

She didn't touch him, though, perhaps understanding that he would be sensitive. Instead, she planted her hand, her thumb around the base, so that her skin met his skin and part of his thick pubic hair. "Mine," she whispered.

In another circumstance, he might have smiled. Instead, though, he met her gaze and covered her hand with his. "Yours, *chérie*. Yours."

She leaned down, flat on her back. She drew her knees up then spread them wide. She would probably never understand how that affected him, that she exposed her greatest vulnerability to him like that, offered herself so willingly, this woman from pristine Boston, this blood slave.

He leaned down and put his lips to her mons and kissed her repeatedly. He felt her hand on his hair, petting him softly.

"Jean-Pierre, this is madness," she whispered once more.

"I know."

What did he have to give her?

What did she have to give him?

Their bodies? *Oui*. For now.

Would it be enough for the future?

He did not want to think of that, not right now.

Every barrier has its own set of teeth.

—*Collected Proverbs,* Beatrice of Fourth

CHAPTER 13

Fiona planted both hands on the tile wall beneath one of several showerheads in Jean-Pierre's massive master bath. She let the water drench her long hair, run down her head, down her face, over her shoulders, her back, hoping that the heat would take some of the tension out of her body and some of the itch from her goddam wing-locks.

She took a deep breath but ended up huffing it out of her lungs because for some reason she was pissed off.

She shouldn't be. She should be happy-happy because she'd just gotten laid. That's what Endelle would have told her.

And yes, it had been wonderful, even extraordinary in a very primitive way, but . . . Yeah, that damn *but* was so big and it was really bugging her right now.

The water had been running a long time.

She turned around and tilted her head back, wishing the hot water would soothe her brain, maybe even shut her brain down.

She couldn't stop thinking about . . . everything.

"Fiona," Jean-Pierre called from the doorway. To his credit, he didn't step into the room but gave her some much-needed space. But even that bugged her. Why did he have to be such a great guy that he gave her space when she needed it?

He continued, "Endelle wants to see us both again in her office. Evidently, she has an apology she wishes to make."

"She said that?"

"No. Marcus did. I just spoke with him. Thorne told him what happened so that Marcus was able to enlighten Her Supremeness as to the nature of the problem . . . with me."

The problem . . . with him.

She shut the water off. She couldn't hide in there forever.

She folded a towel from the sink. She knew he still stood in the doorway. She could see him from the mirror above the sink, but he was turned away, again, as if he could read her mind, as if he understood she needed this separation.

She whisked herself dry, quick hard rubs with both hands until her skin looked like she'd been in the sun for about an hour. She threw the towel on the floor then folded another towel to wrap up her hair.

When she was done with that, and still huffing out each breath, she folded her cream chenille robe from the back of the door then shrugged into it, punching her arms through each sleeve like she was ready to do her own round of boxing.

Maybe she was.

She stepped out of the shower at last and adjusted the collar of the robe—part of it was caught underneath.

But when she saw her reflection in the mirror, with her hair still wrapped up in the towel on top of her head, she had a wide-open view of the bruises on both sides of her neck. She let loose with a long loud shriek-like groan. "Look at this," she cried. "Look at this. Look at what you did to me."

He turned into the room and met her gaze in the mirror, but he looked confused.

"What do you mean? What is wrong?"

She shifted and held the collar wider then presented each side of her throat to him. "You marked me."

He narrowed his gaze. *"Oui, c'est vrai."*

"Oh, would you stop it with the charming French bullshit."

"You seem distressed." A smile played at his ridiculously sensual lips. He leaned against the doorjamb and crossed his arms over his chest, a move that drew her attention to his pecs. He wore another ribbed T-shirt, long-sleeved, an excellent look for him, which also pissed the hell out of her.

Her gaze fell lower.

"And why do you have to wear jeans and no shoes?"

He shrugged. "Jeans are very comfortable and my floors are very clean. I like the feel of the polished wood under my toes."

"And another thing, why does everything you say have to sound so fantastic. Couldn't you just once try for a little crudity?"

"If you wish." But his lips quirked.

"If I wish? I wish you would go to hell, that's what I wish."

He smiled. "Would you please just tell me what is wrong, Fiona? Be honest with me. Speak the truth. These things you are saying are ridiculous."

Her shoulders slumped. She put her hands on the counter and leaned forward, her head hanging low. "I don't want to do this. I want all of this to stop. It's too much. I can't catch my breath. I need to find my bearings." She straightened and looked up at him. "And I really do hate that everyone will see that you took my blood. I can tell that Endelle thinks everything's so funny, and she thought it was just hilarious to take me into that locker room, but I hated it, Jean-Pierre. I'm not that woman." She tugged at her collar. "And I'm not this woman to be paraded in front of everyone else like a . . . a cow you branded."

"A cow?" His lips twitched.

"You know what I mean."

"Yes, I suppose I do. But I believe I can fix this situation."

"How?"

He moved to stand beside her. "I do not have very strong healing skills, as some of the brothers do, but if you will permit me I can take away these bruises and the puncture marks."

"But you wouldn't have minded me wearing them?"

"Truth?"

"Oui," she said. "Truth."

He shook his head. "I am in this terrible place, as well. I want you with the ferocity of an animal and a little while ago, I took you the way I have been wanting you since I first caught your wonderful scent in Toulouse. But I am not proud of it. I despise being caught in this same trap of the *breh-hedden* in which you are caught. At the same time, I am loving every second of it because I like you and I respect you. For that reason, this terrible part of me would have loved letting everyone see that I took your blood . . . twice. That, yes, I marked you. That you were mine."

He had stated her feelings exactly.

She finally took a regular breath and pushed the collar of her robe out to her shoulders. He moved in behind her, understanding her signal. She faced the mirror now and watched as he settled his hands over the sides of her throat. He had long beautiful fingers, sexy fingers.

She felt the warmth begin and she closed her eyes. Her breathing settled down and her temper eased back. She didn't speak. She just let the moment happen.

She was troubled; there was no other way to describe what she felt, how confused she was, how torn, and how angry. She wanted life to just stop. Ever since she'd been rescued, instead of life growing simpler and gentler, she felt as though she'd been thrown into the spin cycle of a washing machine.

When he removed his hands, she opened her eyes and her throat was as it had been before. Only instead of feeling grateful, she felt sad, as though the healing of the bruises and the punctures made from his fangs had erased what had just happened between them.

He slid his arms around her. *"Chérie,* do not be sad. I can put them back, right now if you like."

At that she laughed. "I am being absurd, aren't I?"

"You have been through so much and you have shown

such courage and such grace. You have my permission to be as absurd as you need to be."

She met his gaze in the mirror. "If that's the case, then there's something else I'd like you to do for me."

He laughed, and she was pretty sure he knew exactly what she was going to ask of him. "Only if you drop the robe that I might gaze on your body. That is the payment I require for this ongoing service."

He grinned, showing all those big beautiful teeth of his. Why the hell did she have to like him so much?

But she dropped the robe, and he offered a very satisfied groan in response. Then he suggested she bend over slightly so that he could get the exact angle he needed.

She once more put her hands on the counter. "Will this do?" She rounded her shoulders just so.

"Oui, c'est parfait."

She closed her eyes. He began at the upper left wing-lock and began to scratch. She released a long loud groan that must have reverberated around the car-wash-sized bathroom at least three times.

The paralysis had finally worn off but the effects of first drugs, then Sister Quena's little mind trick, had taken a toll.

Marguerite lay limp and exhausted, staring up at a cottage-cheese ceiling with a fluorescent light box running straight down the middle. Sweet Christ, how the hell old was this place?

She closed her eyes against the glare, then opened them. She saw a switch by the door and mentally hit it. The light went out, *thank you, God,* leaving behind a very dim natural light.

She twisted to look up at the wall with the window and groaned. Barely a slit, not even wide enough to put a shoulder through, never mind her fucking head.

She felt the weight of her ankle guard. Apparently, Stanny wasn't taking any more chances than Quenny had. This one was new, heavier.

As prisons went, Marguerite thought her new home might

actually be worse than the Creator's Convent, and she really didn't think that was possible. At least she had her own cell this time, but what good would that do when Thorne wouldn't be able to get in here every morning to give her some good old-fashioned, bumping-uglies relief?

Instead of a wooden bed and lumpy mattress, she had a concrete platform and about an inch of foam. *Perfect.*

She struggled to lift up on her elbows. What was that smell?

Ugh. Urine. Oh, dear God.

She slid her legs over the side of the tall platform. Her toes just touched the floor. Her gaze landed on that which had offended her nose. She tilted her head. This so could not be what she was looking at. A pissing pot? In the twenty-first century?

Of course, given the nature of the odor in the room, she couldn't be far off.

The room was white, and the texture peeling off the cement-block walls. Yep, this was definitely worse than the Convent.

Prison was right.

The door opened and Stannett himself walked in. "You don't need to worry," he said, closing the door behind him. "Endelle may have thought she negotiated rights to enter the facility, but I'm sure I can prevent that from happening."

Why on earth would Stanny think those words would offer her even a small degree of comfort?

He removed his red embroidered leather coat and hung it on one of the pegs by the door.

He unbuttoned the first button of his black silk shirt, then the second.

Uh, she didn't like where this was headed. She enjoyed men but she'd never really thought of Owen Stannett, with the curling wave along the side of his head, as a man.

A lot of chest hair appeared.

"Hold up there, Stanny. I never agreed to sex."

"I didn't ask you to agree to anything. You're here. Life is simple at the Superstition Fortress; everyone does what I want them to do, just like I did what I was told all those centuries ago. It's just my turn and I'm making the most of it. So we can do this however you want to do it, but this is my call. Do you prefer all fours or missionary?"

Marguerite understood something and she suddenly had a little more respect for Sister Quena. If Stannett had ever touched Marguerite during one of their sessions, one word of accusation would have disallowed Stannett from the Convent. He'd been circumspect all those decades. Now he didn't have to be.

"You're not afraid of Madame Endelle finding anything out here?"

"No. I'm not. I have friends in high places. Specifically, COPASS."

"How convenient for you but you're not gettin' any from me today, not now, not ever."

He merely smiled and unbuttoned and unzipped his snug embroidered red leather pants. He had to work them down his skinny legs and she about puked when she saw he wore tight ball-huggers, also in red. Talk about overkill.

She swung her legs, dragging her toes back and forth on the floor. "I didn't think you liked women."

"I don't . . . especially. But you have something I need."

As though on cue, she heard a baby cry. "Aw, shit, Stanny. You set up a nursery in this goddam facility."

"Genetics is a beautiful thing."

"You're creating a race of super-Seers."

He shucked his tight briefs. As for size, he was somewhere in the middle. But she was used to Thorne and he was warrior-sized. She frowned. Worse, he still wore his socks. There was just something so unattractive about a naked man standing around in his socks. Well, that and he had a chest that bear cubs could snuggle against and not realize their ma was somewhere else.

She wrinkled up her nose. "How about I just donate some eggs?"

"Can't justify the medical expense to the committee without them finding out what I'm up to. Now, just to keep you informed, I will need a little oral stimulation to get things firmed up. If you refuse, I must warn you, I have about a dozen different ways to make you willing to do what needs to be done."

He drew close, which was a good thing, because she just smiled, reached for his left ball, and squeezed. She decided then and there that Owen Stannett must be something of an idiot to have allowed her to get this close and think she would just acquiesce.

His face turned the color of his leather jacket, pants, and briefs fast, much faster than the scream left his throat. She didn't stop squeezing, either. She just held on and waited. He hit her arm, hard, but she added a little twist to the experience.

Nature had given the physically weaker woman a simple way to sustain balance in any relationship with a man.

She kept holding, squeezing, and twisting until the bastard passed out and dropped to the floor.

She sank down beside him and burrowed into his mind. She found him curled up and sucking his mental thumb, whimpering. She sent, *You always were a bit of a lightweight. Now let's get one thing straight. I've been keeping a lot of secrets from you over the years, so I'm going to share a couple of them with you now. I have darkening abilities. You know what those are, right? Which means that if you ever pull this shit on me again, I'm coming after you in the darkening, and I'll find you because we inhabit the same facility. I also recently discovered that I'm the red variety of obsidian flame. Now, I haven't begun to explore those abilities, but I suspect there's enough power somewhere in my mind or my body to make a goddam eunuch out of you.*

So what do you say, Stanny? Are you going to leave me alone or is this just going to be the beginning of a long, painful, contentious relationship?

Even though she was just in his mind, she felt him look at her, really look at her. Good.

After a long moment, he nodded. *Truce,* he sent.

Like hell he'd leave her alone. All she'd done was buy herself some time. He'd probably drug the first meal she ate.

Not to be too cliché, but man did she need to get the hell out of this place. Stannett made sister-bitch look like Mother Teresa.

Jean-Pierre once more stood near the door in Endelle's office, his arms over his chest, monitoring Endelle's actions with Fiona. She had made her apologies and did not wink or smile when she said them so he could only presume she was somewhat sincere. It did not mean that her behavior would remain respectful, but for now she seemed to be very serious with Fiona, asking her many questions about her channeling experiences so far.

While they spoke, Thorne paced in front of the far enormous plate-glass window, the one that overlooked the desert to the east. He stopped in his pacing and turned to face the windows, his hands on his hips. Jean-Pierre observed the slight lowering of the warrior's shoulders. Despair.

Jean-Pierre knew what was to the east, far to the east: the Superstition Mountain Seers Fortress.

From the moment Jean-Pierre had learned that Thorne had made a devotiate from the Convent his lover, and that he had been with her for a hundred years, Jean-Pierre had questioned what was really happening to his brother. Thorne denied that Marguerite was his *breh.* He insisted she was too short and did not have a scent that he could perceive. He believed she was just a woman he made love to and cared about, even loved. *Oui,* he confessed to loving her very much. But he did not believe she was fated to be his vampire bond-mate.

So why then did Thorne once more pace in front of the east window and why did he seem so lost to his surroundings. Jean-Pierre knew those sensations, an almost desperate anxious need to get to his woman. He felt certain these were Thorne's present thoughts.

Because Fiona and Endelle seemed to be conversing without hostility, he crossed the room to join the brother by the window but was not very surprised when Thorne started and stared at him as though he had seen a specter. He even held his right hand up as though to draw his sword into his hand.

"You seem a little tense," Jean-Pierre said.

Thorne released a terrible huff of air. "You noticed, huh?"

"You are thinking of Marguerite," he said in a low voice.

"Of course. Stannett—" He paused, blinked a couple of times and huffed another piece of air. "He's a real shit. He has a long, difficult history in the world. Damn, I knew him when he was kept as a slave in a rogue lair for a century, really bad shit. But he had Seer ability and went into a Fortress after that. He rose in the ranks. His prophecies had a really high accuracy rate, in the high eighties.

He shook his head, then continued, "Greaves is a real bastard. I mean the worst. But you have a pretty good idea what he's going to do next, like even if he's devious, he's out front with it, if that makes sense.

"Stannett, shit, he's not right in the head. Not that Greaves is either, but Stannett's just plain old fucked up."

"And he has your woman."

Thorne shook his head. His eyes were red-rimmed and pinched as he stared out into the growing morning light of the vast creosote wasteland beyond the window. "She's not my woman. I mean, she is, but not like Fiona is yours."

"So you have said."

At that he turned to scowl at Jean-Pierre. "You don't believe me?"

Jean-Pierre shrugged. "I do not know what to believe about the *breh-hedden* except that it is a terrible master."

"Then I hope I never have to endure it because this is bad enough."

"You fear for her safety."

"I do. She may have hated the Convent, but she was safe there. She's under a man's thumb now, a very powerful, dangerous man, and there's nothing I can do about it." He took a deep breath and closed his eyes. "This is hell."

Endelle called from across the room. "I hate to break up your little *tête-à-tête*, boys, but I've got work to do. Jean-

Pierre, take Fiona over to Militia HQ. Thorne, you can head to bed."

Thorne turned back to her. "But you're going over to the Fortress, right?"

"Damn straight. Stannett is giving me access, that's the deal."

"Fine. Fine." He pulled the *cadroen* from his hair and scrubbed the sides of his head until his hair hung loose well past his shoulders. "Fuck. I'm heading to Sedona. Call if you need me."

He didn't even lift his arm. He just vanished.

Jean-Pierre glanced at Endelle. She stared into the empty space where Thorne had been. For just a moment, her face began to collapse, the muscles of her cheeks sagging, her lips drooping. Then she gave herself a shake and turned back to Fiona. "I want you working with Jean-Pierre this afternoon. Of all the warriors, he seems to have an ability to assess the powers of others and to draw them out. I've often wished he had the Third Earth facilitation power, but I've never known a Second ascender who possessed that shit. Whatever.

"As for Alison, she's been whining about not spending enough time with Helena so I only get her services for about four hours in the afternoon."

Fiona's lips quirked. "Hey. I thought you said there's no whining in ascension. Forgive me, Your Supremeness, but that sounded damn close to a whine."

Jean-Pierre felt certain he needed to give Fiona a hint about not poking at rattlesnakes or scorpions, but for some reason Endelle laughed. "All right, smart-ass, get the hell out of here and take your boyfriend with you."

Jean-Pierre did not need to be invited a second time. He crossed the room quickly to Fiona and slid his left arm around her waist. "Ready, *chérie*?"

She smiled and nodded. He lifted his arm and felt the smooth, swishing glide through nether-space, his heart warm as he held Fiona next to him. For this moment, she was here, she was with him, and she was safe.

* * *

Fiona strove to settle her temper down. Her *boyfriend* had been working her channeling powers for the past two hours, but now he wanted to attempt something new, something he was certain she could do. But she wasn't having it, not one little bit.

"Even if I *could* let a possession occur," she cried. "The hell I will."

Jean-Pierre wanted her to see if together they could take her obsidian flame abilities to the next level, one that involved possession, in which he would slide the metaphysical part of his being over hers, possess her, and make use of her powers in concert with his.

No way in hell and all this session had done was taken her temper down to a cold hard place. Her boyfriend, it seemed, took any kind of *training* seriously, and right now he was really pissing her off. "I won't do it. I won't."

"Having ascended in 1793, I am still young by ascended terms," he said, his chin low, his eyes glittering in the dim light of the room. "But this I can tell you: Each power you have must be pushed to its limits, its farthest boundaries. This is one of the lessons of our world. To hold back in this way can allow the enemy an advantage, a terrible advantage."

She pinched her lips together. "I don't see how."

"Because the more powerful you are, the more the enemy will want you dead. If your powers are not fully expressed, then do you not see how you are left exposed like a weak flank in an offensive? That is where the enemy will attack, hurting you where you are at your most vulnerable."

Fiona turned away from him and paced in front of the closed blinds. Seriffe had given them the same room as before, but the door was closed and she was alone with Jean-Pierre. At first, she thought it might be difficult given the I-can't-keep-my-hands-off-you nature of the *breh-hedden,* but almost from the beginning Jean-Pierre had browbeaten her with her need to engage more fully with obsidian flame.

What he said sort of made sense. "This is just all so new

to me. The day I left the hospital, I was floating because I thought now I could have a life, you know, maybe work as a waitress, something simple, basic, straightforward. Start over." She chuckled, "You know, fly under the radar." So much irony since she couldn't even mount her wings. Whatever. "Now I'm something that I can't really begin to comprehend, obsidian flame, and you're here telling me I have to allow a kind of possession in order to truly express my powers.

"Jean-Pierre, the first time we made love you had to enthrall me because I couldn't bear the weight of you on me. And these last two times, well, first I rode you, then this last time you took me from behind. I know, *I know,* that if we tried to do it the regular way"—she looked up at him and gestured first to his chest, then to hers—"I'd freak out again."

Of course bringing up sex was a mistake, because a heavy roll of his delicious coffee scent poured over her. "Would you stop that?"

"*Désolé, chérie.* Though I understand the reason behind the reference, the images caught me by surprise."

"But you know what I mean, right?"

"Yes, of course."

She moved to sit down in the chair she'd used the afternoon before when she had worked with Alison. She bent over and shaded her eyes with her hands. This was too much. All too much, but it had been from the first anyway, from having been taken from the streets of Boston in 1886, used as a blood slave, rescued by one of the hunkiest men she had ever seen, until right now with her vampire *breh* standing in the center of the room, waiting for her to calm down so that they could continue the training. All too much.

Absently, she fingered the gold locket that she wore around her neck, trying to find an anchor. Her husband had warned her repeatedly not to go shopping by herself, that a woman on the streets alone would always invite danger. And so it had, but not in a way that Terence could have ever predicted. Was there a lesson here for her, then? And just how right was Jean-Pierre?

The trouble was, she wasn't sure she could do it period. Not just because she resisted the idea; she also thought it possible she would really struggle to learn the skill in the first place.

She looked up at him. He waited so patiently, a slight furrow on his brow, solemn. He was a good teacher; he had skills, because here she was ready to do what she had pretty much vowed never to do. "All right, Obi-Wan, let's do this thing."

Then he smiled, all those big beautiful teeth.

"You know, you could have been a model or something."

He chuckled. "I think I would rather make war."

At that she laughed but his expression grew serious. "You are so beautiful, Fiona. Sometimes looking at you makes my heart ache."

She rose to her feet and her breathing seemed to stall in her chest. He always gave her the most wonderful compliments because he tied them to his heart. Did he know he did that?

He closed his eyes and his nostrils flared. "I wish you could smell what it is that I smell. There is nothing like a bakery first thing in the morning when the aroma of all that goodness fills the dawn air. That is what I smell when you are near me like this. All that goodness." He opened his eyes. "And that is who you are, Fiona. When I see you with your daughter, Carolyn, and her children, I think, *Oui, all that goodness.*"

He crossed to her and she let him take her in his arms, let his lips find hers, let his tongue pierce her mouth. She slid her arms around his neck and he wrapped his arms around her so that she was pressed front-to-front against him; his heavy muscled pecs to her breasts, his rippled abdomen to hers, his now very firm cock tempting her very low, his strong thighs pushing into her thighs, making demands they couldn't possibly follow up on, not here in this room at Militia Warrior HQ.

Does this make you feel trapped? he sent.

No.

She didn't say the rest: that what he was doing made her feel *loved*. Oh, God, how deep could this well get?

He held her for a long time, the seconds dragging into a minute, then two. She breathed against him and he breathed against her, his body, hers, living, alive, here and present.

Finally, he pulled back and looked into her eyes. "Can you trust me and try? Can you trust that in my two hundred years of living as an ascended vampire I know what I am speaking of when I say that each power must be taken to its greatest breadth of expression, that this is necessary? That when we do this, as individuals, we make our world, our society stronger?"

"You want me to think of the whole?"

He nodded. "To some degree, yes, but mostly I want you to think of yourself and trust me that this will be the very best for you as well, that place where you will find the greatest joy as well as the greatest strength."

She looked into his eyes and for a moment thought that he could sell her swampland in Florida. She smiled. "I'll try."

"Good. Let's begin with preternatural speed, something I know you do not hold as a power."

The truth was, she didn't have a great number of powers like any of the extremely powerful ascenders she knew. Alison, for instance, had all of the Second Earth preternatural powers and a few that were at Third Earth level, like her ability to capture pockets of time and reverse them. Fiona could fold herself from place to place, but she wasn't powerful enough to take anyone else with her.

Still, she was the gold variety of obsidian flame, which for her apparently meant that she could channel the powers of others, even though she didn't have the powers herself. However, this was early in the process. Who knew what would emerge as the days and weeks progressed?

Fiona closed her eyes. As she drew near to Jean-Pierre in a preternatural sense, her being up against his being, this part of the process made complete sense to her. She didn't know why exactly, but when she felt herself almost locked against him, shoulder-to-shoulder, hip-to-hip, she knew that this was the first part of the channeling gift . . . proximity.

But as she relaxed and thought about allowing the possession, she felt a strange vibration of new energy—not the hard sweep of gold power, but something cooler washing over her skin, which seemed to pull Jean-Pierre even closer to her.

But as the power increased, it began to feel *suffocating.* She drew back and back until she no longer rested beside him.

She opened her eyes, and he frowned down at her. "Why did you stop? I felt it, as though I was being drawn into you. Fiona, you have this power. I can feel it in you now." His eyes held an almost wild light of excitement.

She whirled around and returned to her chair. She sat down and crossed her legs and folded her arms over her chest. She wagged her head. "No. I felt as though I couldn't breathe. I can't do this, Jean-Pierre. I won't do it." She couldn't meet his gaze. She didn't want to see either the reprimand in his eyes or the disappointment. Besides, why did this have to be on her? Why?

There was no answer. Why did Jean-Pierre have to be a Warrior of the Blood and battle every night at the Borderlands in order to keep Second Earth and Mortal Earth from falling into the hands of a monster? Why had Endelle been essentially forced to a rule a world for so many millennia when clearly, *clearly,* she'd rather be doing a million other things, like starting her own roadkill fashion line accompanied by rattlesnake accessories.

But instead of shouting at her, as surely Endelle would have done, he moved to sit beside her. He slid his hand up beneath her long waterfall of hair and rubbed the back of her neck with his long beautiful fingers. She closed her eyes, but a couple of tears slipped from beneath her eyelids.

"I wish this was easier for me," she said.

"I know. I understand. I got very excited, though, when I felt your power drawing me to you, into you. I was a little carried away by the possibilities, even by the pleasure of feeling connected to you in that manner."

"You're not mad at me?"

She still couldn't look at him, but she heard his frustrated sigh. "I am angry that our world is built like this. I remember being this angry about a year ago when Alison, our wonderful Alison, was required by the rules of COPASS to submit to an arena battle, using a sword she had only had command of for a day or so. She was forced to battle the traitor Leto, a former Warrior of the Blood. I can remember thinking the same thing: that this was not just unfair, it was a great sin against Alison, against all ascenders that anyone should be treated so cruelly.

"After everything you have been through, all you have suffered, I think it cruel that you must now do something that is abhorrent to you. Beyond that, if we were not at war, there would be no rush to bring your powers to the fore. You could take centuries exploring your gifts. But no, you must hurry and do this thing or perhaps the world will fall because you did not. It is absurd and it is a sin."

A chill went straight down her back and not because Jean-Pierre still touched her, still rubbed her neck.

Fiona rarely experienced anything close to prescience or clairvoyance but she had the worst feeling that what he had just said was true.

She suppressed the thought, however. If she honestly embraced the notion that the fate of the world depended on her, she thought she might just go insane. So instead she looked at him and said, "Then for now, why don't we practice that part of the channeling skill that I can use, so that when I am next to you, in that strange way of mine, I can still make use of the powers you possess. Okay?"

He nodded. "I think it a good idea."

But as she looked at him, she said. "You know, you reminded me of Alison just now. Are you empathic?"

He shook his head. "Not that I am aware."

She laughed. "Maybe not. I guess you're just a great guy."

But he squeezed her neck then pushed against her playfully, side-to-side. "Well, that is very true. I am most definitely a great guy."

A number of sudden unexpected thoughts flowed through her, images of what they had done so recently, and another image she wanted to explore, of Jean-Pierre in his bedroom and some bindings fashioned out of silk. Of course, being a woman from Boston so long ago, these new thoughts brought a flame to her cheek.

"Your scent is intoxicating, *chérie*." His voice was a low whisper right against her neck. "What were you thinking? Tell me what you were thinking? Tell me in detail."

She looked at him, met his gaze. She had never been so bold. "I saw the most beautiful gray-green-blue silk, the color of your eyes, only I wrapped it around your wrists and held you captive on your bed."

His eyes fluttered in his head and she watched him shudder and shiver. His scent didn't just flow; it pounded over her until she was suddenly in his arms and clawing at his pastel brocade *cadroen,* trying to release it with one hand, but failing. At the same time, he held her almost cradled in his arms, his mouth on hers, his tongue bruising the inside of her mouth until she whimpered and writhed.

After a moment, she drew back breathless and put a hand on his chest. "I . . . shouldn't have said that."

"*Mais non.* I think it would be perfect for you to have that kind of power over me." His voice dropped about a foot as he continued, "And I want to be bound and in your power. I want you to do to me whatever you desire. Anything."

She may have just passed out. She wasn't sure. She was very dizzy and now he sucked on the side of her neck. She wanted to leave with him, to go back to his house, to find some new space to explore with him and yes, to find a length of silk or maybe two, or four. Oh, God, four. To have him so bound that he couldn't move and she could do whatever she wanted.

He was breathing hard as he pulled back and set her in her seat. "I am sorry, *chérie,* but my phone is buzzing."

He reached into his pocket and drew out his warrior phone. "*Allô,* Bev." He met Fiona's gaze.

She sat forward, her brows raised, her heart rate climbing

even higher than it already was. Because it was daytime at HQ, Bev would be running the grid.

He thumbed his phone and replaced it in his pocket, then smiled. "Another anomaly."

Fiona couldn't believe it. "But that makes three in three days. I would be exhilarated but I have to say I'm a little suspicious."

He leaned back in his chair and worked at his breathing. She was able to stand but she was pretty sure Jean-Pierre still needed another minute. He smiled up at her. "Go ahead, *chérie,* this will take some time." But his expression was so warm, so disarming, and she felt such a profound affection for him that she moved between his legs and held his face in her hands. "Thank you. Just . . . thank you."

She kissed him.

When his hands found her hips, she knew this would not help his condition at all. Beyond that, she had a sociopath to find.

She pulled away. He let her go.

She ran to the door and then to the grid, a prayer flowing through her mind, *Dear Creator, let this be the day that we get that bastard Rith.*

The most satisfying deception
always includes a surprise.

—*Notes on Dark Spectacle,* the Amazing Rimizac

CHAPTER 14

"Where are we? Which country?" Fiona asked, staring down at the anomaly.

Bev spoke from her perch above the grid. "Australia. Brisbane."

Fiona searched through what looked like a smudge on the electronic field. After a moment the blue-green of Rith's intricate mist pattern emerged, outlining a very specific area. So in the space of three days, they'd found three blood slave facilities. This had to be a new record, but to say she felt uneasy all over again was to say the least.

Seriffe left his office to stand at the end of the grid. "So we've got another one?"

Fiona met his gaze and nodded but he scowled. She didn't blame him. This was just too good to be true.

"I'll get Gideon on the com."

Bev called out in an excited voice, "A powerful signature just arrived, stronger than just a death vampire."

"No shit," Seriffe said.

Fiona's heart began to thrum. Could this be Rith, at long last? Could they have found the moment in time when Rith would be at the facility they currently had on their radar?

Jean-Pierre walked up the hall, having left the room they'd shared, but he'd changed to flight battle gear. He looked very serious, somber-eyed as he moved to stand by the wall nearest the foot of the grid.

He waved her over.

She frowned. Usually he came directly to her. She wondered what was wrong.

Several Militia Warriors also stared down into the grid. Seriffe began issuing orders into his com, ordering Gideon to get his team together for another rescue operation.

Bev called out, "The signature disappeared."

Fiona looked up at her. Bev shrugged. Maybe Rith had folded in then left. So what did this mean?

Fiona moved in Jean-Pierre's direction but the hairs on her nape rose. She stopped in her tracks and looked around. Something was really wrong, but what? No one else seemed to be disturbed. She shook her head at Jean-Pierre but he shrugged.

Once more she headed toward him, but the uneasiness remained. Just as she reached him, the door to the room they shared, maybe thirty feet away, opened once more and . . . Jean-Pierre stepped out, wearing what he'd been wearing earlier.

She didn't understand.

She looked up at the battle-ready version of Jean-Pierre next to her. He smiled, but his smile was very different. His smile was . . . *familiar* and not Rith's.

Deep sonorous church bells began to sound. Recognition dawned.

The Upper ascender.

She stepped away just as her real boyfriend blurred toward her. At the exact same moment, warning sirens shrieked through the grid room. But before her Jean-Pierre could reach her, time appeared to slow all around her, something that just didn't make sense. She saw *her* Jean-Pierre pause as if in mid-run, his expression intense, his eyes pinched, mouth wide as though screaming.

The false Jean-Pierre put a hand on her shoulder and the next moment she was flying through nether-space, a smooth glide, but this time no pleasure accompanied the trip, only a terrible panic at what had just happened to her.

She barely had time to collect her thoughts as she touched down on a solid stone floor. She glanced around. A cavern. She was in some sort of cavern, lit by a few scattered, wall-mounted lanterns. Underground locations made excellent hiding places since the grid could only detect surface activity.

The fake Jean-Pierre stood next to her. She turned toward him and backed up. The image of her warrior, her man, wavered. The Upper ascender shook himself like a dog emerging from water.

"Well, that was fun, but the security alarm was so loud. Ouch. My ears hurt." He laughed.

She took another step back.

The Upper ascender was exactly as both Jean-Pierre and Marguerite had described him: long curly dark hair, a narrow nose, quite handsome, full, sensual lips, deep brown eyes, almost black. He wore very snug pants and she kept her gaze away from what he must be intent on displaying. She felt her cheeks grow warm.

So how exactly was she supposed to escape a vampire with Third or Fourth powers?

The man's gaze drifted down her face, her throat, her breasts, all the way down then back up. "I like that you're tall."

She swallowed hard and gathered what remained of her courage. She lifted her chin. "I know of you, but we haven't met. I'm Fiona Gaines, taken from Boston in the late 1800s. And you are?"

"Casimir." His smile was slow, lascivious. "Eastern Europe, from sometime in the middle of, oh, the third millennium BC, I guess. Yes I think that's right. Time takes on such a different meaning as the years wear on. They call it 'millennial adjustment.'" He still smiled and for good measure his tongue made an appearance, rubbing back and forth over his lower lip.

Jean-Pierre would have gone ballistic at the sight of Casimir's smile alone. His tongue? A declaration of war.

He walked in a circle around her, a very slow circle until he faced her. He hooked his thumb in his pants, which of course drew her gaze right where he wanted it. She looked away. The man was aroused.

"How sweet," he crooned as he circled once more. "You're actually blushing. I think that's adorable."

When he was behind her, the hairs on the nape of her neck rose once more. She felt the urge to run. She would have bolted but suddenly he took hold of her arms and she couldn't move. The snakes in the pit of her stomach began to writhe. Her heart pumped hard and she had to part her lips to breathe.

"I would never hurt you, Fiona of Boston. Really." But he laughed deep into the well of his throat. "I feel you trembling. So frightened. I confess, it's an elixir." He breathed in, a slow hissing sound, close to her neck.

She felt his mind against her mind. *I have known obsidian flames before. Your kind is rare, very rare, and quite unpredictable. I can feel the power inside you, very deep, and building. I'd like to be inside all that power. Can you feel your power building?*

No. And that was the truth.

Interesting. Aloud, he said, "But then, this is all very new to you, isn't it?"

"Yes." So the man liked to chitchat before he slit her throat or whatever it was he had planned for her.

Fiona took deep breaths and tried to still the slamming of her heart. She couldn't believe this had happened to her again, that she was once more in the power of a man. But no ordinary man. An Upper ascender.

What the hell was she supposed to do now? She didn't have power like Alison, certainly not like Endelle. She couldn't throw a hand-blast and hope to drop the man to the floor.

Her folding skills were nominal. So exactly how was she supposed to defend herself?

She could channel the powers of others, but whose power in this situation? She needed outside help. She really did, some power she could channel.

"So where exactly is this place?" she asked, thinking she would be wise to gather information.

"Las Vegas Two, beneath one of my favorite theaters. Do you like it? I had it carved out for my own personal use." She glanced at a long slab of dark granite supported by a massive boulder. An altar? She shivered.

"Come out, Rith."

Fiona grew very still at the mention of Rith's name. She glanced around and there he was. The man she had been hunting for so long suddenly emerged from between an almost invisible breach in the cavern wall. He was followed by—*oh, God*—two pretty-boys, and they were all focused on her.

She had never seen a death vampire this close before.

The two looked almost identical: porcelain skin with a bluish cast, long wavy black hair, dark eyes, and so much beauty. Her heart began to feel tremendous ease and well-being as she looked at them.

Enthrallment.

The specialty of death vampires.

She closed her eyes and fought the strange pulsing sense of peace that flowed over her, that made her legs and arms feel limp and useless, that spilled euphoria over her mind.

She drew upon her new power, reaching deep into the gold stream of obsidian flame. The power flowed up and up, covering her, flooding her thoughts, pushing all that false ease out of her head. She opened her eyes and the death vampires were . . . just men.

Very nice, Casimir sent. "I'm impressed." He released her arms and moved to stand beside Rith.

Fiona settled her gaze on the man who had been her captor for so many decades, who had essentially killed hundreds of women to acquire dying blood. She forgot about Casimir and about the death vampires, even though the latter moved to create a semicircle around her, one on each side. All she could see was Rith, and the long list of women who had died in his Burma blood slave facility.

She felt her power begin to build deep within, a faint rumbling in her soul. She wanted this man dead more than anything in the world. She wanted him to pay for what he'd done and she wanted him incapable of enslaving any more women.

His eyes flared and he took a step back.

"Are you afraid of obsidian flame?" Casimir asked. "You needn't be. She's young in her power. She doesn't yet know what she can do. She may never know. It happens with this particular variety."

"She's glowing."

"Yes, she is."

Fiona hardly heard this exchange. All she could think was that Rith was here and if she could just channel the right kind of power, she could take him down right now.

Her mind flew, picking up ideas and casting them aside. Her instincts spread to encompass all four vampires. She couldn't physically overpower any of them; nor did she have the power to blast her way out. She couldn't fold out of the cavern and, most important, she knew she would be unable to contact Jean-Pierre or Seriffe or even Endelle—she could sense the shield that Casimir had placed around this location.

But as her intention of doing harm to Rith became more and more focused, her power sharpened and she knew there was one entity she could contact, nothing could prevent her, not Casimir's Fourth ability, nothing.

There was just one problem.

She shifted her gaze to Casimir and saw the determined light in his eye. He had no intention of letting her live.

He glanced at the death vampire to his right and said, "Do it."

Fiona's life flashed before her eyes as swords appeared in the hands of each of the death vampires; she saw Boston,

Burma, Carolyn and her children, and finally, Jean-Pierre. Time did a slow dance as sharp thirty-inch swords arced in the air.

Her time had come.

Except . . . Jean-Pierre's beautiful smile suddenly rose in her mind. Like hell she was ready to just accept her death. From deep within the rumbling came that golden rush of obsidian power that flowed within her until a wave burst from her in all directions and all four vampires flew back, away from her, hitting various parts of the cavern's stone hard.

She turned, as if to run, but all she met was another stone wall not ten feet from her. Whirling back, she thought maybe the breach on the other side could lead somewhere, but her enemy wasn't dead, wasn't even unconscious.

Each vampire slowly began to recover and to rise. She didn't exactly understand what she had just done, but her power wasn't lethal, which went to the larger conundrum: She could channel but not produce.

Worse, she might have held death at bay for this first round, but she could tell her power had weakened. Exactly how many waves like that could she release to protect herself? And what the hell was she supposed to do now?

She needed help, but could she bypass the shield around the place?

Jean-Pierre had been in this place before, five months ago in the back bedroom of the farmhouse in Toulouse. He had seen Rith with Fiona in his arms, he had watched them vanish and had cast himself into nether-space, following the gold glitter of Fiona's trace, only to be thrown back again and again. Rith had blocked her trace then as her trace was blocked even now and he could not follow after her to save her.

How had Rith, if it was Rith, gotten past the security system?

But he tried, repeatedly, to throw himself against what was essentially a preternatural brick wall. He slammed against the block in the trace over and over, but to no avail.

How had this happened? Why was he back where he had started?

When on the twelfth attempt he landed on his back, at the foot of the grid, the wind knocked out of him, he ceased the futile effort. He could not breathe and his body trembled.

Seriffe squatted beside him, his dark eyes haunted. At least the alarm had stopped shrieking through the building. "We'll find her, Jean-Pierre. If we have to storm the gates of hell, we'll find her."

Jean-Pierre opened his mouth wide but could not bring air into his lungs.

"Just relax. This will pass in a few more seconds."

He nodded.

This will pass. What will pass? His world on edge perpetually? His greatest fear realized over and over again, that his woman would be taken because the enemy grew stronger and more devious with each new sunrise?

Finally, air eased into his lungs and he sat up. "Do we have any idea where she has gone? Where she has been taken?"

Seriffe shook his head. He looked wrecked—and why wouldn't he? Last night he had lost another man, a good man, and now Fiona was taken straight from his HQ. How the hell were any of them to be safe?

"Fuck," Seriffe said. He rose then extended a hand to Jean-Pierre.

He took it and let the man pull him to his feet. "The trace was blocked."

"Yeah. We all got that. What do we do now? Do you have a link with her? Can you contact her? If we can get her position, we can send a goddam army after her."

Jean-Pierre, still weakened from attempting the impossible, turned into the grid and leaned his forearms on the wide side railing. "I will try," he said. He closed his eyes and focused on Fiona, on her lovely face, her silver-blue eyes, her long elegant chestnut hair.

He worked hard at conjuring her image, creating a portrait of her in his mind, and reaching out, casting a wide net, into telepathic space and hunting for her.

But she could not be found.

He tried and tried, but no answering voice returned to invade his mind. Just silence; the worst sound in the world.

Marguerite paced her cell. Her stomach rumbled. She hadn't eaten since yesterday, but like hell she was going to take any of the food placed before her by a zombie-like servant. At least the servant had taken the piss-pot with her.

Still, she chewed on one of her nails, just to ease the gnawing sensation in her stomach.

She was debating whether to start on the thumbnail of her left hand when she felt Fiona's presence right up beside her, shoulder-to-shoulder, hip-to-hip. She could tell that the woman's powers had expanded since the last time they'd communicated, which was only a day ago, at the most. Wow.

What's cookin', Fee? she sent. *And how come I can communicate with you, but I can't reach Thorne or Grace or anyone else?*

Uh, I've got a little problem and I need your help.

I don't like to spoil your buzz, but I'm incarcerated now in the Superstitions.

I know. But I just got abducted by the Upper ascender, Casimir, and he's got two death vampires ready to attack . . . again. To top it off, that bastard Rith is here, smiling at me. I can't reach anyone but you so I thought maybe we could try out some of our shared power.

Holy fuck.

Marguerite processed all that Fiona had just said to her. She blinked. Shit, if she couldn't help Fiona right now, the woman was dead.

You mean our flame gift?

So you know about that?

Yep.

Thank God.

What do you have in mind? I can't see how I can possibly help you.

My gift is channeling. Have you got anything I can channel to escape these losers?

Have you tried just folding the hell out of there?

Uh, I can't.

What do you mean you can't?

I can only fold from room to room and I don't know where this is or where to go from here. Oh, God. In fact, I'm really short on most powers. I can only channel powers. And there's one more issue, but it might not be a hindrance; Casimir has a shield around the place, which is why I couldn't reach anyone else. So I'm hoping this will work.

Okay. She put her hands on her hips. *I can fold. You want to try channeling a fold?*

Absolutely. But make it fast because they're coming at me again.

Chill, Fee. We can do this. Just tell me how it works.

Fiona's heart beat like a jackhammer. All four vampires were on their feet.

To Marguerite, she sent, *You feel me next to you, right?*

Right.

In as few words as possible, she told Marguerite what her previous experiences had been like with Alison and Jean-Pierre.

Got it. Let's do it.

Fiona kept backing up, since both death vampires had gained their feet and looked really pissed off. At the same time, she remained focused on Marguerite, on the level of power that had begun vibrating between the two women.

I'm holding in my mind that I want to fold, Marguerite sent. *Can you feel it?*

Yes. Oh, God. We gotta do this now. I think Rith is winding up for a hand-blast.

Picture where you want to go, Fee.

Fiona released her fears and pictured the landing platform at Militia HQ. She closed her eyes and—what do you know, the glide began. She sped through nether-space, relief hitting her like a flash flood during a monsoon storm.

The next moment, she was staring at five Militia Warriors, all with swords drawn. "It's just me," she cried. "But we might have incoming."

One of the Militia Warriors blurred toward her, caught her arm, then pulled her behind him.

She moved toward the back wall then waited. The warriors all stood, facing the platform, swords still drawn, bodies hunched.

Seconds passed.

No one came. Her heart was still racing, but she was here and she was safe.

Did it work, Fee?

Yes, yes, yes! Thank you, Marguerite! You saved my life!

Good, but I'm signing off. If Stannett figures out that you and I can communicate, he might put me someplace even worse.

Okay, but thank you! I won't forget this . . . ever!

Fee, I may ask for a favor one day.

Anything, sister. Anything!

Gotta go.

Fiona felt the telepathic thread snap at the very end, like a hang-up. She drew in a deep breath.

She had another message to send. *Jean-Pierre, I'm at the landing platform.*

Within the space of a heartbeat, he folded next to her and immediately he was touching her arms, her legs, her hips, then back up to touch the sides of her head, then down to her neck. He kept asking her things in French.

"Anglais, chéri," she finally said.

He huffed a laugh. "Are you all right? How did you get back? I could not reach you. Where did he take you? Was it Rith?"

She shook her head. "It was our friend from Copán. The Upper ascender. His name is Casimir. But Rith was there and two death vampires."

"Mon Dieu, mon Dieu, mon Dieu." Another string of

French followed until he caught himself and reverted to English. "Where did you go? Where did he take you?"

She kept her explanation brief, dwelling on how Marguerite, the newly avowed second leg of their obsidian flame triad, had helped her channel a fold in order to escape.

She met his gaze. "Jean-Pierre, they intended to kill me. If I hadn't been practicing my channeling ability, I'd be dead."

He nodded, a brisk series of nods, then dragged her into his arms. *"Merde,"* he said, one slap of French profanity against her ear. Finally, he added, "But you found your way out. You did this, Fiona. You embraced your power, you kept your head very clear, and you did this impossible thing. Thank you, *chérie,* more than words can express for coming back to me."

Casimir shouted a string of profanities into the cavern. He might have begun the abduction with a casual attitude but by the time he'd ordered the death vamps to finish her off, he wanted nothing more than to eliminate this emerging and terrifying obstacle to his plans.

He'd been so close to seeing her killed. The swords had been spinning in Fiona's direction—then suddenly her power was just there, an enormous wave of energy. He'd been slammed against the wall of rock. Several of his ribs were broken, which was no doubt what had happened to the others as well.

But each of them had self-healed and he'd already sent the death vampires back to their lair in Geneva, Mortal Earth.

Rith sat on the floor, a hand to the back of his neck.

Casimir stared at him. He and Greaves had already discussed the next step in this journey, for all of them. Rith would have a new role. First he would deliver an invitation to Fiona and her warrior, then he would be delivered elsewhere by Endelle's faction to hopefully initiate Greaves's worldwide publicity campaign against Rith-the-scapegoat.

At least in that sense Caz would know some relief.

The man's smell really did irritate the hell out of him.

He folded an extra-large dog crate into the cavern.

"As soon as you're healed, Greaves wants you to crawl inside. It's time we moved our plans forward."

Rith dropped both hands to his lap and smiled at Casimir. "Just remember what I have said to you. The future streams have been very clear about your future. No, I did not say that correctly. The future streams say you do not have a future."

Caz wasn't a Fourth ascender for nothing. He knew that the future was like a prism catching light—and that light split apart and bounced in every direction imaginable. "You don't get to be my age, asshole, without learning to ignore the future streams."

But Rith just laughed at him then crawled inside the cage.

Fiona had her arm around Jean-Pierre's waist, her hand on his chest, and her face turned into his shoulder.

Seriffe and at least ten more Militia Warriors stood near the landing platform, all with swords drawn.

She was calmer now. Several minutes had passed since her arrival at Militia HQ, but she didn't want to leave the landing platform area just yet. Jean-Pierre had asked her twice if she wanted to retire to the room they had been using for practice, but she shook her head. For just a moment, she wanted to stay here, feel the heat and strength of his body.

She kept replaying the brief terrifying abduction over and over in her mind. Each time she would come to the moment when she dove inside what she had come to think of as her golden rush of power, and she would marvel at what lived inside her, what existed deep inside her.

She had power now, something she could tap, something she could use to make herself safe, something she could possibly use to keep others safe as well. She looked up into Jean-Pierre's face. Maybe she could even keep him safe as well?

The snakes that writhed in the bottom of her stomach stopped moving, then shriveled to the size of peas—then simply vanished. She had done this thing today. Through her own effort, she had escaped another horrible abduction and now she was back with her man. Maybe she could have a life on Second Earth, a real life. Maybe, just maybe she had sufficient power to stay alive and to live.

Could she therefore have a life with Jean-Pierre?

He met her gaze and frowned slightly. *What is it,* chérie*?* he sent.

Movement on the platform shifted her gaze in the direction of the Militia Warriors who still stood battle-ready and waiting.

"Incoming," one of the men shouted.

Fiona drew in a sharp breath.

The next moment a cage appeared, a supersized dog kennel with an enormous gold metallic bow on the top.

In the cage was . . . Rith, bound and trussed.

She understood. A gift from Casimir.

The lead warrior moved toward the kennel. He turned back to Seriffe. "There's a letter here."

"Give it to me."

The warrior plucked it from the top of the kennel and handed it to the colonel. Seriffe glanced back at her. "It's addressed to you, Fiona."

She left Jean-Pierre and went straight to her son-in-law. She withdrew the elegant card that bore Casimir's name in raised black script on the front. She turned the card over.

May you enjoy your newfound powers. As for Rith, decapitation then cremation on separate pyres. Best wishes, C.

She handed the note to Seriffe. A moment later, he muttered, "Jesus H. Christ."

Her gaze fell to Rith, who lay on his side, his hands bound, his ankles bound, and his knees drawn up tight.

Rith, her enemy. The one she had been seeking all this time. Casimir had simply offered him up.

Why?

She knew the question needed answering, but right now all she could do was stare at the man who had kept her prisoner for over a hundred years, who had month after month seen that she was drained for her dying blood then brought back to life.

Rage suddenly boiled through her, rising from so deep within her body that she didn't need to be told that her aura was on fire. She could feel the heat all over her skin, and a golden glow now enveloped the room.

The Militia Warriors all started talking at once, commenting on her aura. The alarms shrieked once more, evidence no doubt of the sudden surge of power she emitted.

Seriffe was on the com talking to Bev, and within seconds the alarms stopped.

She moved close to the cage. "Rith Do'onwa," she called out in a strong voice, "you will answer today for the women you murdered in the Burma facility where you held me captive. What do you have to say to me?"

"That I murdered no one," he responded. "The women were weak and chose death. They died when they lost the will to live."

Splitting fucking hairs.

She put her hands on the cage. She wasn't sure what she wanted to do. She thought maybe she would pick it up and throw it against the wall.

Instead she dropped to her knees, put her hands in her lap, then held his gaze. Again, in a strong voice, she said, "I am Fiona Gaines, the first woman taken into your captivity and used by both you and Greaves to harvest the first vials of enslaved dying blood.

"I am Fiona Gaines taken from Boston, torn from my husband of eleven years and from my two children, Carolyn and Peter.

"The second woman to come to your Burma facility, but this time to die, was named Mary Sisk. She was from Virginia. She had six children, six who grew up without their mother or ever knowing what happened to her.

"The third was an elegant African American woman you took from Mississippi. She had just given birth and left behind an infant daughter. She died heartbroken, craving the feel of her baby in her arms.

"The fourth woman to live and die under your hand came from Barbados. Victoria. She was just seventeen, newly married. She died soon after. Most of the women in the early years couldn't take the hand-blasts to the chests. Your hand-blasts, remember?"

And on she spoke, detailing the lives of those she held in her heart and in her mind, a living memorial to the dead in Burma.

Jean-Pierre had remained near the back wall, perhaps twenty feet from Fiona. He used his warrior phone to call Carla at Central Command.

"Carla here. How can I help?"

"We have a situation at Militia Warrior HQ." He explained what had happened then added, "Please advise Endelle and Thorne. We're not sure what to do with the prisoner but I feel certain Endelle will want to be involved in this. If she desires to come, please have her fold to my position."

"You got it."

He didn't try to explain that Fiona had begun a recitation that could take a very long time. He certainly did not feel it would be right to disrupt her, but he also needed Endelle to witness what was happening.

Endelle folded to the doorway barely a minute later. He caught her gaze just as she opened her mouth, no doubt to say something inappropriate.

He shook his head and gestured to Fiona.

She drew close to Jean-Pierre and in a surprisingly quiet voice, her brows drawn into a knot, she asked, "What the fuck is going on here? And is that Rith in a dog cage?"

Jean-Pierre connected with her telepathically and told her the story from the moment he had left the practice room to find Fiona being abducted by a version of himself.

Endelle stared at Fiona and the bright golden glow of her aura. *But what the fuck is she doing? I'm hearing names and events but what does this mean? I don't understand. What the hell is she doing?*

She is speaking his conscience for him, since he does not have one.

So, she's reciting the names of the women who died.

All during her captivity, she cared for them. She was a mother to each of them. She loved them and tried to help them live. Now she carries them with her.

Jean-Pierre expected Endelle to roll her eyes and fold out of there, or worse start yelling at Fiona. Instead, in her truly unpredictable manner, she kicked off her stilettos and moved forward to sink to her knees beside Fiona. She put an arm around the younger woman and supported her. She even bowed her head as if in prayer.

Fiona didn't waver. She merely continued speaking the names of the women, where they were from, and if they left children behind or if their babies died in utero after the first drain of dying blood.

He didn't know exactly when his cheeks grew wet but so they did. And he didn't weep just for those Fiona spoke of but for all who had died since he had served as a Warrior of the Blood.

The Militia Warriors, one by one, sank to their knees as well. But Jean-Pierre remained standing and folded his sword into his hand while the rest honored those who had died. If the enemy chose at this moment to attack, he would be ready, goddammit. He would be ready.

When his phone buzzed, Carla patched Thorne through and he gave him the details in a quiet voice. He told him of Marguerite's role and of the cage and Casimir's most suspicious gift.

Thorne said to call him when the impromptu ceremony ended. Fiona's list was long, so he warned Thorne that it could be another hour, perhaps longer.

More and more Militia Warriors came to the landing area, to watch the golden hue of obsidian flame, to observe the incomprehensible act of the Ruler of Second Earth kneeling and supporting the woman. They knelt themselves as Jean-Pierre stood guard over them all. No place could have held a more sanctified air. In all the experiences of his mortal and ascended lives, no place ever had.

Pride swelled once more as he listened to the strong voice of his woman, as he marveled at what she had endured and survived, as he honored her care of all her fellow slaves. His heart began to expand, truly expand for the first time since his wife's betrayal all those decades and centuries ago.

Could he love this woman, Fiona? Could he love her as he had once loved, with his heart wide open?

He was a man who knew what it was to give everything to a woman and as he watched Fiona, the light pouring from her body, and her voice calling out each name with great dignity, yes, he thought it possible.

If he held back, God help him, it was only because he lived in a world at war, so that even the thought of losing her tore his soul to shreds.

Find the deepest place, live there, then rise.

—*Collected Proverbs,* Beatrice of Fourth

CHAPTER 15

When Fiona finished her litany, her voice almost hoarse from the effort, she rose slowly to her feet. Her knees ached from the hard cement, but she didn't care. Rith had passed out. For a long time, from halfway through her recitation, he had taken to trembling and weeping and calling for his mother, and all she had done was place his sins before him. She'd made him look at the lives he had destroyed—not just the women who died, but all their families who would never know what happened to their wives and mothers, sisters and aunts, even grandmothers.

Yes, he had passed out, rolled his black eyes and disappeared into unconsciousness.

But she felt better than she had since the day she'd been taken from her hometown, from the life she had loved, from her children, her husband, her mother and father, sisters and brothers, her family, her friends, the world she and Terence had built together.

She knew that Casimir had sent Rith with no good intention. His was a devious soul. Some evil was sure to follow. But right now, she could feel grateful to him because this was good, confronting the man who had held her enslaved, and all the others, for so very long.

She blinked a couple of times and became aware that Her Supremeness now stood beside her and that she had been with her from shortly after the beginning. She turned to her. "Thank you."

Endelle's eyes had never looked more ancient or more lined. She nodded a few times, but she didn't say anything.

The air seemed so quiet.

Fiona turned around and was shocked by how many Militia Warriors were now gathered in the large space, all on their knees, some faces wet, some eyes hollow, some chins set and determined, facing the future of war and more war.

She wanted to offer them something. She wanted to thank them for joining with her, because this was an enormous show of kindness and respect for the unseen and usually unacknowledged victims of the war.

She lifted both of her arms—and only then did she realize that she bore the golden glow of the power she carried as obsidian flame.

She prayed to the Creator for the words to say, then began, "Most beloved warriors, who fight against those who have used these our fallen women, may you be strengthened and blessed by this observance today. I wish you Godspeed as you continue to fight and to train and to grow in your own power." As she spoke this last word, she moved through the men to stand in front of Jean-Pierre. He folded his sword away and opened his arms to her.

She walked into them and he held her fast. *"Je t'aime,* Fiona. *Je t'aime."*

Her tears came and she couldn't stop them. Somewhere in the back of her mind, she knew that the Militia Warriors had begun to rise and to head back into the main part of the building, but her weeping continued.

In the end, she stood with Jean-Pierre, held in his arms, weeping until she could weep no more.

Even Rith was gone, taken by Endelle to be delivered to COPASS in Prague where he would stand trial for his war crimes.

She had no doubt that trouble loomed, because Casimir had made himself fully known to everyone.

But for this moment, as the tears finally subsided, she rejoiced that her enemy was at long last brought to earth and imprisoned and that she was still alive. That part of her life was finally over and it seemed well and fitting to her that she should be standing here, with her *breh*'s arms around her, holding her tight.

Thorne stood on the opposite side of the crate from Endelle. Despite the fact that Rith had remained unconscious, apparently from the time Fiona had recited his crimes to him, Endelle had placed a tight preternatural shield around the cage, one more layer that would prevent Rith from folding away.

They were in Prague half a world away, at the landing entrance to the COPASS Eurasian division awaiting clearance, which seemed to Thorne one of the biggest farces in the world. As though the present security, standing guard at the landing platform, didn't recognize who they were.

To the landing security's credit, they were deeply apologetic and avoided meeting Endelle's gaze. Smart warriors.

Endelle, however, was in a strange indefinable mood, maybe because she'd knelt with Fiona for an impromptu soul-bending ceremony, not exactly Endelle's cup of tea.

Thorne wanted to be more sympathetic. He really did. But he hadn't had a drink since his woman got transferred to the Superstition Mountain Seers Fortress, and as far as he knew Endelle hadn't made much of an effort to get her ass over there and make Stannett keep his end of the bargain. Endelle was supposed to have access. So why hadn't she made face-to-face contact with Marguerite yet?

His gaze swept the length of the black-and-white tile

floor, thinking that the landing area of this building could have housed a small jet. Finally; he turned to Endelle, because he had to know. "So, what the fuck's going on over at the Fortress?" Surely she knew something by now.

"Stannett's up to his old tricks."

He tried to meet her gaze but she wouldn't turn her head. She stared straight in front of her. Her jaw worked. He was about to yell at her, to tell her she was being played, but there was something odd about that jaw and the way it shifted from side to side, like she was rolling pea gravel around in her mouth. A muscle close to her ear twitched.

"So we're not talking about this?" he asked.

"No. We're not." Her voice. With resonance.

The words punched his ears good and hard. He tried to read her but empathy was at the bottom of his skill set. Still, of all the ascenders now living on Second Earth, he knew this woman best—and something had happened. Something had changed.

His mind skated to the Superstitions. He'd flown out to the Fortress an hour ago, just doing a flyby. He'd forgotten how locked down it was. The cells housing a hundred Seers were around the perimeter, but the windows were maybe four inches tall, by three feet wide. A cat would have had trouble escaping.

One section on the northeast side was cloaked in mist, no doubt Stannett's creation. Whatever else he might be, he was one powerful sonofabitch.

He'd come away from the recon mission with lead sinking his gut. He'd need dynamite to break in and even if he did, COPASS would have the right to prosecute him—and who knows how that would end up. At the very least, he'd spend some time in prison. At the most, he could be executed for breaching the sanctity of an institution heavily regulated by COPASS law.

And now Endelle was in a state he couldn't read and his woman was incarcerated by a sociopath.

Perfect.

He knew one thing for sure. He wouldn't sit much longer

with his thumb up his ass. If Endelle didn't act, didn't get this travesty figured out, he would blow a hole in the Fortress and get Marguerite the hell out of there.

"You're in a weird fucking mood," Endelle said.

"Right back atcha."

Then Darian Greaves and an entourage of twenty of his uniformed Militia Warriors marched through the door.

Thorne crouched, threw his left arm in front of Endelle, and folded his sword into his right hand.

But *the little peach* smiled and lifted both hands as if in surrender. "I come in peace and with a reward, for it would seem the Ruler of Second Earth has brought to justice one of the most deplorable war criminals of the past century."

The cage rattled. Rith tried to sit up but Greaves merely looked at the man and he settled back down, his eyes once more rolling back in his head.

"We brought your pet back," Endelle said. "Thought you might be missing him."

His large brown eyes opened wider still. "I am sorry, but I don't take your meaning. But never mind that, we have a presentation to make."

As if on cue, another entourage entered, or rather poured into the landing area. Music started, a lively march, Sousa maybe. Lots of trumpets. There must have been at least forty scantily clad beauties, all in full-mount and chosen, no doubt for matching wingspan and color, for the wings were all in shades of cream and white, but average in size. They arrayed themselves in equal numbers on opposite sides of the cage.

Thorne growled. "What the fuck is this, Greaves?"

But Darian moved close to Endelle and two more beauties, not sporting wings this time, moved in front of them both. They carried one of those ridiculously oversized checks.

"I will apologize for keeping you waiting, but it took a few minutes to print your name on the check."

A host of reporters and flashing cameras came next, also like a flood that had been restrained then unleashed, many of them calling out questions that none of them would answer.

"Who caught the monster?"

"Will he stand trial?"

"Madame Endelle, is PETA suing you?"

Thorne wanted to get the hell out of there. He was the only real security for Endelle in this huge farce, though, so he stuck close but folded his sword away. The blade was extremely sharp and the grip, identified only to him, was always a potential danger to anyone who got too close and accidentally made contact.

Endelle, still to Thorne's surprise, didn't seem to be reacting to much of anything. He didn't get it. Usually, she'd be snarking away, snapping at Greaves and never for a second tolerating his present proximity.

"You still smell like lemon furniture polish," Endelle muttered. But she smiled for the cameras.

The cameras flashed away.

Greaves didn't respond to the snipe, but stepped forward and made a rousing speech about the Coming Order, his plans to *assist* the Ruler of Second Earth in improving all of Second Society, blah, blah, blah.

When Greaves was finished, however, he made a sweeping gesture and the entire press corps reversed direction and headed back into the hallway beyond. The winged beauties followed, as well as the two lovelies carrying the oversized check.

Greaves's uniformed warriors took charge of the cage. Without even looking at them, he lifted his arm and vanished.

Just like that, Thorne was once more alone with Endelle, except for the landing area security detail. They squatted near the side wall shooting craps over a pair of tickets to Dark Spectacle.

Endelle turned to him, her jaw still grinding. "I think we've just been had."

"Ya think?" She was being way too calm given what had just happened.

"Well, you don't have public enemy number one show up in a cage with a bow and expect anything else. My guess is that Greaves will have COPASS do a monthlong trial, televised of course, presided over by Greaves himself, staged, filmed, edited. Maybe he'll even throw in a few spectacle-grade flying swans and geese for good measure."

Finally, Thorne took her elbow and squeezed. Hard. He rarely touched Endelle, but she was bugging the shit out of him. "What the hell is the matter with you?"

"With me? Nothing much. Did I tell you Braulio came to call?"

"Who the fuck is Braulio?"

Endelle lifted her arm and vanished.

Thorne folded after her, following her trace, straight to her office. He found her leaning over her desk, her hands planted on the marble.

Now he was fucking worried. "All right. Give. Who the hell is Braulio and why are you acting like this? You're not yourself or haven't you noticed?"

She lifted up and turned toward him. "Everything is changing, heating up. I've got a sick-gut feeling now, Thorne, like things are going to start moving . . . fast . . . and there's nothing I can do about it. I can't stop it. I can't fix it. I can't do a damn thing. I can't even get into the Superstitions and something's going on over there."

He would sift through most of what she'd just said later. For now, he addressed the one thing that possessed his mind. "Give me the word, and I'll use my best hand-blast and take the front door off the Fortress."

"Can you contact Marguerite telepathically?"

"No. And believe me, I've tried."

"Fuck. All right." She looked up at the clock. "Shit. You've got to get out to the Borderlands."

"This is more important."

"No. It's not. Not yet. Let me talk this over with Fiona. She was able to contact Marguerite when no one else could. Marguerite has to be the red variety of obsidian flame.

Thorne shaded his face with his hand. He kept shaking his head, back and forth. "She's been incarcerated for a hundred years. This isn't fair to her." And it wasn't fair to him.

He needed her. He wanted things back the way they were so that he could keep seeing her, keep in control of his demons.

"Then you probably understand what Fiona's feeling. Her life hasn't been any different. She was a blood slave for over a hundred years and now she's saddled with all this *gold* shit."

"Then Jean-Pierre must be in hell."

"Understatement."

He moved to lean his ass against the edge of the desk as well. He was six-five and weighed in at 260. He was one of the most powerful vampires on the face of Second Earth, but this situation made him feel about as powerful as a fucking cockroach.

He drove a hand through his hair and pulled out his *cadroen*. "What the hell am I supposed to do now?"

"Are you sure Marguerite isn't your *breh*? Because you're acting like all these other assholes."

"She isn't fragrant, so no, she's not my *breh*, but we've been lovers for a century and I love her. All that just doesn't go away because you moved her somewhere else."

Endelle's shoulders slumped. "Well, shit, motherfucker."

Yep, that about summed it up.

Jean-Pierre extended his preternatural hearing, listening for Fiona. He smiled. He had her back in his house, and Endelle's mist covered his entire property. He had his woman as safe as he could make her. And . . . she had kept herself safe as well without his help.

She hummed while she was in the shower, and the sound was *très jolie*.

He stood in his kitchen preparing a simple meal for her for this early part of the evening. He would grill chicken over mesquite wood chips later, but for now, *oui*, something simple.

He had taken her to Alison's for the afternoon then had left her there so that he could purchase a gift for her, something he hoped would please her very much. He did not mean it to be serious at all. He needed to keep their relationship very light, simple, like the food they would eat.

If he could learn to manage things between them, perhaps the next few days or weeks would show them both how to move forward without being so enmeshed in the *brehhedden,* without feeling the need to complete it. Perhaps the sensations would pass and he could go back to making war, and she could serve Endelle in the capacity of obsidian flame without needing his constant protection as a Guardian of Ascension.

This was what he wanted, to keep everything simple so that he could continue to make war. Perhaps he would even return to the Blood and Bite and to all the women he once made love to night after night. *Oui,* now it began to seem as though each of their lives could return to some sort of normalcy.

He rinsed a container of strawberries in a stainless-steel colander. He scooped the little leaves off some and sliced them. Other smaller strawberries he cut in half, while still others he left whole. The largest strawberry, the size of a small fist, he left whole as well.

He extended his hearing and this time heard the blow dryer and more humming. He listened a little harder and realized she was humming *"La Vie en Rose."*

He put a hand to his chest. He wished to God that he did not like this woman so very much, that he did not love her.

He believed in many kinds of love. His for Fiona he decided was a soft version of passionate love, very tender. He thought it beautiful in its way and so he had said, *Je t'aime.*

But tonight, he would not speak of love. Words were not necessary for what he planned for Fiona, the gift he had purchased for her, and the champagne he would pour for her.

Tonight was for celebration because the great evil known as Rith Do'onwa had been caged and taken to COPASS in Prague Two, where he would be tried at the International Court for his crimes against humanity. Thorne had told him of the farce at the landing area, that Greaves had arranged a disgusting ceremony for the supposed capture of Rith, so it was a very questionable success. Marcus had even texted that he'd seen the footage on the evening news. Such complete bullshit.

Or as the Americans liked to say, *Whatever.*

In March, in high country, the air was cool enough so that he had a fire crackling on the hearth. But he also left the window open to let the moist creek air rise into the living room. The couch was a soft brown leather, and over the lounge portion, he had draped something called a throw, knitted of every color of the rainbow with long fringe. He had put it there for several reasons.

He looked at the throw and one image came to him, full of prescience, so strong that he had to put down the sharp paring knife and plant his hands on the counter to catch his breath. How beautiful Fiona would look on that throw, so close to the fire, the shifting light moving over her golden skin and chestnut hair, catching perhaps the silver-blue of her eyes.

Her scent drifted toward him and he closed his eyes and drank in the light smell of the *patisserie.*

He was not surprised when she called out to him, "Something *particular* on your mind, Warrior?"

His chest swelled. He loved her melodic voice, in the lower timbres. He loved that she referred so quickly to the scent he must be giving off. He loved that she called him *Warrior.*

He rinsed his fingers and dried them on the towel he had sitting on the sink.

He rounded the striated beige granite island and crossed to her. She stood very still, not far from the fireplace, her eyes wide, her lips parted as she took in his hair caught loosely behind, many of the strands now in disarray and curling around his face. Her gaze drifted lower, taking in his bare chest, his abs.

"You're wearing jeans," she said, her voice almost a whisper. "It's such a good look for you."

He rounded the lounge part of the couch and took her hand. He drew her toward the knitted throw. "Please, sit down.

I have prepared a meal for you, not too heavy. I have brought you champagne as well because I know you enjoy it."

Her eyes lit up as she sat on the throw and stretched her legs out. "Yes, I do."

He nodded several times. Her chestnut hair wasn't completely dry, but even wet, just as he suspected, the light from the fire caught the red and gold glints. *"Bon,"* he murmured, but he couldn't seem to let go of her hand.

She wore jeans as well and a red silk halter, cut low, which showed beautiful cleavage. Almost, he could not move.

Then he thought of the strawberries and champagne and he headed back to the kitchen, even though his mind felt full of clouds. He could hardly think. He could only draw air into his nose and savor her sweet dangerous scent.

Fiona tracked Jean-Pierre's movements like a woman who hadn't eaten for days and was now presented with a nine-course meal. She felt starved, but not for food. She hadn't wanted to release his hand and felt desolate when he let go and moved quickly back to the kitchen.

She wanted to tell him to forget about the food and stretch out beside her so that she could put her hands on his thick, muscled pecs, then put her lips in the same places, maybe spend the next hour just exploring what was so beautifully built because her man was a warrior.

He moved to the fridge and for the next minute or so wrestled oh-so-carefully with the bottle of champagne. He poured the sparkling wine into a pair of fluted goblets, thin glass, very simple—fitting, she thought, for his glass-and-wood house.

He brought the glasses with him, holding each by the stem. He rounded the lounge so that as he sat down beside her, his knees faced the fire. He handed her the glass and she held it up.

He raised his glass to her. "To my beautiful Fiona, who brought Rith to justice. But more than that, who laid his sins so eloquently at his feet. You were magnificent today."

He tapped her glass.

She sipped and watched the rim of his glass touch his perfect lips, the lower full portion and the upper that formed such exquisite peaks. He held her gaze as he drank.

When he drew the glass away, he leaned over her and planted his free hand on the couch to his left. He kissed her, his lips wet from the champagne. She kissed him back, reaching up. He dipped down again and pushed his tongue into her mouth. She moaned because it always took so little.

But he withdrew and smiled down at her. He still held his champagne glass in his right hand. "Let me feed you," he said, his eyes glittering in the firelight.

"Yes, you should definitely feed me."

He chuckled, kissed her once more, then rose from the lounge. He turned and headed back to the kitchen, but slow enough that she had a wonderful view of his back rippling as he walked, the broad expanse of shoulders tapering in beautiful lines to his lean waist, his long hair hanging down the center and barely held in place by a loose piece of light green brocade.

Then there was the sight of his buttocks moving beneath the jeans. She knew what he looked like without anything on and it was so not difficult to picture him out of his jeans. Besides, if he ran true to form, he'd probably gone commando. In some ways Jean-Pierre, with all his sophisticated French accent and speech patterns, was remarkably basic and down to earth, hence the house made by his hands, that he was barefoot, and that he probably wore nothing under his jeans.

She sipped her champagne and loved that for just this moment, the wine relaxed her, let her breathe. That Rith was in custody in Prague sent her spirits flying toward the ceiling. Despite the abduction, this was one of the best days of her life.

When he returned to her, he placed a platter on the end table by the lounge. She leaned to look at the platter and stared at the prettiest arrangement of . . . strawberries.

He had prepared her a meal of champagne and strawberries.

She felt dizzy, as though her body was making sense of this before her mind could articulate the meaning.

"I found these in an organic roadside stand not far from Medichi's villa. I was hoping to find some that were very ripe, sweet, and juicy, but you must judge for yourself."

He sat down as he had before but this time he scrutinized the platter and picked up a small strawberry, one free of the leaves.

He turned to her and held the strawberry for her to see. "May I feed you, Fiona? Will you permit me this intimacy?"

She met his gaze and for just this moment, time seemed to stop. As she looked into the kindest eyes she had ever known in her life, she realized that she loved Jean-Pierre. She really loved him, who he was, all his many kindnesses toward her, that with his smiles and charm he eased her heart, that he asked for permission when in many ways it wasn't necessary. She loved him.

There could be no other explanation for the warmth that moved through her, flowing in a beautiful circle around and around her heart. She loved that he asked permission and that even now he waited for her answer.

"I would like nothing more than for you to feed me." She parted her lips. He moved in slowly and as the strawberry touched her lips, he didn't just let it hang there but he held it while she took a bite.

The strawberry was just as he had described, succulent and sweet. She moaned as she chewed so he smiled, showing her all those big teeth and that wonderful smile. She lifted her arm and put her hand low on his shoulder. She leaned into him and kissed him on his left nipple, just a kiss.

An answering swell of his exotic male-and-coffee scent returned to her. She loved that they exchanged scents, that the *breh-hedden* had given her this clue to his desire and response to her actions.

"More?" he asked.

She nodded. Definitely more. He held the rest of the berry for her to take in her mouth. She chewed, savored, and swallowed.

"Jean-Pierre, I must ask you something very important."

"Anything, *chérie*," and again he smiled as though he knew she was being absurd and not at all serious.

She traced a series of circles on his jeans just above his knee. "Wouldn't you be much more comfortable without these?"

"I must ponder this idea." He paused. "I think my answer must be that I would only be comfortable if you were undressed in the exact same manner."

She released a sigh and sank back a little more into the leather cushions. "I think that would only be fair."

"And if nothing more, this should be *fair* tonight."

"Very mutual, yes." She leaned forward and unbuttoned the single button that held the shimmery halter top together in the back. Another button at the neck and the silky fabric slid down her front to rest on the swell of her breasts. She didn't try to move it herself since Jean-Pierre's gaze had fallen to the rumpled line of the red silk. He now leaned down to her, down and down until his lips brushed her breasts just above the fabric and in a wet line across her chest.

Your beautiful scent is flooding my nostrils, Fiona. So beautiful.

She loved telepathy, that while his lips were otherwise engaged, he could share his thoughts with her. She arched her back and with her left hand tugged at the fabric, lower and lower. His lips followed until he suckled the nipple of her right breast. Then, to be fair, he moved to the left. Yes, tonight would be fair, very fair.

She wanted him to continue but he drew back.

"You have exquisite breasts. I have been meaning to say that to you, beautiful large nipples, full round areolas." He slid his hand beneath her right breast. "And all this weight. This is the meal that will satisfy me tonight." Once more he dipped low and again suckled.

She closed her eyes and savored the feel of his mouth working her breasts, and working her up, so that again her back arched and she leaned into him, pressing her breast harder into his mouth.

But once more he drew back and held her breast in a light touch. He lifted his eyes to her and pulled back his lips just a little. His fangs emerged.

She gasped. Low, so very low, her muscles tightened in a series of hard tugs that almost brought her. "Yes," she whispered. "Please."

Once more he lowered his head and she closed her eyes. He struck and released the potion. There was nothing like it on Mortal Earth. This was one of the surest ways she knew she had entered the world of the vampire: that he could pierce her skin and release a potion into her. The pleasure seeped and burned and felt wonderful.

"Open your eyes, *chérie*."

She found it difficult. Already she felt lethargic and all he'd done was kiss, suckle, and strike with his fangs. Then she saw the strawberry, this one cut in half.

"I'm hungry," he said. Then he lowered the berry to her nipple. The strawberry was cold and the sensation drew more little ripples down deep inside her. He rubbed the strawberry well over her nipple then outward to let the juice cover her.

Then he put the strawberry to her lips. He pushed it inside.

She struggled to draw air as he lowered his head and licked at her breast in long sweeps of his soft wet tongue working from an outer perimeter to an inside one until once more he suckled.

The combination of the potion now teasing the inside of her breast, and his tongue and mouth stimulating the outside, bowed her back once more. She cried out, "I'm close."

He slid his hand between her legs, cupped her and worked her in several brisk, drawing movements so that the orgasm was simply *there*. She released a long cry and he kept working her, kept suckling her nipple, and the potion now had her entire breast on fire. He brought her again and again.

She'd eaten two strawberries, sipped her champagne three times, and the man had made her come. She had the truly unholy thought that for these skills alone, she ought to complete the *breh-hedden* with him.

She chuckled as his hand slowed and he released her breast from his mouth.

"That was divine," she said.

"I want your pants off . . . now."

"But you're still wearing your pants. This isn't fair." She smiled.

He just growled at her and dipped his chin.

She chuckled.

She thought he would simply fold her jeans off, but instead he did this part the old-fashioned way: button, zipper, and alternate tugs at her hips. He leaned down at the same time and kissed his way across her lower abdomen with each tug, from hip to hip.

I'm getting very hungry, he sent.

Then you should definitely have something to eat.

I wish to eat until I am completely satisfied.

But will the strawberries be enough? she teased.

He tugged her pants down and kissed the uppermost line of her pubic hair, then kept tugging. *You will soon see just how much the strawberries will sustain me.*

Certain images slipped through her mind. Did he mean? Could he possibly mean?

Her hips bucked at the thought and he chuckled as he drew her pants down her buttocks and thighs. He stood up and pulled them off the rest of the way. He looked down at her then looked inside the jeans. "You went commando?" he asked.

"I thought it only fair."

His smile was slow this time. He started to sit down, but she lifted a hand. "No. You promised and now I'd like you to do it slow. Let me watch." For good measure, she sent, *You have the most amazing body.*

His smile was crooked this time as he unbuttoned then slowly unzipped. Yep, no sign of briefs, just his skin and then his thick animal hair that always made her sigh. He was fully erect, which meant he had to move the jeans around to get them down and off.

She enjoyed the show. He was big; when he was on his

back, his erect cock reached his navel. Right now he held it in his hand, a very loose support. She looked up at him and saw that he was waiting for her to make the next call.

This time she smiled. "I'd like one of the strawberry halves, please."

He looked at the plate and picked up one for her. She held out her hand.

"Come closer," she said. "Very close. Put your knee on the lounge and lean your hips as close to me as you can."

He was very obedient. She rubbed the strawberry over the tip of his cock and then the crown. Afterward, she put the strawberry to her lips and with her tongue pulled it into her mouth.

He groaned.

"Now feed me," she said. "And I don't mean another strawberry."

He braced his hands on the back of the sofa and moved into her, his hips flexing as she parted her lips. He pushed himself into her mouth then pulled back. She put her arms and hands on the back of the couch. He continued to push then withdraw. She sucked both ways but fixed her gaze on his eyes as he looked down at her.

Everyone has secrets,
Especially those who have passed from this world.

—*Collected Proverbs,* Beatrice of Fourth

CHAPTER 16

What was it about the mouth of a woman that so pleased a man, to have his cock thrusting in and out, to feel the pull of her suckles, to watch her cheeks flex, to see the cock disappear then reappear.

He was moved by her willingness, but he had her in a cage of his body and he was worried. *Do you feel trapped?*

No, she responded.

Good.

He threaded his fingers through hers and moved in a little closer so that she could take him deeper.

She drew her hands out of his and he pulled away, fearing that he had pushed too hard, but she grabbed his buttocks and dug her nails in then brought him toward her. He hissed.

Mon Dieu.

That she savored him and wanted him and dug her nails into his flesh—it was too much suddenly. *You must stop,* he sent.

She released the sucking motion but still held him within her mouth. *I love you here,* she sent.

He did not move. He could not, otherwise he would spill into her and he did not want this night to move so fast.

But he took his hands and drifted them down the sides of her head to her neck, then touched her cheeks with the backs of his fingers. *I love that you take me in your mouth.*

Slowly, he began to draw back. He was stiff and so close. She seemed to understand. When he was fully out, she smiled. "You almost came."

He nodded. "Too soon, *chérie.*"

She relaxed back into the cushions and sighed. "I'm so happy right now. Thank you for this, for the strawberries and the champagne. I love you for that."

But the moment the words left her mouth, a blush climbed her cheeks and her gaze fell away, as though embarrassed she had spoken the words. Did she love him? Did she love him as he loved her, in that tender way?

"I don't want to make too much of this," she added, her gaze again shifting to look up at him.

He sat down beside her. "It is for the best to keep everything very simple, but, Fiona, I do love you. I cannot say how deeply, but I care so much about you. I wish you to know that."

She tilted her head. "I feel the same way. You are very dear to me. I truly wish that our situation was different, that there wasn't a war or dimensional worlds or all this horror."

He petted her head again. "So tell me, how is the potion in your breast?"

"A wonderful fire."

"Do you wish for more?"

"All that you can give me."

"*Bon.* But, I need you in a different position." He held his hand down to her, she took it, and in an easy motion he lifted her to her feet. He meant to lay her out on the couch in a different way, but the moment she stood next to him, he opened his arms and she pressed herself against him, her arms around his waist. She was just tall enough that the top of her head came to his chin.

She fit him. That is what he thought. She fit him so perfectly.

After a moment, he released her but only enough so that he could slip an arm behind her knees, lift her up, then move to settle her low on the lounge.

I am so hungry, Fiona.

You must eat, then.

Oui.

He shifted to the end of the lounge and moved between her legs. A soft whimper left her throat and he smiled. She had lifted up to support herself on her elbows. He slid his arms beneath her legs then, still holding her gaze, he kissed her low, and licked between her folds.

She threw her head back.

He did not wait, but with his fangs struck her at the top of her clitoris and released a potion. He had to hold her down with his arm because her body reacted with a long writhing wave that bowed her back. She cried out, contorting. "Oh, God. So good. So good." Her voice was a series of breathy punches.

He smiled and relaxed as he withdrew his fangs.

She grunted low in her throat. He looked up at her. Her face was twisted as if in pain, but he knew it was not pain she felt. He teased her with the tip of his tongue, flicking over every sensitive part of her until her hips pushed hard against his arm over and over.

He removed his arms from beneath her legs. He needed his hands free for what he wanted to do next.

He folded one of the large strawberries into his hand. "Fiona," he called to her softly. "I am so hungry."

She looked down at him wild-eyed, and when he held the strawberry up she gave a little cry. He dipped low and at her opening he swirled the whole fruit, swirled and pushed, just a little. He loved the cries she made.

He removed the strawberry. *Look at me,* he commanded.

Again, her gaze was panicky. He held the strawberry in

his left hand high enough that she could see it. She was breathing hard and so very close. At the same time, he carefully slipped two fingers inside her and began to work her body, in and out. More whimpers.

He then he put his mouth around the strawberry. She cried out and at the same time he shifted to work her with his fingers.

When he bit the strawberry, the juice flowing down his chin, as he held her gaze and drove into her with his fingers, she came screaming for him, writhing as he pistoned his hand and brought her. The broken fruit he rubbed on her stomach so that she came and came and came, her hands on his hands, her fingers exploring his mouth, her body riding the waves of ecstasy, on and on, until finally she began to settle.

But her body jerked and twitched. She was breathing hard yet her face looked relaxed, her lips curved in a satisfied smile. It took him several mental gyrations, but he brought a damp washcloth into his hands and wiped all the juice off her stomach and anywhere else.

"I have a gift for you," he said.

Her eyes were closed and her hands resting at her sides as she laughed and said, "You just gave me a gift. Several in fact."

But he rose up. He crossed to the kitchen and washed all the sweet juices, hers and the strawberry, from his hands and his lips. He left her lying there, sprawled and at ease. From the table in the entry, across from the piano, he retrieved what he hoped would give her a different kind of pleasure.

The gold box was very light.

But when he returned she had shifted position. She lay on her side facing the fire so that her body was outlined in the soft flickering light. He loved this view of a woman, with the dip of her waist accentuating the swell of her hip. She was beautiful from behind and he loved taking her in that position, but for what he had in mind next, he doubted he would have the opportunity. In fact, he hoped he did not, but this would be up to Fiona.

He moved to kneel in front of her. She looked so beautiful in the soft light, her lips swollen, her eyes lethargic. She put her hand on his face and rubbed her thumb over his lower lip. Her gaze fell to the square box.

"You didn't have to get me anything."

"Oh, but I did, for I believe you asked for this most specifically. It would have been very thoughtless of me not to have bought you such a gift."

Her brows rose. She lifted up on her elbow and as he placed the box in front of her, she pulled the bow with one hand. He helped since he didn't want her to sit up. He didn't want his view of her waist and hips, of her beautiful naked breasts, disturbed by anything.

She lifted the lid and her brows rose. She drew a long narrow scarf from the box. "Oh, Jean-Pierre," she whispered, her eyes wide. She laid the scarf over her waist, then pulled out the second one. She let this elegant piece of silk join the other. She pulled out a third and shuddered when she withdrew a fourth.

She met his gaze, her lips parted. A heavy wave of buttery croissant almost pushed him flat on his back.

"I love my gift," she said, sliding her arm up around his neck. She drew him close and kissed him. Against his lips, she said, "Where do you want to do this, *chéri*?"

"I will fold you to the room." Once more, he took her hand and lifted her to her feet.

He gathered up three of the scarves. With Fiona holding the fourth, he folded them to a bedroom she would not have seen before, a guest room in black toile and white.

The bed had a black wrought-iron frame, at both the head and the foot. She stepped away from him and scrutinized the bed. She took the scarves in hand and looked up at him. "I want you on your back, arms and legs spread wide."

Where was all this boldness coming from?

Fiona marveled that she was this person who could demand of her lover something so . . . sensual. But he smiled and with a wave of his hand managed to dispense with the bedding except for the bottom sheet, which was black.

She shivered as this naked man rolled into position, everything on display, his hair now loose about his shoulders, his cock still partially erect.

She stood at the side of the bed, trembling but not with fear. She clutched the long silky swaths as Jean-Pierre threw his arms wide and smiled at her.

She had to stop staring but he was a thing of beauty, part vampire, part man, part muscled animal, and he was all hers, to do with as she willed.

She forced herself to move to the ankle nearest her. She tied one end of the scarf up, then hooked the other around the tallest iron post at the foot of the bed.

"Is this where you have always wanted me, *chérie*?"

His voice weakened her fingers but she formed the knot anyway. He had once told her to speak the truth, so she did. "I have always wanted you like this." She met his gaze, being bold with him, because she knew he would like it, he would approve.

She approved. She liked this woman she had become. She stroked his ankle and ran her fingers up his leg. She loved the feel of his hair. "In my fantasies, yes, you're tied up and I do whatever pleases me."

His jaw quivered as he groaned and a heavy roll of his coffee male scent nearly knocked her backward a few feet. As it was, she caught the iron post, steadied herself, then took the remaining scarves to the head of the bed. She leaned over and wrapped the second scarf around his left wrist. She secured him to the upper rail, but left him enough room to bend at the elbow and still rest his shoulders and arms on the bed.

She completed the chore and her body wept for him. Whatever the fantasy had been, this was so much more, because he was flesh and blood and real.

She crawled onto the bed. He was hers to feast upon and so she feasted.

She used her hands first, feeling every muscle, every rise and dip of his body, over his arms, his shoulders, his chest and lower, to caress what was so very male, to draw her hands down his heavily corded thighs, his calves, his feet.

The entire time he was aroused, and at times he trembled and made strange grunt-like sounds. She smiled and then she applied her tongue and explored once more. She took her time, sucking at certain parts, licking the rest, until he wept from the tip of his cock and pulled on the scarves.

But there was one thing she had always wanted to do, a very small thing, from the first time he had kissed her.

She put her fingers in his lips and stroked back and forth. His tongue made an appearance but she forbade him. "I want to know your lips. I love these lips." She leaned down and placed very small kisses on his lower lip, the full sensual part, beginning at one side and progressing to the opposite.

Then she worked on the upper lip, digging her tongue into the points and using just the tip to outline.

When he was bowing off the bed and crying his frustration in deep groans, only then did she kiss him. She kissed him and kissed him, driving her tongue into his mouth over and over. She still held his face, her fingers close to his mouth. She let her fingers replace her tongue and her lips.

She drew back and looked at him as she worked two of her fingers in and out of his mouth. His eyes had a frantic, wild look and her body wept a little more. The potion still worked over her breasts and tightened her body very low, where more potion tingled. She was very close to another climax, just stroking his mouth.

He was close as well.

Then she knew exactly what she wanted to do.

"You'll need to be brave," she whispered.

His eyes flared, but she continued to thrust her fingers into his mouth. *Why,* chérie*?*

"Because I need you to do something to me, but you'll be afraid to do it."

What, chérie*? I could not hurt you, if that is what you're asking, but* mon Dieu, *your fingers in my mouth. I am so close. Tell me what you desire.*

"When I tell you, I want you to break free of the scarves and take me, on my back, but don't enthrall me. Do you understand? I want to feel you, all of you, as I was meant to feel you. Do you understand?"

He nodded.

"But not until I tell you."

He nodded again.

She removed her fingers and at the same time, she shifted her hips to position herself above his cock.

He groaned as she eased down on him, as she took him into her very wet opening. She cried out, arching her back, because he felt so good and she was so ready. The potion, very low, still teased all her nerve endings and nearly brought her.

She put her hands on his shoulders. She met his gaze, his wild intent gaze, and she cried, "Do it. Now."

The illusion that he was truly bound shattered instantly, as all four scarves tore in a blur of movement. The bed shook, creating a little earthquake. She was airborne but still connected as he used whatever this particular preternatural power was and flipped her onto her back.

Fiona was a new person. She felt it now, the new power she possessed. Maybe it was because Rith had been carted away, or maybe because she had survived an abduction by an Upper ascender, but whatever the case, as Jean-Pierre moved over her, his body pressed to her, holding her down, pinning her, she felt only a profound sense of release and even accomplishment.

"Stretch out over me. Lay yourself down on top of me."

He didn't argue. He simply eased down until the full weight of him was on her chest. It was heaven.

She couldn't remember, even a little, why this had ever bothered her. She felt his shins rubbing against hers, his heavy muscled thighs pressed to her, his hips, his stomach, the thick pecs that always made her lips tingle with promise.

"You're heavy on me," she said, but she smiled and he gave her an answering grin.

He even took her hands in his and threaded his fingers

through her fingers then held her arms far out to the sides so that his weight grew.

But instead of feeling the whirling snakes in the pit of her stomach, she felt an airiness in her chest, a warmth within, a glow that brought a wonderful sigh flowing out of her.

Then he kissed her and captured her breath and possessed her mouth. Her hips responded, pushing against him. He moved inside her, drew back, and thrust hard.

She groaned but there was just one more thing. *Take my blood,* she whispered through his mind.

A heavy groan rumbled in his throat and before she had taken a breath, he had pierced her neck and was sucking. *I won't last,* came as a cry through her head.

But already the orgasm swelled within her so that she spoke into his ear. "Come for me, Jean-Pierre. Come with me. Come now."

He drew back from her throat and as pleasure streaked through her body, as she gripped him deep, holding all that was so strong, so powerful, so forceful, she watched him rise up off her and cry out as he came.

"Look at me," she said.

He brought his gaze to her and when that happened, it was as though all the sensation tripled and a second orgasm barreled down on her. He became fierce in his movements, thrusting hard and bringing her a second time and a third, writhing over her.

He was hard again. Oh, God.

"Your blood," he murmured. "Like a fire in me." He drove her once more, looking into her eyes and bringing her so that she rose up and surrounded him with her arms and pulled him down to her to once more press her into the bed, a heavy weight, anchoring her, shielding her, caring for her.

Only then did the sensations start to drift away, as he lay on top of her, his body slack now, breathing hard, his work done.

"Chérie," he murmured, kissing her shoulder.

"Mon amour," she responded. His mouth was on her

shoulder and she felt him smile. Then his ribs rose and fell in a breath and a sigh.

He rose up just a little and looked at her neck. "Do you want me to heal your throat?"

She shook her head. "Not yet. Maybe later. I want to enjoy it for a while."

"Bon." He lay back down on her.

She marveled again that she no longer felt the oppressive fear of being trapped. She surrounded him with her arms and fell into a doze.

She dreamed of flying high above the White Tanks. The day was clear and sunny, very dry, of course. The lake beneath was a glittering diamond and she felt such peace.

But from the east storm clouds, black and furious, rolled over the tops of the White Tank Mountains and descended toward her at a perilous rate. She was suddenly engulfed and thrown down into the lake, below the surface of the waters. She struggled to swim, to rise to the surface, but she was bound and each movement made her bonds even tighter.

Words flowed through her mind: *Find the deepest place, live there, then rise.*

She jerked awake, and the memory of the waters and storm flowed away from her. *Find the deepest place and rise.*

Jean-Pierre's arm covered her. He lay on his side facing her, his long hair hiding the lower half of his face. Part of his lower lip was visible. She wanted to kiss it, but what else was new?

She sat up and took a few deep breaths. Dreams were an important part of ascended life. She knew that. But what did it mean that a storm would come from the east and try to drown her?

She wasn't a fan of symbolism. She preferred things to be open and straightforward. And what could it possibly mean to find the deepest place and rise? The deepest place of what? The bottom of White Lake?

That made no sense at all.

"What is it, *chérie*? I can hear your thoughts."

"You can hear my thoughts in your head?"

He laughed and turned over on his back. "*Non.* It was just an expression. You are thinking very hard."

"I had a dream about White Lake."

A pause. "I am not surprised. White Lake is a place of great power, and yours are emerging."

"I was drowning."

At that, he lifted up on his elbow. "Drowning, *chérie*?"

"Sort of. I was beneath the waters and drowning. Do you think it's just a leftover from my captivity?" She turned to look at him. She stretched her preternatural vision and there he was, sitting in a glow of light. So gorgeous. Her heart hurt, as it seemed to be doing a lot lately, just looking at him.

He opened his left arm wide. "Come to me."

It was the easiest, most natural thing in the world to fall into that arm and let him pull her against his big warm body. They were still in the same bed, in the toile bedroom, beneath a sheet and cuddled together. "Jean-Pierre, would you tell me something?"

"Anything, *chérie*?"

"What happened all those years ago that such a good kind man, such a noble man didn't marry again? I've met a lot of fine women since I've been here on Second Earth, several who would have made you a good wife, a warrior's wife. For you to have remained unattached all these decades, I know something went wrong for you."

"It was a long time ago." His arm was no longer lax around her. The muscles rippled as he flexed and tried to relax only to flex again.

She had touched a nerve, but that was not always a bad thing. "Truth, Jean-Pierre, remember? You wanted me to speak the truth."

"La vérité," he murmured.

"Yes, the truth."

Jean-Pierre tried to still the rising beat of his heart. He tried to take a deep breath, but could not. Fiona had awakened from a dream, perhaps even a nightmare, and now wished him to speak of the unspeakable, the unforgivable. To his surprise, the words flowed from him.

"She betrayed me, my wife. I . . . loved her so very much." Fiona lay very still beside him, only her fingers moving as she plucked at the sheet over his chest.

"What was her name?"

"Isabelle. Very pretty. She was beautiful in a flirtatious way, a pointed chin and such dancing eyes that crinkled almost shut when she laughed. She laughed a lot. She could flirt with her fan better than any woman I knew. And such flirting, so long ago, was an art."

"She was enchanting."

A faint chuckle left his throat. "*Oui,* she was enchanting. But not with me. I mean I was enchanted but she always spoke the truth to me. Hard words to hear at times. I believe she corrected a great many of my flaws in the years we were married. I was lazy and she pushed me. I grew more disciplined. I was sometimes thoughtless in my speech, in my words—"

At that, Fiona tilted her head up to look at him. "I would find that very hard to believe. You are always so careful around me and with me. I think it one of your finest qualities."

He chuckled again, but gave her a squeeze. "You would have to thank Isabelle for that. I sometimes said the most foolish things, hurtful words. No, she made of me a better man. I am convinced of that."

He didn't want to say more, so he remained silent.

"Were you together long?"

"Eleven years. We married very young by today's standards."

Again she twisted to look up at him. "How old were you?"

"I was nineteen and terribly in love."

"How old was she?"

"Seventeen."

"Did you have any children?"

"Our second greatest failure that we did not."

She went back to plucking at the sheet. He could feel the

question coming but he wished with all his heart she would not ask it. But perhaps it was necessary. She would need to understand him better. So he waited.

"What was your greatest failure, Jean-Pierre?"

He sighed before he could speak. "That for some reason our love was not strong enough to prevail against the winds of the revolution." He took a deep breath and spoke the terrible words, "She betrayed me to the devil Robespierre. She signed documents indicating that I had acted against the will of the people. She sent me to the guillotine."

When she remained silent, but still plucking, as though her fingers reflected the workings of her mind, he said, "She was not herself the entire month before she did this thing. I would say she was hysterical. I believe now that she knew what she would do, and during that time she wrestled with her conscience. I will give her at least that much, that she seemed to suffer before she betrayed me. I often wondered if she heard rumors of one of the condemned disappearing before the blade could complete its work."

The plucking fingers pulled harder. He caught her hand and stilled it. "Say what it is you do not want to say."

This time she pulled back to recline her head on his arm so that she could look at him. He pulled back as well; otherwise they would be almost nose-to-nose.

"What if . . . what if she had a reason for what she did?"

"Do you think I have not thought of that?"

"Maybe she was protecting other members of her family? Maybe her only choice was her life or yours?"

"I would never make such a choice against her."

She put a hand on his face. He saw her eyes well with tears. "I'll tell you what I know. If Isabelle knew you as I know you then she could never have betrayed you without a profound reason. Something enormous must have been at stake. I'm convinced of it. Otherwise it makes no sense to me."

"Of course you would speak with such grace. Of course. But I will never know. How can I? She did not ascend."

"Do you know for certain?"

"I have visited her grave in a small church in Sussex, in

the south of Britain. She emigrated the same night that I went to my death." He sounded bitter. He supposed that he was.

"How did you know she'd done even that much? Did you follow her?"

"*Oui.* That first week. I kept at a distance. I watched her board the small ship to cross the channel. That was all I needed to see."

"How did you know she died? Or when or even where she lived?"

"She kept her married name, my name, Isabelle Robillard. A few decades ago I went through the death certificates in Britain and found her in a place called Rottingdean in the south of England."

"Then she didn't remarry?"

"No, she lived less than a year." He could hardly bear to think of it, that she had sent him to his death and he had lived all these decades, yet she had died but a few months later in a land not her own. He wanted to think of it as a form of justice. Instead, it was only pathetic. And very sad.

He felt Fiona's finger on the side of his face. It was wet.

Fuck. He had not meant to weep but he so rarely spoke of her, of his beautiful vivacious wife, whom he had loved with all of his heart, so passionately. She was his first love and should have been his last in every good sense.

Fiona inched toward him and kissed his cheek all the way up to the corner of his eye. He turned into her and kissed her on the mouth, hard.

She opened for him, a flower blossoming so that he could penetrate her mouth. The faint whimpers, and that she spoke his name so sweetly within his mind, a very soft *Jean-Pierre, Jean-Pierre,* gave him permission to do what was in his heart to do.

He pushed her onto her back and took her, perhaps not as gently as he should have, but she clung to him, and shed her beautiful croissant scent, and cried into his hair, and dug her nails into the flesh of his ass.

What he knew for certain, as he spent himself inside her

yet again, was that his heart reached for her much too often. He needed to be more careful, to restrain himself, but with her lovely cries and her sweet kisses and the tenderness in her eyes when she held his face as he came, *mon Dieu,* what was he supposed to do?

The use of the word obsidian, *in the mythical triad known as obsidian flame, has a long history. Ultimately, the word became synonymous with truth, as in cutting to the truth, or bearing the weight of truth. The concept in my opinion is more poetic than scientific.*

—*Treatise on Ascension,* by Philippe Reynard

CHAPTER 17

The following morning, Fiona sat across from Seriffe, in his office. He leaned forward in his chair, elbows on the desk, head in his hands. In the five months she had been on Second Earth, for most of that time living in his home, she had never seen him this distraught, this sad.

"I knew Greg," he said. "Carolyn is best friends with his wife and now that poor woman is left to raise her kids without their father. Shit. I brought him on board, you know. Maybe two decades ago. He was a good fighter, the best of men, honorable, hardworking. Jesus, I can't believe he's gone. He was fucking careful in the field."

Jean-Pierre stood off to the side, his arms folded over his chest, sentinel-like. Fiona glanced up at him. His gaze was solemn, his nostrils flaring. His jaw shifted a couple of times, back and forth.

She turned her attention back to Seriffe. She had no words for him. What could be said? The funeral would be held in a couple of days, a weekly ritual now. Too many Militia Warrior deaths. The Grand Canyon battle, just a few months ago, had taken the lives of over a thousand Militia Warriors, many of them based in Phoenix. But a good number of them had been flown in from around the world.

Greaves had mounted a major attack, but his army, composed as it was of both a militia contingent as well as hundreds of death vampires, had been a formidable opposing force.

Only the appearance of Warrior Medichi and his *breh,* Parisa, as they took on their finest combined quality of *royle* wings, had ended the battle. For whatever mystical reason, the phenomenon of *royle* wings had brought an end to the fighting, as though the presence of this preternatural power forbade violence.

She hadn't been there, but Jean-Pierre had. He'd described it as a soft wind so full of peace that every sword had fallen from the hand metaphorically. So many lives had been saved because of Antony and Parisa, which was why Endelle had sent them on their ambassadorial tour, to display this power to all her allied High Administrators as a reason to remain aligned with her.

The war was a mess and now here she was, another kind of phenomenon, the purpose of which she still didn't really understand. Endelle had seemed excited enough initially, but what good was obsidian flame in this situation? How could she possibly keep more Militia Warriors from getting killed?

Though she was reluctant to admit it, she couldn't. Whatever obsidian flame was, the purpose was not like *royle* wings. She didn't have the kind of power that could stop violence, put an end to a battle, halt a war.

So what could she do?

Seriffe sat back in his chair. He looked wounded as he dragged a few breaths into his lungs. Finally, he rose from his chair, like rising from a bed of ashes. He gathered himself, pulling in his grief, straightening his shoulders, setting his chin, the warrior that he was.

"You would leave this job if you could," Jean-Pierre said.

Fiona shot a glance to him as Seriffe said, "I'll confess that was exactly what I was thinking, but how could you tell?"

Jean-Pierre shook his head. "I am not sure, but it was not a difficult guess."

"Yes, but I haven't felt this way before today. For some reason, Greg's death had an impact. I need things to change. If his death has affected my morale, then there's a good chance that effect is moving through the ranks. Sometimes there is a last straw.

"Shit, I hope to hell this isn't it. We've had a lot of transfers since the Grand Canyon battle and I don't blame any of them. How the hell are my men supposed to take wives, have families, with the fucking mortality rate so high?"

Fiona knew Seriffe spoke, but her attention was fixed on Jean-Pierre. His statement about Seriffe wasn't casual. Something was going on with him. With a jolt, she realized he was changing or perhaps had changed, as though a new power had come online.

She had asked him recently if he experienced empathy as one of his powers. He had denied it, but now she wasn't so sure. Maybe he didn't even know what was going on with him, but she could feel it, see it. His gaze was fixed on Seriffe, the way Alison would fix her gaze, as though looking into the soul. This meant something, but what?

"I would help you, Seriffe, if it were in my power. I, too, see the need among your warriors. Some are so very close to Warrior of the Blood status: Gideon, Duncan, others. And the need in our ranks is terrible as well. Greaves has been successful at turning vampires, so many of them. You know the hours we fight, every night."

Seriffe shook his head. "Something has to change. Jesus."

Fiona stood up. "I wish I could help."

Both men looked at her. Jean-Pierre's gaze now became stuck to her, his ocean-eyes shifting over hers, almost piercing her. "Perhaps your emerging power is meant to help."

But she shook her head. "That's just it. I don't think it can help in this way, not with the Militia Warriors." She looked away from him and as Seriffe had done, she shook her head. "I just don't know what good it will do the war effort, to be obsidian flame."

"Fiona, you have helped," Seriffe said. "So very much. The rehab center, identifying all the blood slave facilities, even with this guy." He jerked his thumb in Jean-Pierre's direction. "You saved his ass in Copán Two."

She knew all that, but it wasn't good enough. "Still, with this new power, I just wish there was more I could do."

"We all feel that way."

Jean-Pierre said, "If we continue to work your powers, perhaps you will learn more of the application, the purpose for obsidian flame. Maybe there is something you can do beyond just channeling the powers of others."

She shrugged. "Maybe, and of course I'll keep trying. Of course."

Endelle was kicking herself for taking Braulio's advice.

Braulio. Long-lived lucky bastard.

What the hell had she been thinking to negotiate a deal with Owen fucking Stannett?

She stood outside the doors of the Superstition Mountain Seers Fortress, in the middle of the goddam cactus-and-rattlesnake-infested Superstition Mountains, banging on a rusted iron door complete with rusted rivets and rusted everything.

The place looked like a run-down Spanish presidio, a square structure, absurdly tall walls, flaking plaster on the outside. The only thing it lacked was bars over every window, but the windows were so small, bars weren't needed. Nothing could get in . . . or out.

She pounded on the door again, then shouted, "Stannett, if you're not letting me in then get yourself out here and explain yourself, you motherfucker."

She could feel him inside . . . gloating.

COPASS law forbade her to cross the threshold without express invitation from the High Administrator of the Fortress.

Fuck.

Owen knew how to savor a moment. He leaned back in his executive chair, in his office, his booted legs propped up on his desk and crossed at the ankles. His new boots were beautiful: red leather heavily embroidered with black, yellow, and green thread.

He sipped a Starbucks nonfat latte as he listened to Endelle pound on his front door and assail his Fortress with a wholly improper string of profanity.

Did she really think he would let her inside *his* Fortress?

He smiled. He'd seen this moment in the future streams. He'd seen many moments, some that had shrunk his nuts to the size of peas. But this moment he'd worked hard to bring to fruition, just so that he could sit here, sip, and savor Endelle's shouts.

The front door was a hundred yards away, about as far from his office as you could get, so he used a combination of preternatural hearing and some good old-fashioned voyeurism to see her and listen to her and generally bask in the perfection of the moment.

The Ruler of Second Earth stood outside *his* Fortress and had no legal way to breach his front door.

Hallelujah! Sometimes the heavens answered his prayers.

But the pounding stopped and the obscenities trailed off, and then she was gone.

Which meant that the next part of his life's nightmare was getting ready to heat up.

He needed to get into the future streams to see what battles he had to face next. He really did. For one thing, though he had always known that one day Marguerite would reside within his Fortress, she was completely unpredictable, both in life and in the future streams. So he was at something of a loss as to what to do with her.

Besides, she'd hurt him. Though he was no longer in pain,

the mere thought of getting near her again brought his nuts once more tight up against his ass, quivering in fear. In whatever way he moved forward with her, she would have to be knocked out, something he'd certainly be able to do within the next day or so.

She wasn't eating, which of course meant she suspected he'd drugged her food. He had.

But that was not his only recourse. He could simply have a couple of his minions hold her down while he injected her. He was always amazed how far a little brute force could take a man. Although he shouldn't have been since he'd been on the receiving end a few centuries ago.

He waved a hand in the air, pushing all his troubles to the side. For the moment, he sipped and savored a little more. The future would come whether he wanted it to or not, but for now, the pleasure of having this much power, having the most powerful Seer in the world under his thumb, and of having refused entrance to the most powerful vampire on earth—yes, these things satisfied his soul.

Thorne sat on a stool at the Cave, a half-emptied bottle of Ketel One sitting within fingers' reach.

He waited for Endelle's call. She'd promised to try to get into the Fortress, to make sure Marguerite was okay. He had little hope, but fuck, he couldn't do anything, not legally. By COPASS's decree, no one could go into the Superstition Fortress unless given permission by the High Administrator, and he believed Stannett would cut off his dick before he allowed Endelle or any of the Warriors of the Blood on his property.

At least that was one thing he respected about the bastard. He'd staked out his territory and he protected it like a man should.

Unfortunately, he had sociopath written all over him, so on a very instinctive level Thorne knew that evil resided in that facility. He knew it the way he knew that a death vampire's complexion always paled to a faint bluish state once he started drinking dying blood.

Thorne was bleary-eyed, dizzy, almost completely drunk, and mad at the world. Yet he was anything but sleepy.

In fact, he couldn't recall having had much sleep in the past forty-eight hours. Even when he went home, the longest he could keep his eyes closed was maybe two hours. Then he'd wake up.

This had been going on for so long, for so many years, that he couldn't recall a time when he knew what it was to sleep.

But today felt like a ton of boulders had landed on each shoulder and he wasn't bearing the load very well. Fuck. But then, when had he ever carried his burdens well?

Maybe in the beginning, when he'd taken on the responsibility as Endelle's second-in-command. He'd been young in ascended terms, hopeful, full of enthusiasm like anyone starting out in a field of endeavor. His field had been war, battling death vampires, a noble one and he was built for it. Surely, with just enough diligence, he'd be able to end the struggle, hunt the last death vampire down to earth, slay him, then move on, maybe have a family, a real life.

That had been so long ago; he couldn't even remember which century. And he sure as hell couldn't remember the day he'd lost hope, all hope, that things would change.

Then he'd met Marguerite.

He sipped his tumbler and smiled. These memories at least still had the power to give him some ease.

You ready for me, Warrior? Those had been the first words she'd ever spoken to him, right after, *How happy I am to meet Grace's brother.* Imagine meeting a beautiful woman for the first time, in a fucking Convent, and that's what she says, *You ready for me, Warrior?*

What he'd done after still smote his goddam conscience because as soon as Grace left to do Sister Quena's bidding, he'd taken Marguerite. He'd taken a goddam devotiate in a goddam Convent.

He was going to hell, no two ways around that. But then he was in hell, so what was the difference?

Somehow he'd lost his innocence along the way. Any

man who'd lived for a couple of millennia had a lot of skeletons in his outbuildings, but this had to be his worst yet.

But Marguerite had been a willing, panting, back-scratching participant. When he'd met her, she'd been half hidden behind the door. When his sister had turned away, Marguerite had bared a breast to him.

The image of that breast had become forever fixed in his head, burned there like a silver cross against the bare skin of a fictional vampire. There had been such perfection in that shape, beautifully round but with the slightest hint of teardrop, sloped inward at the top and weighted at the bottom. The nipple had been hard and puckered, as though she'd just had an orgasm. That's when it hit him and that's what had done him in. Sister Marguerite had just shown him her orgasm.

He jerked off to that breast almost every night and any other time the mood struck him, which was often.

He loved and hated this obsession. She hadn't lived long enough to really know her mind—not even thirteen decades. And for at least a century she'd been trapped inside a Convent. But he just couldn't keep away from her.

Another memory returned, the first time they'd made love. *You gonna talk to me, Warrior? Use that fucking voice of yours? The one that makes me come?*

Shit, yeah.

He'd split his resonance twice. He'd work up to fifteen through the decades, just for her. She'd be screaming against the palm of his hand at fifteen, shaking, convulsing. God, he loved fucking her.

Her family had discovered her excessive love of males and had put her away in the Convent for rehabilitation. That's when the sisters had detected her Seer gift and called in Stannett to monitor her progress. Thorne still didn't know why Stannett hadn't done it sooner. But thank God for whatever reason the bastard had.

But that's when Thorne's treachery had begun because he could have told Endelle about Marguerite, and her Seer powers, a century ago, maybe even altered the course of the war. But he'd feared losing her. She was the only thing in all this time that had kept him sane and loose so he could keep on saving the world.

Yeah, that's right. Keep thinking that way, asshole.

But why shouldn't he be allowed some peace of mind, some relief? Marguerite had eased his twitches when his head spun hard, when Darian's heinous plans piled up on him, when Endelle griped at him for hours on end, when he had to account for another batch of dead Militia Warriors, when years of loneliness stretched before him like a vast ocean of fucking cactus-infested desert. Yeah, Marguerite kept him loose. She almost made him believe in a divine plan.

He threw back a hefty shot of his Ketel One and poured another two fingers.

So now his woman was locked up in the Fortress.

He took his Droid from the deep pocket of his kilt and checked the time. Ten forty-five and Endelle still hadn't given him a mental shout. He shared a mind-link with her. Why the hell hadn't she contacted him?

He sipped again. He hated waiting.

Then he felt the vibration deep within his mind.

Yo, Thorne. Endelle kept things simple.

I'm here. Fucking waiting, Endelle.

You sound slurred, even in your head. You need to cut back.

How about you cut the shit and tell me what happened.

Nothing happened, not a goddam thing. I'm still locked out and the bastard won't even show his face at the door.

He felt her anger like a white-hot stream of fire through his head. He sat back on his stool. The woman was pissed and sometimes all that rage gave him a headache. *What are you going to do?*

Fuck if I know.

Then his rage kicked in, meeting her fury with an answering flaming bolt of his own.

Settle down, she snapped, which felt like a boomerang flying through his head.

The hell I will. The hell if I can. He's going to hurt her. You know he will.

I'm contacting Daniel Harding.

What? He shouted the word through her head. Greaves owned Harding, and as head of COPASS he was about as useful as a bug on a windshield.

I have to go through channels. Don't have a choice.

And neither did he.

Apparently, Endelle knew that as well, because she sent, *Just give me a few more hours, that's all I ask, then*—here she offered a mental sigh—*well, then you gotta do what you gotta do.*

He grew very still, his tumbler poised in the air. Endelle had just given him permission to break the law. The only trouble was, busting into a Seers Fortress could be a death sentence.

On the other hand, right now he didn't fucking care.

Jean-Pierre was just a little pissed off. He could not get through Fiona's very thick skull.

During the most recent training session, in the now familiar room in Militia HQ, he had pushed her . . . hard. He spoke to her about the need to engage in a full-possession while channeling. He spoke of the advantages: the most certain increase of power and the possibility that she might have great need of possession-based channeling at some point in the immediate future. He reminded her, more quietly, of their recent lovemaking, that she no longer had the same fears of feeling trapped as she once had, even that she could allow him to take her blood. All to no avail.

Fiona was a very stubborn woman, now more than ever it would seem.

She even stood chest-to-chest with him, her arms back, and her face like a fury ready to take his head off. "I won't do it, Jean-Pierre. I've made up my mind about this. I'm keeping this part for myself."

"You are being ridiculous and very willful, like a child."

"Like a child? You would say that to me? Simply because

I am telling you that I am unwilling to do something, you tell me I'm like a child?"

There was only one response he could give, but it came out like a dog's bark. *"Oui."*

"Oui?"

"Oui."

She planted a finger on his chest. "Let me tell you something, buddy, you're the one who's being stubborn and you're not listening to me. I have spent the past two hours channeling every one of your abilities, from hand-blast to preternatural speed to kinetic movement of objects around this room, and not once did you need to possess me in order for me to get the job done. What do you have to say to that?"

What could he say? She was right. "You are right." He dropped his hand to his abdomen. "But what I feel here, as a man who has battled in this war for over two centuries, is a powerful instinct that tells me you are wrong. Very wrong."

She drew back, maybe three inches. "That's your opinion."

"Why will you not trust me, that I might know better in this situation, this circumstance? You have only known your powers for a few months now."

"I've been telepathic since I arrived on Second Earth all those decades ago."

He nodded. "But you cannot even mount your wings when the doctor said you should. What if your resistance to working your obsidian flame power is connected?"

At that, she stepped back perhaps an entire foot and stared at him, her eyes wide, her lips parted in something like horror. "You know how hard I've tried to mount my wings. That is unfair of you, Jean-Pierre."

He closed the distance between them. "But what if they are connected? Please listen to me, *chérie*. Take your obsidian power the distance."

She whirled away from him and put her hands to her face. He hoped she did not cry. He watched her back move up and down as she took very deep breaths but he did not hear the sounds of weeping.

But he also knew that he was right. In this, he was right.

As he watched her, as he thought how hard he pushed her, he felt confident in not just his position, but also exactly how he was treating her, as though he understood very deep things about her.

His gaze shifted to the carpeted floor. He had felt the same way earlier, when speaking with Seriffe, as though he could see into the very core of the man, as though he could understand in what ways the man suffered and what he should say and should not say. This was peculiar. He wondered if there was a meaning to this, something he did not yet perceive.

A wind swept through his mind, leaving him dizzy. Change had come to him, he could feel it, but he did not understand what it meant.

Fiona's shoulders fell as she turned back toward him. Neither her eyes nor her cheeks were wet as her hands dropped away from her face. Good. This was good.

"Let me think on what you've said. And I do trust you, Jean-Pierre, very much. I respect you . . . infinitely."

Infinitely. His heart warmed and he put a hand to his chest. To be respected. That was a good thing.

He nodded several times, and once more drew close to her. He took her hands in his and kissed the backs of her fingers, one hand to the next.

Her lovely patisserie scent floated toward him, and something more, that which was just Fiona, that which he carried in his mind and as a beautiful flavor on his tongue. His body responded. *Merde.* It took so little for him to be suddenly ready for her, to desire above all things to take her back to his house and into his bed, to keep her there for, *mon Dieu,* all eternity.

But these things were not practical, not in this moment, not in this war. Still, he could not help taking her in his arms and bending down to possess her lips, her mouth, and to penetrate her with his tongue at least in this way.

A knock on the door drew him back. Fiona had a blush on her cheek as she smiled up at him.

He didn't turn toward the door as he called out, "Enter, please."

He knew Fiona could guess his difficulty because her blush deepened. She took a step sideways as she said, "Hey, Bev. What have you got there?"

"Something for you."

Jean-Pierre shifted slightly to glance at Bev. He scowled since she held a gold box in her hand, bearing a very pretty white bow. "What is this? Who is it from?"

Every sense was on alert. If a man had sent her this present, he had reason to be angry all over again. Did one of the Militia Warriors believe he had a chance with his Fiona? Did he need to address one of Seriffe's men?

"This arrived at the landing area. We had security scan it. There isn't a danger here."

"Then it appeared anonymously?"

"Not exactly." She stepped into the room and let the door close behind her. "There's a card but we didn't open it. We thought maybe Carolyn sent it to Fiona."

Jean-Pierre looked down at Fiona. "Will you permit me in case there is some danger here that we cannot know? Cannot see?"

She nodded. "Yes, of course."

Jean-Pierre, calmer now, turned to Bev. She stood perhaps five-three and had to go a long distance to meet his gaze. In stature, however, she was very tall, a woman he trusted, that all the Militia Warriors trusted. She was a person of great kindness and restraint. She had wavy dark hair she wore to her shoulders and cornflower-blue eyes that sparkled with something close to mischief. She was perfect in her position among so many difficult men.

He crossed to her then took the package. He lifted the lid. Inside lay an envelope. Terrible things could be sent like this.

He looked at Bev. "Was this tested for pulmonary toxic inhalants?"

Bev nodded. "Everything. It's clean."

He blew air from his cheeks. He glanced at Fiona and gave his head a small jerk, beckoning her to join him. He held the box for her and she withdrew the envelope.

The same card as before came out first, with black raised lettering. She read it aloud, "A small peace offering. Casimir."

She looked at Jean-Pierre. "What do you think?"

"I think I do not trust this vampire, especially since he tried to kill you."

She looked inside the envelope and frowned. "Oh, my God. There are four tickets . . . to Dark Spectacle Phantasmagoria. This must have cost a fortune and how did he get them?" Then she read the front of the ticket, "The amazing Rimizac, one night only." She looked up at Jean-Pierre and shook her head. "Rimizac."

Jean-Pierre frowned then rolled his eyes. "Casimir."

"So our Fourth ascender is the creator of Dark Spectacle. Somehow I'm not surprised."

"He cannot mean any good by this." He glanced at the back of the card. "There is more. Look."

Fiona turned the card over then gasped. "Impossible."

The hairs on the nape of Jean-Pierre's neck stood up. "What?"

Fiona met his gaze, her silver-blue eyes suddenly full of concern, even fear. "Rith escaped from COPASS." She glanced back at the card and read aloud, "Rith escaped. He is more powerful than even Greaves suspected. I wished to warn you."

Jean-Pierre let out a very loud, "Fuck." He turned in a circle and threw the box on the floor. "It was too good to be true."

"Is all of this a trap?"

Jean-Pierre turned toward her. "Of course it is. It could be nothing more."

She waved the envelope back and forth. "Do we attend?"

"Of course not."

But she tilted her head at him. "Wouldn't it be better to meet the enemy on the field than to wait for him to steal in through the window at night?"

In this moment, he hated that she was right. He hated it more than anything in the world because he knew what it would mean. His woman would insist on going.

But he had one last refuge, one last hope that this could turn out differently. "We must discuss this with Endelle. This must be her call."

Endelle stared at the tickets, which she held in her hand, and which burned her ass.

An imbecile could smell a trap, but that wasn't the discussion at hand. Everyone knew this was an invitation to battle the devil.

But what the fuck did it mean that Rith had escaped?

Her blood boiled. She thought of Braulio's brief appearance, insisting she should negotiate with Stannett, and now the Superstition Fortress was locked down and Daniel Harding was playing hide-and-seek. She couldn't reach him, COPASS refused to comment on the supposed rumor that Rith had escaped the well-guarded Prague jail, and now she had to decide what to do about Dark Spectacle.

Goddammit.

Should she send Jean-Pierre and Fiona into the lion's den?

There were four tickets. Should she send two of her Warriors of the Blood to accompany them?

Fiona and Jean-Pierre stood near the fireplace and seemed to be arguing something in low tones, something about obsidian flame.

Thorne stood in the same place he had the last time they were all together, over by the east-facing window, staring off into the distance. He had his hands behind his back. He was half-blitzed, maybe three-quarters.

Shit, he was her best friend and he was hanging on by a thread, a very narrow thread, a thread with holes in it.

Goddam, this whole thing was coming down on her head. She could feel it.

Her gaze snapped back to Fiona. "All right, Goldie, get your ass over here."

Fiona turned from scowling at Jean-Pierre to meet her gaze, her brows lifted.

"Yes . . . you. You know, gold variety of obsidian flame?

We have some work to do. I want to check on Marguerite and you're gonna help."

From the corner of her vision, she saw Thorne turn from the window and head back in her direction. She shifted her gaze in his direction. He was just about out of his mind, his chin down, his fists clenched. Didn't this beat the shit out of her?

But what she really wanted to know was how he could be so crazed about Marguerite, yet she wasn't his *breh*.

Thorne drew up on Endelle's left side. They formed a tight little square, with Jean-Pierre glaring at Thorne because of how close he stood to Fiona.

Eventually, Thorne got the message, because he took a step back.

Endelle rolled her eyes then focused on Fiona. She had tried voyeuring Marguerite herself, but she couldn't get past Stannett's shields. The man had power, way too much power. "All right, ascender. I want you to make contact and I want you to use my preternatural voyeurism so we can see what's goin' on. Got it?"

"Yes," Fiona said.

Endelle smiled. She liked the woman, she really did. She had a confident air, something she hadn't really expected from a former blood slave.

Fiona closed her eyes and the next moment Endelle felt the woman's being right next to hers as though she stood shoulder-to-shoulder and hip-to-hip. A subtle vibration made a strong connection, even a powerful one. Very cool.

She felt a second vibration as Fiona's mind extended in the direction of the Superstition Fortress.

Fiona sent, *I'm next to Marguerite. Open your window.*

Fiona was commanding her? She wasn't just strong; the woman had balls.

Fine, Endelle sent. She opened her preternatural window and about two seconds later, she was looking at an abysmally bare cell of a room, very dim, worse than even the Creator's Convent.

Fiona began a slow pan to the left and up. There was one of those long windows, maybe four inches tall. Sweet Jesus.

Fiona kept panning down to the left and there on a platform Marguerite lay curled up. She'd been sleeping but now lifted up on her elbow.

Fiona? Marguerite asked telepathically.

We're here. Endelle and I. She has her voyeur's window open so that we can see you, both of us, right, Endelle?

Endelle jumped in. *Is this the shit-box Stannett moved you to? That lying sonofabitch. He said his facility was like a Mexican vacation.*

Marguerite smiled then laughed. *Mexican, all right, but more like one of their prisons. So when are you guys busting me out of this joint? Oh, and just so ya know, lover boy came in here yesterday expecting some nookie, but I got my hands around his left jewel. I didn't so much polish his little diamond as grind him to a sparkling shine. He passed out.*

Endelle approved so much she couldn't speak for a moment. When she did, she expressed her surprise. *I didn't think he liked women. Or men. He's kind of the opposite of bisexual.*

Asexual. Yeah, I got that, too. But Stanny's a man with a plan. He's got himself a nursery in here. Did you know he's into baby-making big time? He's genetically engineering Seers.

Holy fuck. So that was his game. So that was why he kept the Fortress locked down. Well, well, well.

Suddenly Marguerite sat up and backed herself against the wall.

Fiona panned to the left. Stannett himself walked in, but there was nothing casual about this visit. He looked around. "What's going on in here? I can feel that something's not right. Tell me, Marguerite."

"I'm a little bored so I've been practicing some of my powers." In a quick move she flicked her wrist and sent a hand-blast firework up to the ceiling, a very pretty red color.

Clever girl.

Stannett looked around. He frowned. He walked in Endelle's

direction, as though he could sense her presence or Fiona's or both.

Endelle tried to back her window out of there, but she wasn't driving. *Fiona, you've got the controls. Let's give him some space.*

Fiona moved backward until once more they glided through nether-space and Endelle stood staring at Fiona, back in her office.

She looked into silver-blue eyes but neither said a word.

Endelle turned the situation over and over in her mind.

"What the hell did you see?" Thorne asked, a frown heavy on his brow, as he looked from one to the other.

Endelle shook her head. "Marguerite's fine but we just learned Stannett's been busy making babies. Apparently, that's his plan with Marguerite." She wasn't thinking when she said this.

After nine thousand years, Endelle knew she should have learned some restraint, a little perception, something close to discretion. Instead, she felt a wave of heat flow from Thorne.

"Babies?" Thorne blended all the gravel in his voice with his resonance so that Endelle took a step backward.

Fiona covered her ears. "No, Thorne! Please don't start this."

Jean-Pierre jumped in front of Fiona and got in Thorne's face. "Would you please not use your resonance when Fiona is near? Dammit, Thorne!"

But Thorne's nostrils flared. "Move it," he shouted. His eyes were bloodshot and red-rimmed.

Endelle knew exactly where this would end, so, shit.

"Settle down, boys." She put a hand on each shoulder then gripped them hard, painfully hard, until both Jean-Pierre and Thorne dipped in her direction and spewed a few profanities.

Fiona sighed and moved back to the fireplace. She rubbed both of her ears, though. So damn sensitive.

Once her warriors had settled down, she released them. Thorne returned to the window, Jean-Pierre to stand next to

Fiona. He crossed his arms over his chest and glared at Thorne.

Fine. Whatever.

She glanced at the tickets. The spectacle event was to-night so what the hell was she supposed to do? And what the hell was she supposed to do about Marguerite?

The only event I've ever stolen down to Second Earth to watch was Dark Spectacle. I consider this a true aberration in my spiritual development. But as is supremely human, I could not resist the event year after year, despite my annual vows to set aside such foolishness.

—*Memoirs,* Beatrice of Fourth

CHAPTER 18

Fiona rubbed her ears a little more. At least they weren't bleeding this time.

She looked at the tickets splayed in Endelle's right hand. She thought she understood her dilemma. If it was a trap, and what else could it be, then Endelle would be sending people she cared about into an extremely dangerous, possibly even deadly, situation.

But Fiona didn't have the same dilemma. "I intend to go," she called across the room. "If that's what you're wondering. Call it a date with destiny."

"You cannot go," Jean-Pierre said.

"Why not?"

"Because it would be madness."

Fiona shrugged. "I think it would be madness not to go. Besides, aren't you just a little curious?"

"To find out what your friend Casimir has in store for you? No, not at all."

"You're being stubborn again."

"As are you." But he looked down at her and she thought she saw his lips twitch.

She put her hand on his forearm, the muscles taut from having crossed his arms. "Don't you see? If Rith is there, if Rith intends to be there, then I must go. I don't know why or how he escaped from Prague, but I have no doubt that if he can find me he will hurt me. And I believe Casimir spoke truly. I believe Rith is more powerful than any of us know."

"I do not think you are ready, Fiona."

She rubbed over his arm and stared at his chest, his broad beautiful chest. A terrible feeling descended on her—that if she went tonight, it was possible she would never know Jean-Pierre again as she had, in bed with him, locked in ecstasy, crying out his name, weeping because he was so beautiful. She might not survive. He might not, either.

But Casimir's presence had changed the game. As had Rith's sudden escape.

"I have to go. Not one more woman is to be harmed by Rith's hands, and I don't care if you tell me that Greaves probably already has another organization set up to handle the supply and demand. We'll take this one step at a time. First Rith, then whatever else we have to deal with."

"What about me?" Endelle called out. "Don't I get a say?"

Fiona met Endelle's gaze. She saw the knowing look in her eye. "Of course," she said. But she already knew the answer.

"You have to go. No, Jean-Pierre, you don't get a say in this one. I want you to take Santiago and Zacharius with you. Thorne, are you in agreement?"

Thorne glanced back at her over his shoulder. Fiona had never seen him look quite this wrecked before. "You have to go. This is war."

An hour before showtime, Fiona finished getting dressed. She once more stood in front of the mirror in the guest room at Carolyn's house. Her daughter had dressed her hair in waves and curls that hung over her arms and down her back.

Since Dark Spectacle was essentially the Super Bowl of events for Second Earth, and tickets were incredibly expensive and hard to get, the cream of Second Earth society attended from all over the world. For that reason, she wore an evening gown despite the fact that she had every reason to believe she'd be facing the enemy tonight.

Jean-Pierre had already arrived but she hadn't seen him yet, although Carolyn said she nearly swooned when she saw all three of the warriors. "And Jean-Pierre is wearing a Brioni tux and looks magnificent. I want Seriffe to buy one. No. I'll buy it for him myself."

Carolyn helped her don a pearl-and-diamond necklace, sliding it beneath her curls. She secured the clasp and met Fiona's gaze in the mirror. "You look beautiful, and I'm so jealous that you get to go to Dark Spectacle." Carolyn didn't know the real reason for her attendance, and she had no intention of worrying her.

But Seriffe knew.

"The tickets were such a surprise."

Fiona caught Carolyn's hands and, as she had done the morning of baby Helena's christening, she wrapped Carolyn's arms around her, pulling her daughter into another awkward back-to-front hug. "You'll ruin your hair," Carolyn complained.

"I don't care. I love you so much."

But Carolyn pulled away laughing. "And you're going to ruin your makeup if you start weeping, which I can tell you're just about to do."

Fiona took a deep breath. Carolyn was right. Besides, if she dwelled too much on the spiderweb she was walking into, her resolve might falter.

She focused instead on the moment, on appreciating that Carolyn had brought in any number of favors from the higher-end shops in Scottsdale Two, so that over the course of the afternoon they'd had at least a dozen evening gowns to choose from.

At four, they'd found *the one*. The gown of cream silk, beaded with Austrian crystals, clung to her curves and was cut with a deep V that gave her a beautiful line of cleavage, which Jean-Pierre would love. The skirt of the gown hugged her thighs then flared from the knees down to her heels in generous pleats. Of course what Fiona didn't say to her daughter was that the loose fabric around her lower legs would allow her a freedom of movement that many of the other gowns simply didn't.

A knock on the door forced Fiona to turn away from the mirror. "Come in."

Seriffe opened the door and poked his head in. "I've got three WhatBees in my living room, all strung tight as piano wires." He looked Fiona up and down and smiled. "You look lovely, but I think Jean-Pierre will probably pass out when he sees you."

That made Fiona's heart jump. Whatever else this night would be, she wanted Jean-Pierre to see her at her best, just this once.

She left the bedroom and made the long march down the hall. She could hear the men: Santiago's gorgeous Latin cadence, Zacharius's strong, bold speech, and then the voice that never failed to turn her knees to water.

"You can never speak of a dagger, *mon ami,* without making some reference to your . . . personal assets."

Men, she thought, but she smiled.

She saw Jean-Pierre in profile first. All his long, blond, wavy, and somewhat unruly hair was slicked back and pulled tight in the *cadroen.* His cheekbones, one of his finest features, were made more prominent, which gave his face a stronger look.

Nudged by Zach, he turned in her direction so that she saw him from the front. He looked . . . magnificent.

The coat had a very narrow lapel, but it emphasized the wonderful breadth of his chest and shoulders and the narrowness of hips. His lips were parted and she saw that he was taking in her appearance as well, his gaze falling first to her cleavage then lower and lower until he made his way to her feet, then slowly back up.

He met her gaze and for a moment time fell into a huge

hole. She saw only him, the man who was her *breh,* the man who had carried her out of New Zealand, who had served for so many months as her Guardian of Ascension, who challenged her about her powers, who scratched her wing-locks, and who made love to her so tenderly.

Affection blossomed so sharply that she took a step back and even Carolyn slid an arm around her waist to steady her. "You okay?" she asked.

Was she okay?

She hardly knew.

Jean-Pierre stood very still as though to move would shatter the image before him. Fiona was perfection, the dark of her long hair now curled at the ends, a strong counterpoint to the creamy sparkling shade of her gown.

She looked like a princess, a soft elegant princess who belonged in a court from years ago. All the love he felt for her swelled in his chest and squeezed his heart. He wished more than anything that this was not a world at war. He would ask her to marry him, he would drop on one knee right now, take her hand, kiss her fingers, and beg her to become his wife.

But this *was* a world at war, and he was this man who had been through too much to ever so simply give his heart, all his trust, to a woman again.

Still, for this moment, as his feet put him in motion before his rational thoughts caught up with him, Fiona belonged to him, tonight and, God willing, tomorrow.

He forgot all about his brother warriors who stood nearby, about Seriffe and his wife, Carolyn. All he could see was Fiona, and her loveliness, all that she had suffered, all that she had overcome, and the woman she was this night.

He took her hands in his and kissed the backs of each. "You look so very beautiful. I thank you for that."

Fiona smiled and there was laughter in her silver-blue eyes as she said, "Right back atcha. You look . . . *magnifique.*"

"I want to kiss you," he whispered, as though everyone in the room couldn't hear him.

"Later, you can kiss me all you like."

"All? Are you certain, because that would be a lot of kissing, perhaps hours of it?"

Everywhere, he sent for good measure.

A lovely wave of buttery croissant wafted over him, which in turn caused him to draw his breath in deeply. He watched her sigh, and her lips parted as though she struggled to draw air.

Santiago said, "*Lo siento, mi amigo,* but the hour grows late and the landing platforms close on time. They do not care that you wish to kiss your woman."

Fiona chuckled but rolled her eyes.

"Santiago is very right," Jean-Pierre said. "We should go." He pulled his phone from the pocket of his pants and touched the screen a couple of times. He touched again to connect with the Las Vegas Two arena theater to set up the folding time for their party of four. He'd preset the ticket numbers so that as a group they were already confirmed and identified. Because of his status as a Warrior of the Blood, and because the ticket numbers were courtesy seats provided by the owner of Dark Spectacle, they did not have long to wait.

Fiona clung to his arm as she said good-bye to her daughter.

A minute passed.

A return call allowed them to fold to the VIP landing platform as a group.

They were greeted by a tall dark beauty, wearing a skimpy red silk dress. She opened her mouth to speak then blinked a couple of times as she looked first at Jean-Pierre, then Santiago and Zacharius.

Jean-Pierre knew that look: the eyes that widened almost in shock, the lips that parted. A blush soon covered her cheeks, but he doubted she was embarrassed. He was a man who knew women and when he glanced back at Zach and Santiago, each appraised the woman, her willingness, her level of *interest.* Had the circumstance been different, she appeared to be just the sort of woman any of them would have taken into the red velvet booths at the Blood and Bite.

Fiona glanced up at him and narrowed her gaze. He opened his eyes very wide, but she shook her head at him and laughed.

When the hostess had collected herself, she pushed back a wave of her long, flowing brown hair. She inclined her head slightly and began her speech, greeting them in her special VIP voice and manner.

"Welcome, most exalted Warriors of the Blood and Ms. Fiona Gaines. The proprietor, the Amazing Rimizac, wishes me to take you to the box he has set aside for your use tonight. Champagne and a fine selection of delicacies imported from Mortal Earth await you. If you will follow me."

She turned and headed down a short flight of stairs.

At intervals, security personnel nodded to the hostess as she led their group to the right, up a shallow ramp covered in a very fine scarlet carpet. Jean-Pierre did not know whether to be impressed or concerned. The owner showed a tendency to attend to details, not a good thing in an enemy.

Given the size of the arena theater, the walk was long. In the distance, he heard an orchestra tuning their instruments.

As he walked, he kept his left arm around Fiona, low on her waist, but very light. His right hand remained free so that he could draw his sword into his hand if needed.

The box was low as boxes went yet it was situated, as all the boxes were, a considerable distance from the central stage. This was not an average production by any means.

This was spectacle.

Fiona sat in the front row of the box to his right. Zach and Santiago took the chairs behind them. He scanned the enormous theater, going from box to box and the less expensive seats high in the galleries. He extended his vision. By habit he hunted for death vampires, but given the level of security he doubted any were present, certainly not visible.

He turned back to Santiago, who in turn leaned forward and whispered, "I do not see the enemy—do you?"

Jean-Pierre shook his head.

The theater was built in a deep horseshoe with a ceiling

that rose at least ten stories in height to allow for a true spectacle performance, which always involved genetically altered swans and geese.

Zach also leaned forward. "There's something wrong here. Have you looked at the next four boxes to the left of us?"

Jean-Pierre shifted his gaze. He had scanned them but he had not paid attention to the occupants. Before, he had been looking for the pale, almost bluish complexion and overall beauty of death vampires. Now he saw something else and as he continued shifting his gaze from box to box, he cursed beneath his breath.

"Mon Dieu," he murmured.

Fiona slipped her hand in his, her fingers cool against his palm. "What's the matter? You're scowling and muttering."

Of course she could not have known. "In many of the boxes on our level, the entire distance around the theater, are High Administrators from Territories known to be allied with Endelle."

"Oh, no," Fiona whispered, her fingers clasping his tightly.

"We should go," he said, turning toward her. "I should take you home immediately. I believe there is much more going on here than just Casimir's interest in you."

"We can't leave, Jean-Pierre. We just can't."

He admired her conviction but he hated that she was beside him and in danger.

She leaned toward him and whispered. "You know, I think everyone is staring into this box."

He glanced around and realized that what she said was true. He had been so concerned about determining any overt threat that he did not realize their box had become a matter of interest. Great interest. He was surprised and did not quite know what to make of it.

After a long minute, one by one, spectators began rising out of their seats. At first, he thought it might be in some sort of protest of their war efforts, perhaps an expression of disapproval of Endelle's policies or the recent battle at the Grand Canyon.

Instead, however, applause began, and more and more

people rose to their feet turning to face their box. This was not disapprobation. Quite the opposite.

He was stunned, feeling as though a sharp breeze had just struck his face. He looked back at Zacharius who was now smiling. He leaned forward and said, "I think they might be expressing their appreciation for what we do. Imagine that."

A full minute passed and nearly every person had risen to their feet. Whistles started up as well until soon the arena theater was a sea of thunderous applause, shouting, and hoots.

Then Fiona stood, stepping away from him, from his brother warriors, and also offering her applause. Her eyes were drenched with tears as she smiled down at him.

He turned and waved Santiago and Zach forward to stand beside him, which they did. The applause escalated into a roar.

Jean-Pierre had never experienced anything like this in his life. He was moved beyond words. He put his hand over his heart and offered a bow. More shouts and whistles. All three warriors bowed repeatedly. He did not know how long it would continue, but finally the lights in the theater dimmed, a sure signal that Dark Spectacle was about to begin, and at last the audience returned to their seats.

Fiona sat down again and wiped away her tears. She was so moved by what had just happened, for such an outward and enormous show of support for the warriors. Given that she and Jean-Pierre both believed there was significant danger in the event this evening, and that it was possible some of that danger might be directed toward the notables present, she was grateful she had insisted on coming tonight. She had no idea what was about to happen, but that her presence might be necessary weighed on her.

She didn't understand all that living on Second Earth entailed, but five months had taught her that increased power often demanded an intuitive approach. Her intuition had screamed at her to attend Dark Spectacle and with so many notables present, she began to understand that the scope of the situation could certainly be much larger than she had imagined.

She folded her hands on her lap and took a deep breath. She relaxed her shoulders and sank inward, focusing her thoughts on all that was around her, all the people leaning forward in their seats, the vibrations of excitement in the air.

Off to the right some fifty feet was the entrance point for the performers, an enormous black tunnel that had been given the shape of a dark cave, the underworld spilling forth its secrets.

From the opening, a long black pathway, perhaps thirty yards in length, rose at a steep angle. The path was maybe ten feet wide and led to an expansive central, circular stage that had to be fifteen yards across.

To the left of the round stage in a semicircle was a huge double orchestra that rose from the depths.

A heavy roll of drums began. Shivers and goose bumps traveled up and down Fiona's body. Jean-Pierre reached for her hand and she gave it to him gratefully. She leaned close. She had heard so much about Dark Spectacle and if just this pounding of drums was any indication, the show would astonish and terrify even on its own merit.

What else the evening might have in store for them, she didn't want to imagine.

The music began, filling the entire space, driving hard. She touched Jean-Pierre's sleeve and looked at him. To his mind, she sent, *I don't know this music.*

Holst's The Planets. *I believe it is "Mars."*

If she made it through this night, she wanted to listen to it again. *It's amazing,* she sent.

Yes, it is.

From the cave, and lit with dim spotlights, came a sudden brisk flow of women flying in full-mount, all bearing dark gray wings, all wearing strange gray costumes that looked both ethereal and dirty, like substantial cobwebs that hung for thirty feet from their arms and legs as they flew up the ramped path. Once they reached the circle they began to fly in an ever-increasing spiral up and up. There must have been fifty of these women, flying in formation so tight and exact through the spiral that one error would send them all spinning out of control.

But by the time they were essentially flying in this enormous whirlwind of movement, the audience was crying out and applauding like mad. Lights from the ceiling above grew from white to pink to red until the whole image shifted to the appearance of flames flickering above the round stage.

The music thumped through the arena.

The women flew.

And from the center of the stage, a man appeared, rising on a small circular platform no more than five feet across, rising up into the center of the flame.

As he ascended, his costume began to flow past the edge of the circle for several feet until the bottom edge suddenly burst into flame. Cries went up from all around the audience, but the central performer merely turned in a circle and the flames stayed burning just at the hem of the garment.

"Welcome," the man called out.

"Casimir," Fiona said.

"I am Rimizac, your host for tonight." He spread his arms wide. "Welcome to Dark Spectacle."

The applause resounded through the vast length of the theater. Even though Fiona knew she was seeing and hearing Casimir, she was amazed by what she saw and applauded with everyone else.

The women flying in the red flame-like tornado around him now began to depart as seamlessly as they had come, one by one, flying back down the ramp at amazing speed into the cave.

The music subsided then drifted into the most exquisite and strange melancholy tone, very impressionistic. Casimir held his arms wide; the flames at the hem of his robe exploded then turned to large white puffs of smoke that drifted into the air. "Bring the sacrificial lamb to me," he called out. "Bring her to me."

He extended both his hands in the direction of the cave's mouth.

Two enormous men, bodies gleaming and oiled and wearing only loincloths, were in full-mount. Their wings were identical and almost pure white, very large, magnificent. Between them they held aloft a woman whose costume was nothing more than a few streamers of a green mesh fabric. She was otherwise naked.

"She's naked," Fiona said aloud. She was stunned.

Her legs thrashed in the air as the two men flew her in the direction of Casimir.

"Her wings are not mounted," Jean-Pierre added.

Fiona clung to his arm. She didn't like where this was headed.

The two men flew the woman to Casimir and dumped her at his feet on the platform. The woman either was unconscious now or pretended to be. She rolled to the side and fell limply off the small raised circular platform.

Many women screamed at the sight of what would mean certain death.

But Casimir extended a hand down in her direction and just as she would have struck the circular stage, she stopped in midair. Slowly, through the force of his power, he drew her back toward him in a feat of pure levitation that she knew did not exist on Second Earth.

"How is he doing that?"

Jean-Pierre leaned close. "Remember that he is an Upper ascender. You and I know that, but no doubt most everyone here will believe he is using ropes or some other trick. He is believed to be a magician."

Slowly the woman rose, on her back, her legs splayed wide open, a few wisps of the green gauzy fabric barely disguising her nakedness.

The music shifted and what had been somewhat mystical now turned very heavy, more about wild drums and timpani than melody.

As the woman breached the side of the platform, Casimir leaped off, which sent another cry rising from the audience, but he merely floated in the air. At the same time, he shed what was the voluminous cloak so that it fell in a heap to the stage below.

He wore just a loincloth as he approached the floating woman. He moved between her legs, and if Fiona hadn't been embarrassed by the obviously sexual nature of the theatrics she would have been astounded by the levitation alone.

At the same moment, the drums and timpani grew louder, and developed a driving rhythm. From somewhere guttural grunts emerged, probably offstage.

He bent over the woman, pushing her head to one side. He appeared to sink his fangs, which brought the woman to life as she slipped her legs around his buttocks. Casimir's hips began to move.

Fiona wanted to look away, but probably like everyone else she was mesmerized by the audacity of the act. Just as she was about to shade her eyes, several winged men emerged from the cave, also in loincloths, bodies glistening, nine men in all, with long hair that flowed behind them. Hundreds of trained swans flew behind the men in close formation.

She had only heard of the trained birds that were used during spectacle. The lights shining on them were red. The men were their trainers and took up patterns that brought squadrons of the swans flying in intricate circles up and around the copulating image of Casimir and the woman.

At the same time, an enormous flood of red confetti descended from the tall ceiling so that the couple was soon completely disguised by the flocks of birds in flight and the red rain of confetti.

The music still pounded the wild rhythms. Whether they were actually engaged in the act, Fiona would probably never know. She didn't want to know.

But the rain of confetti stopped and the birds and their trainers began widening their patterns until they were making large circles well over much of the audience then finally they headed back to the cave.

The music slowed then halted as the last of the swans disappeared.

In the center, Casimir and the woman were simply gone, probably folded somewhere.

The effect, however, was astonishing. The small round platform that Casimir had occupied was now covered in red confetti and descended slowly to the large circular stage, also covered in red so that by the time the smaller platform reentered the stage, the whole effect was like looking at a lake of blood.

Suddenly, a body fell from the distance of the ceiling, the woman again, in the same strange pose.

Just as she would have struck the lake of blood, Casimir appeared and caught her in his arms.

The applause was thunderous. He kissed her, which seemed to revive her. Even Fiona couldn't help but put her hands together. In terms of drama, the whole thing was amazing. And for this small moment, she was enchanted.

Santiago leaned forward. "Jean-Pierre, I think that's Crace's widow, you know, Julianna."

"I think you are right, *mon ami.* Yes, it is her. I did not know she had become a performer, but then I suppose as the wife of a High Administrator one could call her role a performance—and she did excel at that. She was very well connected in the greater Chicago Territory. She always had the most beautiful brea—that is, a lovely figure."

Fiona shook her head but couldn't help extending her vision as well, something she was certain most of the vampires in the building were doing. The woman's breasts, barely covered by the gauze, were indeed pretty great, and as Casimir turned them both in a circle, she thrust her chest forward. She lifted her arm and vanished.

As the show progressed, Fiona understood one thing: Casimir was a true showman. How unfortunate he had aligned himself with Greaves. If all this time he had been the force behind Dark Spectacle, why on earth, any dimension, did he need to forge an alliance with the devil incarnate?

Since Casimir was very old, maybe he'd simply grown bored with life. She said as much to Jean-Pierre.

"It happens, *chérie,* especially for those rogue vampires

who no longer inhabit the dimensions for which they are suited. Casimir is a Fourth ascender, which means that the scope of his powers probably makes his life on either Mortal Earth or Second rather dull."

Fiona tried to imagine living for even several hundred years, never mind *thousands* of years. She thought of Endelle, and her complete disregard for propriety, for appropriateness of conduct in just about every situation. The woman was the leader of all Second Earth and wore mini skirts made out of boar's hide, for God's sake.

Maybe that's what happened over time: boredom, indifference.

Then she wondered if she would even have the luxury of finding out what tomorrow would be like, never mind a thousand years.

She glanced at Jean-Pierre's profile. She sat beside one of the most powerful men on Second Earth, a Warrior of the Blood. This sort of proximity alone put her life in jeopardy, just as her own extraordinary emerging powers put her at risk.

Would she even have years to grow jaded like Endelle or a complete hedonist like Casimir?

For some reason, still looking at Jean-Pierre, at his handsome profile, at the lips that rose in two kissable points, at the sheer strength of the set of his jaw and the way he held his head high, his gaze moving back and forth over the audience, the central stage, the dark cave, her chest seemed to collapse as emotion, unexpected, swamped her. She loved him. She *loved* him.

Her heart beat erratically, leaping around. Of course she knew she loved him, but right now what she felt seemed much, much greater, a living thing inside her swirling as the swans had swirled in circles, rising up and up.

She squeezed his arm, which brought his gaze to hers. Even though the orchestra had begun a powerful symphony, something like Beethoven, perhaps, Jean-Pierre leaned down and kissed her. It was not a simple kiss. No, he kissed her as though he understood the cry of her heart for him, his lips a pressure that kept increasing. She pushed back and parted her lips. That he pierced her mouth sent all those familiar sensations flowing through her, erupting so suddenly that she let him hear her body's response as a soft moan through his head, *I'm coming.*

So he used his tongue and worked her in that way only he could, drawing out the sudden physical response so peculiar to her, that she could orgasm with just a kiss. Tears brimmed in her eyes.

Maybe it was Dark Spectacle. Maybe it was the music, or the moment, or the knowledge that death lived off her right shoulder ready to swing the scythe, or maybe it was just Jean-Pierre in a gorgeous tux, but as he drew back from her and smiled that tender smile of his, she sent, Je t'aime. *I love you, so very much. You have my heart.*

His expression changed, his ocean eyes narrowing, his cheeks drawing in, his breath a sigh. Je t'aime, aussi, he sent. *You have my heart as well,* ma chérie.

But something began to change. His eyelashes batted as if in slow motion. He spoke as he turned back to the music. "The . . . music . . . is . . . Beethoven's . . ." The last word was so low and so garbled she could make no sense of it. Then he simply froze.

She didn't know what was happening. She turned to glance down the long curved row of boxes. No one blinked, spoke, or moved in any perceptible manner.

She glanced behind her intending to ask Santiago or Zach what was happening, but they were frozen as well, Santiago looking at his phone. Zach frowning at the stage.

She looked back at the stage. Casimir stood there alone, facing in her direction. He waved at her.

So he could move.

What on earth was going on?

She stretched her vision and saw his smile, the arrogant curve of his lips and set of his shoulders. He wore snug black leather pants, black boots with pointed toes, no shirt, just his long, thick hair loose about his shoulders, his muscular pecs on display.

"Come join me," he called to her. There was no music

because even the orchestra appeared stuck in mid-motion. "I have done this for you, Fiona. Now come to me."

She shook her head. She didn't know what to do.

But before she could gather her wits to even figure out what was happening, the two white-winged men flew from the cave and sped in her direction. She felt panicky, queasy. If she rose, they would grab her. But if she stayed put, they'd do the same and there seemed to be no time, just three seconds to make a decision.

Instinctively, she put a hand on Jean-Pierre's arm and leaned back farther in her chair.

The men arrived. She shook her head and said, "No. Don't do this." But neither looked at her.

Instead they swooped down on Jean-Pierre, took him underneath his arms, and flew away with him.

She vaulted out of her seat reaching for him. If she had been able to mount her wings, she would have flown after them, but she couldn't. All she could do was cry out another helpless, useless, "No!"

Casimir was suddenly next to her. She moved backward, bumping into her chair. She tried to move around the chair, but he simply caught her arm and held her fast.

"What are you doing? What have you done with Jean-Pierre?"

He smiled. "You weren't supposed to be immune to my stasis skills." He shrugged. "But I don't think this is a bad thing. If anything, I expect to have a little more fun. And isn't that what life is all about?"

Fiona felt the smooth glide, saw the darkness, and knew she was moving through nether-space.

When she arrived, with Casimir still holding her by the arm, she blinked at the familiar dark space, the stone walls, the smooth floor, the slab of dark granite upon which Jean-Pierre was stretched out, beautiful in his tux, but held in stasis.

She jerked away from Casimir.

"You should thank me. I've made him more comfortable. I stretched out his legs, his arms."

She turned and faced the monster, the hedonist, the Fourth ascender. "Have you no conscience?"

He pursed his lips, shook his head, and shrugged. "Uh, that would be a no." He chuckled.

"Then what do you want?"

"That is an excellent question and to tell you the truth I often have the worst time answering it. I can say this: I want to feel pleasure, a lot of pleasure, and as often as possible. Is that something you can offer me?" As he had the last time she was with him, he hooked his thumb in the waistband of his pants and tapped his zipper with long fingers.

She refused to look down. "No," she replied.

"Pity." He turned to the men, who had retracted their wings. They each were as tall as Jean-Pierre, but more muscled, like Warrior Luken. She would have been more frightened but their eyes were dull, enthralled.

"Your minions?" she asked.

"Of course. Are they not magnificent? Russian and as physically powerful as your WhatBee here."

He moved toward the table in the direction of Jean-Pierre's head. "Nice tux. I've seen this. I believe it is the latest Brioni. Yes, very nice. Your man is quite beautiful." Casimir put his hand on Jean-Pierre's shoulder and caressed him.

Fiona's instincts flared. She didn't want Casimir touching him, not like that, not like he wished to possess her man. She moved toward him.

Casimir glanced at her and laughed. "Jealous?" he asked.

"Take your hand off him. Now." She had never heard so much force in her voice before.

"Oh, I think I've hit one of your buttons." He looked back at Jean-Pierre, leaned down and kissed his forehead. At the same time, Jean-Pierre's coat, bow tie, and shirt disappeared, leaving him bare-chested. Casimir moved in behind Jean-Pierre's head, bent low, and slid his hands down Jean-Pierre's chest.

Fiona wasn't thinking when she leaped onto the table and threw herself on Jean-Pierre. She bared her fangs to Casimir.

What he saw seemed to startle him because he actually

moved backward, his hands flying away from Jean-Pierre. He held them up in surrender. "Extraordinary," he murmured. "But then given what you demonstrated earlier, I shouldn't be surprised. You're glowing again."

She hardly cared. She only knew he was not to touch her man, her warrior, her vampire.

She remained in that position, protectively above Jean-Pierre.

Casimir shifted his gaze to his oversized minions, snapped his fingers, and said, "Secure the woman. Bind the man."

Before she could plot a countermove, the two men moved with preternatural speed and she was dragged off the table and her arms pinned behind her back. The other worked a strange kind of white tape around Jean-Pierre's throat and torso, lifting him up, raising his arms in a series of quick moves as though he flipped a rag doll.

She thought she saw the smallest flicker of Jean-Pierre's eye in her direction.

She gave a little cry then sent, *Jean-Pierre, can you hear me? Oh, God, please hear me. Hear me. I don't know what to do. I don't have the power to battle these men.*

I am here, he returned. *But I cannot move.*

He put you and the entire audience in stasis.

My breathing, what is happening?

She looked at his throat and chest and she saw the brilliance of the trap. *The bindings are tightening with each breath you take.*

Are you all right?

Yes. But for how long? *I don't know what to do.*

What of your channeling power?

Yes. Of course. She moved her mind next to his and felt all the miraculous vibrations.

"Hold her tighter," Casimir called out.

Fiona, your aura is glowing again.

Casimir said as much. Can you feel me next to you?

Yes.

I want to try a hand-blast.

Do it.

She could feel a faint vibration travel down his arm, very weak, nothing like before when they used the hand-blast together.

She opened her palm and let the sensation fly, but barely anything happened.

Casimir laughed. "I saw a little burst of gold from your hand. Surely you can do better than that." He crossed his arms over his chest. He looked arrogant again, his lips almost a sneer.

Fiona knew she couldn't channel Jean-Pierre, not in this situation, because of the stasis.

She reached out for the one woman who could help her: Endelle. She sent her telepathic thread flying in the direction of Phoenix Two, but before she'd gotten a few feet, she stumbled mentally, such a strange preternatural sensation that her head actually jerked forward.

"Not gonna happen, Fiona," Casimir called out to her. "I've shielded the building. Nobody in. Nobody out. No preternatural phone calls."

Oh, dear God.

Freedom has many faces.

—*Collected Proverbs,* Beatrice of Fourth

CHAPTER 19

Fiona. Jean-Pierre's voice was a mere whisper through her mind. *I cannot breathe.*

She looked down at Jean-Pierre. His face was red and the bands had again tightened around his throat.

She looked at Casimir. "You're killing him."

But he lifted up both hands and shook his head. "I'm not allowed to kill anyone on Second Earth or Mortal Earth. To do so would be a death warrant."

"But you are the instrument of his death. How is that any different?"

Casimir shrugged. "It's a loophole and it's worked quite well for centuries."

Fiona looked down at the man she loved. She felt her power pulsing around her and through her. She knew her aura glowed, that her preternatural channeling power was at full bore, but what good could it do her when she couldn't channel anyone?

She felt completely helpless, even useless. She might as well be strapped down on Rith's bloodletting table for all the power she could wield in this situation. She slid off the table and sank to her knees. She held Jean-Pierre's limp hand in hers and brought his fingers to her lips.

She loved this man, this dying man. She loved him with all her heart, yet there was nothing she could do.

Tears fell, dampening his fingers as she rubbed them back and forth over her cheeks. *I love you,* she sent.

Je t'aime, returned faint, so very faint.

Jean-Pierre drew the smallest breath, but the band tightened even more. His mind skated about uneasily. He could not see a way out of this situation.

He knew only one thing: He would miss Fiona. He did not know what the afterlife would hold for him and perhaps this was his time, but already, even in this moment, he knew he would miss her, all the years he did not have with her, perhaps even the children they would not birth and raise together. Yes, he would miss it all.

He did not understand the power that the *breh-hedden* had wielded over his life since he first caught Fiona's lovely patisserie scent. He had at times been a crazed man, a vampire searching to be satisfied with only what she had to give. Taking her blood had been one of the finest experiences of his life, giving power to his body, and to his spirit. That was the true mystery between them: that somehow *she* empowered him and forced him to think in larger terms.

Even his desire to see the Militia Warrior force improved had expanded during his pursuit of Fiona, by all their conversations together over the past five months. *Oui,* so many conversations about life and about the war, about what each of them could do, desired to do, to make a difference in their society.

To lose all that now seemed tragic.

And yet who was to blame? He had only himself, always holding back, always restraining himself because of things that had happened so long ago, things that had forged a wall of bitterness around his heart, things that had prevented him from really loving Fiona the way this woman deserved to be loved, with nothing held back, with his heart on fire in true passion, in true commitment, in true love.

How much he wished even for just a moment to reclaim his life, that he might give himself fully to her as he had once given himself to his wife. Whatever Isabelle's reasons had been for her betrayal, he should never have closed his heart and his life to love because of it. That had been his real foolishness.

As his ability to breathe diminished, his mind seemed to grow and expand. He allowed himself to love Fiona. He gave his heart, so that it was as if a cool breeze swept through him and he could see things he had not seen before: that he had diminished his own life by not giving himself to love, that his own powers had been hindered because he had been restrained, even bitter.

How strange at the point of death to be so overcome by truth. He understood something about his real power. Fiona had even alluded to it several times—how much he was like Alison in empathic abilities. He felt them now and they were strong, very strong.

Understanding.

Of others, of their strengths and weaknesses, of what they needed in the moment of greatest stress.

As he released the past, as he embraced love truly for the first time in so very long, his mind flowed back to the last time he had trained Fiona. Though he had been right that she needed to allow possession during channeling to truly gain access to the power of obsidian flame, he had been wrong to pressure her. The last thing that she had needed or could have absorbed was that pressure.

As her teacher he had erred, he could see that now. He even saw that if he had covered her in his love, in his full acceptance of who she was, she might even now have complete access to her powers.

If he could go back, he would undo the mistake.

If he had been open and loving with Fiona, instead of proud in his defiance against love, would they be here, right now, trapped?

Fiona, he whispered through her mind.

I'm here.

You must forgive me.

For what? For what? What could you have possibly done that would need forgiveness.

I should not have pressured you about allowing a possession of your channeling abilities. It was wrong of me. I am so sorry.

What do I care about that, she sent, *when you have been so tender and forbearing and I've been so stubborn.*

Chérie, he sent, *you must listen. I do not have much time. I kept my heart closed to you because of something that happened so long ago. I wish that I could have opened myself to you, truly given you all of my heart. This you deserve, to have all that is in my heart, in my soul. I give it to you even now.*

"Jean-Pierre," she whispered aloud, her voice catching on a sob.

I will miss you, chérie. *In whatever plane I go to, ah,* chérie, *I will miss you so very much.*

Fiona couldn't bear the words he spoke. They were like a sharp knife slicing through her heart, her chest, down and down until she felt split into two parts. The pain was enormous.

What had she done? Dear God, what had she done?

More important, what was she doing?

From the time she had been rescued from New Zealand, she had made herself a promise to hold to her freedom, something that had sustained her for the past five months as she grappled with her recovery. She had come to understand how important, even critical, a sense of autonomy, of freedom, and personal control had been for her to come to terms with her slavery. For that reason she had recovered so very fast and had been able to set her sights on those things she could control—like being able to identify Rith's remarkable mist signatures on the Militia grid.

But something had been lost as well; she could feel it as a truth rising from her spirit to invade her mind. She didn't understand all that the ascended world of the vampire was meant to be, and her emerging powers had become a terrible burden. But here she was, with so much power, yet without the ability to save the man she loved.

What was she missing, not seeing?

Jean-Pierre had begged her forgiveness for not opening his heart to her but she had never felt unloved. He was so incredibly tender with her, so patient, an excellent teacher.

The only time he had pushed her had been where her powers were concerned, about obsidian flame and allowing . . . a complete . . . possession.

Her brain lit with a thousand little lights. She held Jean-Pierre's fingers tight. A path out of this terrible trap streaked through her mind.

Possession. Her ascended life had always been about possession, about feeling trapped. Even the early lovemaking with Jean-Pierre had required a thrall so that she could tolerate the sensation of his weight on her. So much of her fear of being trapped had disappeared, but not about letting Jean-Pierre or anyone possess her in order to explore and expand her obsidian power.

But tonight that would change.

Jean-Pierre. She called to him, but would he answer? Could he?

She tried again. *Jean-Pierre, hear me please.*

Fiona . . . so tired.

Possess me. She slid her mind next to his, and felt his shoulder against her shoulder, his hip against hers in that strange obsidian way.

Possess you?

If we worked together, right now, if I allowed you to take possession of me as you wanted to, then I think we can get out of this.

No. This would hurt you.

Not anymore. Please. I've erred, I can see that now. If you've held back, so have I. Please, do this thing. You can possess me and together maybe we can break these bonds.

He didn't speak. Instead, she felt his energy rise and begin the strange vibration next to her. She felt him push against her. Before, she would have pushed back and held him at bay. This time she simply let him come to her, all his energy, all that he was, and he took possession of her. All his power was now her power and his mind was her mind. She was no longer just Fiona, but she was both Fiona and Jean-Pierre.

She rose up and looked at Casimir, at his arrogance as he stood examining his nails waiting for Jean-Pierre's death.

Casimir lifted his gaze. "Is he gone?"

"Not yet." Fiona looked down at Jean-Pierre, then reached to the binding around his throat. All that Jean-Pierre was came into focus as vast vibrating energy within her body. She put her hand next to the strangling tape, touched it, and felt his power, her power, flow down that arm, and in a very small hand-blast she severed the plastic.

Jean-Pierre took in a deep breath and another and another.

Down his body, together they severed binding after binding.

"What the hell are you doing?"

She looked up at Casimir. It was so strange to see him both from her eyes and Jean-Pierre's.

She held her right hand out and a sword appeared in it. Another flash of thought and she wore her black yoga pants and a white tank top. Black flats.

Casimir sent his minions to attack her and now they had swords. But she was no longer Fiona, she was Jean-Pierre and she moved like lightning until two heads rolled on the black stone floor.

She moved past them and headed toward Casimir. She had never felt such power before, more than she could have imagined. She could even see the future in small increments, just a second or two before things happened. She held out her left hand and it wasn't a hand-blast she sent toward him, but a wave of her obsidian power that cascaded over him and dropped him to the floor, his eyes rolling in his head.

She kept the same power pulsing over him. She knew she could take his life.

Casimir, she sent. *You should not have done this tonight. Release the audience at once.*

She held his mind in a firm grip and felt his own wave of power as he tried to thwart her. But she knew her strength now, at least in this moment, possessed as she was by Jean-Pierre.

"Release them," she cried, using resonance, her voice, and mind-speak all at one time.

He rolled back and forth, screaming with the pain of what she had just done, in the way she would cry out in agony when someone used the same skills near her. Blood poured from his ears.

But still he remained stubborn, refusing to obey her. He held his hands to his ears.

She moved closer and this time she split her resonance three times. *"Release them!"* she shouted.

The hold he had over the entire assemblage broke, a snap that felt like a huge whip in the fabric of space and time. A roar of applause could be heard from above the cavern, a distant noise like a waterfall. For the audience, only a split second had passed, and they were marveling at Casimir's recent feats.

She released Casimir and he rolled on his side to look at her, his ears still streaming. He could hardly move, she could see that. He was in her power. She flexed her sword and lifted it high. She felt all of Jean-Pierre's strength in her body.

She was about to bring the blade down on Casimir's exposed neck when she realized that the shields around the Las Vegas arena had disappeared. Marguerite shrieked at her from the distance of the Superstitions.

She held the bloodied sword in her hand and Jean-Pierre's mind flowed over hers. *I can feel it as well. Marguerite is shouting for you, crying out for you, for us to stop the killing. What does it mean?*

Fiona extended the thread of her telepathy swiftly through nether-space until she touched Marguerite's mind.

I'm here. Jean-Pierre is with me.

You have less than two minutes, Marguerite cried. *And Casimir must live. There is something he will do in the future that must be done. But right now Greaves intends for Casimir and for all the High Administrators in the theater to die. Explosives have been set throughout the building. I've seen all this in the future streams, so go, fold everyone out of the building.*

At that moment Jean-Pierre separated from Fiona, pulling back, folding the sword from her hand.

He was off the table now and moved to stand over Casimir.

"Casimir, you must leave," he said. "A very powerful Seer has prophesied that you must live, that you have a role in the future to play. We are trusting this Seer to be right, so leave. Go."

Casimir stared up at him. "Greaves will be here soon. I summoned him."

Fiona shook her head. "No, Casimir. He will not. His intention is for you to die, for all of us, in an explosion. We only have a minute to change all of this. So do as Jean-Pierre has said. Fold."

Casimir frowned, his brow heavy over his dark eyes. He didn't lift a hand or an arm. She didn't think he could. But suddenly he was gone.

She turned to Jean-Pierre. "I think I know how we can do this."

"I do not think I have the capacity to fold all these people out of here, all the performers, the animals. I am so sorry, but I know I do not."

She smiled. "But I know someone who does."

At that, he smiled as well. "Of course."

With the shield around the building gone, she sent her telepathic thread streaking in the direction of the McDowell Mountains, to the white rotundas of Endelle's palace.

She found Endelle in a split-self configuration, as the ruler of Second Earth hunted Greaves through the darkening.

Sorry to intrude, she sent. She could feel the disruption of the hunt and Endelle's quick rage.

Fiona, what the fuck are you doing here and how the hell did you break through my security shields? Shit, I'm fucking dizzy. Don't ever—

We have an emergency in Las Vegas. I need you here in about five seconds or half your High Administrators and their significant others will be vaporized at Dark Spectacle.

A very slight pause, then, *Why the fuck didn't you say so?*

A moment later Endelle materialized right next to Fiona. She wore a long purple linen gown, which apparently she used while doing her darkening work. Of course the movement of air caused Jean-Pierre to crouch and draw his sword into his hand once more. At the sight of him, Endelle looked him up and down. "That's a different take on a tux, just the pants. I *like* it."

Fiona didn't try to admonish Endelle. Instead, she just slid next to her mentally, shoulder-to-shoulder, hip-to-hip. Endelle's vibration was so extraordinary, so powerful, that Fiona knew this would be the work of a second or two.

When she felt Endelle's awareness of her, she explained about Marguerite's warning and their current task. *Take possession of me. Now.*

Just like that?

Yes. Now. Do it so we can fold about twenty thousand people and a few hundred animals out of this place.

I don't think I have that much power.

Fiona felt joy as she sent, *But together,* we *do. Trust me.*

As Fiona let all her restraint go, as she lowered her mental shields, as she gave herself to the possession of the toughest bitch on Second Earth, she felt obsidian flame lock into place.

Endelle, bless her, didn't hesitate or question or argue. She simply took charge and the ride began. She grabbed Fiona's hand and folded her to the large central platform in the center of the arena. Fiona lifted her free arm, Endelle lifted hers.

Just as a rumbling began, as the explosion erupted, the gold rush of power flowed through her, combined with Endelle's Third ability. Together they captured everyone, and all the animals, in the immediate vicinity. As one, they folded the crowd to the desert at the foot of the palace.

Hundreds of swans, geese, and ducks, disoriented by the sudden fold, took to the air, their trainers shortly afterward mounting their wings and taking off as well.

Fiona remained in her possessed state with Endelle, no longer afraid of joining her spirit to the power of another. She felt strangely free, the exact opposite of what she had expected. Instead of oppression, her heart felt light, her spirit buoyant as new possibilities opened themselves up to her. Could she make a difference in the war?

Everyone she knew asked that question. *How can I make a difference in the war?* How many times had she heard Jean-Pierre express this as the deepest wish of his heart? What if *together* they could make a difference? How tremendous would that be?

What next? Endelle sent.

I don't know. Address the crowd? Fill them in?

What am I supposed to tell them?

Fiona took a moment to replay the Dark Spectacle event for Endelle, up to the point when Casimir put the entire audience in stasis. *None of the High Administrators knows what really happened.*

Okay. I get it now. Stasis . . . wow, that bastard has power. You should have killed him.

Marguerite was adamant and I trust her.

Fine. Whatever. I'll take over from here.

Fiona separated from Endelle. The ruler of Second Earth looked down at her purple gown and clucked her tongue. She waved her hand and changed into a new ensemble.

"Oh, no," Fiona murmured before she could catch herself.

Endelle grinned. "You no like?"

Fiona just stared at her, incredulous. She wore strange orange-feathered capri pants and a black leather bustier cut really low. Once more, she sported stilettos.

Fiona opened her mouth, then closed it.

There simply were no words.

But Endelle chucked her chin and whispered, "You need to have more fun." Then she whirled into the air, levitating higher and higher until she could address the crowd in front of her.

Fiona was not surprised at the number of gasps that filled the air, and not because Endelle was levitating.

She began speaking of the event, of what had so recently been avoided. She had an excellent, strong voice as a public speaker and even used her arms expressively. There actually were times when she could function in her role. Sort of.

Fiona stepped away, shaking her head. The ruler of Second Earth was a conundrum in so many respects.

High Administrators began to move forward, creating an arc around her. Fiona remained close, but she noticed that Jean-Pierre, Santiago, and Zacharius all mounted their wings and took off to form a protective triangle around the crowd, hunting, as they were designed to do, for the sudden, unexpected presence of death vampires.

Of course, the frightened birds darted over the crowd, creating a lot of chaos. But the trainers were busy as well, drawing the swans and geese, one by one, under their control.

Fiona remained near Madame Endelle.

And she smiled.

Jean-Pierre hovered in the air to the north of the crowd, his wings moving slowly. He listed left then right, his gaze shifting back and forth over the crowd, then around him as he turned in a slow circle. His wings moved in concert with his thoughts, making infinitesimal adjustments to keep him thirty feet in the air and pivoting so that he could watch the crowd and scan the skies.

He slipped his warrior phone from his battle kilt and swiped his thumb over the front.

"Jeannie here. How can I help?"

"Jeannie, would you send Thorne to my position as soon as possible, when he has a break in the fighting?"

"You got it. Hey, I didn't think Dark Spectacle would be over this early—and what are you doing near the palace?"

"Move the grid to the McDowells."

He heard tapping, then, "Holy shit. It's lit up with more power signatures than I've ever seen. What's going on? Death vampires?"

Jean-Pierre explained in a few brief sentences. By the end, Jeannie whistled. "No shit. Wow. Okay, sounds like I have a few calls to make. I'll let Thorne know. Seriffe covered three of the Borderlands with Militia Warriors. I'll contact him as well, and get some warriors over there."

"How are the Thunder God Warriors doing?"

"You know, I like that you're using their nickname. But they're doing great. They really are. No mortalities, and only one skin burn."

"That is good, very good. *Bon.*" Except his stomach tightened at the thought of Militia Warriors battling the usual number of death vampires that entered the Trough at night, all during the night. And it was very early still, not even nine o'clock.

"I'll give everyone a shout, update the brothers, and I'll get Thorne to you ASAP."

"*Merci,* Jeannie."

He thought he heard her sigh, that soft feminine lilt. Women seemed to like his French accent. He smiled as he slid his phone back in his pocket.

A moment later, not even ten seconds, he felt a powerful vibration beneath him. He drew in his wings to close-mount, folded his sword into his hand, and aimed at a spot next to whatever entity was folding so close to the crowds.

Fortunately, it was Thorne.

Jean-Pierre touched down.

"Tell me everything. Holy fuck, how many people are here and why don't the trainers have command of all the swans yet?" His gaze was fixed into the dark night sky. As if on cue, one out-of-control goose buzzed the crowd from the south heading straight in their direction.

A roll of cries came out of the crowd where the poor creature, wild-eyed, searched for a piece of normalcy. Jean-Pierre held his arm out in the shape of a crook, something he had seen the trainers do hundreds of times over the decades. For whatever reason, the goose dove toward him, flapping his arms wildly but settling his big body in that crook. He was a heavy, muscular bird and his heart beat like it would soon burst.

"What the fuck," Thorne muttered.

"Ça va, ça va," Jean-Pierre whispered. He stroked the bird's chest. The goose let out one serious huff and settled down, breathing hard.

"What are you now, the bird-master?"

Jean-Pierre shrugged but smiled. "He has gone through a trauma. Most animals never glide through nether-space. Is not that so, *mon petit*?"

"Jesus," Thorne muttered.

A moment later one of the trainers flew close, touched down, then called softly to the bird. The goose turned toward the trainer and dipped his neck.

The trainer very gently took the goose from Jean-Pierre's arm. "Thank you, *duhuro*."

Jean-Pierre almost opened his mouth to refute the ancient, extremely respectful form of address, but he bit his tongue then said, "Of course. They are very frightened right now."

Thorne scowled. He had blood spatter across the bare portions of his chest and arms, as well as the black leather weapons harness. "What the hell kind of circus is this anyway? I guess you'd better tell me what happened."

Jean-Pierre related the details, including the point at which Marguerite issued her warning about the need to keep Casimir alive.

Thorne's eyes flared at the mention of Marguerite and his lips tightened into a grim line; beyond that he just listened. At the end, he glanced in Endelle's direction.

Jean-Pierre also turned. Fiona stood well back from her.

He didn't like that she was in the shadows and suddenly the hairs on the nape of his neck stood up. "Shit," he murmured.

He folded straight to her, but by then she was gone.

Endelle turned around. "What just happened?" She was scowling as well.

"I think Rith just took Fiona."

"Aw, fuck," Endelle muttered.

Fiona faced her enemy. She stood in a garden she knew very, very well, a place where she had lived for decades. She smelled garlic and turmeric, and her stomach turned.

Rith looked as he always did, fully in control.

"Did Greaves let you off your leash?"

"I have foreseen this, that you would come back to me, and we would begin again." He gestured with his hand in the direction of the sky. "Look up?"

She knew what he wanted her to see, but she feared taking her eyes off him. She took several steps back and glanced in the direction of the sky. "Oh, my God," she murmured.

Three layers of mist this time, the inside an exquisite shimmering gold.

"I had to do something to put everything back the way it was."

She looked back at him and frowned slightly. "Greaves doesn't know you're here, does he?"

He shook his head, his straight black hair swaying against his ears and neck. "Greaves was finished with me. I was to be laid on the altar of his ambitions, so you mustn't blame him for this. He didn't know that I would be able to escape from Prague."

"Then you weren't at Dark Spectacle?"

"Yes, of course I was there, looking for you, watching, waiting for my opportunity. And most fortunately, I got swept up in the mass fold to Scottsdale Two."

"Who set the explosives then?"

Rith shrugged. "I don't know, but Greaves has an entire army who serves him without question, just as I once did."

He seemed strangely despondent.

"He held you captive, didn't he?"

"Yes."

"It's not pleasant, is it, to live without freedom?"

"I never cared about freedom."

She understood then. Whether or not Rith and Greaves were lovers, she was looking at a broken heart. The man he loved had betrayed him.

Of course, she might have felt a little more sympathy for him if he hadn't been her jailer for over a hundred years. "Are you keeping a new set of blood slaves here?"

"I intend to keep only one." His lips curved faintly. "I always admired you, Fiona. You outlived them all, but I also think you kept many of the women alive far beyond normal expectancy. Your compassion had a good effect. Yes, I confess that I admired and respected you."

Fiona frowned. "So you're not setting up another facility?"

"Of course not. There is no reason to now. I only did so to please Greaves. Actually, I have something different in mind for you and me. Because of your emerging powers, your dying blood will mean my salvation."

"But . . . you don't take dying blood."

He sighed. His black eyes took on a distant expression. "My only hope for survival now is to become a death vampire, but I won't drink just anyone's blood. Yours is the blood I want. It will add to my powers considerably with each taking, and as I said before, I respect and admire you. Your blood is acceptable to me, and I know from past experience that you have the ability to thrive, even in captivity.

"I should also add that I understand the limitations of your obsidian abilities—that you can only channel power, not express it yourself. At least that is what I have observed."

Fiona stared at a madman, one who had chosen her as the vessel of his transformation, and the ongoing nourishment by which he intended to grow strong enough to sustain his own life in the face of Greaves's intention that he should die.

She was appalled and disgusted, but this was the least of her concerns. She could be properly outraged later. Right now, she had her own survival to consider.

"You do understand that I have only begun to explore my obsidian power."

"Yes, of course. I'm counting on the breadth of that power to push me beyond even Greaves's achievements."

She took deep breaths and relaxed her shoulders. She knew that the three layers of mist would undoubtedly keep her from reaching out to anyone else for help. Her only hope of defeating the powerful vampire in front of her would have to come from within herself.

Jean-Pierre tried to follow Fiona's golden trail only once. When he was kicked back to the same spot where she had dematerialized, he knew who the adversary was and he also knew that he needed help.

Endelle still levitated ten or so yards away, answering questions from her High Administrators.

Thorne materialized beside him. Jean-Pierre was so overwrought, he had his sword in hand ready to take his enemy's head off and just barely kept himself from decapitating Thorne.

"What the fuck happened?" Thorne asked.

"Rith took her . . . again."

Thorne drove a hand through his hair. "Aw, shit."

But Jean-Pierre stared at him . . . hard. "I think I know what we can do, the way we can maneuver around Rith in this situation."

"How?"

"We need your woman. We need Marguerite. She prevented a complete annihilation at the outdoor chapel in Prescott Two because she saw into the future streams. She warned Fiona about the explosion at the arena and the women have a strong connection. If she uses her Seer ability to search for Fiona, I think we might be able to find her."

Thorne scowled and searched Jean-Pierre's eyes. He glanced at Endelle, who was now arguing with one of her

High Administrators. "What the hell is Endelle wearing? She's about one fruit basket away from belonging in the Caribbean. Shit. Okay. I gotta take care of this . . . now. Shit."

He whipped his warrior phone from the pocket of his kilt and thumbed the slick surface.

"Hey, Jeannie. Has Endelle asked for Marcus tonight?" He rolled his eyes. "That's what I thought. You need to get him over here right away. Havily, too. This mess calls for administrators." His gaze shifted to Endelle whose face was bright red as she told one of her High Administrators to take his goddam head out of his ass. He added, "Not profane Voodoo priestesses."

He put his phone away then turned back to Jean-Pierre. "We have to get Endelle's go-ahead. What we need to do will involve breaking a big law."

A moment later Marcus and Havily arrived looking very tousled: hair not in the usual tidy order, clothes less than immaculate. Generally the couple could've come from the pages of *GQ* or *Cosmo*. Marcus thumbed a line of lipstick off Havily's cheek then kissed her.

The scene was so tender, so intimate, that Jean-Pierre had to look away.

Thorne called them both over. "Did Jeannie give you the scoop?"

"The short version," Marcus said. "Sorry. We were a little . . . tied up."

Havily coughed behind her hand, but Jean-Pierre could see she was blushing.

Marcus's gaze slid to Jean-Pierre. "Hear we've got one of our own missing."

Jean-Pierre nodded, but said nothing more. His throat was far too tight and his eyes burned.

Thorne filled him in. Marcus, his eyebrows slashed low over his light brown eyes, listened intently. Every few seconds his gaze would take in the crowd, then Endelle, then back to Thorne.

Finally, Marcus stared at Havily. Her expression was

serious as well. Jean-Pierre knew they were talking it over telepathically. After a long minute, Havily nodded.

"We've got this," Marcus said. He then called out to Endelle, "Madame Supreme High Administrator, you have an important phone call. It's urgent."

Had to be some sort of code.

Endelle glared at him, her cheeks still rosy from the ongoing argument. At last she made her excuses and floated toward them. Her administrative style did not help her at all, but such a demonstration of levitation power—something most Second ascenders could not do—would be talked about for a very long time.

"What do you mean, a phone? Why the fuck did you disrupt my meeting?"

Marcus offered her a profound you've-got-to-be-kidding look, then spoke rapidly. He outlined a disembarkation procedure for the High Administrators. Havily was already on the phone, initiating some kind of preset emergency strategy.

Jean-Pierre wasn't surprised when off to his left, and away from the group, Marcus's team began to appear.

A moment later Marcus spoke with three senior members of his team then levitated and took over Endelle's place among the High Administrators.

For a long moment, as Havily joined Marcus's staff, Endelle stood with her back to Jean-Pierre. Her fingers plucked at the feathers of her calf-length pants. She watched and listened to Marcus for about thirty seconds. Jean-Pierre wanted to interrupt her, to press her over their current disaster, but Thorne shook his head.

Finally, Endelle shifted to face Jean-Pierre and Thorne. "Guess I should have called Marcus right away."

Thorne nodded.

Jean-Pierre felt ready to jump out of his skin.

Thorne put a hand on her shoulder and very quietly said, "We need permission to break into the Superstition Fortress."

She opened her mouth to speak, but Thorne filled her in on Fiona's sudden abduction and Endelle listened.

Finally she turned to Jean-Pierre and said eloquently, "Well, shit motherfucker."

"We will never find her," Jean-Pierre said, "without the aid of Marguerite. Rith blocked his trace as he did in Toulouse. Please tell us we may go to the Superstitions and do this thing."

Thunder drifted down the valley,
Only an echo now.
The last of the rain fell to earth.
She crawled into the safety of her bed
And slept.

—*Collected Poems,* Beatrice of Fourth

CHAPTER 20

Endelle turned and looked at the crowd that she and Fiona had saved, over twenty thousand people. If Fiona hadn't come through in that moment, if she hadn't grown into her obsidian flame abilities, if she hadn't allowed Endelle to possess her so that together they forged sufficient power to move all these people through time and space as though they were slicing soft butter, not one of them would be alive.

Marcus had told her that the explosion had rocked Las Vegas Two; he'd seen a special report that included helicopter views of the scene not five minutes ago.

If Greaves had succeeded in his plan, if the explosion had happened a minute sooner, if Fiona and Marguerite hadn't worked in beautiful tandem to get the information to Endelle, all these important High Administrators aligned with her government would be dead. The ensuing chaos would have cost her the war. She had no doubt about that.

She owed Fiona everything right now.

As for the Fortress, she turned back to look at Thorne, at his red-rimmed eyes and the way he breathed hard through his nostrils waiting for her to say the word, just say the fucking word. His woman was imprisoned by a sociopath apparently intent on creating a super-race of Seers. If Endelle didn't stop Owen Stannett right now, what would she have to face in the coming months or years? Just how much power had Stannett amassed?

She had tried throughout the afternoon to talk sense to Stannett, to force him to own up to his end of the bargain, but he was making use of his old tricks, stalling and ho-humming until she had mentally pulverized his nuts, in her hands, about a thousand times.

And there was something more. She'd also tried contacting COPASS again, trying to impress on that worthless entity that Owen Stannett needed to be removed from service as High Administrator of the Fortress, but all that came back to her was a voicemail from Daniel Harding, chairman of COPASS and secret death vampire, in which he spoke one word: "Nonsense."

So here she was, hamstrung for the one millionth time.

And as she once more cast her gaze at the crowd, as she watched the High Administrator of Mongolia Two Territory, his very pregnant wife, and their small entourage fold into the night, she drew a deep settling breath.

"No more," she whispered.

She turned back to her men, two of her tough, powerful Warriors of the Blood, two who had been so faithful, who fought every night against death vampires that Darian Greaves sent to wear them down, night after night at the Borderlands, battling to keep two worlds safe. And now each of them was fighting to save the woman he loved.

Fine.

She called out, "Havily, get your ass over here."

Havily left her place near Marcus's execs and moved to stand beside Endelle. The woman waited for instructions, which was exactly what she needed.

Damn, her heart felt heavy. What she was about to do could land her in prison, perhaps even worse.

She turned back to Jean-Pierre and Thorne. She put a hand on Jean-Pierre's left shoulder then cupped Thorne's face.

She nodded and let her hands fall away, back to her sides. To Havily, she said, "I want you to witness what I have to say to my men. Do you understand? This is a serious legal matter and you will be called upon in the future to answer for what you have heard here tonight. Do you understand?"

"Yes, Madame Endelle."

She nodded. She glanced from Jean-Pierre to Thorne and back. "I hereby grant you permission to breach the Superstition Mountain Seers Fortress, to take in hand and remove from that place the gifted Seer and recent transfer from the Creator's Convent, Marguerite, bringing her to my office as soon as you have apprehended her. I understand the legal ramifications of taking this action. May any subsequent suit against this action fall exclusively on my head." She nodded briskly several times. "Go get Marguerite then bring Fiona home where she belongs."

Thorne changed into clean battle gear. He wished he had time to shower, to clean the blood off his skin, rinse it the hell out of his hair. Not that Marguerite would give a rat's ass. How many times had he gone straight from battle to the Convent, pulled her out of bed, and taken her in just this state.

He'd tried apologizing once, but she'd told him to *shut the fuck up and do me*. No, Marguerite wouldn't care. But the flight gear, yeah that was fresh.

His heart hammered in his chest at the thought of busting her out of the Superstition Fortress, having her with him, keeping her by his side.

But as Jean-Pierre talked over the situation with Jeannie, orchestrating a tight fold to the entrance to the Fortress, he slammed the brakes on all his hopes about what Marguerite would do and where she'd go once he got her the hell out of that place.

He realized that the moment Endelle gave permission for the invasion, he'd turned about sixteen again, excited to see *his girlfriend.* He'd even had the ridiculous thought that once she was out, she'd move in with him, live with him in his Sedona house.

But there was a greater truth to Marguerite, something that only he knew. Above all things she craved her freedom, to do what she wanted to do, to go where she wanted to go, *to be with other men.* For a long, terrible moment, he wished she was locked up back at the Creator's Convent, where he could keep her to himself.

Fuck.

Endelle stared at him hard. "Bring her back to me, Thorne. We'll get her set up in some new place, a place of her choosing, but God help me, I need her. I've got to have the use of the future streams. What happened here tonight, well, we were damn lucky. If Fiona hadn't been in the right place at the right time, if she hadn't had her powers come online like that, Jesus H. Christ, we'd be in Las Vegas picking up body parts instead of sending people back to their homes."

He nodded, but his gaze fell to the dirt.

"We need her, Thorne. Tell me you intend to bring her to me."

He lifted his gaze to her, but his heart felt like it was being held in the fist of a giant and squeezed. "You know I will," he said. And he meant it. But didn't that make him a selfish bastard—because in the most secret place of his selfish heart he was hoping that Endelle would lock her up again.

Jean-Pierre nodded to Thorne. "Jeannie can send us now."

Thorne nodded, his gaze still on Endelle. "Let's do it." As he slid through nether-space, he had one last view of Endelle, her lips curved about a quarter of an inch as she flipped him off.

He arrived at the doors to the fortress, the tall, arched iron doors, rusted from the weather. If this was any indication of the state of the facility inside, his stomach lurched.

"Back up with me," Thorne said. "There's only one way to do this."

Jean-Pierre moved about twenty feet away, and Thorne laughed as he joined him. Jean-Pierre knew Thorne's style. This wasn't going to be a gentle break-in.

Thorne didn't do the blast first thing, though. He knew better than that. He called Jeannie and asked her to scan for life-forms near the entrance. He didn't want one of the Seers accidentally hurt or even killed because he was so anxious to get this job done.

He held his phone to his ear. A moment later Jeannie gave him the all-clear.

He put his phone away and aimed his palm at the door. He didn't mess around. He gathered energy from all around him, let it sing through his arm, and in a quick flying bolt blasted the damn thing off the hinges.

To Marguerite, he sent, *Honey, I'm home.*

Marguerite heard the explosion and instinctively backed up against the wall of her room. She was hungry as hell and a couple of flies were enjoying the second tray of food she'd refused to touch. She'd just been wondering how long she could go without eating, or how soon she could expect Stannett to visit her with some serious muscle in tow to subdue her, when the vibration of the explosion shook her sad little platform bed.

Then Thorne's voice rang through her mind, *Honey, I'm home,* and she smiled. Well, dayam! Her man had come to bust her out of this shithole. But wasn't that like some kind of death sentence or something? Didn't COPASS frown on trespassing in Seers Fortresses?

Aw, what the hell did she care? The cavalry had come.

I have no idea where I am in this place, she sent.

Honey, we're checking every cell . . . except, oh, God, Jean-Pierre, is she alive? He just nodded back at me.

What is it? Tell me? Is who alive?

The first cell we opened has this godawful smell and there's a woman curled up into a ball, thin as a stick, ex-

cept, shit, she's pregnant. Oh, my God. I'm getting Horace and his team over here. I'm coming for you. Oh, my God.

She felt him shut down and now she sat with her arms hooked around her knees and her forehead pressed against her legs. What a nightmare, what a goddam, fucking nightmare.

She'd always hated Owen. She'd always known he had sociopathic tendencies. But to be impregnating women just to make a super-race? Her stomach turned over a couple of times.

"Your boyfriend's here," Stannett said.

She looked up. Stanny stood there, calm as you please, as though he'd foreseen this moment.

"So what happens next?" she asked. "You must know."

He shrugged. "I'm not as good as you. Why don't you check into the future streams then you tell me?"

"Why are you so calm? Don't you realize that your life, all these plans, has just been blown to hell?"

But he just smiled. "Do you seriously think this place is the beginning and end of my vision?" He smirked. "I'll be seeing you real soon, Marguerite." And with that, he lifted his arm and vanished.

Marguerite unfolded her legs and slid them over the side of the platform. She dropped the few remaining inches to the floor, walked to the door, her mind dizzy and full of thoughts about freedom. This was just too easy. Too damn easy.

But she opened her door and looked left down the long hall. Others were emerging from their rooms. She looked right and standing at the end, like a god, was her man.

She stepped into the hall, turned in his direction, and planted her hands on her hips. "About time, asshole."

He grinned. She'd never seen him look so young.

He didn't walk to her, though. Instead he folded straight in front of her and took her in his big powerful arms, lifting her straight up off the cold cement floor.

"This your room?"

She nodded. He carried her backward, her feet dangling.

She was too short for him, but he always made it work. He didn't close the door but he kissed her in that warrior way of his, the way he had from the first—like he was going to devour her from the inside out.

She loved it, that hard tongue of his driving into her mouth. She whimpered and threw her arms around his neck. She kissed him back, biting his lip and making him bleed.

He laughed. "Wildcat," he said, but he kissed her again.

"Does this mean I'm free?" she asked against lips that kept pushing at her mouth.

"Please stay," he said. "Not here. I mean on Second. Please come back with me to Endelle's office. She wants to talk to you, then please stay."

"Of course I'm staying." Not.

He kissed her again. "I want you to stay. Please. I need you, Marguerite. I don't know what I'll do if you go."

"I'm not going anywhere." She didn't know exactly why she was lying to him. Maybe the piercing desperation in his voice, or the trembling of his arms as he about squeezed the life out of her.

"Thorne, I am so sorry to intrude, but we must find Fiona."

At that, Marguerite jerked out of his arms and pushed past him to stare at Jean-Pierre. Well, wasn't he one hunk of a man? She loved the color of his eyes, similar to Thorne's but bluer—or would that be greener? Yes, the man had great eyes. And those lips. Fuck, but she could kiss those lips for about a century.

She heard a low growling sound beside her and turned to see that Thorne was watching her watching the warrior in the doorway. Uh-oh. She wasn't the most discreet woman on the planet but there was no point rattling the lion's cage.

"So . . . what were you saying about Fiona? Is she in some kind of trouble?"

"*Duhuro* warrior," a man's voice called from behind Jean-Pierre.

"Horace," Thorne called out. Jean-Pierre stepped aside and the healer named Horace came into view. Marguerite had known of him for decades. He was the one who kept the warriors mobile every night, going from one Borderland to the next and healing their *skin burns*—as they called the deep sword cuts that happened now and again.

She looked the healer up and down. Horace had a look to him that Marguerite really liked. He had longish wavy brown hair, not as long as these warrior brutes, but wavy and quite beautiful. He had a long neck. Her gaze fell to his vein and she suddenly wanted some of what he had to give.

But as she looked at him, ignoring the conversation among the men, Thorne was suddenly in front of her. "What are you looking at, Marguerite?"

She blinked up at him. His fangs had emerged. And all that sudden interest in Horace shifted until all she could see was Thorne's fangs wet from his mouth. Shit. All that need she felt coalesced, and she couldn't exactly help that she threw herself on him and wrapped her legs around his waist.

"Thorne," Jean-Pierre called out.

He drew back from her, his hazel eyes wild. "We can do this later. Shit. Sweetheart, we need you to find Fiona in the future streams. Rith took her."

"Rith has Fiona? Why the fuck didn't you say so?" She didn't exactly release Thorne since now she was a woman with *two* critical missions. She locked her ankles around his waist then sank into the future streams.

She found Fiona's golden ribbon and dove in. The images came at her faster than she wanted them to, but she got the gist. She collected them and released the golden pathway. She opened her eyes. "Don't let me go," she told Thorne.

"I've got you."

She nodded. "But I have to touch Jean-Pierre." He had hold of her ass and pressed her against him so that she could feel all the promise of his body.

"Jean-Pierre," she said, still holding Thorne's rough gaze. "Come here, and let me show you what you need to see. I'm not letting go of Thorne. Don't look at me, just put your face against my hand, do you understand?" Multi-tasking was just plain fun.

"*Oui.*" She felt his face. Thorne's arms tightened around

her. She felt Jean-Pierre's mind though she heard Thorne growling against her neck now. With her eyes closed, she let the vision flow toward him.

The process took less than five seconds, images being a kind of movie that sped up the communication in light-speed increments.

"Fuck," Jean-Pierre cried. "He has got her back in Burma, that sonofabitch. When does the vision take place?"

She savored how Thorne ran the sides of his fangs up and down her neck. "I'd say you've got about three minutes, maybe a little more." But her gaze was fixed on Thorne's sandy-colored hair as she picked at the *cadroen* that held it together. "Shut the door on your way out, Jean-Pierre. Thorne and I have something to discuss."

She heard the door slam.

Thorne backed her up against the wall. *Good. Good.* She was already panting hard and her thighs were wet, so ready. He jerked her nightgown up and lost his kilt and the briefs he wore to do battle in so that he was right there, his cock hard as a rock as it had been for the past century with her.

She tilted her hips. *Give it to me. Give it to me. Give it to me.* He drove in hard. *Oh, God.*

She loved it the best when he was like this. He'd been jealous and it soothed her feminine soul because an animal couldn't have been more powerful right now as he pumped her hard. He was big, thick, hard, exactly what she liked, what she needed. She clung to him. "What are you waiting for, asshole? Take my blood . . . now."

And he did.

Her back arched against the wall. Thorne slammed into her and drank her down. He made huge grunting noises and the slap of his skin against hers was the only music she really liked, or vowed she ever would.

He brought her, a rush of sensation as she ground her muscles against him, pulling him deeper into her well. She dug her nails into his back, barely avoiding his wing-locks. She felt the skin break and when it did, he came, drawing his fangs out of her and pounding into her, giving her what only he could give.

She cried out at the ceiling as pleasure spilled over her, a wave of sensation through her chest that washed her overboard and let her swim and swim and swim. Her mind filled with euphoria so that she knew happiness and peace.

She sighed over his back, savoring the feel of him deep within. She felt his cock twitch. He drew a quick breath then released a quicker sigh. "I love you" came from his absurdly gravelly voice.

"I love you, too." The lies came so easily.

"Please stay."

"I said I would and I will."

"I mean it."

"Of course you do and I mean that I'm staying."

"Like hell you are."

"I'm staying, Thorne." Maybe if she said it enough, she'd start to believe it as well.

Jean-Pierre stood outside an impenetrable wall of mist. It was raining in Burma, hard. He was already soaked. He had tried several times to reach Fiona telepathically, but he could not break through the barrier of mist that once more covered Rith's house. He had even mounted his wings searching for an entry point over the outer dome, but Rith had changed the structure of the shield and unlike most walls of mist, he could not pass through.

So now he waited, playing the vision over and over in his mind, of two knives and Fiona. *Mon Dieu,* he prayed to the Creator that Marguerite was right and that he was exactly where he needed to be.

Fiona looked around the living room of Rith's house. She stood just inside the door and gazed. She had only been in this part of the British Colonial replica once, when she had battled with Rith physically all those months ago. She had overpowered him by shattering a vase over his head, then ran into the garden, the place where she had first met Parisa, the woman who had engineered her eventual rescue.

She looked around at the polished mahogany floors, at the quiet serenity of the Burmese house, of the orange cat half hidden behind a chair, his tail flipping.

The house felt like a home, yet downstairs, in the damp stone basement, was the place she had resided for over a hundred years in blood slavery. She had of course many times seen the front room or lounge from the gardens, where she took an hour of exercise each day. She had seen the small dark Burmese women cleaning, polishing, performing a different kind of slavery for Rith, day in and day out.

And here she was again.

But like a river you could never step into twice, this was not the same room she had been in before. She was not the same woman.

"I have a request," she stated. She moved into the living space and sat down in a chair overlooking the garden. "I'd like a cup of tea." She looked up at him. "Would you be so good—"

"You want a cup of tea?"

He now stood to her left. His brows were lifted, almost in surprise, maybe disdain. He didn't like women very much. Certainly he had no respect for them and no particular use except as submissive slaves. He was a man of boxes.

So she would play this box.

She watched him turn on his heel, a slight shrug to his shoulders. He even chuckled, an unusual sound for him.

Fiona stared at the wall opposite now and drew inward. She felt her obsidian power, the mass of golden light that was becoming so familiar to her. She had barely begun to scratch the surface of its meaning and uses.

She sent her telepathic thread outward several times, reaching in turn for Marguerite, for Endelle, for Jean-Pierre, but the signal simply returned in a brisk boomerang of sensation that left her with a slight headache just above her right eye.

She hadn't expected to connect. Rith wouldn't have been that stupid.

But she turned inward once more, settled herself very deeply against her obsidian power, the power of truth. She pondered the two recent "possessions," by Jean-Pierre and by Endelle. The resulting power had been extraordinary.

She went deeper still and explored the memory of having been possessed by Jean-Pierre, when she had wielded the sword in her hand, when she had essentially killed two men, both infinitely bigger than she.

She felt the vibrations of the experience within her body, her bones, her muscles, all the connective tissues.

Without thinking, she held the vibrations very close within her body. She rose from the chair. She could hear the sudden scream of the teakettle. She remembered Rith's chuckle. She felt something else, as well: the way Jean-Pierre could read people. And so she read Rith now, the web of his emotions. She understood just how much he believed women to be inferior, silly, easily overpowered.

She moved into the kitchen. She looked around. There were three knives in a wooden block.

He saw her. He had the kettle in his hand, but he put it back on the stove. He turned toward her, assessing.

"You seem different."

"You do not. *Pas du tout.*"

"French?" He cocked his head. She noticed a sheen of perspiration on his forehead. The next moment he had a knife in his hand and blurred toward her at preternatural speed.

She allowed all the vibrations of Jean-Pierre's two hundred years of warrior service on Second Earth to live, beat, and breathe within her. The knife was just suddenly in her right hand and with her left, she blocked the blurring arm, pushing the stabbing thrust away from her neck. Her blade found purchase in the soft belly of Rith's body. She thrust up and up until his back bowed, and she pushed the blade through something meatier and pulsing.

As a warrior might, she gave a twist.

Rith's body jerked hard. He fell backward and she released the knife so that it would stay within him.

She had no particular reaction as his head slapped the tile

hard. He shook from head to toe, his eyes wild for a few seconds. But soon his body fell still and the light in his eye disappeared. Blood poured from the wound, spreading in a beautiful red blossom on the fine white line of his shirt, around the ebony handle of the knife.

But she wasn't done.

She put her foot on his neck and looked outside. Rain now pelted the garden. The dome of mist was gone.

She sent her telepathic thread flying through nether-space, reaching for Jean-Pierre. She found him almost instantly. Which meant he was close by.

Come to me now. Help me finish this, she sent.

She understood Rith's power. She felt in her bones that he could undo this. No, she *knew* he could undo this, that he was undoing it even now.

Jean-Pierre watched the mist crumble before his eyes. He did not question what he saw. He focused on Fiona and folded.

A split second later he stood beside her.

Rith lay on the floor, a knife up through his abdomen, blood seeping. But he understood at once why Fiona had sounded desperate. Rith was healing his heart and slowly pushing the blade out.

Jean-Pierre had but seconds. A vampire with this amount of power, which he understood to be a Fourth ability, would not take long.

He drew his sword into his right hand and with a single swift arcing swipe, severed Rith's head from his body.

Only then, as blood poured from the head and from the neck, did Rith's body finally slump into the stillness of real death.

Fiona slid her arm about his waist. He looked down at her. "Are you all right?"

"He was deranged," Fiona said.

He folded his sword away. "*Oui*. At the very least, he was deranged." He withdrew his thin warrior phone from the pocket of his kilt and thumbed it.

"Jeannie, here. How may I serve?"

"Jeannie, we have Rith at last and he is dead. I want you to transfer his body to the morgue. His head is severed but would you be so kind as to transport them separately and alert the doctor to send the head immediately into the crematorium? Do you understand?"

"Tell you what, *duhuro*. Let's do the head first. We'll leave the body right where it is until I have confirmation that the head has been disposed of. Is that okay with you?"

"*Oui*. A much better idea."

"Good. I have a fix. Are you ready?"

"Do it." Rith's head vanished. And as though his body understood that the separation was now complete, a shudder passed through it.

He felt Fiona lean into him a little more. He slid his arm around her shoulder and held her close. Both of them stood over the gore, staring and watching. Waiting until Jeannie called back. A morbid vigil.

"I wish Parisa was here," she said softly. "She would want to know that he's dead."

"Do you want to call her?"

"Yes." He felt her nod against him.

He drew his Epic from the deep pocket of his kilt and handed it to Fiona. She sighed heavily as she put in Parisa's number. She looked up at him. She had tears in her eyes.

"Hi, it's me," Fiona said. "No, everything's fine. Better than fine." She paused, drawing in another breath. "We got him, Parisa. We got the monster."

Jean-Pierre was still holding his warrior phone next to his ear. Jeannie came back online. "You there?"

"Oui."

"The doctor put the head in the crematorium personally. This boy is toast. He's only waiting now for the rest of the corpse. Shall I take it?"

"I have a favor to ask."

"Anything, *duhuro*."

"The Militia Warriors have a different morgue, *non*?"

"That's right. Are you thinking what I'm thinking you're thinking?"

He smiled, a little. "That makes no sense to me. But I would like you to send the remainder of Rith's body to a different morgue, to Militia HQ morgue. Will you do that?"

"With pleasure. Let me make the arrangements. Hold on."

He looked down at Fiona, who held the phone loosely in her hand. Her shoulders shook. He turned into her and gathered her into his arms, though awkwardly because he still had his warrior phone pressed to his ear. She sobbed against his chest. With one eye on Rith's remains, he held her tight.

At last, Jeannie came back on. "Ready?"

"Yes."

"This will be a complete cleanup job. Close your peepers."

He warned Fiona then closed his eyes.

"Ready," he said.

The flash of light behind his eyelids was blinding, but when he opened his eyes Rith, and all his blood, was just gone. "Thank you, Jeannie."

"My pleasure. Call if you need me."

He put his phone away. "It is over. At long last, it is over."

Fiona pulled back to look up at him. Her face was streaked and her nose red but she had never looked more beautiful. She was alive and she was safe. "I asked Parisa to join us here."

"And is she coming? Now?"

"Yes. Antony as well. Parisa was held captive here for three months and this was . . . my home, for over a century."

"This is good," Jean-Pierre said. "I suppose Alison would call this *closure*."

Fiona offered a faint curve of her lips as she said, *"Oui."*

Review the past,
Learn the lessons,
Forgive the self,
Forgive others,
Dwell in peace.

—*Collected Proverbs,* Beatrice of Fourth

CHAPTER 21

Fiona looked up at the kitchen ceiling. She had never heard rain on the house before, ever. Rith's creation of mist had prevented the property from experiencing any extreme of weather.

A movement of air, and suddenly Parisa and Antony materialized. Because she still had her arm around Jean-Pierre, she felt his sudden tensing then release.

"*Allô,* Medichi. Parisa."

Fiona put her fingers to her chin. Her lips quivered. There she was, the woman, her friend, who had made it possible for Fiona to have a new life. Her heart was suddenly so full, unbearably full, and more tears tracked down her cheeks.

"Fiona," Parisa cried. "Is it true? Is it really true?"

Fiona nodded. "Yes, he's dead."

Parisa's shoulders fell as she released a sigh. "Thank God. He can't hurt anyone else. Ever."

Fiona went to Parisa and took her in a tight embrace.

Parisa held her equally as hard. All Fiona could think to say was "Thank you," over and over.

Parisa responded, "Of course. Of course. Of course."

Finally she drew back, folded tissues into her hands, and gave a couple to Fiona. She dabbed at her eyes and her face. "I can't believe it. I just can't believe it. But I want to know everything about your life here. Would you be willing to share that with me?"

At first, Fiona thought it would be impossible, that she felt too much, that her wounds were still too raw. But after a moment's consideration, she said, "If you'll tell me about yours."

"I want to do that," Parisa said, nodding. "I think it would be a good thing . . . for both of us."

So for the next hour, Fiona walked through the house with Parisa. She took her into the basement and told her stories about the women she'd known who had died there. Afterward, climbing the stairs, Parisa showed her the perfect bedroom in which she had lived out her three months of captivity.

"It hardly seems like anything," Parisa said, "compared with what you went through."

Fiona let her gaze drift over the four-poster bed and the silk quilted coverlet. "I think at least fifty of the slaves died before the three-month mark. Don't minimize the time of your captivity. Slavery is slavery."

Parisa looked at her. "Do you know what I think? I think I was brought here to make sure you got home. That's what I think."

"I would never wish such a fate on anyone, but I will always be grateful that I met you, no matter what the circumstances."

Turning, she saw that the rain had stopped. In Burma, it was morning. Through the windows she could see that the sun sparkled on the wet feathery leaves of the tamarind tree.

"Come outside with me."

She took Parisa out into the wet garden. For a long moment, they stood shoulder-to-shoulder and stared at the teak bench beneath the enormous old tree where they had met for the first time just five months ago.

"I sat there for hours," Parisa said, "the first day of my abduction because Rith told me to. I was afraid to move, afraid to do anything. No one came to me, to talk to me, to tell me what was expected of me.

"When I went in search of Rith, he punished me for my disobedience, piercing my mind and inflicting pain, such pain. How easily he subdued me with that pain. I hated how completely passive I was all those months."

"Try decades."

Parisa took her hand and gave it a squeeze. "You weren't passive the day I met you," she said, smiling. "That day, you fought Rith. I always wondered, why *that* day?"

"I thought I told you."

Parisa shook her head.

Fiona drew in a deep breath. "It was Carolyn's birthday and I had thought her long dead. It never occurred to me that she might have ascended. But that day, the fact that I had been separated from my daughter, from both my children, from my husband, all that I knew as life in Boston, that I had been abducted and used for such a horrible reason—it all crashed down on me. Carolyn would have been a hundred and fifteen." She smiled. "And so she is, but I still have you to thank for everything. Without you and Antony, I would still be here, in this place, serving up an elixir that sustains Greaves's army."

Fiona shook off the heavy sensations, and asked if there was a chance in hell Parisa could come back to Phoenix Two for a couple of days. "I need some girl-time."

Parisa smiled. "Me, too. I love being with Antony but I think even he's getting weary of playing that role, you know, *How do you like my hair? What do you think about these jeans and this shirt?* And how many times has he looked at me in that funny way and asked, 'Are you getting your period?' "

"I know, right? I hate that question. Especially when there's truth behind it."

Parisa sighed. "I need a break."

"Don't we all." But everything seemed to be moving so fast. Events crowded her just as they crowded Parisa.

Fiona looked back at the porch. The men, *their men,* stood on guard duty, bodies tense, foreheads wrinkled, eyes skating back and forth, always looking, searching, hunting. Their voices were quiet as they spoke to each other.

Fiona's heart lurched. Jean-Pierre still had his hair slicked back, and though he wore battle flight gear, she couldn't help but recall that just a little while ago he'd worn a tux that had weakened her knees. Or maybe it was just him.

She shifted her gaze back to Parisa and, dropping her voice to a whisper, asked, "So what's it like . . . the *breh-hedden,* I mean, completing it, going all the way?"

She watched Parisa's complexion change, a very soft blush covering her cheeks while a glow seemed to radiate from beneath her skin. Her amethyst eyes sparkled. "I wish I could explain how magnificent it is. The connection is profound. Like right now, I can *feel* Antony, in an external physical sense—that the *royle* wings exhibition we put on in Puerto Rico Two last night has chafed him under his left arm, that kind of thing. He can feel me as well, probably that the wet grass has made my feet cold.

"And yes, all of that is amazing, but it's so much more. The connection is . . . spiritual, if that makes sense." She tipped her head closer to Fiona and added, "And the sex. Oh. My. God." She then shivered from head to toe.

Antony called out, "Everything okay over there?"

"See what I mean?" she whispered to Fiona, then aloud over her shoulder, she said, "We're fine."

Fiona found it hard to steady herself. She actually spread her fingers on both hands as though trying to find her balance. But the thought of sex being more than it already was with Jean-Pierre had put her mind in a tailspin. She was a small aircraft plummeting to the earth, then righting her wings at the last second and flying upward . . . fast.

Because of all that had happened at Dark Spectacle, the

breh-hedden was suddenly a possibility that it had never been before, and a strong, intense longing gripped her chest.

She turned and met Jean-Pierre's gaze. The christening at the outdoor chapel had happened just a handful of days ago, but the distance she had traveled in her relationship with Jean-Pierre felt like miles and miles. He frowned slightly and dipped his chin, a question in his eye, but she could only look at him and imagine just what the *breh-hedden* would mean for her, or for him.

"Are you thinking of doing it?" Parisa asked, again her voice very low.

Fiona looked back at her. She smiled suddenly. They were like teenage girls asking the age-old questions, *Are you going to do it? What do you think it'll be like? Everyone says it hurts.*

She had only one reasonable response to Parisa's question but it came out as a simple nod.

Parisa squealed. "You'll love it, and believe me it changes everything. I mean, *hello,* we perform a *royle* wings spectacle event nearly every night."

"Does it get old, the *royle* wings show, I mean?"

Her face drew into a knot. She shook her head. "Not really. It's an amazing experience because we bring peace and I can actually feel the crowd's response. But Antony is not happy."

"He doesn't like the performances?"

"It's not that. He hates, I mean he *really hates,* not fighting with his brothers at the Borderlands. I think the whole thing, as important as it is, makes him feel like a traitor. He's not, but he knows what Jean-Pierre and Thorne and the others are going through."

Fiona nodded. "And with Jean-Pierre serving as my guardian, Colonel Seriffe has had to put more of his Militia Warrior squads on the front line. Yeah, the whole thing is out of control. But I guess you know the latest, the explosion in Las Vegas Two."

Parisa nodded. "Marcus let Antony know what was going

on. He said you were instrumental in getting all those people out. How?"

Fiona explained all about obsidian flame and Endelle. "That's why I was able to do what I did here, with Rith I mean."

"But I thought Jean-Pierre—"

Then she explained about the knife and the sensory memory she had acquired from having been possessed by him.

"Wow," Parisa said succinctly.

"You said it."

"Then we both stabbed him."

Fiona was surprised. "When did you—?"

"The day we got you out of the New Zealand facility. He'd intended to abduct me again, but Antony had been training me to use his weapons. It all happened so fast and the next thing I knew I was plunging a dagger into his stomach. I always regretted that I didn't hit his heart, but I can see now that it wouldn't have mattered."

"No, it wouldn't have."

"And he's really gone?"

Fiona felt tears touch her eyes again. "Yes."

The men drew near. Antony was just putting his phone away. "I have some good news, Parisa. I just talked to Endelle. We get a holiday, three days at the villa. Maybe longer. She said that because of the recent incident in Las Vegas, some of the High Administrators have been canceling the *royle* wing exhibitions."

Fiona watched Parisa's shoulders slump in relief. "We get a break."

"Yeah. You do."

"We," she said emphatically, but Antony just looked at her. There was pain in his eyes.

Parisa straightened her spine. "Of course. I wasn't thinking. You'll want to be at the Borderlands. Of course."

Jean-Pierre drew close to Fiona and slipped his hand into hers. She looked down and saw their joined fingers. What would it be like to feel not just his fingers against hers but her fingers against his, all at the same time, a shared external physicality? They had already shared an obsidian flame possession, an internal sharing, but what would the external be like?

She knew from Alison that the strongest benefit of completing the *breh-hedden* was that communication was instantaneous. Because Kerrick could always feel, at will, what Alison was experiencing in a superficial physical way, he could fold to her location in a heartbeat. It was the prime reason that Alison, who had been in the process of her ascension, also became a bona fide Guardian of Ascension in her own right, and felt as secure on Second Earth as she did.

Looking up at Jean-Pierre, meeting his gaze, she wondered if she was looking at her future—that whether she liked it or not, as an obsidian flame, someone capable of channeling the powers of others, she would always need that added layer of connection with the man, the warrior, beside her?

You are thinking very hard, he sent.

She smiled. "I am."

Jean-Pierre felt a warm wind within his chest, moving around in great swirls as he looked down at Fiona, as he held her hand clasped within his own. Who was this woman who had pierced Rith's heart with a blade?

She had been a mother on Mortal Earth, a woman who kept an elegant home in Boston for a very successful businessman. Then she had her life obliterated by Rith's minions who took her from Boston and brought her here, to this house, where she had lived since 1886.

Unfathomable, the sort of spirit required to live all those decades, not to lose hope completely, not to fall into a kind of despair that always led to death. The admiration he felt for her mounted wings of its own and flew up into the sky and beyond, to the stars.

He loved her so very much but what did this mean for them, for the future?

He knew only one thing: that he wanted to complete the *breh-hedden* with her. He had never thought he could do this, even when the terrible mythical experience slammed him hard during those first days and weeks, five months ago. The entire time that he was out of his mind, whether near her or separated from her, he had resisted the call of the *breh-hedden*. He wanted nothing to do with it. On some level, he still did not, as though his spirit understood very well—too well, perhaps—the sacrifices that would be required of him in the coming weeks, months, and years as the bonded *breh* to a woman who had the gift of obsidian flame.

But he no longer held to that part of him that wished to remain aloof and separate, with all his relationships superficial.

He glanced at Medichi, who stared at him with a knowing light in his eye. Medichi nodded to him very faintly. His lips curved just a little. Perhaps the brother could read his mind, dissect his thoughts.

Jean-Pierre had missed Medichi. "I hope this tour of duty ends very soon," he said.

Medichi nodded. "You and me both. I see its value. I do, but"—here he planted a fist on his chest—"everything that I am calls me back to the Borderlands."

Jean-Pierre nodded. Fiona squeezed his hand. When he looked down at her she dipped her chin two times very quickly. He knew she understood that he felt the same way. Not to be fighting, when the rest of the Warriors of the Blood were carrying too heavy a load, was unbearable.

Parisa said, "I'm ready to leave this place. But first, does anyone have a match, or maybe a reckless hand-blast they'd like to throw?"

"Yes!" Fiona cried. "I want to burn this place to the ground, let all this mahogany catch fire and collapse into those horrid basement cells."

Parisa gasped. "You're . . . glowing."

Fiona looked down at her arm. "Yeah. That's been happening a lot lately, especially when I get a little worked up."

Jean-Pierre released Fiona's hand and turned around. "As much as I would like to see this place destroyed, what if we turned it into a rehabilitation center here in Burma? Make something good come of it. There will be such need in the coming years and decades, because who knows all the evil that Greaves has orchestrated during these years."

Fiona chuckled. "Why did you have to say something so reasonable? I was ready to let you possess me again, so that together we could make a nice bonfire."

She hooked her arm in his and he overlaid her forearm with his hand. "But you see, I know you, Fiona. The first thing you did, a week after you were released from the hospital, was to yell at Endelle until she granted funds to create your rehab center for the blood slaves."

Jean-Pierre felt a buzzing at his waist. He slid his warrior phone from the slit in his kilt. He slid his thumb over the front and drew it to his ear. "*Allô,* Jeannie."

"I love it when you speak French," she said. "But I've got one irritable ruler of Second Earth on my ass. She wants the four of you back at her admin offices. I guess it's daylight there in Burma. We're just closing in on ten. Do I have permission to fold the four of you to HQ?"

He relayed the information to the rest of the party and received three nodding acknowledgments in response. "Fold at will, Jeannie."

"You got it. On three."

He still held Fiona's arm as the glide through netherspace moved them swiftly from one location to the next.

Endelle was on her knees, feeling the goddam ankle guard still stuck on Marguerite's foot. She'd been trying for the past half hour to get it off, but nothing worked.

But what she really hated were the thick calluses on the woman's leg from having worn the damn thing for so long.

"Fuck," she muttered. She sat back on the floor in her office. She still wore her fabulous capri pants covered in orange feathers, which came from the red jungle fowl. She wore a black leather bustier on top, something that kept Thorne's gaze turned away from her quite a bit.

Marguerite's first words to her had been, "Whoa, mama! You're the hottest thing I've seen . . . like . . . ever."

Endelle was so fucking pleased. She liked this woman. Marguerite had wide brown eyes and long brown hair and was as short as shit among their tallish group. Yep, the woman was only about five feet five inches in her stockings, but once they got this damn ankle guard off her, Endelle thought she'd let Marguerite borrow a pair of her stilettos. That would jack up her height a solid five inches.

Something about the way Marguerite chewed on her lower lip and kept looking her bustier over in a way that said, *I want to fucking wear that,* led her to believe the powerful Seer was ready for a little party time.

Which of course made Endelle glance at Thorne about a dozen times and wonder what the hell her second-in-command was going to do now. He either stood nearby with his arms compressed over his chest and his hands balled into fists, or he paced the room over by the east window. Something was bugging the shit out of him. So, between his restlessness and Marguerite eyeing the black leather bustier like she meant to steal it off Endelle's chest if she could, she just got a really uneasy feeling about what the fuck was going on.

Whatever.

First things first.

She wanted a full report from Jean-Pierre and Fiona about Rith's demise, but first she needed to get Marguerite situated. Dammit, she couldn't believe she lacked the power to get rid of this fucking ankle guard.

She could hear Parisa and Fiona in the hallway beyond. She stretched her hearing. The women were talking about setting up a rehab center in Burma.

Whatever.

She disliked what she was about to do, since it involved making use of obsidian power to remove a stupid ankle guard, but she was out of options.

She called out, "Fiona, get your ass in here. We need to do your channeling shit for this stupid . . ." She launched into a long stream of profanity that had Marguerite doing some dance-like shoulder moves and making a club-like whistle.

Endelle sat back on her heels and stared at her.

Marguerite just shrugged. "I like the way you roll."

Endelle chuckled.

When Fiona appeared in the doorway, with Parisa, Endelle jerked her head. "In fact, all of you get in here. I can't believe I'm going to say this, but I don't have enough power on my own to break through Stannett's preternatural lock. Goddammit."

The party in the hallway moved into her office.

Now, where exactly had her brains gone, because she'd already taken Marguerite's measure, and Thorne's, and in walked two of the hottest vampires on the face of the earth: Antony Medichi, who was one ancient Italian wet dream walking around on two legs, and Jean-Pierre, whose French accent and mellow timbre had put more females on their backs than there were crumbs at the bottom of a potato chip bag.

Marguerite had been sitting, but now she stood up, which gave Endelle a profile view of a fairly see-through nightgown and a pair of instantly peaked nipples. There wasn't a damn thing left to the imagination, especially when Marguerite arched her back just a little bit, which pushed her breasts out just that extra inch as she called out, "Well, *hello,* boys."

Several things happened at once as sudden preternatural chaos erupted all around her.

Note to self: Never sit on the floor when surrounded by über-powerful vampires, male or female.

Thorne's foot caught her on the side of the head, which shoved her in the direction of the newly arrived foursome, and before she could right herself she had the hard heel of a flat woman's shoe grinding into the back of her hand.

Everyone seemed to be shouting at once.

She had the worst view, and her face as well as her hand hurt like a bitch, so she folded out of the melee and ended up near the fireplace on the west wall.

She opened her eyes wide, because she was as shocked as hell at exactly who had engaged in the battle.

Jean-Pierre and Fiona remained by the door. But Medichi and Parisa had moved right into Thorne.

Thorne shouted incomprehensible things to both Jean-Pierre and Medichi about staying the hell away from his woman, but it was Parisa who had gone into cavewoman mode.

The whole time Thorne shouted at the men, it would seem that something about Marguerite's come-on had flipped a switch in Parisa, the former-librarian-now-*breh*-to-a-Warrior-of-the-Blood. She was an extremely powerful ascender in her own right with her rare preternatural gift of *royle* wings.

Parisa was practically chest-to-chest with Thorne trying as she was to get to Marguerite. She shook her finger around Thorne's shoulder and kept jumping up over and over as she called out, "I don't know who the hell you think you are, but you will never talk to *my man* like that. I didn't ascend to this godforsaken dimensional world, or complete the *breh-hedden,* just so some piece of trash like you could stand there in your goddam nightgown and make a play for him. And don't you even think about giving me that man-never-straying-if-he's-happy-at-homeshit! That's pure bullshit. You hold a man down and stroke him long enough, he'll come."

These last words somehow penetrated Thorne's head, and he fell silent. He even backed up about a foot, even though he held his arms wide and wouldn't let Marguerite get past him.

"Oh, honey," Marguerite said, "if you're that insecure, you've already lost him."

Endelle should have intervened, but damn, this was just too much fun.

She grinned so hard her cheeks hurt.

"The hell if I'm insecure. You're one of those women. The kind myths are born out of, so full of sex and nothing else that even the most rational man in the world hasn't got an ice cube's chance in hell of keeping himself."

Endelle looked back at Marguerite, waiting to see what she'd say. The woman was so satisfied with this portrait, however, that she climbed up on the arm of the chair where she'd been sitting so she could look over Thorne's arm and stare down at Parisa. "Why, thank you," she drawled. "That's the sweetest thing a little uptight bitch could ever have said to me."

Endelle chuckled, but then she had to act, because honest-to-God if Parisa didn't launch herself, preternatural-style, into the air straight at Marguerite, a perfectly executed dive that would put her well over Thorne's shoulder and into the face of the newly rescued Seer.

Aw, shit.

Endelle rarely used her stasis ability, but she used it now, lifting an arm and letting the power fly. She froze everyone in place so that Parisa hung in mid-flight, high in the air, her arms outstretched, her fingers in the shape of claws. She had a look on her face that meant she intended to take the woman apart. *Meow.*

She moved forward, grabbed Parisa around the waist, and pulled her to sit across Endelle's right hip. Sometimes it was a thrill to be a powerful ascended vampire; she could hold the outraged female like she was a feather.

She snapped her fingers and the action resumed, except that Parisa was flailing at her side, screaming and scratching at pure air.

Parisa, totally out of control, writhed, squirmed, and flailed some more as she shouted, "Let me at her. Let me at her."

Endelle stared at Thorne. "I want you to settle down and get a grip. No more yelling at Medichi for something he didn't do."

She turned to Marguerite. "Plant your ass on that chair, young lady. One more word and I'm not taking the ankle guard off because it's getting pretty clear to me why Sister Quena put it on in the first place and why Stanny added his own level of security to the damn thing."

"But I—"

"Not one more fucking word, Marguerite, have you got it? This isn't the Convent and it's not the Seers Fortress. We have all the liberty in the world around here, which means we have to be civilized. So for starters, just keep the fuck away from the warriors who are mated with their *brehs* and you and I will do just fine."

Marguerite shifted her gaze between Medichi and Jean-Pierre. "So these two are spoken for?"

"Yes."

At that, however, Thorne turned back to Marguerite. If ever a man's ego had just been flattened into the flattest point on the face of the goddam flat earth, Thorne's was crêpe-thin right now. Worse, Marguerite didn't even seem to notice—which begged the question, what the hell was wrong with this scarlet variety of obsidian flame? Sweet Jesus, what a goddam fucking mess that her beloved Thorne had somehow gotten tangled up with a horn dog female like Marguerite.

Oh, goody! More fun times ahead.

Marguerite dropped down into her seat and started to examine her nails. "Fine," she said. "No mated warriors. Whatever."

"Fine," Endelle said.

She finally set Parisa on her feet, but held her pinned against her side. Parisa's face was dark red but it wasn't from embarrassment. Whatever had just happened had tripped some internal mechanism of warning in her woman's instinctive heart and she wasn't going down without, apparently, a battle to the death over this one. "You gonna be good for me?" she asked, trying to catch Parisa's gaze.

But Parisa was breathing hard and glared at Marguerite.

Endelle looked at Medichi, wondering how the hell this warrior was taking everything. But the moment she saw the look on his face, his eyes at half-mast as he watched Parisa, and the flush on his cheeks, and his lips actually swollen with lust, she knew how to resolve the whole situation. "Medichi, I think you'd better take Parisa to your villa . . . right now."

"Oh, yeah." His voice rolled through the room, deep, resonant, and with almost as much gravel to the timbre as Thorne employed.

The sound of his voice, however, had a very powerful effect on Parisa. She jerked her head in his direction and her body stilled, then relaxed. Endelle wasn't sure, but she thought Parisa might have murmured, "Sage."

Medichi crossed the few feet that separated him from his woman, pulled her into his arms, and kissed her, a demonstration of interest that honest-to-God sent shivers down all of Endelle's wing-locks. The couple vanished, and the tension in the room just fell away.

Jean-Pierre said, "If you do not have need of me, I believe I will excuse myself. I wish to speak with Seriffe."

"I'll send Fiona to you when we're finished here."

He nodded. He leaned down and kissed Fiona as well, but he didn't just put his lips to hers; he settled his hand on her face as well, which made Endelle sigh. Then he was gone.

Endelle waved Fiona forward and told Thorne to take a chill-pill. Thorne retired once more to the east window.

To Fiona, she said, "I believe you know Marguerite, but you haven't met her. But first, I guess I should ask: Fiona, are you going to behave for me?"

At that, Fiona laughed. "Yes, of course. I didn't quite have the same reaction that Parisa did, but then"—she looked at Marguerite—"Parisa hasn't had the advantage of having Marguerite pull her ass out of the fire a couple of times. I have."

"Well, good. Now make friends, because we've got one motherfucker of an ankle guard to bust through."

In the mythical stories of the breh-hedden, *the precipice preceding the union of body, mind, and blood was considered as significant as the act itself. But then all life-altering decisions are made while standing on a precipice. Only the view is different.*

—*Treatise on Ascension,* by Philippe Reynard

CHAPTER 22

As Fiona met Marguerite's laughing gaze, the gold of her obsidian flame vibrated very gently deep within her, the recognition of a kindred power.

Marguerite's brows rose. "Do you feel that?"

Fiona nodded.

Endelle looked from Fiona to Marguerite. "Feel what?"

"A connection," Fiona said. "Obsidian connection."

Endelle clapped her hands together. "Oh, shit, yes."

Marguerite stood up. "I'm Marguerite Desplat, Twoling out of Iowa 1891."

"Fiona Gaines, mortal out of Boston, ascended 1886. Sort of. I didn't complete my ascension until a few months ago."

Marguerite nodded. "I hear you got Rith."

"We did. Jean-Pierre and I."

"And you're sure the Upper ascender got away from the arena theater?"

"There's no doubt that he escaped. I watched him dematerialize before I contacted Endelle."

"Good." Her expression grew clouded, even distant, as though she was sifting through her memories. She was at least five inches shorter than Fiona, which seemed strange because all the women who surrounded Endelle approached six feet.

But she had every confidence that what Marguerite lacked in relative stature she made up for in sheer force of personality.

"So, what are your plans," Fiona asked, "now that you're free?"

Marguerite's gaze shifted only the tiniest bit in Endelle's direction, a sly glance she wasn't sure Endelle even noticed. Then Marguerite shrugged, a delicate almost flirtatious movement of her shoulders. "I have very strong Seer abilities and I want to help out with the war effort as much as I can. I'm very much beholden to Madame Endelle."

Endelle slapped her hand against her red-feathered thigh and gave a shout. "That's what I'm talkin' about. Marguerite, I'll treat you right. You can live wherever you want to live, just do a good job for me in the future streams, that's all I ask."

Marguerite turned very liquid brown eyes on Endelle. "That sounds wonderful." From across the room, Thorne groaned.

Fiona thought she understood why. Marguerite was saying all the right things. She even looked like the model of sincerity, which itself sent warning sirens shrieking through her head. But Fiona hadn't dealt with hundreds of women over the years without knowing when the column of numbers didn't add up.

The thing was, she understood what Marguerite had suffered because of a hundred years of incarceration, so if the woman was lying, she so got that. She did wonder, however, if she ought to alert Endelle.

Endelle, however, was a big girl, a feathered big girl right now, and she could take care of herself.

"So, how about we get this goddam ankle guard off you."

Marguerite smiled once more. "And that's what *I'm* talkin' about."

A grunt-like groan now slid through the air from the east side of the room. Fiona glanced at Thorne. His gaze was fixed on Marguerite and there was so much pain in his expression, so much anticipated loss and grief, that Fiona once more felt an urgency to warn Endelle that something wasn't right. She even looked in her direction, but Endelle's eyes glittered as she waved Marguerite back into her seat. Then she knelt in front of her. Fiona joined her.

"All right, Goldie," Endelle said. "Let's do it."

"Goldie?" Marguerite asked, her eyes once more alive with laughter.

Fiona explained about the color of her variety of obsidian flame.

"That's right." Marguerite nodded. "Your ribbon in the future streams is a gold color, really beautiful, vibrant. I get it now." Almost to herself, she added, "And mine is red." She even frowned a little.

Fiona had a powerful instinct to follow up on this frown, to coax her to give expression to whatever thoughts might be flitting through her brain, but Endelle intruded. "Enough with the fucking chitchat. Ankle guard. Off. Now."

As Fiona closed her eyes, she realized that there were many reasons why Endelle's rule as Supreme High Administrator tended to teeter on its profane, fashion-challenged foundation.

She focused on Endelle, settling herself in a preternatural way, shoulder-to-shoulder, hip-to-hip, so that she could feel the most essential vibrations of the woman's being.

I'll take possession, Endelle sent, *then we're going to do a carefully aimed hand-blast.*

Ready when you are, Fiona sent.

Power flowed through Fiona as Endelle began to push against her shields and move into her. She had a unique signature to her being, like a warm exotic river, something so comfortable that she was surprised all over again. The earlier possession had been full of such immediacy that she hadn't really paid attention to the experience.

Now she did.

Instead of feeling crowded, she felt as though a good friend had just sat down in her living room and now shared a glass of wine with her. The sensation was easy, even comfortable, which led her to the simple conclusion that she trusted Endelle. Despite the woman's fashion choices, her sailor's mouth, her impatience, the woman could be trusted.

As Fiona settled her gaze on the ankle guard, she looked through both pairs of eyes simultaneously. She moved in concert with Endelle's thoughts and placed her forefinger on the thick plastic. The energy flowed, white hot and precise, as the highly focused hand-blast began cutting. The only real problem was the stink of the plastic. Good Lord, that was a vile smell. Endelle worked hard to keep the beam aimed right where it was needed, but the final cut also brought Marguerite screaming out of her chair, blood flowing down her foot.

Fiona put both hands on Marguerite's foot and felt a different kind of energy from Endelle this time. Healing warmth flowed, and Marguerite let out a deep groan of relief. "Thank God," she whispered. "Wow, that's power."

When the wound was completely healed, Marguerite turned around to kneel in the chair, then extended her leg so that Fiona and Endelle could cut through the opposite side of the guard.

Faced away from Thorne, Marguerite let a few tears slip from her eyes and down her cheeks. But it wasn't because of the cut from the controlled hand-blast. It was knowing what she was doing to Thorne that was beating the shit out of her.

She had her act down pretending he didn't exist. At least in that, she was doing the right thing. She needed him to know that she just didn't have a choice.

She couldn't stay at administrative HQ. She couldn't work with Endelle. She couldn't continue to be Thorne's Convent whore. She couldn't remain in Metro Phoenix Two.

In fact, from the moment she'd landed in Madame Endelle's office, the moment she'd read the woman's formidable powers and the force of who she was in all her glorious nine thousand years, Marguerite had pretty much decided that the only way she could do what she needed to do was by going rogue. She fully intended to slip through the Trough at one of the Borderlands, so that her power signature would be permanently invisible to the electronic grids of Second Earth.

She wanted freedom, anonymity, and men, lots of men.

She couldn't have that here, not with Thorne as powerful and as possessive as he was. No fucking way in hell.

So she pretended to have no further interest in him and no need of him. In fact, she had a very strong feeling that he might even be relieved to see her go.

So, it was all good.

Except she couldn't quite get rid of the knot in her throat.

As for Fiona, she was amazed by the power the woman could create through her obsidian gift and her channeling ability. Completely stunned. But the sure knowledge that she would actually miss her was a new kind of surprise.

Marguerite had never been a woman's woman. Parisa's reaction had been more of the usual. But she would miss Fiona, her sister in obsidian flame, and she'd also miss Grace, Thorne's sister and her Convent roommate.

Part of her, therefore, was sorry about having to take off, and sorry about all the pain and frustration she'd be leaving behind, but she'd envisioned this day for the past hundred years and like hell she was going to let one lover and two friendships alter her plans.

As the final cut scored into the back of her ankle, she screamed long and loud until Fiona, or was that Endelle, gripped her leg and healing flowed.

Once the wound eased up then disappeared, she flipped around in her seat and stared down at the two halves of the guard, at the thing that had kept her bound to both the Creator's Convent and the Superstition Fortress.

"I'm sure the calluses will disappear in the next twenty-four hours," Endelle said.

What the fuck did Marguerite care about calluses? She was free.

Free at last.

Free. At. Last.

Free at long fucking last.

But as she looked at the two smoking pieces of stinking plastic, another smell rolled in her direction, a very strong, strange, but quite pleasant smell of cherry tobacco. Her grandfather used to smoke a pipe that smelled similar, only this scent was sweeter and even kind of gave her a buzz. In fact, it actually tightened her nipples and made her want to put her hand between her legs.

She glanced in the direction of the open door, looking down the hallway. Maybe one of the execs had lit up a pipe.

"Does someone here smoke a pipe?"

She watched Endelle and Fiona exchange a glance, then almost as though they were one person they turned and looked at Thorne. He lifted his head from his hands. "Are you smelling something?"

She shrugged. What did she care for a tobacco smell, or the plastic, or Endelle or Fiona or the red variety of obsidian flame, or gold, or this fucking war? She had some serious dating to do.

She gained her feet and kicked the two pieces of the ankle guard. Both Fiona and Endelle rose as well, but they parted like the Red Sea so that she had a perfect view of Thorne.

That strange tobacco scent seemed to be getting stronger. Whatever.

She turned in a circle, enjoying the feel of her leg without the weight of the ankle guard for the first time in decades. Her other leg now seemed strangely heavy. What an odd sensation. She moved away from the chair and turned in ever-broadening circles.

She saw from her peripheral vision that Thorne had risen from his seat as well.

She sure hoped he didn't intend to prevent her from doing what she needed to do.

She slowly shifted her turning circle in the direction of the open door. "No," Thorne said, but his voice held a restrained note.

She faced Endelle and Fiona and grinned. She called out a resounding, "So long, suckers." She lifted her arm and vanished, at the same time setting up a trace-block. Netherspace, her first ride in a century, felt damn good.

Oh, yeah.

Oh, fucking, yeah.

With preternatural speed, Thorne moved to the exact spot where his woman had just vanished. He'd known from the beginning that this day would come because he'd known his woman's heart and her mind and her spirit from the first second he'd been with her, even before he'd entered her body.

Except she'd asked if someone was smoking a pipe.

And now a new nightmare was on him, because in this space where she had disappeared, he could smell her in a way he had never smelled her before. But it seemed all wrong, because it was a rich floral scent, like the red roses his sister, Patience, had once grown. How could this fire-woman smell of flowers? Beyond that, why the fuck did she smell like anything, for God's sake? Was there to be no peace for him, ever?

He started crying out, shouting. He lost track of himself, of time, of space. His shouting morphed into some kind of strange primal screaming that he couldn't even hear, like maybe he was producing a sound that only dogs could detect.

Then he fell into a hole so deep there simply was no bottom and he screamed the entire way.

Endelle stared at Thorne and then at Fiona whose ears had started to bleed and who was crying and thrashing on the floor. She had to get Fiona out of her office, out of the building, but she was afraid to leave Thorne alone.

Alison. She had to get Alison over here to take Fiona away.

Her phone. Where was her phone?

Oh, yeah.

She leaped on her desk and slid over the marble, knocking her laptop to the floor. She really did need to start carrying her stupid phone with her.

Dammit, her own ears hurt now. She didn't know a man could make a sound like that. He stood very straight, his whole body rigid, but with his neck arched and head thrown back, shouting at the ceiling.

She found her phone on the floor, right where she'd last thrown it, down by one of the curled woolly mammoth tusks that supported the desk. From that position, her head resting against the hard ivory, and with fingers that trembled, she tapped the damn screen.

When a sleepy Alison came online, she shouted, "Get your ass to my office, now. We have an emergency but all I need you to do is fold here then fold Fiona back to your house. Got it?"

"Uh . . . okay . . . got it."

Half a second later, and wearing a long, rumpled blue silk nightgown, Alison appeared. She looked at Thorne and winced. She appeared ready to drop to the floor herself. Then she looked at Fiona.

She went to the latter, put her hand on her shoulder, and the two of them, thank God, vanished.

Endelle used the same phone and tapped for Central. She cut off Jeannie's usual polite greeting. "Fuck that, Jeannie. Listen up. Get Luken over to my office and Horace as well. Now. We've got some kind of something going on. It's sort of—oh, fuck, just do it."

She thumbed her phone and waited.

Luken showed up about ten seconds later, straight from one of the Borderlands where he battled death vampires, his sword in hand, his arms shaking with adrenaline, blood spatter all over him.

He saw Thorne and cried out, "What the hell is this?" Then, "Endelle, where the fuck are you?"

Endelle rose up from beneath her desk, threw her phone back down by the tusk, then put her hands over her ears.

"Don't let him hurt himself. I think, oh, God, I think it's the goddam *breh-hedden.* Shit motherfucker." She rounded the desk to stand a few feet away from Thorne. But Luken was a take-no-prisoners kind of man, and carried more natural brawn, more sheer muscle than any of the other Warriors of the Blood. He had the best heart and when he saw what he needed to do, goddammit, the man just did it!

Despite the painful resonant noises Thorne was making, the high piercing keening sounds, Luken positioned himself in front of Thorne. Thorne's cries kept increasing in resonance and volume until Endelle, as Fiona had done before, dropped to the floor.

Horace arrived next and immediately fell to his knees, also covering his ears.

Endelle crawled under the table so she could see what was happening. Luken, his face pale now, caught Thorne's left arm. When Thorne drew back his right hand and made a fist, Luken moved in with a series of swift preternatural punches that bobbed Thorne's head back a whole bunch of times, until the keening stopped and the leader of the Warriors of the Blood fell on his back at Horace's feet.

Oh, thank God that noise had stopped.

Jesus H. Christ.

Endelle sat back on her heels then crawled around the side of the desk. She'd lost an awful lot of red feathers in the past fifteen minutes, and her fluffy capris now had a bunch of bare patches that would need reworking. Her mind felt like someone had sandblasted her gray matter from one cauliflower-shaped mass to the other. She had a hard time forming coherent thoughts.

A moment later Kerrick appeared. His battle gear was also streaked with blood, black feathers, and other horrible things. His bare muscled arms were the same. In addition, he had a cut that dripped blood onto the hardwood floor near his black battle sandals.

"What's going on?" he asked. "I just talked with Alison. She thought maybe you'd need me."

Endelle released a heavy sigh and flopped an arm in Thorne's direction. "Seen this before? Or something like it?"

Kerrick moved to stand over Thorne. His lips curved and his emerald eyes filled with compassion. "Thorne's turn, I take it?" He glanced at Endelle.

She nodded, then stretched herself out on one of the zebra skins that littered the floor of her office. It felt good to be lying on her back and staring up at the ceiling. She extended her arms then clasped her hands beneath her head.

Her administration was like a goddam three-ring circus. All she lacked were a few elephants trumpeting and monkeys swinging from chandeliers.

Great.

Fucking great.

Now what the hell was she supposed to do?

Fiona thanked the healer for taking care of her busted eardrums, yet again, and watched as he lifted an arm and folded from Alison's library. Rubbing her ears, she went in search of Alison and found her in the living room, sitting in a big comfortable chair and nursing baby Helena. The baby at three months was now a wonderful armful.

Alison's eyes were drooping. The first year with a nursing baby in the house was always a tough time: beautiful, wonderful, exciting, but tough. Add to that Alison's duties as executive assistant to the scorpion queen and yes, it was definitely time to leave mother and daughter alone. It had to be one in the morning.

But as her gaze drifted to the black shock of hair, moving gently with each suckling motion, Fiona's heart squished up into a delicious knot remembering those early months with Carolyn so many years ago. Would she and Jean-Pierre one day have a family?

The thought nearly brought tears to her eyes.

"I should go," she said.

Alison smiled. "You are welcome to stay as long as you like, but you must be exhausted."

Oddly, she wasn't, and yet what a long, strange, frightening night it had been. "I'd better get back to Jean-Pierre."

Alison nodded.

She made a quick call to Militia HQ to let both the landing platform and Jean-Pierre know that she was on her way. Boy, did she have things to tell him. What a show he'd missed when he'd folded on ahead to HQ.

Once she had things settled with Jean-Pierre, she transferred to the night-duty grid monitor, Donna, and got a fold to the platform.

Jean-Pierre stood waiting for her in battle gear. The sight of him was always a jolt to her feminine sensibilities but especially in a uniform that showed a lot of skin: muscled arms, a good portion of his chest, and parts of his legs. He was tall, ripped, lean as hell with sharp cheekbones—so handsome, well, her knees felt watery all over again. She had the strong feeling that no matter what happened in the coming years, that would never change, how the mere sight of him nearly brought her tumbling to the floor.

Her heart started pounding out a new cadence because she realized that right in this moment, they had no more duties for the rest of the night . . . except to go home.

Together.

His thoughts must have been similar because when he approached her, he smelled like a warm cup of coffee.

"Croissants," he murmured, whispering the word next to her ear. He slipped his arms around her and held her close.

She looked up at him. "Is everything okay here? I was a little surprised when you left Endelle's office."

"Yes, I needed to speak with Seriffe . . . about the Militia Warrior training program. I . . . have some ideas I wish to pursue."

"Really?" She saw the light in his eye, something akin to hopefulness. What on earth had happened? What had changed? "What's going on?"

"I am not certain, but I think a new power has emerged for me, something wholly unexpected."

She blinked. "Empathy. Like Alison. I'm right, aren't I?"

He nodded. "I believe so, but the application that keeps flowing through my mind has to do with the Militia Warriors and encouraging not just their skills but their powers as well. We need them to grow stronger if we are to win this war."

"And you think you can help them do that? Sort of *bring* them into their powers?"

"I am not certain, but that is my wish."

She squeezed his arm. "Jean-Pierre, I hope you can do exactly that because I know what this means to you."

His nostrils flared slightly. "I love that you know me in this way, Fiona, that this was your first thought and that you understood how much I want to change the course of the war. I want it as though it is life to me."

She nodded and put a hand on his cheek.

"We should go home now, *non*?"

"Absolutely."

He shifted slightly and waved to the officer on duty.

"Ready?" he asked, looking down at her.

Fiona smiled. She loved that about Jean-Pierre, that he didn't just take off, folding them both, but gave her a warning, which made a huge difference for her. Folding anywhere was still an unsettling experience. Yes, she loved that about him.

She nodded and the smooth glide through nether-space landed them inside his house right next to the piano.

She blinked, staring at the baby grand. "One day, I hope you'll play for me, then I'll play for you."

"You play as well?" he asked.

She lifted her chin. "I'll have you know that every accomplished woman in Boston society played extremely well." But she laughed.

As she took in the piano once more, for a swift moment she was drawn back to her row house in Beacon Hill all those decades ago, to the evening parties, to performing or listening to her dearest friends perform. Those were the requirements of the time and place.

Now she was in Jean-Pierre's house, a very different time,

a very different place. There were new requirements now, one in particular that had been harassing her from the moment she realized that the coffee scent she kept smelling came from him.

Imagine . . . *coffee.*

The whole thing was so extraordinary and demanding and upsetting.

Even now she was just a little pissed off that she didn't seem to have a choice.

"Fiona," he said softly, again close to her ear. "Tell me what you are thinking. You are glaring at my poor piano."

She chuckled. She glanced back at him and he smiled for her, showing her all his beautiful big teeth. She put her hand on his face, stroking her thumb over his cheek. "We crossed some serious territory tonight, didn't we?"

He nodded into her hand, then turned slightly and kissed her palm. She shivered. God, what this man could do to her with just a kiss.

"I have something I must ask you, but I wish you to know that I do not ask this lightly."

She could see that he was suddenly nervous, but she didn't interrupt him.

"I wish to know if you would complete the *breh-hedden* with me?"

Her gaze dropped to his chin. She was afraid to look anywhere else. She already knew what her answer would be, but this was still not a simple thing, not an easy step to take. Marriage would have been a walk in the park compared with this. The joining was so much more involved, more intense, and would come with even greater responsibility.

He rubbed her arms and kissed her forehead.

She loved that he let the moment rest, that he didn't leap in and try to pressure her.

Finally, she lifted her gaze to his. "Is this what you want, Jean-Pierre, truly want with me? I know that what happened so long ago broke your heart, ruined your heart, and I don't want you to feel that you have to do this."

Strangely, his eyes grew wet.

Once more, he kissed her forehead. "Earlier tonight, when I was paralyzed and could not breathe, when I knew that I would die, do you know what I thought?"

She shook her head.

"I thought that no man had been so foolish as I had been in holding my heart back from you. I was already in love with you, but I told myself it was a sweet transient love, not very serious. Lovely, but not meaningful.

"But as I lay there, all I could think was how much I was going to miss you. I could not even imagine what death would hold, but I felt certain I would miss you terribly, that my soul would carry an ache in the very center of my being because I would no longer be with you, have you near, have my arms around you.

"I know it does not make sense, but in that moment I realized that my love for you was . . . enormous, that it filled every corner of my being.

"As for the *breh-hedden,* I know it will bring many difficulties for us both. I know that. I know that our responsibilities to Endelle will be greater, perhaps to Colonel Seriffe and the Militia Warriors as well. This I feel also deep in my soul. And for that, for you, I am so sorry.

"Because I love you, I want something so very different for you—a life of peace for one thing. But I cannot have this, because this is war and we do not know when it will change.

"My answer is simply, *oui,* I want to complete the *breh-hedden* with you. I want you so much in that way that I can hardly breathe. Despite the difficulties that will come, I want to know you, your mind, your body, your blood all at one time and I want you to know me in the same way. And I want to experience where that joining will take us.

"This I believe, Fiona: Something awaits us on the other side of this, something we are meant to know, to experience, perhaps even to accomplish together.

"But mostly, it is you I want, all that you are. So, yes, I want this joining with you, more than life itself."

Fiona had to blink several times so that the tears that had gathered while he spoke would dissipate. She had never thought to hear such a beautiful speech from him, to hear him speak of loving her in such a way, that his love for her filled every corner of his being.

She was moved beyond words. More tears gathered then fell. She swiped at them with her fingertips.

He pulled her close and held her in his familiar warm embrace. She leaned her head against his shoulder.

Her life moved at light speed now, so strangely fast. For over a hundred years the rhythm of her existence had been measured month by month as Rith took her blood, as he drained her to death, then gave it all back again with someone else's blood and the hard, painful jolts of the defibrillators.

But from the time of her release from captivity, life had sped up, or perhaps caught up with the flow of Second Earth and the demands of war.

She was now the gold variety of obsidian flame, able not only to channel someone else's power, but also to allow a full possession and increase that power exponentially.

What she could contribute to the war effort had made Endelle dance a jig on top of her marble desk. She'd even helped release Marguerite from her captivity and rescue twenty thousand people. Surely a woman who could do all this could also give herself to the mysteries of the *breh-hedden.*

She stood on the rim of a canyon ready to leap off into the abyss, hopefully to fly.

He rubbed her back, which of course reminded her of her itchy wing-locks. As though reading her mind, Jean-Pierre began at the upper right and started to scratch at just the right pressure. She trembled then relaxed, settling more deeply against his chest, her soul filling with wonder.

Her mind seemed to open and expand right then and there, in the foyer of Jean-Pierre's house, next to a piano they both knew how to play, held in the arms of the man she loved, having the man who loved her *in every corner of his being* giving her wing-locks some much-needed relief.

When he'd gone over each lock and then just held her once more, when he seemed content just to hold her, when he didn't launch into all the reasons she should complete the *breh-hedden,* and even when her heart began to pound in her chest and throat, she whispered, "Yes."

His body stilled. He didn't draw a breath for a moment.

"Yes," she said more loudly. And finally peace flowed through her, a warm wonderful river of ease that told her she was doing the right thing, the best thing, the most necessary thing for herself and for Jean-Pierre.

He pulled back from her a little so that he could look into her eyes. He frowned. "Are you sure? I do not want you to feel the smallest pressure. This must be your decision and your desire. Truly your desire."

She nodded. "I know." Then she smiled. "I admit this has been a lot to get used to. But I'm ready. Scared, but I'm ready. I want to know you in this way as well, my mind, my body, my blood.

"When Rith died, just a few hours ago, that part of my life ended. Oh, I know that I will work with the rehab center for a long time to come, and I'll continue on at Militia HQ, working to identify blood slave facilities, but I can feel that this is a new beginning, that I, that we, are meant to accomplish more, perhaps have always been destined to accomplish more together."

She shook her head. "But no, I don't feel pressured anymore. I feel—" She paused and put a hand to her chest. "—I feel light and joyous. I know now that I belong here with you and I want to be your *breh* as I want you to be mine."

"So, it is the *breh-hedden.*"

"Yes."

The breh-hedden *always reveals the butterfly.*

—*Collected Proverbs,* Beatrice of Fourth

CHAPTER 23

Jean-Pierre did not move for a long time. He held Fiona in his arms, unable to release her, or to suggest that they retire to his bedroom, or anything. Peace held him immobile, something he had not felt in a very long time, perhaps not since well before the revolution.

He held the moment, as he held Fiona, savoring, wishing that he could make time stop, forever. His breathing was deep, very deep, breaths that seemed to reach into the earth and pull every good thing back up into his body.

He loved Fiona with all his heart.

She was as the stars to him, a vast universe to know and to discover.

Then he knew what he desired, what would satisfy his soul right now, with her.

"I have just realized," he said, "that we have been so busy, I have not shown you my house—just a room or two. I want you to see all of it now."

She lifted her head. "I'd like that." She pulled out of his arms and he took her hand.

He led her room by room, all around the perimeter of the glass-and-wood structure, what he had designed with his mind and built with his hands, through several guest rooms, a media room, a large wine cellar deep in the earth, the locker where he kept his battle flight gear and his weapons, the workroom once more, and the large conservatory filled with plants and trees from around the world.

Closing the glass door, she looked around and said, "Why do I have the feeling that we've walked in a very large circle?"

"Because we have." He gestured in the direction of an arched wooden door. "This is . . . the very center of my house."

He felt so odd speaking the words. His heart made a rushing sound in his ears as he opened the door, holding it wide for her so that she could walk in before him. This room, which was not exactly a room, held special meaning for him. When he could not sleep, he came here. In the past five months, he had come here often.

"I call this the sycamore room."

She did not get far, just a few feet. She looked up and gasped. She looked down and did the same.

She looked up again.

Filling the room and branching out high overhead was an Arizona sycamore, just starting to leaf out, perhaps sixty feet in height. The bark was still white from the winter.

The tree had already been grown when he built this part of his house. The space, forty feet across, was completely open to the sky and subject to the weather no matter the season.

One massive branch hung quite low, at waist height. "I often sit in the crook of this lower branch and meditate, or try to, when sleep escapes me."

She put her hands on her cheeks. "So beautiful," she whispered.

There was no light pollution to impede the view of a black night sky. Nor were there windows on the ten-foot redwood walls.

"I could stay here forever," she said, her voice still hushed.

She could not have spoken sweeter words.

She looked down again and took a few tentative steps. He did not blame her. The floor was constructed of panels of thick, very expensive glass, supported by steel beams, perfectly safe but the illusion of falling was still there. Several decades ago he had created a channel directing water from Oak Creek to create a second stream so that this round central room would be suspended above flowing water. He maintained an island around the tree.

The sky above, water below, a tree through the middle, alive and growing.

She continued to walk until she stood near the tree. "I feel as though I'm in the center of the universe."

"You are the center of mine."

She turned to face him. She released a sigh and smiled.

He went to her, his heart full. He took her in his arms and kissed her, deeply. She leaned into him and her lovely sweet croissant scent rose up and up to surround and engulf him.

"So, the *breh-hedden*?"

"Oui."

She looked around. "Were you thinking we would do this in here?"

"I wasn't thinking of the *breh-hedden* when I brought you here, but you may be right." He turned in a half circle, then back. "I meditate in this room. I look at the stars, I enjoy the cool air, the sound of the creek below. In the summer the tree is fully leafed and fragrant. I would like to do this here but—what is it? Your eyes are very wide."

"Jean-Pierre, would you mount your wings for me?"

"You mean right now? Here?"

She nodded. "I . . . have never seen it done. I mean, I've seen it happen, but never up close. I'm wondering if perhaps I saw the wings emerging—"

She moved around him to his back. When she swept a hand down his wing-locks, he drew in a sharp breath. "*Très* sensitive, *chérie,* especially to your touch." He still wore his flight gear, so the wing-locks were fully exposed.

"Sexual," she stated.

"At times like this, yes."

He heard her sigh.

"But *oui,* I would be more than happy to mount my wings for you."

"Thank you," she whispered, yet again, this time almost reverently. He felt her lips pressed to his back, and his heart seized at the tender gesture. "I just need to ask one more thing."

He knew before she asked. "You wish me to mount my wings without hindrance of clothing."

He heard her soft hiss. "Yes." The accompanying swirl of her scent made him smile.

He folded his battle gear off, sending it to his locker. The cool air above flowed over his body.

Her hands found his waist and he caught them in his. Yes, his heart was so very full.

He focused on his back. He had mounted his wings for two centuries; the process was like breathing and usually the work of a few seconds, sometimes less. But he wanted her to see everything and to feel his back during the process if she wished, so he took it slowly.

"You may touch my back if you like. Just remember that the apertures will weep and of course every touch of yours is like fire."

"Okay," she murmured.

He allowed the muscles and tissues to swell all down his back in a V shape. The wing-locks tingled and he felt a sense of arousal at the base of his spine. Over the years, he had of course learned to keep his cock from responding, from growing stiff, because mounting wings was very close to a sexual experience. But because he was with Fiona and he could smell her own state of arousal, he let his body respond as it wished to respond.

He felt her hands very gently on his back and once more her lips as she kissed him over and over.

His throat grew tight as his desire for her increased. He took deep breaths, prolonging the moment so that she could explore. It became difficult when she touched the apertures then licked one of them.

"No, *chérie,*" he called out. "Or I cannot control what I am doing."

She returned to the thickened flesh just below his shoulder, little kisses that felt like butterflies touching his skin. "Are you ready to mount?" she asked.

"Yes."

"Then let your wings fly."

Jean-Pierre closed his eyes. To do this for his woman meant something, and with a thought he released what he had been holding back.

His wings came in a quick flurry of movement, an extremely sensuous experience, very much like an orgasm, so that when he drew his wings into full-mount, then further extended them to almost touch at the tips overhead, a sense of well-being flowed through his veins.

"Oh, Jean-Pierre, they're so beautiful. I've seen them before, but never up this close. The color is magnificent, almost like—"

"Your eyes," he said. He had not considered it before, but it was true. "My wings are the color of your eyes, silver-blue."

He heard her gasp. He drew in his wings to close-mount, pulling them up tight against his body so that he could turn to face her. Then he let them unfurl to full-mount once more. He wanted her to see them, all of them, front and back.

Her gaze swept over them.

"Your wings are enormous." But her brow grew pinched.

"What is it?"

"Why can't I mount my wings?" She met his gaze and searched his eyes.

"I do not know, *chérie,* but it will happen when it is meant to happen, I promise you that."

She dipped her chin twice then she smiled. "I suppose I shouldn't be worrying about that right now." She reached out and stroked the feathers. "Does this hurt or bother you?"

"No, a light touch is perfectly fine, but pulling hard on a feather hurts very much."

Her gaze raked his chest then drifted lower. When another swell of her heavenly scent flowed over him, his cock, also at full-mount, jerked in response.

She met his gaze once more then lifted up on her feet to kiss him, her hands lightly on his shoulders. "Can you make love in full-mount?"

He smiled. "*Oui, chérie,* most definitely, but it will require some finesse."

She glanced around, her head wagging back and forth. "But . . . how, exactly?"

He saw the confusion on her face and he sought about in his mind. A piece of prescience came to him, a ripple of time that wiggled within his head: He knew what would happen during the *breh-hedden,* something so beautiful, so extraordinary, for a moment his lungs would not work. He also saw something else, the precise reason her most essential power was called obsidian flame.

"Fiona, can you trust me? I must know."

She smiled, almost shyly. "Of course I trust you."

"Good. You will need to."

She took a small step back. "Now you're scaring me."

"I am going to fold something into my arms."

"Okay."

He waved a hand.

"Oh." She laughed then stroked the nubby woven throw from his couch. "I thought maybe you meant to bring the piano in here." She chuckled again. "Okay, so what is this for?"

He drew his wings close once more, turned around, and laid the throw over the low branch of the tree. "I want you here on your stomach. I want to complete the *breh-hedden* in this position. There is a reason for it, but I wish to keep it to myself for now. Can you trust me? Can you do this for me?"

Fiona blinked. Surely, she blinked. But her mind traveled swiftly to the grotto. He had taken her from behind and now it would seem he meant to do it again.

She gasped but only because the desire she felt almost

stung it was so intense, as though a hand gripped her between her legs.

Jean-Pierre moaned and closed the distance. He took her in his arms and kissed her, his tongue thrusting. *You smell of croissants,* chérie.

As his lips played over hers, as his tongue probed her mouth, she sent, *I was in this position in the grotto.*

He groaned and once more everything very low tightened and tugged and pulled. She was so close and all he was doing was kissing her. But then what else was new?

He drew back, and she turned toward the branch.

Fiona shivered. She didn't wait for the suggestion, she simply folded her clothes off. She knew Jean-Pierre. She knew how much he loved the way she looked from behind so she draped herself over the branch, at the hip, and with her bare feet flat on the glass floor she spread her legs.

The sound that came from him was a deep, throaty grunt. She wasn't surprised that what she felt first was the crown of his cock pressing against her opening in small pushes, one after the other, but not quite entering her.

His hands were on her hips and his long fingers began kneading her buttocks on each side. He then slid his hands down her thighs then back up. The whole time she felt the pressure of his cock.

He leaned over her and kissed her back, then began licking her wing-locks and sucking the apertures. She groaned and arched her neck, crying out. Oh, yes, wing-locks were so sensitive. Shivers raced down her sides.

She held on to the wide branch supporting herself. She couldn't seem to catch her breath.

He kissed his way down her back, kissing lower and lower, his lips gliding over her buttocks. Using his thumbs, he spread her wide, then something very soft and wet entered her. His tongue. Oh, God, his tongue.

She cried out as he began to lap at her. His hands moved over her thighs, then up and up to caress her buttocks. The whole time he lapped. *You taste so good, Fiona. A feast for me. A rich, decadent feast.*

I love that you're tasting me, feasting on me.

He drove his tongue into her again and again, until little cries left her mouth. She was so close. He squeezed the flesh of her buttocks. *Come for me,* mon amour. *Come for me.*

His voice, his beautiful resonant voice with the French lilt, took her over the edge. She cried out long and loud, pleasure streaking through her, as he continued to pummel her with his tongue and drive his fingers into her buttocks.

I can feel the depths of you plucking at my tongue, chérie. *So beautiful. Now come for me again.*

Her body responded and she cried out once more, her hips grinding into the branch. Between his tongue and his fingers, she came again. And again.

At last sated, at least for the moment, she lay slack on the branch, her head curved over the side, her knees bent a little, a series of soft sighs puffing from her mouth.

"Such beautiful sounds you make." He now stood up behind her, his hand rubbing down the center of her back. "Your wing-locks are weeping."

She felt his lips next as he kissed her wing-locks one after the next, then shivered when his tongue flicked the apertures.

"Oh" erupted from her mouth. "Jean-Pierre you don't know how good that feels."

"Oh, but I do."

More shivers, like rain down her body.

"The tissues of your back are swollen, Fiona. I think you will mount your wings very soon."

He began to move her hair away from the left side of her neck, and she shivered a little more. Once more, his cock pressed at her opening. She wiggled her hips, trying to help him find his way inside. Not that he needed help, but she suddenly wanted the connection, wanted his cock inside her, wanted it deep.

"You are so anxious, then? You need me to be inside you now?"

She murmured an unintelligible *mmm,* then said, "Yes. Oh, God, yes."

As he dipped low to kiss her neck, he began a slow thrust

of his hips and she felt what she wanted finally enter her. She had always loved sex, the connection, the oneness.

Tonight would be different as well, more intense, more meaningful, and things would happen, unexpected things. Anxiety fluttered in her stomach, but she wouldn't think of that, not now.

Tears welled in her eyes. "I love you," she whispered.

He licked her neck in long strokes above the vein. He shifted her head slightly to create a better angle. He slid his right arm under her chest and supported her. "I need your blood," he whispered. "I want your blood in me, down my throat, entering my veins, strengthening me."

He flexed his hips and reached the end of her. He drew back very slowly. Maybe it was the angle, but as his cock dragged over her, she groaned.

The licks along her neck grew stronger until she felt her vein rise. The moment it did, he struck, a quick pierce that tightened her deep inside. His hips moved in a steady pace now as he drank from her.

Jean-Pierre, she sent, *you'll make me come again.*

Yes, I want you to come. Please come. Ah, your blood, like fire. Mon Dieu.

His hips bucked into her hard now. Even the massive tree moved a little. Each thrust set his wings in motion so that the air flowed over her skin, another layer of sensation.

The orgasm came quick and fast, lightning along her flesh, a swelling ache that kept spilling over and over her. He held her pinned as he drank so she couldn't do anything more than release a long guttural sound.

You are pulling on me, he sent. *So close. So close. Take my wrist, Fiona. Let us see this through to the end.*

She took his arm and with but a whisper of a thought her fangs emerged. She struck, drew blood, and began to drink. He was still buried deep, as hard as a rock, but he didn't move.

Prepare for my mind, he sent.

I'm ready. Oh, your blood. Oh, God. Oh, God.

He tasted of his rich maleness and a hint of coffee; still, it wasn't the flavor but the power in his blood that began to build within her. A fire, yes a fire, that burned hot, that could ignite her and burn her down to nothing.

His mind drew up against hers like a solid wall.

Ready? he sent.

Yes.

He pushed. The smallest push. Then his mind was in her mind. She had felt this before, in the grotto.

He rolled through her mind, a heavy wave of sensation, a type of joining, another connection. His wings wafted, his hips thrust, his mouth suckled at her throat. Groans swirled over her ears.

Pleasure rode Fiona, a fine horse in the home stretch. She had already come several times, but this moment, with Jean-Pierre in her mind, taking her blood, and moving in and out of her, surrounded her like warm bathwater. She could sense the orgasm waiting, as if offshore, for the wind to blow it into port, and it would be powerful.

She was so happy, absurdly happy, to have this man, this vampire, this warrior, taking her blood, entering her, rolling over her mind. She needed a new word for what this felt like, for the fire moving in her veins because of his blood.

Euphoric. Yes, she felt euphoric and peaceful and one with her man.

Come to me, he sent.

She understood his meaning and in a simple way, she pushed into his mind. She could feel how close he was to orgasm, how with the strongest effort he held himself back, waiting for her, perhaps for this moment.

I'm here.

I love you in my mind, Fiona.

I love being here. But, Jean-Pierre, this is it. We've done it all. The breh-hedden.

Oui. *Oh, Fiona, Fiona, my darling,* ma chérie.

Jean-Pierre. Tears fell from her eyes.

He moved his hips faster and suddenly he released her neck and rose upright, the sweep of his wings sending cool air over her weeping back. He held on to the branch and rocked into her, hard.

She retracted her fangs from his wrist and the orgasm barreled down on her. Unlike the others, because her body was on fire, the sensations flash-flooded her, sending series of pleasurable streaks up through the well of her body, little hits of lightning, up and up.

She screamed and the lightning kept striking, leaping, flying.

Jean-Pierre shouted into the room as he came, as he spent himself inside her, his cock jerking. As he came, another orgasm sped through her, flying up and up and bringing another scream out of her throat.

He kissed the back of her neck, his body swaying into her, his body still connected, her mind still richly enshrined within his.

The oneness once more brought tears flowing down her cheeks.

"Jean-Pierre," she said, her voice hoarse.

"Ma chérie," he whispered over her neck, against her ear, into her hair. *"Ma chérie. Ma chérie."*

The feathers of his wings swept over her arms.

The tears continued.

She felt very strange, not quite in her own body. She felt wonderful. She wanted to cry out, to spin in circles, to laugh, to fly.

But as his body stilled, she grew quiet as well.

"Do you feel that?" he asked.

She nodded. "Yes. I think so."

She could feel something at a great distance, hovering, waiting. Finally, it came like a great wind, blowing hard and forceful.

Jean-Pierre, still connected to her, leaned over her, his arms around her.

The wind swept over them both.

She felt the click in the center of her chest. "Do you feel that? A click?"

"Yes, near my heart."

"Yes."

"Fiona, your wing-locks."

She felt it now, the swelling of her back, the weeping of her wing-locks, nothing new and yet everything was new. She had crossed some great barrier. She felt it now as though for so long she had been an island separated from a thriving mainland. Now there was a bridge and she could cross it at will.

Her back no longer itched.

Instead she felt the power within, a new sureness of foot, and an understanding of who she was, who she was meant to be, within herself and in her life.

"I think I can mount my wings," she said.

"Then do it, right now. Nothing would be more beautiful to me."

He started to withdraw from her but she reached back and held his hips. "No. I want to do it for the first time like this, with you inside me. Can you do that?"

She felt him shudder and she realized he was still very much erect. *Jean-Pierre, I can feel you . . . very firm.*

It is your blood.

Her turn to shiver as he very slowly pushed inside, with-drew, then pushed, a new steady rhythm.

Now release your wings.

With his blood like fire in her veins, with her mind still sunk within his, with his body still connected low and stroking her, she closed her eyes and thought the beautiful thought. *Wings.*

He gave a cry. "Your wings are coming. I can feel it from inside you."

And just like that, her wings began to move from within her body, through the wing-locks, flying at tremendous speed so that before she had opened her eyes, the wings were just there, held in place by the attending mesh super-structure.

"Fiona, they are so beautiful! You are so beautiful. But I cannot help myself."

She knew what he meant and because the emergence of

her wings had been, just as he had said, close to a sexual experience, she cried out, "Do it!"

As he held her hips, he pumped her from behind, harder and faster. Before a handful of seconds had passed, she arched her neck and screamed as the orgasm took her again, better than before, better than anything. "Oh, God," came out of her throat in a long keening sound.

Jean-Pierre grunted heavily as once more he released into her, his hips moving at lightning speed, the wind from his wings another layer of erotic sensation.

One last groan and his hips finally stilled against hers.

Jean-Pierre had only one regret: that he had waited so very long to give himself completely to Fiona.

This night had been like nothing he had experienced before. He felt honored to be so close to her at the moment she released her wings for the first time. But this is what he had seen within the brief vision, that she would release her wings tonight. He just hadn't expected to be connected to her so intimately when it happened.

He stroked the length of her back along her spine. He smoothed a hand over the soft black wings with the gold flame markings. This was the meaning of obsidian flame, the beautiful wings that reflected her calling and her gift.

"Can you see your wings, *chérie*? Try to look at them. They are . . . magnificent."

He saw her flex the muscles of her back, and with that flexing her left wing drifted closer to Fiona's body, in the direction her head was turned. "The feathers are black and gold. Oh, I really get it now. Obsidian flame. Wow. Are they as beautiful as I think they are?"

"*Incroyable.* Nothing less. I wish you could see them as I see them."

He leaned down and kissed her between her wings and felt her shiver beneath him. His eyes were wet. He could not help that. His life had just shifted, a turning of the earth to reveal a new arrangement of the stars.

Very carefully, he leaned over her back, pressing his chest

against her skin and against the base of her wings. He mingled the tips of his feathers with hers. "I am so proud of you."

"I want to know only one thing," she said.

"What is that, *ma chérie*?"

"How soon can I fly?"

Casimir sat with the swans and the geese. They were all settled down after a difficult night that included a second fold back to Las Vegas Two, a mode of transportation for which they were poorly suited.

The smell was a bit strong in the massive barn, but . . . whatever. He found their presence soothing, even comforting.

He was not happy.

He sat in the dark with his arms clasped around his knees. He had a shield around him, triple-thick to keep certain powerful Second ascenders from invading his space.

He wasn't used to facing his own death.

He wasn't used to failure.

And he wasn't used to betrayal, not like this anyway, not unexpected.

After the debacle at Dark Spectacle, he'd actually folded back to Paris, to the perimeter of his shielded hotel room, just to see whether or not his children were still alive.

They were.

Once he saw that the hotel room was safe, he fetched Julianna from the outskirts of the palace crowd in Phoenix Two and put her to bed. She'd gotten caught up in the mass fold—otherwise she, too, would have been dead. Her spirits had been depressed by the experience, by the knowledge that Greaves had orchestrated the arena explosion at a time when he would have known she was still in the building.

She hadn't argued too much when he told her he needed some time alone.

But as he sat among the birds, he confessed he didn't know what to do.

"Thought I might find you here, my friend."

And how the fuck did Greaves break through his shield? Just how much power did this Second ascender have anyway?

"Enough," Greaves responded.

So Darian had read his mind? He turned to look at him, his preternatural vision putting Greaves in a halo of light. He stood twenty feet away near a couple of empty swan crates. "Did you come here to finish the job yourself, then?"

"I have no idea what you mean."

"Cut the crap, Darian. I know that you intended for me to die in the explosion."

He heard Greaves sigh. "I confess that was one of the possibilities sent to me from the Mumbai Two Seers Fortress." He started walking in Casimir's direction. "But if I had truly wanted you dead, I would have finished the job myself. COPASS has no rules forbidding me to take the lives of Upper ascenders."

"Then you didn't plan for me to die?"

"I will be honest with you, I had hoped for it, but I wasn't sanguine. These are difficult times as you have now learned, very difficult, almost impossible to navigate with any degree of precision. I mean, seriously, Casimir, could you have predicted that a young ascender would be capable of combining her power with the most uncouth woman on the face of Second Earth and actually succeeding in folding twenty thousand people out of a theater?"

When he put it like that . . . "I suppose not."

"Then you have just defined all my current dilemmas as well as the reason I struck the bargain with you in the first place. When I heard of the vision about your death, I dismissed it."

"But you would not have minded seeing me vaporized."

"No more than you would shed tears at my funeral."

The little peach had a point.

"But I did not come here to discuss the past but rather the future, the somewhat immediate future. All three of my primary Seers Fortresses have provided a very interesting bit of information about our second obsidian flame. I believe you already know who she is."

He nodded. "Marguerite."

"She's missing."

At that he stared at Greaves. He understood the implications at once. "Go on."

"Apparently she's gone rogue and is now wandering around on Mortal Earth, completely unprotected."

Now, that was interesting.

"I want the obsidian triad broken before it has a chance to gain its real power. You are the only one who can do this, Casimir, but I need to know if somehow the night's failure has destroyed your confidence, plucked your oversized balls out of your snug trousers? Hm?"

Casimir's chest tightened as he stared at Greaves. "No," he said.

Greaves returned his stare, no doubt taking his measure. "This one thing I have always known about you, my friend, your hedonism is not your greatest flaw. Vanity holds you in thrall. In this moment, you cannot believe that you actually failed tonight. You had thought your plan infallible and now you can hardly bear the thought that a young female vampire, not even two centuries old, has bested you. Am I right?"

Casimir refused to answer him.

"Do not look so glum. It spoils your beauty. After all, we are not so very different. Imagine what I felt having to ask for your help in the first place."

It disturbed Caz that the bastard was making so much sense. He had all but decided to make Greaves's demise his object rather than continue in his efforts to take down Endelle's administration. Now Greaves was giving him reason to keep up the fight.

"I shall leave you to it, then." Greaves started to lift his arm then lowered it. "I am curious about one thing. Did you actually penetrate Julianna during the performance tonight?"

"I never fuck and tell."

Greaves chuckled. "I think you did, not because I know you that well, but rather because I know Julianna, the lusty creature that she is."

Casimir held his gaze. "Julianna would never have agreed to perform without a measure of . . . compensation."

At that, Greaves laughed again. "No. She would not."

"You miss her."

"I will not deny that we were well suited." The arm rose. The bastard disappeared.

Casimir gained his feet. As pep talks went, Greaves had a knack for it.

Time to return to Paris.

Having lived for over three millennia, I no longer think that variety is the spice of life. In more recent centuries, I've become fond of the unexpected.

—*Memoirs,* Beatrice of Fourth

CHAPTER 24

Endelle stood in the defendant's box, high above the proceedings, cameras trained on her. She wore one of her fav outfits, a silvery gray snakeskin jumpsuit. Marcus had wanted her to don a formal black robe, the one she wore to perform the ascension ceremonies, but she just wasn't feelin' it. She kept sending little zaps of power to her arches since being forced to stand during this little committee hearing for over three hours in her stilettos was one motherfucker of a pain in the ass.

Whatever.

But Marcus kept the proceedings hopping. She'd never been more proud of her longtime friend. He was running circles around these bozos, half of whom were taking dying blood on the sly but keeping the telltale effects at bay by making use of Greaves's famous and not-so-secret antidote.

Although Daniel Harding, chairman of these bullshit proceedings, was looking prettier every day. He'd always been a vain if ugly bastard. Because he was homely by virtue of having the ugliest parents in the world, he couldn't seem to help experimenting by holding off on Greaves's antidote. Even waiting half an hour to take the serum would initiate some physical changes. In time, therefore, Harding's pug-dog features had started to smooth out. The trouble was, he now had a faint bluish line forming in an arc just in front of his ears. Maybe he forgot his Revlon concealer.

"High Administrator Amargi," Harding called out, his cheeks reddening. "You dishonor this assemblage by not owning up to the truth of what occurred the night of the Las Vegas Two explosion. Did you, or did you not, hear Madame Endelle violate COPASS orders by giving permission to Warrior Jean-Pierre and Warrior Thorne to enter the Superstition Mountain Seers Fortress?"

"And I tell you again, I did not," Marcus said, holding Harding's gaze. "But I should remind you that the night was a mass confusion because we were aiding over twenty thousand refugees from around the globe to return to each of over forty allied Territories. You can't expect me to recall everything that happened that night."

He shifted his gaze to the thirty or so cameras and film crews off to the side and smiled. "But I don't need to remind the good people of Second Earth what was found in the Seers Fortress, the devastating truth that the High Administrator had been abusing his Seers, that many were pregnant and malnourished, that there were children without proper care, that the facility itself was condemned by the Health and Safety Board of Southwest Desert Two."

"High Administrator Amargi—"

He continued to address the cameras. "I am fully persuaded that only the most dire of situations would have caused two of our most worthy *duhuro* warriors, elite Warriors of the Blood, men with the highest caliber of integrity, vampires who have served in this war against a growing army of death vampires for hundreds of years, without complaint—yes, only the worst kind of treachery and depravity would have forced Warriors Jean-Pierre and Thorne to violate one of COPASS's most sacred laws. For those who wish more information about this ongoing story of Seer violation, we have extensive footage of the crime on www.madameendelle.com."

"Warrior Marcus, this conduct is outrageous!" Harding shouted. "You are seeking to enflame public opinion."

"Yes, Chairman Harding, I am. I want transparency. I want the good people of Second Earth to know *all* that is going on in high places around this world."

Harding's red cheeks paled.

"And now at this time, we are providing the most esteemed committee copies of over two thousand requests Madame Endelle submitted to COPASS during the past five years, begging repeatedly for a thorough inspection of a Fortress that had not allowed any person within its walls for over fifteen years."

"That is a falsehood. We have answering reports that once each year a thorough inspection was performed."

"Then how do you account for twenty-three offspring genetically proven to be the result of Stannett's repeated rapes?"

The galleries began a serious shout-down of Harding, supported by an answering roar from the hallways beyond.

Endelle crossed her arms over her chest and smiled. She really did like where this was headed. If COPASS even tried to incarcerate Jean-Pierre or Thorne, it would face a revolt.

A quiet masculine voice intruded, right against her ear. "So what do you think?"

She jerked her head to her right, and there, sitting on the edge of the narrow railing as pretty as you please, was Braulio. "What the fuck are you doing here?"

"Wanted to watch the doings."

Endelle looked around. There seemed to be a glitch in the fabric of time, as though everyone else was moving very slowly. "What did you just do?"

"A very small manipulation of the space–time continuum. Wanted to have a little chat with you, is all. So how happy are you that I encouraged you to send Marguerite to the Superstitions? Now you'll get access to some serious Seer shit."

"You seem pretty pleased with yourself."

"I am, but admit it. Sending her there is having some excellent payoffs. This show for one, and now you can start rebuilding your Seer supply."

"I don't like to mention it, Braulio, but those Seers are so screwed up, they can't *see* shit right now. And to top it off, Marguerite folded her ass to who-the-fuck-knows-where, and she was supposed to be the second part of a powerful obsidian flame triad." She then jerked her head in the direction of the current proceedings. "And in case you haven't noticed, I'm on trial for my life, as are my warriors. So forgive me if I don't fawn all over you right now."

But he crossed his arms over his chest, which of course made his biceps flex and look all yummy through his long-sleeved T-shirt. "You can't spoil my buzz," he said. "Things are looking up. James sent a message."

James. The powerful Sixth ascender who had sent Braulio to change things up. Much good either of them were doing. "What? He couldn't come himself?"

Braulio shrugged. "Who knows? He could be here right now."

Whatever.

"So what's his message?"

"He said you'll need to forgive Thorne."

"What the fuck for?" Thorne was her right-hand man. He'd even given up his woman for her sake and for the sake of the war.

Braulio just shrugged. "How the hell should I know?"

She offered a disgusted grunt in response, which only made him laugh. Seeing that he was perched so prettily on the narrow railing, she flung her arm sideways, slugging him hard in the shoulder, which naturally caused him to fall right off. Except the bastard just levitated and moved back in.

"You think you're pretty tough," she said.

"I don't *think*," he corrected her. "I know."

She laughed. "Well, we've got us one fine farce here."

"Yep, but when wasn't it a farce? I don't see your buddy, Greaves, around."

"You never will when one of his pals is in trouble. What do you think of Harding's complexion?"

"Pretty shade of blue right at the hairline."

"Yep. So, you sticking around this time?"

He shook his head. "Can't. Serious time constraints. I only have time do this." He leaned in, grabbed the back of her neck with his hand, pulled her toward him, then put his mouth on hers.

She meant to protest, to shove his sorry ass away from her, maybe spit a small firework into his mouth, but as his lips, so fucking familiar, touched hers, good old-fashioned sensory memory returned and her body lit on fire.

She didn't want to, but she opened her mouth and let him in, the bastard. His tongue made quick work of her, lighting up what hadn't seen much activity in way too long.

He drew back and looked her in the eyes. His lips curved. "Aw, I think you still love me."

But that took all her fire and channeled it into her temper. "Fuck you."

She was going to add a hand-blast, but time seemed to have resumed, Braulio had already disappeared, and silence fell on the entire assembled court.

Every eye, every camera shifted in her direction.

She realized her parting words to Braulio had just been shouted into the courtroom, in real time, and captured on tape.

Goddam that Braulio. She'd get him back if it was the last thing she did.

She glanced at Marcus and watched his eyes do a serious shit-not-again roll.

There was only one thing she could do. She waved an imperious hand over the entire court and in a voice that shimmered with her best resonance, she said, "Please continue." Then she lifted her chin and stared at an astonished Harding.

* * *

Jean-Pierre was in Seriffe's office, talking over the training ideas he had, when his warrior phone buzzed.

"*Allô,* Bev, how are you?"

"Uh . . . I guess you could say I, that is we, are mystified."

"And why is that?" It was not like Bev to speak in riddles.

"There is a man at the landing platform who wishes to speak with you."

"I wasn't expecting anyone. Has he been checked out by security?"

"He's clean. No concerns there."

More riddles.

"Well, tell me then, what is his name?"

"Peter Robillard, from Oxford Two. He says he only wants a word with you and to give you something."

Jean-Pierre listed on his feet. He reached out for Seriffe's desk.

"Hey," Seriffe called out. "What the fuck? You're about as white as a sheet."

Jean-Pierre looked at Seriffe, but he didn't exactly see him. "Bev, please see the gentleman to the conference room. I will be with him shortly. But . . . why are you mystified, if I may ask?"

"You'll know when you see him." She hung up.

His Epic phone rang. He withdrew it from the pocket of his jeans. Fiona. "*Chérie.* What is it?"

"You tell me. I can feel you weaving on your feet. What's wrong? I mean I'm used to the battle training, I know what all that feels like, but this is different, right?"

"*Oui.* Fiona, I know that you are busy at the rehab center but could you come to me right now? Something has happened. I am not certain exactly what it is, but I want you with me."

"Of course."

"I'll have Bev do the fold for you."

When he hung up, he called Bev back and told her what he needed. She promised it would be the work of a moment.

A few minutes later, with Fiona by his side, he walked with her in the direction of the Militia HQ conference room.

He gripped her hand too tightly—he could feel that he caused her pain. He released the stranglehold on her fingers and took a deep breath.

When he opened the door to the conference room, a tall man, at least six-four, perhaps six-five, wearing a conservative black suit, nicely tailored in the British manner of things, turned to face him. His hair was different shades of blond, darker beneath, streaked over the top, very *familiar.*

Fiona gasped and Jean-Pierre started nodding like an idiot. "Who are you?" he said at last because he could think of nothing else to say even though the answer was obvious.

"My name is Peter Robillard," he said, his British accent elegant, refined. "My mother died when I was born, which was of course a very long time ago, over two hundred years. It took me decades after I ascended to find her, to find her grave in a church in Sussex, to take her name, her married name. I have strong reason to believe you might be my father."

He heard a strange sound next to him and looked down at Fiona. She had her fingers to her lips and little sobs escaped her mouth as tears streamed down her cheeks. She looked up at him. "There, you see?" she said.

He was too much in shock to see anything. "See what? My son? Yes, I do see him, so I believe it must be true."

"No. Not that. Isabelle. This is the reason she went crazy. She carried your child. She had been given a choice by the monsters of the revolution. Now tell me she made the right one."

Jean-Pierre moved forward and sank into a chair. The past rose up like an enormous wave and crashed over him, of hearing Isabelle crying out as they took him away, "Forgive me. I have no choice. Forgive me."

She had carried a child, his child, their child. The year, even the month of September when it had all happened, had been a terrible time in the revolution. He understood it all now: that if Isabelle would just confess to a series of lies, then she could go free, even though it meant sending her husband to the guillotine.

He looked up at Peter, at the man who looked so much like him, except for the eyes, and his heart unfolded like a flower blossoming.

"I didn't come to cause you pain," Peter said. "I just wanted to know the truth, to know more about Isabelle and if you were my father, more about you and why I was born in the south of England and not in France. I perhaps should tell you that my wife watched the recent farcical COPASS proceedings and saw your testimony. She thought you and I could not look this much alike and not be related."

Fiona moved to stand in front of Peter. She put her hand on his shoulder and looked up at him in wonder. "He has your mouth, Jean-Pierre, and look at his cheeks, his strong cheekbones, even the line of his jaw. Only his eyes are different."

"Like Isabelle's," he said. "That soft sweet fire in her eyes."

"Then . . . you believe I am your son."

Jean-Pierre shook his head. "You must be my son. How can you be anything else?" Still he stared, unable to move. He stared and searched each feature over and over.

"Do you have children?" Fiona asked.

Peter smiled. "More than one set. I have been married a long time to the same woman. We have eight Twolings, and the oldest three were born at the turn of the last century. There are children and grandchildren, great-grandchildren. Our family is very large indeed."

Fiona returned to Jean-Pierre and dropped to her knees beside him. He shifted to look at her. "You were right, *chérie.* Isabelle had a profound reason for what she did. I understand it all now and I approve. If I had known, I would have agreed with her."

She put her hand on his face as she so often did, "We have both been given our families back. Don't you see? Don't you see?"

He caught her hand and pressed it to his face. He nodded, then finally rose to his feet. He moved to stand next to Peter. He put a hand around the back of his neck and looked at him, really looked at him, searching every facet of his face, every damp glitter in his eye, the way his throat moved up and down in hard swallows, the way his body relented when Jean-Pierre pulled him into an embrace. "My son," he whispered. "My son."

"Father" came as a very soft low sound into his ribbed T-shirt.

After a very long moment, he released Peter, but not completely. He met and held his gaze. "I loved your mother so very much. She was a dance of fire in my life, so warm, so loving. But they were terrible times in France. I had been for the revolution and got caught in the terrible changes of 1793."

Peter nodded.

"I am so sorry that I was not there for you. I ascended at the point of my death. If I had known, thought, even suspected, I would have come for you and for Isabelle. But I thought only that she betrayed me so I made my home on Second Earth and tried to forget all that had hurt me so deeply on Mortal Earth. How grateful I am that you found me."

Peter wiped at his cheeks. "I was raised in an orphanage. It was . . . difficult. About thirty years ago, my wife insisted that I have therapy. She said my anger was irrational. It took me a long time to forgive you and Isabelle." He chuckled softly and his eyes softened with tears once more. "And now to think that my father is a Warrior of the Blood." But at that, a frown entered his eye and he ground his teeth in a way that seemed very familiar.

"What is it, Peter? Do you fear you will now be in danger? You and your family?"

"No, it's my grandson. He's . . . well, he's got some radical ideas about Second Earth. He and his friends have been paying visits to Mortal Earth."

Jean-Pierre was shocked. "Not through the Borderland at Rome. That would be foolish, dangerous." Each continent had an entrance to Mortal Earth, a Trough through which death vampires could descend and not be discovered by the numerous grids around the world.

Peter drew a deep breath. "It's worse than that. He can fold between dimensions."

"Mon Dieu."

"Precisely."

"Could he defend himself against a death vampire?"

"I believe so. I have to trust that he can."

"Has he taken sword training?"

Peter smiled. "He excels at it. He's . . . gifted, probably like his great-grandfather, but he wants nothing to do with the war."

"In that he is wise."

"Warrior Jean-Pierre—" he began.

"Please, *Father*' would do, or the French *Papa*?"

Peter smiled. "Very well. Papa. There is something I wish to say to you. I am so grateful for the work that you and the Warriors of the Blood do on our behalf. I wish you to know that the average ascender understands what is going on, all around the world. We know about the dying blood antidote and that many of our leaders are corrupt.

"I saw the footage of the battle at the Grand Canyon last fall. I saw the number of death vampires in Commander Greaves's army. So many had to be a deliberate undertaking, had to be of his doing. We all know it, we understand it, but there is so little we can do as individuals.

"So we watch and we wait. When the time comes, please believe that you will not be alone, that Madame Endelle, for all her eccentricity, is not alone. There are movements in every Territory on the planet, usually led by Militia Warriors, even in those Territories aligned with Greaves, that work to keep the average ascender informed."

"You are talking underground movements?"

"Nothing less. Greaves and his allies are too involved in the upper rungs of all governments to allow for open dissension."

He was very intense as he said, "She has us, the commoners. We support her even if we can't let our voices be heard right now."

"I will tell her. Your words have given me great comfort."

For the next few minutes, he exchanged phone numbers and email addresses with his son. Though he wanted to know him better, he felt certain that any evidence of a strong familial connection would put Peter and his family in danger.

Jean-Pierre turned toward Fiona and extended an arm. She moved next to him and he held her close. "I wish you to know my *breh,* Fiona Gaines."

Peter offered his hand, but Fiona said, "Nonsense," and slung her arms around his neck.

Peter hugged her back.

Jean-Pierre wiped his cheeks once more. "Look. I have turned into such a woman."

"Hey," Fiona cried, drawing back from his son and giving Jean-Pierre a playful thump to his chest.

Jean-Pierre laughed then drew her up against him, her back to his front. He wrapped his arms around her as he once more looked Peter over: his hair, his forehead, his ears, just like his own ears, his nose, just like his own nose, his chin, so very stubborn and familiar. This was the gift of life, the surprises, like holding his *breh* in his arms while looking at a son he had never known existed, the true answer to a riddle to which he had always assigned the wrong answer.

Yes, this was the true gift of life.

Thorne sat in his usual spot at the Blood and Bite, at the top of the bar so he could keep an eye on his men. He rattled his tumbler around. It now held one finger of seltzer water and two fat ice cubes.

Sam moved forward and refilled.

If any of the brothers noticed he wasn't hitting the Ketel One, no one said a word, but then they rarely did, not to him, not to the goddam leader of the Warriors of the Blood.

He was *the man.* No one questioned him. No one ever questioned him. Why would they? For two thousand years he'd been on duty, serving, loyal, reliable, a good warrior, a consistent leader.

None of the brothers even asked him about Marguerite once it became known she'd been his lover for the past century. He was that trusted among his men, that trusted by Endelle, so trustworthy that no one challenged him about the century's worth of lies he'd been telling—celibacy and all that shit.

He had a full house tonight, one of the rare occasions that all seven of his warriors would be battling, which meant this was exactly the timing he needed to start working things out.

He'd already handed out the night's assignments: Medichi at the Superstitions with Luken, Marcus and Jean-Pierre at New River, Santiago at Awatukee, Kerrick at the White Tanks, and Zacharius downtown.

"Where will you be, *jefe*?" Santiago asked. He had a lovely redhead under his arm. Santiago seemed to like redheads. She had one hand on his chest and was petting him over and over like she meant to wear a hole in his silk shirt.

Well that was the million-dollar question, wasn't it? "I have a meeting with Endelle," he said. A lie, of course. "I'll catch up with the rest of you later." Another lie.

Since the woman practically climbed Santiago's leg, and the brother turned into her and gave her one helluva a deep kiss, he started drifting in the direction of the red velvet booths.

Luken had already disappeared with a blond chick. Zach was on the dance floor. The last Thorne had seen him, he'd had his fangs buried deep. The Blood and Bite, situated in south Phoenix, Mortal Earth, was meant for the warriors of Second Earth, a place Endelle sanctioned for R&R for the Militia Warriors as well as the Warriors of the Blood. Enthrallment of mortals was encouraged in order to keep the nature of their vampire world on the down-low. But any warrior who hurt a mortal suffered major consequences, and Sam Finch, the owner, kept a strict eye on all the doings.

The rest of the brothers, the ones bonded with their goddam *brehs,* huddled at the bar in one big fat happy group, talking about other things, like how to get along with a woman who could feel you all the time, whatever the hell that meant. Jean-Pierre, the latest addition to the club, did more listening than talking.

So Thorne drank his seltzer alone, which was pretty much all he needed right now.

His recent freak-out in Endelle's office, the one that had only ended when Luken had punched his lights out, had actually aided his current mission because the warriors had been giving him a boatload of space.

So it looked like everything was working out for him.

He turned to Sam and said, "I'm headed out to see Endelle."

"I will let them know, *jefe*."

Thorne took one last look around, one last gander at the mated brothers. He felt like a piece of shit for what he was about to do, but he just didn't have a choice. He lifted his arm and dematerialized.

He ended up in the foyer of his home in Sedona. He whipped his warrior phone from the slit in his battle kilt and thumbed it.

"Jeannie, here. How may I serve?"

"Hey, Jeannie."

Silence returned then a very soft, "Please don't do this."

"I'm heading out." He'd shared his plan with Jeannie. He'd known the woman for centuries now and he trusted the hell out of her. She had instructions to let Endelle know what was up.

"Please, Thorne. What will they do without you?"

"I guess they'll have to figure it out."

"How long will you be gone?"

"You know the answer."

"Yeah, as long as it *fucking* takes."

For that, for her use of one of his favorite words, he actually smiled. "Love ya, Jeannie. You're the best."

"Right back atcha, *jefe*."

For a long moment, he held the phone to his ear as though there was something else he needed to say. But after a few more seconds he realized he was just damn sad that he was taking off like this, like a deserter, but he didn't have a choice.

He just didn't have a choice. He'd given two thousand years of his life in service to Second Earth, but this he had to do for himself.

Finally, without another word, he thumbed his phone.

He waved a hand and changed out of his battle flight gear. He wore jeans, a wife-beater shirt, and heavy steel-toed boots. He folded a thick wad of twenty-dollar bills into his hand and stuffed it into his pocket.

He folded straight to the New River Borderland, and with the power of his two thousand years he jumped into the Trough and slammed through nether-space. The ride done this way, through the space between the dimensions, had the effect of wiping out his power signature on Central's or Militia HQ's grids—any grids for that matter, Greaves's Command Center included. No one would be able to locate him on Mortal Earth.

So, yeah, he was going rogue.

When he touched down on New River Mortal Earth, he looked around. Just a few houses. A few cars.

He had only one problem: How the hell was he going to find Marguerite in a dimension that had seven billion people on the goddam planet?

Marguerite drove across the barren stretch of I-10 between Albuquerque and San Antonio One, her right hand on the wheel and her left arm lazing across the door. She had the top down on the vintage Chevy she'd stolen in Phoenix. She had crisscrossed the country a dozen times since folding the hell out of Endelle's office.

She'd left Second Earth via the downtown Phoenix Two Trough, set up mist around her own sweet self, and hunted for just the right vehicle.

Damn, she loved this car.

She loved her freedom.

Freedom was her air.

She had her long hair twisted on top of her head in a banana clip so that the sun could find her shoulders every second of every day. She'd become a sun worshipper since she'd seen the damn thing so infrequently during her prison term.

She wore a bright red halter that revealed a lot of cleavage, and she let her skin burn. At first it had blistered and peeled and blistered and peeled, but she didn't care. She had the power to heal it up, but why? She'd spend hours in front of the mirror in one cheap motel room after another watching her skin tone deepen and darken.

Now she had a dark rich tan and meant to keep it that way. Her really cutoff cutoffs helped as well, since the frayed edge lived in the seam between her hips and legs when she sat down. When she stood up, the pockets dipped below and looked like two flags against her Coppertone skin.

A vast shimmering appeared on the highway a quarter mile distant.

Oh, shit.

She slammed on the brakes and pulled over.

Owen Stannett, wearing the usual embroidered leather, appeared on the hood of her car. She hated that smile so much that she almost puked. But what she really hated was that weird wave of hair on the side of his head. What a freak.

She leaned back in her seat. "What do you want, motherfucker?" She didn't have her leg shackled anymore and she was beginning to figure out that her red variety of obsidian flame carried a lot of power with it. She spent every part of her day working her powers. She had powers no one even dreamed of.

"Darian has big plans for you, honey. He sent me to find you and now I'm here. Time to go to work, sweetheart."

"In your dreams, perv." She waved a hand and Owen flew backward up into the sky until he winked out of sight.

She put her car in gear and drove on. Stannett wasn't a fighter. He wouldn't be back until he was sure he could subdue her. Still, she felt confident she could take him.

There was just one little problem.

If Darian was on her ass, one little orbit flight for the Fortress Fuck wouldn't stop *the little peach*.

Now what was she supposed to do?

Then she smiled. So what if Darian came sniffing around. She was gaining power every day. If she had to, she'd battle him herself, to the death if need be, because like hell was she ever going to be shut up in some fortress or Convent or any other fucking facsimile that one of these shit-eaters dished up for her.

Her smile broadened. There was one thing she was going to do as soon as she hit San Antonio. She was going to find herself a hair salon and get tricked out with something short, wavy, and platinum blond.

Afterward she'd hit a bar. She'd spent the last week getting the lay of the land, flirting with men, figuring out what she was dealing with. But now it was time to get serious, time to start living out all those bed-thumping fantasies that had kept her going for the past ten decades.

Oh . . . yeah.

The purpose of ritual is to train the soul,
And to ease the suffering of the spirit.

—*The Creator's Handbook,* Sister Quena

CHAPTER 25

Jean-Pierre could see within Gideon. He could see where the warrior held back and in what ways he needed to move beyond his present ability. Endelle called this a facilitation power, newly emerged, a gift of the *breh-hedden.* He had seen glimpses of it in prior months, even years, but once he bonded with Fiona, the gift grew stronger and stronger.

Two weeks had passed since he completed the *breh-hedden* with Fiona and so much had changed, for him and within him. He could feel Fiona, just as the other bonded vampires could feel their *brehs.* She was at the rehab center and had a slight pain in her right hip because she had been sitting too long. So strange to know what she experienced at all times.

Gideon sparred with another powerful Militia Warrior as each worked to improve his battling skills. He could see that Gideon, so close to Warrior of the Blood status, still struggled with combining preternatural speed and folding. The skill was critical in battling several death vampires at once. But it was as though Jean-Pierre could see the empty space in his thinking that needed to be filled.

When the men lowered their swords and separated to catch their breaths, he called out, "Gideon. A word with you."

Gideon lowered his chin and scowled. "I'm busy."

Jean-Pierre smiled. He could not help himself. In spirit, Gideon was already a Warrior of the Blood. He was territorial and defensive. He would battle Jean-Pierre to the death over his pride alone.

As Jean-Pierre met his gaze, he swept his emerging empathic ability over the warrior and found what he needed in order to reach the man. "I thought we should have a contest, you and me. A comparison that might end the suspense."

"What the fuck are you talking about?"

"To see whose dick is bigger, of course. What do you say?"

Gideon shook his head then laughed. "Fuck," he muttered. Finally, he said, "What do you want, Warrior?"

"If you would permit me, I believe I can teach you a trick to the speed-and-fold, but only if you wish it. You must choose."

Yes, Gideon must choose, just as Jean-Pierre must choose, as everyone must choose. Jean-Pierre had chosen to love where he had promised never to love again, to open himself, and to grow. But the choice must be offered, must be accepted or declined.

Gideon's gaze shifted away. His jaw worked as he stared at nothing in particular. After a long, tense moment, Gideon crossed the black mats of the workout space. In a low voice, he said, "I don't want to leave the Militia Warriors." He put a fist to his chest. "No matter what happens here, today, my commitment, my loyalty is with the Thunder God Warriors."

Jean-Pierre saw the warrior as though a grid were laid out before him, of flaws and strengths, of hidden desires and open intentions. He felt each of Gideon's words balanced against the lift of his brow, the tightness of his jaw, the dark, concerned light in his eye. Then he understood what Gideon feared: that he would be pushed beyond the boundary he had set for himself where the Militia Warriors were concerned.

Jean-Pierre nodded. "I have felt for a very long time that the future of Second Earth would not be in the hands of the Warriors of the Blood, but in the Militia Warriors and in bringing those who are able up to the same level of skill that we possess. Of course, you will have to do battle with Colonel Seriffe and Madame Endelle. I cannot change that.

"However, I can make you this promise, that I will stand with you, support you, in your bid to remain with your men." He had a sudden swirling of prescience, a small piece of clairvoyance. He saw himself in back of Gideon as the warrior argued with Seriffe about the future of the Militia Warriors. Gideon prevailed. Good. This was good.

Gideon stared at him for a long moment. "I can feel that my powers as a warrior are emerging and I know that I'm obligated to take your instruction by every vow I've made as a warrior, but that you've understood my greatest concern, my commitment, gives me hope."

Jean-Pierre nodded. "I will fight for you to stay here. I make this vow to you."

He watched relief spill over Gideon's face, as though he'd been living with this dilemma for a very long time.

"Thank you and yes, I'll work with you. I need to get this goddam fucking thing figured out."

Oui, he was very much in the mold of the Warriors of the Blood.

Jean-Pierre spent the next two hours showing Gideon the techniques for speed-and-fold; at one point he actually downloaded a memory, something that by its nature would give Gideon the sensory experience of the skill.

After that, progress was swift so that by the time they parted Gideon had a new swagger and a smile.

Jean-Pierre turned the other direction, intent on the landing platform. Fiona had just climbed into the shower at their Sedona home. *Would you like company?* he sent. He could feel the sensation of the warm water on her skin.

He felt her rub the bar of soap between her hands, the soft lather foaming around her fingers.

Oh, I don't know, Fiona returned in a suspicious drawl.

Then, in true bonded fashion, he could feel the soap on her breasts and the pressure of her fingers as she washed herself. He could feel the little pinch she gave her nipples.

What a tease you have become, he sent.

I have no idea what you're talking about. So innocent.

But when he felt her soapy hand glide down her abdomen and slide between her legs he began sprinting in the direction of the landing platform. He was cursing by the time he arrived because her laughter was in his head and he was having a hard time controlling his arousal.

But he made it at last, folding straight to the master bathroom.

She had her hand exactly where he wanted to see it. "Oh, it's you," she said, but she was smiling. "Need something?"

He folded his clothes off and with his own speed-and-fold, he was behind her, his cock pressed between her legs, his hands on her breasts.

"Hey," she cried out. "Give a girl a warning."

But as he fondled her, she leaned her head back. "I am sorry, *chérie,* but I have been working on this skill with one of the Militia Warriors."

Her hips moved up and back, an erotic invitation.

"Not this skill, surely," she said as she leaned forward and tilted her pelvis to give him a better view.

He groaned as he entered her. She planted her hands on the tile beneath the showerhead. He used his mind to shut the water off. He bent over her and sucked one of her wing-locks.

Her groan was long and loud.

Fiona, the sensations, yours and mine . . . it is all too much. I feel you are . . . oh, God, you are coming.

"Yes," she shouted. "And so are you."

He thrust in and out, moving swiftly so that he brought her screaming as he spent himself inside her.

"I think that must be a record," he said, pulling out of her but turning her in his arms and holding her close.

"I know. I know. To experience both at the same time. Do you think we'll ever be able to slow it down?" She was wide-eyed.

He laughed. "Not for a few years, at least."

"Maybe a century or two."

"A millennium."

Fiona leaned her head against his shoulder. "Casimir called it millennial adjustment."

"Do not speak that monster's name when I am holding you."

"Okay." She slid her arms around him and held him tight.

"Shall we retire to the bedroom, *ma chérie*?"

"Oh, yes. You can't think for a moment that I'm letting you off this easily, not with something that lasted about thirty seconds."

He chuckled. "It is your fault. You have the most enticing . . . ass."

"You say the sweetest things." Then she laughed.

A few days later, Fiona knocked on the door to the central sycamore room, the name she'd given to the round indoor–outdoor space where she and Jean-Pierre had completed the *breh-hedden*. "When are you going to show me what you're building in there? The suspense is killing me."

Her *breh* had been working on a top-secret project, something that involved a lot of large rocks—not boulders exactly, smaller than that, but big enough. She'd watched him haul them into the room, refusing all the while to give her even the smallest hint about what he was making.

All she knew was that the job required mortar and some kind of large metal basin. A birdbath maybe?

"I am almost ready" came back to her muffled through the door.

She leaned her head against the wood and drew in a deep breath. The past two and a half weeks had been amazing with Jean-Pierre and with the *breh-hedden*. Love, after all these years, had found her again.

In the distance she heard the front doorbell ring, but she

wasn't expecting anyone. "Jean-Pierre, someone's at the front door."

"That is probably Carolyn and Seriffe. I asked them to come by."

"Why?" She didn't mind, not at all, but this was the first she'd heard of it. What was with all the secrecy?

He came to the door and slipped into the hallway, closing the door behind him. So she still wasn't going to get to see what was in there.

"I am sorry, *chérie,* I should have told you."

She looked him up and down. "You're wearing a suit. Okay, what the hell is going on?"

His smile was slow. "You may wish to change into a dress, that very pretty Halston. The one Havily keeps calling a petal dress."

"But—"

"Trust me. Put it on, *chérie.* I will see to our guests."

"Okay, then."

Stunned, she lifted her arm and folded to the master bedroom. She lived here now, in his house. No, *their* house. He kept correcting her. This was *their* house.

Her heart beat too fast in her chest. Jean-Pierre had something serious planned and he seemed very pleased with himself, but she couldn't imagine what he intended. The whole thing made her nervous.

She dressed in heels and stockings and the cream-colored petal dress. She brushed her long hair, tidied her makeup, and tried to relax, but something about the secrecy of the visit, and the closed door to the sycamore room, told her that what was about to happen was . . . significant.

When at last she was dressed, she walked the entire distance, through several smaller rooms of the rabbit warren house, to the living room, trying to calm her nerves.

Jean-Pierre served champagne, his expression serious. He was a man of good humor most of the time, a lightness of spirit she adored. But at other times, like now, he could overwhelm her with the depths of his soul and his desire for her to understand what he valued in life.

Carolyn wore a lavender silk dress and heels. Seriffe also wore a suit. Both appeared solemn.

"I have no idea what's going on," she said to Carolyn, her voice low.

Carolyn kissed her cheek and squeezed her hand. She nodded several times. "You'll love this, Mother. But you can't blame Jean-Pierre, not entirely. He asked for my opinion and I told him exactly how to go about this."

"How to go about what?"

Carolyn gestured to a long narrow white box on the table near the champagne. "This is for you. In a few minutes, we'll go to the sycamore room and you can open it. Then you'll understand everything." Carolyn squeezed her hand again. "Don't fret. Trust me and trust your *breh*."

"Fine," Fiona muttered. But she wasn't happy about this. She thought she might need to have a conversation later with Jean-Pierre about how much she had never enjoyed surprises.

Jean-Pierre handed her a glass of champagne. He held her gaze. "Lately, I have been thinking of baby Helena's christening and the ritual of the oil and the ash. I recall Sister Quena saying that we are born of ashes to serve Second Earth. I think this is very true, perhaps even in a larger sense, that very often our lives must be burned down to nothing before we can be born to greater acts of service and of love. So this is for you, my beloved Fiona: I dedicate this evening that I might express my profound gratitude that in the ashes of my life, I was born anew to be your *breh,* and to serve you, now and forever."

Fiona blinked up at him. His words were beautiful, even profound. Okay, maybe she didn't need to have that conversation with him after all.

He lifted his glass. "To *ma chérie,*" he said.

Seriffe and Carolyn lifted their glasses as well. "To Fiona," they said, as one.

Each of them drank in her honor and she brought her glass to her lips and sipped as well, overcome. Her heart ached at so much love, at so much expressed respect and honor. She still didn't know what this evening was about or what it was meant to be. And she didn't have the smallest idea what awaited her in the sycamore room, but somehow it no longer mattered. To be with Jean-Pierre, her daughter, and Seriffe was enough.

"Come," he said. He put his glass on the table and took hers as well, settling it beside his. "Come."

Carolyn picked up the long box and smiled her encouragement.

Fiona didn't ask any more questions. She put her arm in his as he led their small processional to the sycamore room.

When he opened the door, and she walked through, she didn't at first understand what she was looking at. Off to the right, a copper basin of sorts sat on top of a broad pillar of mortared stones. Beside the basin, a single tall white candle burned, flickering slightly as currents of air passed through the outdoor space.

With a slight pressure on her waist, he guided her to the strange edifice. "What is this?" she asked.

"I suppose you could call it a pyre."

She met his gaze. "For burning things? You made this for burning things?"

He nodded.

"What are we going to burn here then?" She was lost, totally at sea.

Carolyn held the box up. "I made this for you," she said. "I'm pretty sure I got all the names right. Bev at Militia HQ helped me do this. The landing platform security cameras had a tape of the moment Rith showed up in that cage. I hope—" Suddenly Carolyn's voice got stuck and much to Fiona's shock, her daughter's eyes filled with tears.

"Carolyn—" Fiona began.

But her daughter lifted her hand. "I can do this." She cleared her throat and began again. "Mother, I hope this will give you some peace. When Jean-Pierre told me what he wanted to do, I felt in my heart that it was exactly the right thing. But we both agreed that if it isn't, if you don't want to do this, then we understand. Completely. Neither of us want you to feel pressured."

Seriffe had his arm around Carolyn's waist, a gentle, loving support.

As Carolyn held the box in her arms, Fiona lifted the lid.

Inside, tied together, was a bundle of small pieces of paper, none of them larger than two or three inches. On the first piece was a woman's name. She recognized the name: the first woman who had died in Burma.

Her throat tightened.

When the puzzle came together in her mind, when she finally understood the intention of her *breh* and of her daughter, of the pyre beside her, and of Jean-Pierre's earlier speech, she was moved beyond words.

"This will take time," she said, her voice little more than a whisper.

"Please, *chérie,* take all the time that you need. We are here only for you in this moment."

She carefully untied the bow that held the papers together. She lifted the first one out, spoke the name, then dipped the corner into the candle's flame. The paper ignited. She dropped it into the copper basin.

She drew the next paper out and read the second name. She repeated the process so that the papers burned together.

Within a few minutes a little bonfire blazed in the copper bowl, and with each passing tribute her voice grew stronger. She then asked each of them to participate, to draw a paper, read a name, and offer up the little torches as an honor to those who had died.

She wept, she laughed, and at times she shouted her rage at what had killed so many. But with each burst of flame, as the fire grew, as the breeze sometimes sent sparks into the air, her heart grew lighter and freer. By the time the last of the papers had burned to ashes, as Jean-Pierre held her in a warm embrace from behind, she smiled.

This would not be the last time she performed this ritual, of that she was sure. She suspected there would be days, as the war took its awful toll in countless ways, that she would need to come to this pyre again and again, the names once more inscribed on another set of papers, to create more little bonfires in order to release the terrible burdens of the past.

But for now, with Jean-Pierre's arms holding her tight, with her hands clasped over his arms, with her daughter and Seriffe standing in a similar manner, with the last of the flames dying down to embers and the papers burning to ashes, her heart was at ease. And she knew joy. Great, wondrous, unqualified joy.

ASCENSION TERMINOLOGY

ascender n. A mortal human of earth who has moved permanently to the second dimension.

ascension n. The act of moving permanently from one dimension to a higher dimension.

ascendiate n. A mortal human who has answered the *call to ascension* and thereby commences his or her *rite of ascension.*

rite of ascension n. A three-day period during which time an *ascendiate* contemplates *ascending* to the next highest dimension.

ascension ceremony n. Upon the completion of the *rite of ascension,* the mortal undergoes a ceremony in which loyalty to the laws of Second Society is professed and the attributes of the vampire mantle along with immortality are bestowed.

call to ascension n. A period of time, usually involving several weeks, in which the mortal human has experienced some or all of, but not limited to, the following: specific dreams about the next dimension, deep yearnings and longings of a soulful and inexplicable nature, visions of and possibly visits to any of the dimensional Borderlands, etc. See *Borderlands.*

answering the call to ascension n. The mortal human who experiences the hallmarks of the *call to ascension* will at some point feel compelled to answer, usually by demonstrating significant preternatural power.

Borderlands pr. n. Those geographic areas that form dimensional borders at both ends of a dimensional pathway. The dimensional pathway is an access point through which travel can take place from one dimension to the next. See *Trough.*

breh-hedden **n.** (Term from an ancient language.) A mate-bonding ritual that can only be experienced by the most powerful warriors and the most powerful preternaturally gifted women. Effects of the *breh-hedden* can include but are not limited to: specific scent experience, extreme physical/sexual attraction, loss of rational thought, primal sexual drives, inexplicable need to bond, powerful need to experience deep *mind-engagement,* etc.

cadroen **n.** (Term from an ancient language.) The name for the hair clasp that holds back the ritual long hair of a *Warrior of the Blood.*

Central pr. n. The office of the current administration that tracks movement of *death vampires* in both the second dimension and on *Mortal Earth* for the purpose of alerting the

Warriors of the Blood and the *Militia Warriors* to illegal activities.

the darkening n. An area of *nether-space* that can be found during meditations and/or with strong preternatural darkening capabilities. Such abilities enable the *ascender* to move into nether-space and remain there or to use nether-space in order to be two places at once.

death vampire n. Any vampire, male or female, who partakes of *dying blood* automatically becomes a death vampire. Death vampires can have, but are not limited to, the following characteristics: remarkably increased physical strength, an increasingly porcelain complexion true of all ethnicities so that death vampires have a long-term reputation of looking very similar, a faint bluing of the porcelain complexion, increasing beauty of face, the ability to enthrall, the blackening of *wings* over a period of time. Though death vampires are not gender-specific, most are male. See *vampire.*

dimensional worlds n. Eleven thousand years ago, the first *ascender,* Luchianne, made the difficult transition from *Mortal Earth* to what became known as Second Earth. In the early millennia four more dimensions were discovered, Luchianne always leading the way. Each dimension's ascenders exhibited expanding preternatural power before ascension. Upper dimensions are generally closed off to the dimension or dimensions below.

***duhuro* n.** (Term from an ancient language.) A word of respect that in the old language combines the spiritual offices of both servant and master. To call someone *duhuro* is to offer a profound compliment suggesting great worth.

dying blood n. Blood extracted from a mortal or an *ascender* at the point of death. This blood is highly addictive in nature. There is no known treatment for anyone who partakes of dying blood. The results of ingesting dying blood include, but are not limited to: increased physical, mental, or preternatural power, a sense of extreme euphoria, a deep sense of well-being, a sense of omnipotence and fearlessness, the taking in of the preternatural powers of the host body, etc. If dying blood is not taken on a regular basis, extreme abdominal cramps result without ceasing. Note: Currently there is an antidote not for the addiction to dying blood itself but for the various results of ingesting dying blood. This means that a *death vampire* who drinks dying blood then partakes of the antidote will not show the usual physical side effects of ingesting dying blood; no whitening or faint bluing of the skin, no beautifying of features, no blackening of the *wings*, etc.

***effetne* n.** (Term from an ancient language.) An expression, an intense form of supplication to the gods, an abasement of self and of self-will.

folding v. Slang for dematerialization, since some believe that one does not actually dematerialize self or objects but rather one "folds space" to move self or objects from one place to another. There is much scientific debate on this subject since at present neither theory can be proved.

grid n. The technology used by Central that allows for the tracking of *death vampires* primarily at the *Borderlands* on both *Mortal Earth* and Second Earth. Death vampires by nature carry a strong, trackable signal, unlike normal *vampires*. See *Central.*

Guardian of Ascension pr. n. A prestigious title and rank at present given only to those *Warriors of the Blood* who also serve to guard powerful *ascendiates* during their *rite of ascension.* In millennia past Guardians of Ascension were also those powerful *ascenders* who offered themselves in unique and powerful service to Second Society.

High Administrator pr. n. The designation given to a leader of a Second Earth *Territory.*

identified sword n. A sword made by Second Earth metallurgy that has the preternatural capacity to become identified to a single *ascender.* The identification process involves holding the sword by the grip for several continuous seconds. The identification of a sword to a single ascender means that only that person can touch or hold the sword. If anyone else tries to take possession of the sword, other than the owner, that person will die.

Militia Warrior pr. n. One of hundreds of thousands of warriors who serve Second Earth society as a policing force for the usual civic crimes and as a battling force, in squads only, to fight against the continual depredations of *death vampires* on both *Mortal Earth* and Second Earth.

millennial adjustment n. The phenomenon of time taking on a more fluid aspect with the passing of centuries.

mind-engagement n. The ability to penetrate another mind and experience the thoughts and memories of the other person. The ability to receive another mind and allow that person to experience one's thoughts and memories. These abilities must be present in order to complete the *breh-hedden.*

mist n. A preternatural creation designed to confuse the mind and thereby hide things or people. Most mortals and *ascenders* are unable to see mist. The powerful ascender, however is capable of seeing mist, which usually appears like an intricate mesh, or a cloud, or a web-like covering.

Mortal Earth pr. n The name for First Earth or the current modern world known simply as earth.

nether-space n. The unknowable, unmappable regions of space. The space between dimensions is considered nether-space as well as the space found in *the darkening.*

pretty-boy n. Slang for *death vampire,* since most death vampires are male.

preternatural voyeurism n. The ability to "open a window" with the power of the mind in order to see people and events happening elsewhere in real time. Two of the limits of preternatural voyeurism are: The voyeur must usually know the person or place, and if the voyeur is engaged in darkening work, it is very difficult to make use of preternatural voyeurism at the same time.

***royle* n.** (Term from an ancient language.) The literal translation is: a benevolent wind. More loosely translated, *royle* refers to the specific capacity to create a state of benevolence, of goodwill, within an entire people or culture. See *royle adj.*

***royle* adj.** (Term from an ancient language.) This term is generally used to describe a specific coloration of *wings:* cream with three narrow bands at the outer tips when in full span. The bands are always burnished gold, amethyst, and black. Because Luchianne, the first *ascender* and first *vampire,* had this coloration on her wings, anyone, therefore, whose wings matched Luchianne's was said to have *royle* wings. Having *royle* wings was considered a tremendous gift, holding great promise for the world.

Seer pr. n. An *ascender* gifted with the preternatural ability to ride the future streams and report on future events.

Seers Fortress pr. n. *Seers* have traditionally been gathered into compounds designed to provide a highly peaceful environment, thereby enhancing the *Seer*'s ability to ride the future streams. The information gathered at a Seers Fortress benefits the local *High Administrator.* Some believe that the term *fortress* emerged as a protest to the prison-like conditions the Seers often have to endure.

spectacle n. The name given to events of gigantic proportion that include but are not limited to: trained squadrons of DNA-altered geese, swans, and ducks, *ascenders* with the specialized and dangerous skills of flight performance, intricate and often massive light and fireworks displays, as well as various forms of music.

Supreme High Administrator pr. n. The ruler of Second Earth. See *High Administrator.*

Territory pr. n. For the purpose of governance, Second Earth is divided up into groups of countries called Territories. Because the total population of Second Earth is only 1 percent of *Mortal Earth,* Territories were established as a simpler means of administering Second Society law. See *High Administrator.*

Trough pr. n. A slang term for a dimensional pathway. See *Borderlands.*

Twoling pr. n. Anyone born on Second Earth is a Twoling.

vampire n. The natural state of the *ascended* human. Every ascender is a vampire. The qualities of being a vampire include but are not limited to: immortality, the use of fangs to take blood, the use of fangs to release potent chemicals, increased physical power, increased preternatural ability, etc. Luchianne created the word *vampire* upon her *ascension* to Second Earth to identify in one word the totality of the changes she experienced upon that ascension. From the first, the taking of blood was viewed as an act of reverence and bonding, not as a means of death. The *Mortal Earth* myths surrounding the word *vampire* for the most part personify the Second Earth death vampire. See *death vampire.*

Warriors of the Blood pr. n. An elite fighting unit of usually seven powerful warriors, each with phenomenal preternatural ability and capable of battling several *death vampires* at any one time.

wings n. All *ascenders* eventually produce wings from wing-locks. *Wing-lock* is the term used to describe the apertures on the ascender's back from which the feathers and attending mesh-like superstructure emerge. Mounting wings involves a hormonal rush that some liken to sexual release. Flight is one of the finest experiences of ascended life. Wings can be held in a variety of positions including but not limited to: full-mount, close-mount, aggressive mount, etc. Wings emerge over a period of time from one year to several hundred years. Wings can, but do not always, begin small in one decade then grow larger in later decades.

Don't miss the other novels in the
Guardians of Ascension series from

CARIS ROANE

ASCENSION
ISBN: 978-0-312-53371-7

WINGS OF FIRE
ISBN: 978-0-312-53373-1

BURNING SKIES
ISBN: 978-0-312-53372-4

Available from St. Martin's Paperbacks

And look for

OBSIDIAN FLAME
ISBN: 978-1-250-00853-4

Coming in May 2012 from St. Martin's Paperbacks